THE L

The Lost
and
the Dreamer

NAOMI STARKEY

MINSTREL

Eastbourne

First published 1990
Reprinted 1991

Front cover illustration and design by Rodney Matthews

British Library Cataloguing in Publication Data

Starkey, Naomi
 The lost and the dreamer.
 I. Title
 823′.914 [F]

 ISBN 1–85424–014–5

Printed in Great Britain for
Minstrel, an imprint of Monarch Publications Ltd
1 St Anne's Road, Eastbourne, E Sussex BN21 3UN by
BPCC Hazell Books
Aylesbury, Bucks, England
Member of BPCC Ltd.
Typeset by Watermark, Norfolk House, Cromer

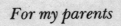

For my parents

PART I

The Settlement

He has also set eternity
in the hearts of men.
(Ecclesiastes 3:11)

Chapter One

'It was dark when we came,' said the old woman in a voice as frail as a withered leaf. 'You couldn't see your hand in front of your face. And quiet too, except for the wind rushing on and on over the empty desert. It blew the terrible red dust into your eyes and nose and filled your throat with it, so that you couldn't go outside the ship without a cloth tied over your mouth.'

'And how old were you then?' asked the girl, her bright dark eyes fixed on the old woman's shrivelled face.

'I was young, very young. No bigger than Jenna.' She glanced over at the thin little girl who was playing quietly in a corner of the hut, stripes of light shining through the cracked walls onto her faded brown shift.

'Yes, very young. A poor baby girl born on Earth and taken off beyond the stars in one of the last ships, off into Deep Space, to Osiris.' The old voice mumbled on, quavering in self-pity. 'We were going to join the colony here and start a new life, but we didn't know about the terrible dust storms. We crash-landed in the cruel desert and, worst of all, the others who followed us in Orion, the second ship, got lost and never came to join us. There were just us poor castaways. We couldn't go

9

back to the old world with its poisonous air and fire and disease, but there was nothing for us here except Sirius, the big ship we'd travelled in.' She fell silent, and the girl waited patiently for her to continue.

'And then?' she prompted, shifting from one foot to the other and drawing her jacket round her more tightly.

'Our ship would never fly again, so all we could do was wait and see if the others came down from the sky after all, when the storms were over. So we moved everything from the ship, bit by bit, far away to this place where there was shelter in the hollow of the mountains and forests of rua trees, and water and enough soil for growing things. We built huts and raised a few crops and reared the animals we'd brought with us. I lived in my mother's and father's hut until they died and then I stayed on alone, except when there were little ones with nobody to care for them and I took them in.'

'You mean like us?' asked the girl, frowning slightly.

'Like you, Cara, my dear, and your sister Minna and now Jenna, but before that there was Mora who died in the cradle, and Amund who went off to explore and never came back, and his brother Medwin with the crippled leg, who has that great brood of children now . . . .' The old woman's voice faded away again. Sighing, she rose from her stool by the smoking fire and limped across the uneven floor to where Jenna crouched, and gathered the little girl in her arms.

'Finish the story, Holly,' urged Cara, shivering as the wind blew under the door and shook the ash-coloured blanket which hung as a screen.

'Finish . . . ' The old woman's voice was weary. 'We waited for two long winters, gazing into the skies till our eyes ached, hoping to see Orion come down onto the

10

desert with the rest of our people on board. But there was only the emptiness and the wind biting our faces and hands till the skin was red raw. Then we knew they were lost, and we are left here all forgotten and nobody will remember when we are gone.'

Cara turned abruptly and left the hut, shielding her eyes against the noon-time glare outside. Holly's home was perched awkwardly on a knoll, some distance from the rest of the settlement, and from where she stood, Cara could see a tapestry of makeshift roofs, well-trodden paths and the bare red earth of the vegetable gardens and bean fields, already seeded in preparation for the coming spring. The sprawling dwellings were huddled in a narrow valley, partly shielded on both sides by steep slopes which eventually rose up to meet the first crags and peaks of the distant mountains. The harsh croaking of a colony of gryfons echoed among the rocks, and Cara saw some of the ungainly carrion birds wheeling above their cliff-top nests.

Every morning for as long as she could remember, she had looked down on that scene as she clambered up the steep track from the well at the bottom of the valley, staggering under the weight of the water bucket she carried with Minna. In winter, the same wind always blew clouds of gritty brown dust into their sting-ing eyes. In summer, the first fierce beams of Sol, the Osirian sun-star, were always shining over the moun-tains, glancing like lightning off the quartz boulders on the lower slopes, and, summer and winter, there was always a pencil-thin column of smoke wavering up from the squat chimney of the hut as Holly baked the morning loaves.

Waving her foster-mother a brief farewell, Cara set off back to the settlement where she and her sister shared a hut together. Her straggling brown hair kept

11

falling into her eyes as she walked along, and she pushed it back impatiently. She wore a thickly padded dog-skin jacket to shield her against the cold wind gusting through the valley, and her sturdy green boots were packed with strips of blanket for added warmth. There had been one storm already that morning, and she noticed the thick yellow clouds swirling overhead, showing that fouler weather was in store. Even as she neared the first cluster of huts, a few fat raindrops began to fall, swiftly becoming an icy deluge and turning the muddy path into a liquid red-brown quagmire which would stain skin and clothing for days. Hastily, she dodged into the open doorway of one hut which had stood empty since its old, embittered owner killed himself two summers before. It boasted a sheet-iron roof and was quite dry inside, although the ground was littered with chicken feathers and goat dung. A bristle-backed, long-snouted chargul, one of the scavenger creatures of the desert margin, bolted from a corner and ran out squealing into the downpour. Cara leaned against the wall, folded her arms inside her sleeves and watched the solid walls of rain close in on the valley.

Then hurried footsteps sounded on the path and a tall figure, huddled up in a patched and work-stained cloak, almost knocked her down in the rush to shelter from the storm.

'Your pardon,' said Cara stiffly, moving aside to let the stranger in.

'Please excuse me.' The stranger pulled back his hood and wiped the raindrops off his face. 'These winter storms are not good to walk out in.'

They stood in silence for a while, as the rain turned into hailstones as large as a clenched fist, battering the roof until it rang like a gong. Cara recognised the young man as a distant cousin of hers—but then

12

almost all the settlement people were related in some way. She remembered that his name was Gethin and that he had left Lesson Hall long before the other students, turning his hand to repairing the more ramshackle of the dwellings, as well as mending broken stools and tables. The storm eased a little and Gethin turned to look at her.

'Cara, isn't it?' he said. 'We were at Lesson Hall together.'

'A good while ago,' Cara replied. 'But Anno is still as distant and stern as if we were all just seven summers old.'

Gethin laughed. 'I've heard you're still working there, while the Assembly can't even get the smallest children to start learning these days. Sometimes I see the ones who still attend come running down the street at sunrise, clutching their little mats and eating their morning bread as they go, and quaking at the thought of old Anno's frown if they are late.'

'And is it any better to spend all day shivering in the wind and mending a broken roof?' Cara retorted scornfully. 'I have no skills like weaving or making pots or growing food, so why should I not study while there is Anno to teach me?'

'You were the girl who said she would disobey the Assembly and go off over the mountains and explore,' Gethin replied. 'I can still remember that day. Everyone was shouting and you were standing on the table and shouting back, with tears running down your face, and then Anno walked in.'

'And he gave me a beating for unruly behaviour, and old Holly sobbed for a week because she thought I would go the way of her favourite boy who walked off and was never seen again,' said Cara with a grin.

They fell silent once more. The storm clouds were

13

already breaking up at the far end of the valley, revealing the bleached sky above. Cara straightened up and was about to say a polite farewell when Gethin put out a hand as if to stop her.

'Are you going home now?' He looked down as he continued, tracing a pattern on the dusty floor with his boot. 'Because I'd be glad if I could come with you and meet your sister again.'

Cara stared in surprise. 'See Minna again?'

'Yes, if it's no trouble to you.'

She shrugged. 'No trouble. You may eat with us, if you wish.' Unfolding her arms from inside her jacket, she stepped out of the hut onto the sodden track leading to the rest of the settlement. Gethin strode beside her, a battered sack of tools under one arm.

Chapter Two

The downpour had not improved the settlement's appearance. Mud, thrown up by the feet of passers-by, was beginning to splatter the already piebald walls of the huts, carelessly repaired with crumbling brown plaster or rusty scraps of sheet-iron. Rubbish piles sank into wet heaps, oozing putrid slime into the gutters where shiny hordes of raches swarmed, their armoured black bodies as thick as a man's wrist. Children ran screaming out of gaping doorways to dabble in the filth, their bare legs mottled with cold. The air was thick with smoke from freshly kindled fires—not the aromatic smell of burning rua bark which Cara could still remember from her childhood, but the metallic odours of nameless refuse. At first the Assembly tried to regulate what was burned, but the people had to have fires and when rua wood became scarce, they kindled whatever they could find.

As Cara and Gethin trudged along the street, watched indifferently by two old men resting on their haunches under the eaves of the Assembly Hall, Cara thought how the dirt and squalor had gradually blighted the settlement. Even she could recall a time when things had not been so bad, when huts were wind-and

15

weather-proof, when all the children had come to learn their letters at Lesson Hall, when there had been enough wood to burn and plenty of fresh meat to eat, when babies had thrived instead of drooping and dying like sickly seedlings within a few weeks of birth.

They went over the crossroads and passed the graveyard where a small forest of quartz arrows rose out of the hard ground, pointing skyward to show that the decaying remains beneath were not of Osiris but descended from the real world, Earth, far beyond the stars.

'It is strange,' Cara said suddenly, 'how the young and old seem to die at the same time now, always weakening and shrivelling in spite of the best remedies.'

A young woman was being buried in the stony soil as they went by. Her family stood round weeping noisily while the graveyard keeper carefully stripped the body of the precious woven garments before lowering it into the shallow grave, bare and pitiful in the harsh light.

Gethin pointed at the mourners. 'That's my neighbour's daughter being buried there. She had the wasting sickness like her three brothers before her, and her father.'

Cara sighed. 'Do you not worry sometimes at how this wasting sickness is wiping out whole families in one winter? Surely you can remember when just a few people sickened and the Assembly said it was bad water, and then it was not enough green food and we all had to grow cabbages on every spare patch of ground, but none of that stopped the people from dying!'

Gethin nodded in agreement. 'Some say that more are dying every day. Others think there are already too many in the settlement. Women have six, eight, even

16

ten children and at least half reach their fourteenth year and start breeding themselves.'

Even as he spoke, they turned a corner and found themselves in the middle of a screaming rabble of young children who were playing a rough game of catch. There were several bloodied noses and torn tunics and one group of small boys wrestled fiercely in the mud, five or six bodies in a squirming heap. Cara and Gethin pushed their way through, fighting off the cluthching hands of some of the larger girls who tried to hold them back, asking for food, twine, scraps of cloth, anything the two could spare as a ransom. It had always been a midwinter custom that settlement children would pretend to take people hostage in the street, for a ransom of a simple gift like a polished nugget of quartz or a lump of cheese. It was not so long since Cara had done it herself.

Now the harmless tradition was becoming an excuse for constant begging and even robbery. There were a few gangs of children who spent all their time roaming the settlement, half-starved and sleeping rough wherever they found shelter. They had been known to snatch garments off the backs of unwary travellers who strayed into the winding side streets after dusk. Careless traders, hurrying back from the sprawling market, were sometimes pinned in a dark corner and threatened with rocks until they gave up their precious supplies of cured meat and oil, bought only that morning. The children would devour the meat in greedy mouthfuls and trade the oil for several jars of tappa, the fiery distilled liquid which the Assembly was always trying to ban.

Cara and Gethin managed to tear themselves away from the crowd without losing anything, although one grimy little girl, screaming in triumph, ran off with a

17

long strip from the hem of Gethin's cloak. They hurried through the crooked alleys of Alden, the dirtiest and most dilapidated quarter of the settlement, and then the way widened and started to zigzag up a hill, passing under the crumbling gateway leading to Eden, where the oldest dwellings stood. Eden was surrounded by a high wall, built to protect the first settlers from the unknown dangers of the new world. There were fewer huts here and many were in better repair than the rest of the settlement. Some even had carefully tended gardens beside the door. One or two women greeted Cara as they leaned out of a window to throw a pail of water into the gutter or shake the dirt from a faded blanket. As she drew near the red mud brick Lesson Hall, she crossed the street and suddenly turned right down the short path leading to her hut, Gethin hurrying to keep up. The hut stood apart from the others, just inside the encircling wall, with its back to the mountains beyond.

When they got to the door, they could hear someone singing inside to the accompaniment of the thud and creak of a loom. Cara knocked firmly four times, and the singing stopped. They heard footsteps crossing to the threshold and then the screech of bolts drawn back.

'Is that you, Cara?' a voice called.

'With a guest.'

The heavy door swung back on protesting hinges and they stepped in out of the cold. The room was lit by a flickering candle in a small dish, as well as by the leaping flames of the fire beneath a large black pot in the hearth. Shutters sealed windows because of the howling gale outside, and in the dimness Gethin stumbled over some bolts of cloth lying carelessly heaped in the middle of the floor. Cara held up the candle to light the way over to a round table near the fire where a

18

couple of stools were drawn up. Gethin courteously chose the stool farthest away from the heat and slung down his tool sack at his feet. As his eyes grew accustomed to the dimness, he saw that fringed rugs hung on every wall, woven in bold patterns and bright colours, and other rugs were spread underfoot, muffling the draughts and hiding the hard-packed earth floor. He caught his breath in astonishment. Although he knew that Minna was a weaver, he had not known she had a fortune in fine cloth hidden in her home. He still thought of her as the quiet, pretty girl at the back of the Lesson Hall, always daydreaming with a wistful expression on her face.

Cara noticed his stare and said warningly, 'Not a word of this outside, or the whole settlement will be tearing our hut apart.'

Minna now emerged from the shadows after rebolting the door and dragging across a thick curtain to keep out the wind. She smiled at the expression on Gethin's face. 'I could sell every one of these rugs at the market before spring,' she said. 'But I never show all my wares at once. I would either be robbed of my earnings on the way home, or thieves would break in here to see how much more I had stored away.'

'That one is—beautiful,' said Gethin, gazing at the swirling stars and rainbows on a hanging over the fireplace.

Minna shrugged. 'I weave whatever comes into my head. Some things I sell to buy food; others I keep because I like to look at them.'

Cara explained that Gethin was to eat with them, and Minna busied herself with the contents of the black pot which she ladled out into earthenware bowls. It was the kind of stew common in every settlement household, generous in watery gravy and thick with yellow anak

19

beans which were simmered until soft and swollen and bursting out of their tough skins. Minna had added a handful of thumon, gathered from the rocky crevices of the valley for the fiery taste of its tiny brown leaves. She drew up a third stool, and they began to eat in silence as was customary, mopping up the gravy with lumps of doughy beanmeal bread.

Gethin looked at Minna while they ate. Her hair was a lighter brown than her sister's and it hung in a long plait over her shoulder, tied with a scarlet hogskin thong. She was also shorter and thinner than Cara, and her eyes flashed violet in the firelight. As he stared at the hollow at the base of her throat, above the quartz pin which fastened the neck of her dark green gown, she glanced up and he hastily dropped his gaze to the scarred wooden table.

When they had finished, they pushed away the empty bowls and Minna filled three cups with freshly fermented anak beer. Now was the time for talk, and Gethin told Minna about what he had been doing since he left Lesson Hall and heard how she spent most of her time doing loomwork to support herself and her sister. They talked of the doings of the settlement—the lawless gangs of urchins, the decaying huts and the growing scarcity of food as the soil grew less fruitful and the relentless wind pared it away to the bare rock. Cara's Lesson Hall work was the compiling of a history of the people, with the help of Anno, and she told the others how in the minds of the oldest inhabitants there still lingered memories of nearly fifty years ago, when the settlement was surrounded by towering rua Forests that covered the land as far as the skirts of the mountains. In the easily tilled soil under the forests eaves, crops of grains, roots and fruit had grown plentifully, once the settlers had cleared away the trees. The timber was burnt in roaring log fires, and the settlers' own hogs and goats, brought from Earth, grazed on the rich grasses which grew swiftly in the brief spring. The chickens scratched about beneath the trees and laid many eggs.

Cara recounted how that morning she had ventured to visit a wrinkled old woman living in Alden, who had sobbed as she huddled over a smoking fire of dried dung while the inevitable pot of bean stew went cold in the ashes. She told how she had been raised on wheaten bread, handfuls of achingly sweet roh berries and oatmeal with as much fresh milk as she had wanted—in the olden days. Then the forests had sheltered the cluster of huts from the gales, and the gentle rain showers pattered on the rustling green leaves which fell in orange drifts when winter came. She remembered how low, bushy groves of nadel trees used to soften the foothills, and how star-shaped sida flowers had bloomed yellow and white across the valley every summer. But when the forests were gone, Sol seemed to burn hotter, and the rain fell in violent storms, carrying the soil away into the desert. In the space of a few years, crop after crop failed, leaving the people with little to tend except a few stunted vegetables and the anak bean vines, which continued to thrive in a climate that froze the settlement for three quarters of the year and roasted it for almost all the remaining time. The livestock had dwindled too, and now meat and eggs were jealously guarded and bartered at the highest prices. Saddest of all was the disappearance of the svala birds whose scarlet wings had flashed among the forest branches and whose fluting voices had once filled every twilight with song.

'And what is the Assembly doing about it all?' Cara finished. 'They probably hoard the best food so that they can feast at leisure.'

'The Assembly knows of your work,' said Minna suddenly.

Cara looked at her in surprise. 'Of course they do. Anno would never allow me to carry out a task which breaks one of their petty laws.'

'Oh Cara! The way you speak will get you into trouble one day!' Minna sighed. 'A message came for you at mid-morning from the Assembly. The aldermen have heard about the stories you gather and the things you have been saying about dirt and decay.'

'And so? Why did you not tell me this before?' said Cara crossly.

'They wish to see you at noon tomorrow. Anno must go as well. All the messenger would say was that they wish to discuss important matters with you.'

Meanwhile, Gethin was growing more and more uncomfortable. His old Lesson Hall companions clearly lived in a rebellious, troublesome world, very different from his own, with their gloomy tales and fear of robbery and hoard of expensive cloths. He cleared his throat and rose to leave, thanking the sisters for their hospitality. Cara stayed sitting at the table, staring moodily into the fire, but Minna smiled as she opened the door and said they would be pleased to see him again. As he set off down the path, the wind cutting through his cloak, he heard behind him the door slam shut and a heavy bolt sliding across. He quickened his step and turned homewards as the short winter afternoon darkened to nightfall.

Chapter Three

Morning dawned chilly and grey. The settlement people rose early during the winter months to work while the brief day lasted and save their fuel stores. Cara was woken as usual by their nearest neighbour whose hut boasted an ancient clock in a worn gilt case which had somehow survived the years and was inscribed on the bottom with the mysterious words 'A hand-made timepiece from England'. The clock face had lost most of the numbers but the battered hands still kept to the time-scheme of the old world. The neighbour—a plump farmer named Marris—banged on the sisters' door as he passed by on his way to climbing through a gap in the encircling wall and trudging off to his stony fields where he tended crops of anak beans, potatoes and a tiny, spindly patch of wheat from which he dreamed of making his fortune.

In her dreams Cara heard the knock and woke with a start. She unrolled herself from her layers of thick blankets and, shuddering with cold, hurried to the water jar to splash her face and neck before dressing in an assortment of goat hair leggings and warm tunics. She belted her jacket snugly round her waist and laced her boots tight, knowing from long experience how the wind would bite to the skin as soon as she set foot outside and would howl all day long in the Lesson Hall chimney. She had no time to sit and eat, so she grabbed a hunk of bread left over from the night before and hastily drank a cup of milk and water. Minna sat up sleepily in her corner bed, yawning and stretching. Cara smiled a brief farewell to her before unlocking the door and stepping out into the bitter midwinter day, remembering at the last moment to snatch up her rolled floor mat. She heard the door bolts screech home behind her.

The sky hung a blank ceiling of cloud over the settlement, and the people walked through the streets with heads bowed and shoulders hunched against the cold. The ceaseless wind drowned the early morning sounds of grumbling voices behind the thin hut walls, the bleating herds of goats anxious for milking-time and the rattle of cart wheels carrying grim-faced men and women off to work on their fields.

As Cara turned onto the main street, she saw hurrying in front of her one of the older girls who had stayed on at Lesson Hall when her companions left to start raising their own families or earn a living with some sort of menial labour. Cara liked Amma because she was eager to help with compiling the settlement history—but before she could call out a greeting, the thought of the history reminded her of the Assembly summons.

Even the possibility of Assembly interference with her work enraged Cara. She kicked hard at a clod of dried mud, sending it sailing through the air to explode in dusky red fragments against a nearby hut. A large rach wriggled indignantly out of a hole in the blotched wall, its orange tail poised to sting. Ignoring it, Cara clenched her hands into fists and walked faster and faster until she caught up with Amma. The other girl looked round at her approach, but her smile drooped at the sight of Cara's glowering face.

Cara sighed with exasperation as she fell into step beside her. 'This is not a good morning, Amma, so I shall spare you a greeting. I have been summoned before the Assembly.'

'Do you know why?' asked Amma timidly.

"They wish to discuss important matters with me and also with Anno. I think it is about my work—perhaps they are trying to find some reason to stop it, in case stirring up old memories makes the people discontented.'

By this time they had reached the arched Lesson Hall doorway and Amma hung back to let Cara enter first, according to Hall custom. Cara fell silent as they entered the small lobby where muddied boots and damp outer garments were stored. As the two girls fumbled at their laces with wind-stiffened fingers, they could hear someone pacing up and down the inner room, stockinged feet muffling the heavy tread. Cara went on in ahead of Amma, pausing on the threshold to bow politely to Anno, the instructor, who had stopped his pacing to scrutinise the pages of a manuscript which he held carefully, almost tenderly, in both hands. The room was quite bare apart from his three-legged stool, placed commandingly at one end. Cara remembered two rows of wooden benches and even a table in her first days at Lesson Hall, but they had all long since disappeared—sold or stolen for fuel.

Anno acknowledged her greeting with a brief nod and turned back to his manuscript. Cara hesitated. Although she was reluctant to disturb him, she was desperate to know whether the Assembly had sent word to him as well. She cleared her throat, but got no further than 'Excuse me, sir' when he interrupted.

'I presume the Assembly have sent their summons to you,' She nodded.

'I for one expected this to happen sooner,' he continued drily. 'There has been some talk of you and your work, and the Assembly always takes note when a matter arouses more than passing interest.'

He looked down at the manuscript again and turned a page so that Cara knew she was dismissed. She went down to the opposite end of the room and unrolled her mat in its customary place, close to the wide hearth where a small fire was crackling, sending showers of sparks up the chimney. She seated herself cross-legged on the mat, preparing to recall all the stories she had gathered during the previous day, and laid out the treasured pen which had belonged to her father, a pot of amber writing fluid and a square of goat-hide parchment, already half-filled with recollections. Then, as often happened when she was about to begin working, she was seized by an urge to daydream. She stared across at Anno and wondered, as she often did, about his past life. She liked gathering facts, and her interest in the instructor had first quickened when she had heard, quite by chance, that he had been an adventurer years before, when he was scarcely older than she was now.

It was Holly who told her that he used to travel up into the mountains, exploring farther than any had dared go before. He believed that there were greener, softer lands beyond and had hoped to find them, but suddenly the Assembly took fright and banned all journeys passing beyond a day's march from the settlement, on the grounds that too many strong young men and women never returned from their explorations, and the settlement could not afford to lose more.

26

According to Holly, however, Anno raged so furiously against the ban that the aldermen had ordered his imprisonment in the old settlement lock-up.

Cara had only ever known him as the taciturn Lesson Hall instructor who was half-feared, half-respected by the children and secretly laughed at by more than half the settlement for spending his time absorbed in learned matters which had little to do with everyday life. She had been gazing at the pale flames flickering in the hearth as she pondered, and when she looked up, she saw that a handful of children were now seated on their mats in the middle of the room, waiting for lessons to begin. Each balanced a writing board on his knees—a slab of wind-dried mud which was moistened with water and then marked with a sharpened stick, a scrap of metal or even a fingernail. The day's lessons were rubbed off back at home when the children had committed theirs to memory.

Cara had a morning's work to do before her appointment with the Assembly so she bent her head over her parchment and began, weighing each word before she wrote it. Meanwhile, Anno started to teach the eight children seated in front of him, ranging in age from Amma, who was in her seventeenth year, to little Jenna who was only six winters old. These days, lessons consisted of learning the workings of letters and numbers, reciting word-perfect the small part of settlement history which Cara had completed, and listening while Anno told a story about Earth or read aloud from his own manuscripts. The younger children knew no better than to accept as true the tales he told about their own settlement world—tales about the winged feys who were the colour of light and made the wind blow, about the dog, black as night, who howled for the passing of every Earth-born soul, and about Kalkona,

27

the terrible red-eyed beast which lived out on the desert plains and was only held back from destroying them all by its fear of fire.

This morning, Anno told them about the last Earth wars and gave them long lists of dates and names to remember, showing how petty quarrels turned to nation feuding against nation. 'The last wars happened because of pride and distrust. The great cities and fertile lands were destroyed, all because the people could not put aside their pride and distrust,' he said. He told them again about the plans to rebuild the lost glory of Earth on the planet of Osiris which had been found and settled by a brave band of colonists not many years before, and about the terrible storms which had driven off-course and separated the two huge starships carrying the remnant of Earth people to their new home.

Anno surveyed his pupils gravely. 'All of us, all of our settlement, came from the ship Sirius. But without Orion—the second ship that was lost—and without all its supplies, we can scratch out only a castaway life here.' The smallest children stared back at the instructor with bored or puzzled faces, but the older ones worked away busily at their writing boards, slowly piecing together a picture of Earth, the half-forgotten mother-world.

'For,' said Anno, 'the first settlers here were foolish and cut down the sheltering forests and exhausted the land by growing too many crops, and one day our valley will turn to desert.'

The room was very quiet and some of the children close to tears at the horrifying thought of the desert swallowing up their homes and leaving them alone in the wind and the roaring dark. The fire had sunk to a nest of glowing cinders and the only sound was the scratch of Cara's pen on the parchment. Then they heard voices and footsteps in the street outside. Doors banged and dogs barked. It was noon, and time for the settlement to stop work and eat the midday meal.

Chapter Four

The heavy Lesson Hall door swung shut behind Cara as she followed Anno into the street, huddling into her jacket against the cold and pushing her hands deep into the pockets. As they started down towards the gateway leading to the rest of the settlement, jostled by the crowds hurrying back to the shelter of their huts for a noon-time rest, she ventured to speak.

'Sir,' she began in a breathless voice, hesitated, and then began again. 'Sir, do you know why we are being summoned?'

Anno frowned and said nothing until they had passed under the old gateway where their feet crunched fragments of the bricks which had fallen in the winter storms. When he did reply, he did not answer her question.

'Many laugh at the Assembly behind the aldermen's backs, but they rule over us and their authority is one of the few things still holding our settlement back from chaos. We must respect them. Years ago, when I was young, matters were very different. Then the Assemly could still wield enough power to do whatever it wished. I myself felt that power.'

Cara said without thinking, 'You wanted to explore

beyond the mountains and, when they forbade you, you fought against them until you were thrown into the lock-up.' Then she bit her lip in embarrassment at revealing her secretly gathered knowledge.

Anno gave her a glance tinged with amusement. 'So you have been studying my own history as well? But I suspect the whole settlement has talked of it ever since. A fine tale for a long winter evening round the fire—how the foolhardy Anno got his just reward.'

Cara's cheeks burned. 'I don't waste my time with stupid gossip, but old Holly will talk to the clouds if there is no one else to listen, and she has filled my ears with all the stories she has ever gathered.'

Anno lowered his voice. 'She may not have told you the truth of it, then. The aldermen said my wilfulness would lead the people astray because I talked of reckless adventure, not building up the life of the settlement here. They told me that if I continued to disobey, they would have no choice but to have me publicly disgraced and if that were not enough, they could even execute me. I have not been Lesson Hall instructor all these years just for the love of learning. When they first released me from the lock-up, I was too weak for any other kind of work, and most people were afraid to associate with me.'

Cara stared at him, amazed at his frankness. He had never revealed so much of himself before. She realised for the first time how terrible the lock-up must have been and why the older people always spoke of it with a shudder. The dreary edifice had been built using part of the metal hull of the ship so that the inmates froze in winter and roasted when summer came. A mob had broken the doors and ransacked it two winters ago, during the annual Karnavale when normally timid men and women were inflamed by heavy drinking and the more belligerent-minded worked themselves into a frenzy. The Assembly had ordered its rebuilding and posted stewards to guard the ruins, but thieves still managed to carry off scraps of the precious metal. The lock-up remained unfinished and semi-derelict.

'Much has changed since that time,' said Anno. 'The aldermen's power has dwindled as the settlement has grown, and I think I have grown a little wiser with the passing of time. I used to dream of overthrowing the Assembly, and I know that there are many who might even now be willing to try rebellion—but I do not think the settlement would be a happier place because of it.'

'But—' Cara said in bewilderment, 'but you could get rid of the stupid, pompous aldermen and—and form a good Assembly which will let us alone and repair the huts and see that everybody has enough food to eat and let you—'

'And let me journey away?' Anno's grey eyes smiled at her suddenly. 'I am too old now, and the time for such adventure has gone. Besides,' he grew serious again, 'I fear that far more evil than good would come of such an uprising. I have come to see the Assembly's power can be a safeguard as well as a restraint.'

They fell silent as their way led them through the broken streets of Alden. Curiously, no children were running about, and every door and shutter was fastened, although Cara felt that eyes were peering through the cracks and watching their progress. The sky boiled with grey clouds, turbulent in the high wind and gathering in a purple stain over the desert. Somewhere far out on that sterile plain lay the last battered remnants of Sirius, scattered over the barren rock by years of winter storms and bleached by the fierce summer heat.

They were passing the graveyard, where only a heap

of freshly turned soil marked the place where Gethin's neighbour was buried, when Cara spoke again. She was not afraid of Anno, after years of observing his abrupt moods, but she did not want to make a fool of herself by speaking her private thoughts if he had retreated into his usual distant, formal self.

'I have sometimes wished for more than my place at the back of the Lesson Hall, sir,' she began. 'I have sometimes looked at the mountains at the end of the valley and the desert plain and longed to go and see what might be there.'

Anno said nothing and for the second time in their conversation Cara felt overwhelmed with shame at her forwardness. She was vowing never to speak openly to him again, when he halted and gazed at her for a moment without speaking. She looked down, suddenly embarrassed. Then he stepped closer to her and laid a firm hand on her shoulder.

His voice was stern. 'Listen to me, Cara. A time may come when we can talk openly of leaving and journeying away, perhaps leaving the settlement forever. But for the moment we must work to safeguard our people. We must respect the Assembly and its laws, even if they do not fit our own wishes.' As they continued down the muddy alley which was a short cut to the Assembly Hall, he said, 'I will tell you one more thing. I think that before many winters have passed, the settlement we know will have gone. There are too many people and less and less food. Those aldermen who are a little wiser than their fellows may perceive this and fight disruption while they can, or they may not. Consider that, Cara, and speak of it to no one!'

His voice sank to a whisper as he finished, because they were now back in the main street where the faded red walls of the Assembly Hall loomed high above the other buildings. In turn these seemed to lean towards it, as if trying to shelter under its sagging eaves. There was always a group of old men resting on the cracked strip of quartz paving which ran round the hall, watching the people pass by, drinking watery beer and reminiscing endlessly about their youth. Cara had spoken to them in the course of her work, and one of them waved a shaky greeting as she climbed the flight of steps leading to the gloomy chamber where those with Assembly business had to wait until the grey-robed stewards called them in.

The airless room was packed with women shuffling back and forth, and noisy with a mingled weeping and cursing. Tearful, anxious voices disputed with the stewards guarding the doors of the inner hall where the aldermen sat. Anno shouldered a path through the crowd to where the chief steward perched on his high stool, a heavy register on his knees, directing who might be allowed in and out. Carà followed as best she could.

'What is all this confusion?' she asked as soon as she reached Anno's side.

'It seems that half the women of the settlement are here today to try and speak in defence of their children who have been rounded up along with the urchin gangs for punishment,' he shouted back over the din.

The reason for the silence in the normally bustling streets of Alden became clear. Cara looked at the crowd and saw strained, frightened faces, some hollow-cheeked and some round and flushed with the heat of the thronged room. Most of the women clutched babies, enveloped in tattered shawls, and many had two or three small children clutching at their legs as well. The chief steward was telling Anno that the Assembly had been at work all morning, sitting in

34

judgement first on petty offenders who received fines for stealing loaves of bread or allowing their dogs to run wild. Now they were dealing with the lawless children.

'Forty of them are in there now, little dirty wretches, more like wild animals. The aldermen had to call in extra stewards to keep order, and they've been sentencing them five at a time, in rows with a steward at each end. Most of them will escape with a good beating, but some say—' the chief steward paused significantly, clutching at his register to keep it from sliding to the floor, 'some say there might even be a hanging or two—in public, perhaps, to teach the rest of them a lesson.' He nudged Anno in the ribs. 'And who knows? You might get a few more youngsters at Lesson Hall after this, dragged there by frightened mothers to keep them out of mischief.'

Anno moved back, his mouth curled in distaste. 'We were summoned here to speak to the Assembly on a matter of private business and have left our work to do so. Kindly inform the aldermen that Anno is waiting to see them and cannot wait till nightfall.'

Just then the inner doors were flung open. Struggling to see over the heads of the crowd, Cara noticed a short, earnest-looking girl steward emerging from the Assembly room. She called shrilly for silence and announced that the aldermen were having a brief recess and that she had orders to read out the sentences passed on the children. Judgements were always declared in this way even if there was no one in the outer chamber except a handful of stewards and one or two old men come in to shelter from heat or cold. Cara recognised the steward as an old friend of Minna's, a dull, hard-working girl who achieved her sole ambition when she gained a steward's post. The list of forty names droned on—ten of the children were pronounced innocent and allowed to rush into the arms of their sobbing mothers. Thirteen were convicted of theft and lawless behaviour and sentenced to a dozen strokes of the rod. Eleven other children were allotted two dozen strokes, which the aldermen judged a severe beating, for their part in a number of violent robberies.

The steward paused, wetting her lips nervously, and Cara guessed that she was reluctant to read out the judgements on the remaining six children, even though the room was now almost empty as many mothers hurried off to fetch the usual bribes of cheap blankets and sticks of firewood for the stewards in the hope that their children would be let off unharmed.

'The Assembly decrees that for the crime of lawlessly taking the life of Elmo the labourer in a back street of the district of Alden sixteen nights ago, the urchins known as Kez, Lora, Tem, Melia, Ley and Cal will be shut up from this day on in a safe and secret place until the Assembly decrees otherwise.' The steward hastily rolled up the list and darted back into the inner hall, closing the door behind her.

In the utter silence that followed, Cara tensed herself for the screams of outrage, but the women who had been waiting for the judgement seemed too stunned to make a sound. One pale girl, heavy with child, fainted and was carried out by her companions. Then, in the same numbed silence, the room emptied save for Anno, Cara and the stewards, who had expected an angry mob to form and exchanged puzzled glances as the last woman descended the steps into the street, her face strained with bewilderment and grief. The chief steward was shaking his head.

'This is bad for the Assembly, very bad,' he said to

36

Anno. 'Lawlessness must be punished but at what price? They might have reason to imprison one or two, but six! We'll see rioting over this matter, even before the Karnavale.' He glanced down at his register. 'You and your young friend can go in now, but don't expect a long hearing. The aldermen are tired and want to finish their day's work soon.'

At Anno's brisk knock, the doors were flung open and Cara saw for the first time the chamber where the governing of the settlement took place. As yet another steward came forward and beckoned them to stand before the aldermen's benches, she glanced round at the crumbling walls and the high vaulted roof where ancient cobwebs swayed slowly in the draughts. The walls were covered with large frescoes, depicting settlement history in a series of crudely painted scenes, beginning with a shapeless silver-coloured object which Cara guessed was Sirius, surrounded by a sea of smiling pink and brown faces. The next picture showed the happy settlers rushing to build their new homes at the foot of impossibly steep, streaky red mountains. Although she could see no sign of the lost rua forests, Cara was sure that if she examined the walls closely, she would be able to find where the trees had been discreetly painted over. Elsewhere, patches of livid green damp spoiled many of the frescoes, and the plaster had cracked and was flaking away to expose the mud bricks underneath.

The heat from the tiny fire at the far end of the hall did not reach far and Cara began to shiver, partly with cold and partly with nervousness. To calm herself, she began studying the aldermen's benches, which were narrow and backless, with the sole comfort of torn brown cushions. She was trying to calculate the immense value of the quantity of wood when a small

37

door opened and the twenty-five aldermen filed in, stumbling over their long saffron robes and blowing on their numb fingers. While they found their places, their elected spokesman for the day took his place in the only chair, placed on the left of the benches and distinguished by richly carved armrests and an inlaid back.

'Let the proceedings of the Osirian Assembly commence.' The spokesman, whose exhausted face mirrored his tired voice, began reading hurriedly from a book even larger and thicker than the chief steward's register. 'Anno, Lesson Hall instructor, and Cara, Lesson Hall pupil. It has come to the attention of this Assembly that you have been stirring up discontent among the older settlers by asking them to dwell on past days as part of a so-called history of the settlement. The aldermen have had many reports of this causing great distress to these settlers, as well as tempting their sons and daughters to use the supposed decline of our community to justify their own laziness and selfishness. The aldermen feel this is a threat to the safety of our people. Have you anything to say before the Assembly passes judgement?'

Looking at Anno's grim expression, Cara guessed that the words of the announcement startled even him. She could not think what to say, and her eyes ranged over the seated rows of aldermen, many with their heads resting wearily in their hands or gazing back at her with heavy-lidded expressions. Anno, however, addressed himself to the whole gathering.

'Cara undertook the work with my permission, to extend her own studies and provide matter for the younger children to learn. Far from meaning harm to settlement life, we intended to give our people the dignity of a history of their own instead of leaving them

38

feeling that they were no more than remnants of an older civilisation and–' He was interrupted by a short, red-faced alderman on the second row who fidgeted irritably with the sleeve of his robe as he spoke.

'Very honourable, I am sure, but it alarms and upsets the people. Two young men accosted me on my doorstep this morning with the rumour that nobody is allowed more than a day's journey from the valley because the Assembly has its own secret supplies of grain and timber over the mountains. We cannot afford such rumours spreading in these days.'

He shut his mouth with a snap and sat down heavily. A stout woman on the front row leaned towards the spokesman and whispered something. The spokesman nodded several times, noting a remark in the margin of his book.

'Have you anything further to say?' he asked Anno and without pausing for a reply added, 'I have been reminded that the Assembly has already discussed the matter at length, and it is not proper for debate to begin again among the aldermen themselves.' He frowned at the red-faced man who was muttering to his neighbour.

Anno's mouth was tight with exasperation as he answered, 'Since, O learned Assembly, the matter is settled already, why waste breath? Since my pleading is useless, I will not offer it.'

He stood with folded arms, staring hard at the spokesman while the judgement was read out. Cara was to cease immediately all activities concerned with the writing of the history, and Anno was banned from giving her encouragement or guidance for that work. The aldermen noted the devotion of the instructor to his duties and regretted the decreasing number of children attending Lesson Hall. They suggested that Cara could be appointed as an apprentice instructor and spend her time visiting settlement households in search of recruits for new classes which she could then teach.

'Salute!' A steward's voice rang out and Cara, dazed by the suddenness of it all, bowed her head while the aldermen retreated through the little door, leaving behind an overpowering smell of musty cloth. She followed Anno out through the main door, down the steps and into the cold street where she was momentarily dazzled by the brightness of Sol, escaped from behind the clouds and glinting off the quartz paving. Judging by the light, it was midway through the afternoon.

'You may have the rest of the day to yourself, if you wish.' Anno's voice came from far away. 'I can only say that I am sorry that this should happen to you, Cara, but do not allow yourself to be too bitter.' Then he turned and set off back to the Lesson Hall. Cara remained standing desolately at the edge of the street, the wind whipping her long hair across her face. She watched his retreating figure until he vanished round a corner.

Chapter Five

Burning in a vast cloudless sky, the mid-morning sun turned the smudged walls of the huts into glittering mirrors of light. The crisp air was bright with cold, and Minna's sage green wrap was a vivid patch of colour as she toiled up the hill towards Eden, carrying a heavy sack over one shoulder. A single gryfon sailed overhead on dirty brown wings, but she ignored its harsh cry. She had risen early to forage among the stalls at the labyrinthine market where some of the settlement people spent their days trading and stealing everything from sturdy hogskin boots to torn pages from ancient books, brought from Earth long ago and offered for barter at hugely inflated prices. Even though few could read, and the pages were usually so dirty as to be illegible, many people believed that a scrap of print pinned above the hearth lent a prosperous air to a household.

Ever cautious about revealing her full store of woven goods, Minna only took two small rugs for bartering, each flecked and striped in a different pattern and brilliant with dyes that would eventually fade to duller hues through everyday use. After an hour or so of skilful bargaining, she had exchanged them for generous portions of anak beans and potatoes, a sliver of smoked pork, a sealed pot of soured milk and, most precious of all, several bundles of unspun hair. Since the demand for clothing had risen far beyond the existing supplies of goat and dog hair, quite a few people had taken to letting their own hair grow long and selling it to the spinners and weavers for as much as they could make.

When Minna reached the Eden gateway, she paused to shift the sack onto her other shoulder and then turned left down a side-street which led to a spacious courtyard formed by three long huts. A group of little children, stout with layers of clothing, were hunting raches but stopped and came running to greet her with shouts of recognition. She laughed at their eagerness as they clustered round to escort her into the hut across the courtyard, the home of Minna's foster-brother Medwin and his wife Hanni, who worked as a spinner to help feed and clothe their expanding family.

As Minna entered, Hanni was busy pinning her long yellow hair into an untidy bun, but she stopped to embrace her visitor warmly and to seat her before the fire in the front room, which ran the length of the hut. A large window at one end let in the light and kept out the cold with two precious panes of glass. Medwin guarded the panes jealously and took them out every night in case of thieves. He had built the hut himself, adding two smaller sleeping chambers behind the bright front room. Although they had eight children and a ninth due before the summer, Medwin and Hanni tried to run an orderly household and even insisted on all their children spending some time at Lesson Hall, if only to learn how to write their names. Hanni was Minna's only close companion beside Cara, and she showed her gratitude for the other woman's friendship by making clothes for the children and occasionally pressing a gift of food into her hands as she left. Now she delved into her sack and produced five snugly woven little smocks, worked in the brightest colours she could find.

Hanni laughed and shook her head at Minna's generosity. 'I suppose I must accept these for being your friend?'

'Just something for the children, because the wind is colder than ever this winter,' Minna pleaded, beckoning over six-year-old Feya and struggling to pull one of the smocks over her small golden head. Hanni relented and handed out the other garments to whichever of the children was nearest, before offering Minna her usual cup of fresh milk from the family goat who lived a pampered life in a draught-free shed at the back of the hut, sheltered from both heat and storms.

Minna handed over the bundles of hair which she would return to collect a few days later as neatly wound balls of yarn, ready for threading onto the loom. After Hanni had stacked them in a corner for combing and sorting, she seated herself at her spinning wheel, ordered the children outside again and set to work on the last hanks of some coarse black dog hair. The creak of the treadle and the crackling of the fire filled the room with drowsiness and Minna cupped her chin in her hands, watching her friend's fingers skilfully twisting the hair into a fine thread.

'I rose before dawn to get to the market in time to find good bargains,' she remarked.

Hanni surveyed the bundles of hair with an expert eye. 'You always bring me good quality, never that twice-woven and shredded rubbish which some traders try to pass off as new shearing.' It was acceptable to unravel and rework old garments and blankets, but some unscrupulous dealers would spend hours pulling the yarn to pieces so that careless buyers thought they were getting unspun hair at a fair price.

'How has your sister been keeping these past few days?' Hanni asked after a pause.

'She had gone out even before I woke this morning, without a word. Maybe to attend Lesson Hall—but I'm beginning to think she has not set foot there since the Assembly ban on her work. She took that very hard.' Minna spoke softly, gazing into the hearth where the fire was dying into feathery ashes. Hanni shook her head sympathetically and carried on spinning.

Minna suddenly found she had to fight hard to choke back a sob as she remembered Cara's recent behaviour, alternating between sullen silence and black rages which burst out at the slightest provocation. 'She is very angry at being forbidden to continue with her history. She says that there is nothing else she wants to do.'

Hanni sighed. 'She has an independent nature and hasn't been checked before. She should be glad that the Assembly's power is less than it was. Once it might have decided to break her spirit, like it broke the spirit of the Lesson Hall instructor.'

'You think Anno has a broken spirit? I thought that Cara took some of her own fierceness and freedom from watching him.'

'All I know is what I remember from when I was a young girl of about ten winters, same age as my Hal. The Assembly threw Anno into the lock-up for defying the ban on long journeys. He was in there five years, partly because he had no close family or friends to offer bribes for his release.' Hanni's kindly face was full of concern. 'When he came out, he was all wasted and weak and didn't say a word to anyone but quietly took himself off to the Lesson Hall.'

Mina made no reply, and the laughter and excited

44

cries of the children floated in from the courtyard. Then she rose, gathering up her sack.

'I must return home now,' she said. 'Have you heard the rumours about riots over those Alden children who've been imprisoned?'

Hanni nodded. 'Medwin promised to come back from the fields well before dark because there might be trouble. Did anybody talk of it in the market?'

'Not openly, but I saw many anxious faces about, and one of the meat traders told me I should take care to bolt my door and window shutters tightly tonight.'

Minna kissed Hanni goodbye and set off for her own hut, pursued by the voices of the children calling farewells after her. The sky had filled with enormous swollen clouds which came scudding from over the mountains on the rising wind, and Minna paused as she neared the Lesson Hall to look down over the rest of the settlement and watch the rapidly shifting shadows on the walls and rooftops. She wondered whether to stop at the Hall and see whether Cara was there, but when she tried the door, it was locked. She noticed too that no smoke was rising from the chimney. No doubt Anno had given the children a half-day holiday and Cara would be waiting for her back at the hut.

The door of the hut was also locked, however, and when Minna entered, she found the room in darkness and the air cold and stale. She opened the shutters of the window facing away from the nearby dwellings, offering a glimpse of the mountains over the crumbling outer wall. There was no sign that Cara had been back since daybreak. Minna revived the fire, trimmed and lit a lamp, and set about straightening the disorder of bedding, garments and dirty bowls and plates in the small room. Then she drew the loom out of its corner and arranged a half-finished strip of coarse blanket to make it look as if she were in the middle of working. After checking that the door was securely bolted, she fastened the rest of the shutters as tightly as possible, wedging the cracks with folded rags.

At last she drew a deep breath and, pulling aside the star- and rainbow-patterned cloth hanging above the hearth, she tugged a large loose brick out of the wall. Reaching into the dark cavity behind, she brought out a small wooden box with a carved lid. It was the one heirloom given by her parents, who had died long before she could remember them. But it was chiefly precious for what it contained. Cara knew nothing of it, and even if she had discovered it and asked her sister what the treasure was, Minna would not have told her. There were few secrets in the overcrowded settlement, but this was perhaps one of the most closely guarded.

Seating herself at the table, she took out a length of fine-woven material, swathed in an old piece of sacking to protect it from dust. She unfolded it carefully and studied it, starting at one end. A series of needle-worked pictures lay before her, joined together by a meticulously stitched seam. Each picture was different, but the same details recurred—a slender brown-haired girl; a bare, wintry landscape of a valley lying between bleak hills; a shabby hut with thin smoke trickling from the chimney; a tall man robed in dark blue, holding out his arms to the girl who ran towards him with light in her face. The man's face was always turned away so that only the girl in the picture could see it. Minna had worked each scene with a tiny steel needle which Holly had given her long ago and the finest thread she could find.

She first began one empty afternoon, not long after she had left Lesson Hall to begin work as a weaver. Sit-

46

ting alone and forlorn in the cold hut, she had been suddenly overcome by black despair at the thought of all the hours and days, all the summers and winters which she would have to fill with some sort of purpose. She had always been a dreamer, and was shaken by the knowledge that the dream-time was over and she had to start struggling from darkness to darkness to provide for herself and her sister, locked forever in the grimy settlement world.

Then, as she sat crying into her folded arms on the unyielding tabletop, she remembered a tale told by Anno one long Lesson Hall morning, about a young girl kept locked in a tower until a man Anno called a prince passed by and heard her singing. After many trials, he rescued her and carried her off to his enchanted kingdom where she forgot her days of sadness in a lifetime of bliss. The tale had sunk deep into Minna's heart and returned to comfort her, and she had resolved to create her own tale to dream in—a tale of herself as the beloved found by the prince wandering in a lonely land, in exile from his enchanted realm. He would meet her and declare his love, and she would wait for his return, when his labours would be over and he would summon her to his bright kingdom where the sun shone on grassy meadows, swift rivers and the silver roof of his lofty hall.

Each picture told a different part of the story, and Minna would gaze at them and weave the dream in her mind, or sometimes make a new one—the last piece of cloth was blank except for an outline of hut and hills worked in black thread.

She closed her eyes, trying to decide what to do with the short time left before she must set to work on the muted stripes of a cloak she was weaving for one of the aldermen. He had stopped her in the market that

47

morning and ordered her to have it ready at noon on the following day. Looking down, she saw one of her favourite scenes. She began to dream.

The lonely girl stood at the door of her little hut, feeling the rough wood of the threshold under her bare feet. Behind her was the sparsely furnished room, containing only a narrow bed, a table and a stool. She gazed out at a landscape of brown sameness, where the rounded hills rose on either side against a sky entirely void of colour. She was watching the crest of the hill where the path from the wide world crossed over to descend into her valley, and in the emptiness of her heart a tiny hope welled-up, as it did each day until the blue-black shadows crept across the rocky ground and night came down like sudden blindness.

Then she caught her breath, and her fingers tightened on the doorpost as a figure outlined itself against the hill-top, pausing on the path to survey the valley spread out beneath. Before he raised a hand to wave at her, she knew who it was and started to run towards him. Her prince had come back, and she forgot in that instant of recognition all the long days and nights of waiting. When she reached him, he opened his arms and held her tightly, and she looked up into the eyes which she feared she had forgotten and saw that they shone with the joy and tenderness of the reunion.

He was footsore and weary after his journey, and he leaned on her arm as they went slowly down the path back to her door. His voice was as gentle as she remembered, as he told her that his labours continued, fighting to regain his kingdom from the dark forces. One day, though, the battles would be over and he would call her to come and make her home with him.

'This is a hard, cold land to leave you in, beloved,' he said. 'but you can dwell here safely until all is ready for your homecoming.'

'Tell me what has befallen you in the days since we last met.

At least I can share in the story of it,' she replied. They entered the little hut and sat side by side on the bed, and he began.

Minna's closed eyes flew open and she jumped up from the table, hastily folding the pictures and thrusting the little box back into its hiding place. A soft knocking at the door. Now it came again—someone trying to attract her attention without alerting the whole neighbourhood. She struggled with the bolts and opened the door a crack, peering out to see who the visitor was. To her surprise she found an anxious-looking Gethin standing on the threshold, pinched with cold and carrying a small bundle under his arm.

'Gethin! Are you not working this morning?' Then she saw by the light that it was the noon-time break and beckoned him inside. He handed her the bundle, saying it was a gift in return for her hospitality the other day, and shiveringly went to stand in front of the fire which had settled to a bed of glowing ashes. The bundle proved to be a piece of hard brown cheese, a settlement delicacy because of its sweet taste. Minna thanked him and said that he must stay and eat some of it with her. While she built up the fire and set out a half-loaf of bread and some beer, Gethin wandered round the hut, examining the rugs strewn over the floor and hanging on the walls.

'Where's Cara?' he asked carelessly, twisting the fringes on a purple and moss green blanket spread over one of the beds.

Minna straightened up from tending the fire. 'I have not seen her today. The Lesson Hall is closed, so I think she must have business elsewhere.'

Gethin's anxious look returned. 'I've heard there could be trouble in the streets of Alden tonight. I felt I should come and warn you.'

Minna tried to hide a smile. 'Thank you for your thoughtfulness, but I have already heard the rumours this morning in the market, and I'm sure Cara will have heard something as well. Come and eat.'

After they had finished the slabs of crumbly yellow bean bread and thin slices of cheese, Gethin told Minna about the doings in Alden, the settlement quarter where the Assembly Hall lay and where he shared a spacious hut with three friends. His building and repairing skills were much in demand as the people grew more distrustful of one another and wanted stronger doors and tightly fitting shutters. Families spoke in secret of the Assembly's loss of power and the need for each household to start fighting for its own safety.

'And did you know, Minna, that some are even talking of leaving the settlement and going to find another valley, perhaps travelling over the mountains?'

Minna shook her head. 'I think that is Cara's secret dream, and it is consuming her heart, but even she must see that it would be a terrible choice to make—to leave the little that we know here to go in search of what may be no more than certain death.'

Gethin smiled, 'I have plenty to keep me content in the settlement, and now that I'm finding new companions . . . ' He hesitated, and Minna felt her cheeks burning. They were both silent for a moment and then Gethin reluctantly rose to his feet. 'I must be off now and finish my day's work. I wouldn't want to be out in the streets after nightfall, and I shall look out for Cara and tell her to hurry home.' Minna decided to accompany him as far as the gateway to stretch her limbs in the cold sunshine, and he waited while she found her wrap and locked the door from the outside. She took his proferred arm shyly and they set out along the path leading to the main street, chased by light and shadow as the great clouds sailed overhead.

As they neared the gate, overlooking the sprawling mass of huts and fields below, they saw that the lower streets were swarming with unusual activity. Shouts and screams were carried up to them on the wind and when they looked towards the rusty iron roof of the Assembly Hall, they saw thickening columns of smoke rising. As they turned to one another in disbelief and horror, they noticed a man who came running up the slope in their direction. Minna clutched Gethin's arm, but it was only her neighbour Marris who stumbled towards them, his face yellow with exhaustion and fear.

'It's started,' he moaned, his breath coming in sobbing gasps. 'They're setting fire to the Assembly Hall, and they have blood on their hands already.'

Chapter Six

The desert floor of finely ground red dust sparkled with tiny fragments of quartz, clinging to Cara's boots and glittering on her garments. She stumbled over half-submerged rocks or the twisted stumps of long-dead trees in the path of her headlong, reckless running.

She had started running when approaching nightfall would hide her flight from prying settlement eyes, although most people had joined the stampeding hordes in front of the burning Assembly Hall. She had returned home after a futile day spent wandering through the back alleys, when she was caught up in the tumult. At first she was filled with a kind of horrified delight at what was happening. A crowd of Alden men and women had finally dared to show their hatred of the aldermen openly by trying to burn down the Assembly Hall. Although stray vagabands and bored children soon swelled the crowd to a mob, a good many loyal citizens were roused by the sight of their hall being mistreated by a dirty rabble. They dispersed the mob and extinguished the fire, but not before it had badly charred the venerable main door. When the excitement was over, stewards found the mutilated body of a white-haired alderman lying in the street. He had ventured out in his ceremonial robes to remonstrate with the rioters.

Watching from a sheltering doorway, Cara saw the chaos being tidied up and was suddenly overwhelmed by numbing despair. Nothing would ever change in the settlement. It was untidy, miserable and sometimes dangerous, but common sense would always prevail. Nobody was upset by being forced to see the true wretchedness of their lives, and everybody had enough spirit-breaking work to keep them too tired to try and change anything. She did not want to go back to the hut and hear Minna exclaiming over how fortunate they had all been, so she started walking, taking turnings at random. When it began to grow dark, she found that she had come to the very edge of the settlement, where ramshackle huts and stony fields came to an abrupt end on the waterless red shore of the desert. She did not need to return home for food because she carried a flask of water and half a bean-cake left over from her noon meal. Without another thought, she broke into a run.

It was deepest night now, and she did not know how far she had travelled. Her feet had carried her on, always away from the settlement and into the heart of the desert, hour after hour, as the last light vanished and the huge Osirian stars came out one by one. One of old Holly's choruses of regret at the lost Earth-world beat in her mind in rhythm with the crunch of her boots on the gritty rock: 'I cried when they said there's no moon on Osiris. The stars burn bright, but there's no moon and, oh, I cried when they said . . . ' As her legs moved mechanically, one in front of the other, she tried to gather her thoughts, to explain to herself what she was doing. She saw herself presenting her case to

53

Anno in the echoing Lesson Hall, with his stern grey eyes fixed enquiringly upon her.

Her voice was high-pitched and breathless in the cold air. 'Sir, I am going into the desert. I want to find where the ship landed. I want to prove for myself that there once was more for us than the settlement and the valley, that we were once part of a wiser, stronger people.'

She stopped speaking; the silence of the desert closed round her like a trap. There was no wind, and each breath she took thundered in her ears. She did not know where to go to look for the First Ship except to carry straight on, keeping the far-off black line of the mountains at her back. Her body felt light and tireless, carried along by a fierce flood of hope which overflowed because she was at last doing something to fulfil a long-held dream. She wanted to find for herself just one small token to show that the past was true, something more tangible than a crumbling Assembly Hall fresco or a Lesson Hall tale. Deep down, she feared that if she found nothing to show that there had ever been a ship from another world, her hopes would finally collapse. She would choose to die in the desert rather than go back to the settlement for a life of squalor and ugliness and disappointment.

Her run slowed to a walk and then to a hesitant stumbling and scrambling as the uneven ground became a tortured maze of craters and jutting rocks, with the fleshy stems of juss bushes thrusting their way out of the cracked ground. The starlight and the midnight sky were slowly disappearing behind a fine haze of cloud, and gusts of wind began to raise little eddies of dust in the still air.

Tired out, she decided to halt for a rest beneath the shelter of a huge boulder. Huddling deep into her jacket to keep warm, she leaned back and gazed at the troubled sky, trying to pick out the familiar constellations—the Sword, the Sickle, the Golden Rain. Then she looked further, searching out specks of light so remote that they were almost invisible. Maybe Earth lay even further off. She wondered if any humankind still lingered on the home world, and whether they ever thought of the band of people who flew away into the night and were never heard of again.

Then as she crouched against the boulder, she thought she heard a faint scuffling sound coming from somewhere in front. She held her breath to listen, and the sound came again, like fingers scrabbling in the dust. She clenched her fists to stop herself crying out— and a tiny hunched shape scurried round the boulder and stopped right in front of her, rearing up on its hind legs to inspect her. Then it dropped down, and the scratching sound began again. Cara strained to see in the dimness and realised that she was looking at a bora, so named by the first settlers. Holly had often told her about the boras, little hairless creatures with shiny black skin, short scaly tails and inquisitive eyes. The children had tried to keep them as pets, but they pined and died in captivity, and soon they were all but forgotten and left to scamper on the desert plains as they had always done.

The bora was not very interested in Cara and scuttled back behind the boulder where the sound broke out again, even louder than before. Peering round the corner, Cara saw that the creature had rejoined a group of about ten others, all busily working with their forepaws, trying to dig holes, perhaps, or find food. As she watched, one caught sight of her. Instantly, all the heads turned, their eyes glinting faintly in the starlight. Cautiously rising to her feet, she started walking slowly towards them. Then the two largest creatures gave a squeak of alarm. Suddenly every bora vanished, moving so fast that she could not see where they had hidden. She waited, but they did not come back although she thought for a moment that she heard the scuffling sound start again in the distance.

Glancing up at the skies, she suddenly realised that the night had changed. Heavy clouds were swiftly blotting out the last of the stars and the wind had risen to an ominous moan, blowing stinging dust into heaps against the rocks. A sudden rush of heavy wings passed just over her head—a pair of gryfons fleeing to the shelter of the mountains. She hesitated, unsure whether to look for shelter or to carry on, or even to turn back. Most of her anger had burned itself out, replaced by growing exhaustion, hunger and a sharpening edge of fear. Then she remembered the sullen faces of the aldermen sitting in uncaring judgement on her and her work, and she resolved to fight her own lack of courage and continue as long as she could, and find a place to sleep when her feet would carry her no further.

Before long, however, Cara was groping her way in impenetrable darkness, while the air became so choked with swirling dust that she could hardly breathe. Blindly, she felt about her, bruising her fingers against boulders which seemed to crowd against her, determined not to let her pass. She tried hard not to think of the stories of strange beasts Anno had told them in Lesson Hall, stories which had amused the children on a bright morning, but which made her heart thud painfully as she stumbled along in the dark wilderness while the wind sobbed between the rocks. She was suddenly afraid that if she reached out her hand, she would find coarse hair instead of cold stone, and feel

56

the hot breath of Kalkona on her face as it slowly turned its red eyes towards her. A pebble tumbling into a gully behind her became the footfall of the black dog as it stalked her, waiting for her to fall before it would spring.

And then the storm broke. One moment she was inching across a smooth plateau of rock which appeared to stretch out some way on either side of her, and the next she was sprawling on her face as the wind unleashed its full power. She dug her fingers into chinks in the ground to keep herself from being flung against the boulders. As the note of the wind rose steadily to a shriek, she heard the dull rumble and crash of stones shifting and falling under the force, and knew that she was probably safer spread-eagled where she lay. She burrowed her face between her arms as the dust became a dense cloud, sweeping over her and bringing hails of sharp stones which bit into her unprotected head and scored deep cuts in her hands. Confused thoughts whirled in her mind as she fought for breath, trying to check her rising panic. Her mind seized on a fleeting memory—Anno saying calmly, 'Sometimes the great storms of the desert can last for days.' The panic mastered her and she cried out, her mouth and nostrils filling with dust. The scream was torn from her throat and whirled away, disembodied, by the wind. Raging terror took possession of her and she lay retching and and choking on grit and tears, utterly alone and lost in the dark. Time ceased.

At last the wind died, and the veils of debris began to settle. After a while the first pale rays of daylight filtered through from the hidden sky. Cara slowly raised her head. The plateau where she lay had been blown clean, but the storm had piled great banks of soil and broken rock against the boulders which rose on either side, and she was coated in red dust, mingled with blood on the backs of her hands. Her hair felt wet; she reached up and found blood there too. Painfully raising herself into a sitting position, she unfastened her jacket and wiped her face clean on the lining. Through the hazy air, she could see that the plateau stretched away in front of her like a table of rock, furrowed here and there with yawning cracks and marked with what looked like black scorches in the middle. In places, the rock was curiously patterned, almost as if it had partly melted under some intense heat.

Cara's legs felt too unsteady to carry her, so she had to crawl over to one of the cracks to examine it more closely. It was deep and wide and, on an impulse, she thrust her hand in to see if it held any secret. Her fingers found something hard and sharp, and she clutched at it and drew it out. A twisted piece of grey metal. She stared at it, turning it over and over, unable to believe what her eyes told her. A scrap of metal like every other scrap she had seen in the settlement, taken from the broken shell of Sirius, the first ship. She clutched it tightly as a wave of dizziness swept over her. This was the place she had been seeking, where Holly first stepped onto the new world, where the ship landed with its despairing band of settlers, lost in a storm even more terrible than the one just past.

Fighting her own weakness, Cara forced herself to crawl into the middle of the plateau and looked at the scarred rock where the ship must have landed with the blazing engines which had powered its flight. She wondered what had happened to those engines. Had they burned out like smoking torches or had they been taken to pieces like the rest of the ship, made to carry the last heroes and then reduced to being used for leaky huts and crude carts? The sense of the past was so heavy on that plateau that Cara felt the weight of it forcing her to the ground. She found herself crying again, feeling the horror that her own forebears might have felt when they saw the empty land to which they had come.

Something glittered through her tears. She wiped her eyes and noticed a bright round object wedged in another of the deep cracks. When she eased it out, she saw that it was the token she had sought—a delicately shaped clasp studded with three unclouded green stones in a tracery of tarnished silvery metal. Maybe it had fallen from one of the women as she struggled away from the ship, dragging frightened children and an armload of belongings. Although she was light-headed and near fainting with hunger and fatigue, Cara still managed to push the clasp and the metal scrap into one of her pockets before her remaining strength gave way and she fell down into a trance of confusion and tormenting dreams.

That was how Anno found her, when the dusky sky was bathed in sunset crimsons and purples. When Cara opened her eyes and saw him leaning over her, she thought it was another dream and did not speak. He helped her to eat and drink a little, and then cleaned her face and hands with a rag and water. He lifted her to her feet and, half-carrying her, began the long journey back to the settlement. As they walked, she gradually came to her senses and was dimly surprised that he had managed to find her. When she was too tired to go on, he made her lie wrapped in a blanket for a while as the stars flamed overhead in a sky which was finally clearing. Pretending to sleep, she gazed at him through half-closed eyes as he sat hunched in his cloak, watching over her.

Before half the night was gone, they started walking again, and only then did he tell her how Minna and Gethin had secretly come and begged for his help after she failed to return home. He had set out at once, but they had to return to the settlement as soon as possible, before anyone else discovered that they were missing.

A question formed in Cara's dazed mind. 'How . . . did you . . . know . . . where . . . to find me?'

Anno's hand was firm under her arm and his voice was gentle as he replied, 'Because I too once journeyed into the desert.'

Chapter Seven

Spring always came slowly to the settlement, beginning
with a gradual lengthening of the daylight as Sol crept
over the mountains a little earlier each morning and
lingered a moment longer in a sunset haze over the
desert. The biting winter wind began to blow more
softly, and the first frail green shoots started to poke
above the stony red soil in the carefully tended fields
and vegetable gardens. The pounding hail storms
became rain showers, bringing floods to the low-lying
parts of the settlement where the people laughed as
they mopped up the water with old blankets—it happened every spring, and they had no possessions which
were spoilt by a soaking; anyway they saw it as a sign
that winter was over for another year. The settlement
valley could almost be called beautiful for a brief time,
when the ground was covered with a delicate flush of
grasses reaching up to the foothills of the mountains.
Rough fences saved as much of the new growth as
possible for winter fodder, but the hogs and goats
roamed freely over the rest in a frenzy of eating after
months of semi-starvation. The scavenging charguls
followed behind on their stumpy legs, quick to pull
down any of the weaker, smaller animals who strayed

too far from the rest.

A special Assembly was called to set the date of the Karnavale—three days of high spirits, feasting and drinking to celebrate the end of winter and an accepted part of the settlement calendar for as long as anyone could remember. Every spring the aldermen issued decrees forbidding the brewing of tappa and exhorting the people to enjoy themselves without what they called riotous behaviour. In the old days this meant vomiting in the street or beating your neighbour in a drunken rage, and stewards had the power to lock up offenders. Cara remembered Medwin coming home shamefaced after two nights' imprisonment for knocking out the front teeth of a girl who shouted an insult at him because of his limp. After the lock-up was destroyed, however, the stewards had nowhere to put wrongdoers and had to content themselves with shouted warnings as they patrolled the streets. And somehow the steward patrol had lapsed in the past few springs so that the only remaining sign of authority was the announcement of the Karnavale and a list of decrees nailed to the Assembly Hall door.

Cara passed the Hall as she went to visit Holly on the day before the Karnavale commenced and saw that someone had already defaced the list with an indecipherable scrawl. An undercurrent of tension ran through the streets. Mingled anger and fear showed in strained faces and nervous voices. Doors were hastily bolted, and rumours spread about increasingly brutal and open robberies in other quarters of the settlement besides the back streets of Alden. The softening air seemed to stir up a reckless, anarchic spirit, a loosening of the winter restraints, a burst of unchannelled energy before spring mildness gave way to the enervating blast of summer heat which left the people burnt and gaspsing for the chill of winter again. Despite the Assembly ban on tappa, Cara could smell the sharp tang of the hot liquid hanging in the air as she went along, and in the alleyways, women were brewing beer in huge jars for the festivities.

Cara had recovered from her desert ordeal. Few people bothered to ask why the Lesson Hall had been shut for three days, and she soon reappeared in her usual place at the back of the hall, where she now taught the youngest children to read. Anno maintained his usual gravely courteous manner towards her and dismissed her faltering attempts to thank him for saving her life.

'There is no need for gratitude, but,' he paused, 'I am glad to hear your life has some value in your eyes. Do not speak further of it.' He watched her, though, and let her rest from her teaching work when she grew too impatient with her stumbling pupils. Then she would quietly slip away between the huts and gardens and out into the fields, to walk round the very edge of the settlement. She would climb up to the far end of the valley where the foothills began and wander on the little paths worn by some of the goats who had slipped their tethers and escaped to start breeding in the wild. Men and women working in the fields had at first stopped and stared at her as she strode by, but after a while they grew used to seeing her and would shout greetings when she passed. Sometimes she would go on to the top of one of the higher hills and sit there hunched in her jacket, staring down at the untidy settlement or up at the mountains, as she fingered the silvery clasp with the green stones which she always wore pinned on her tunic.

Anno's concern surprised and warmed her, and she puzzled over the change in his manner. Lately she had begun allowing herself half-formed daydreams about the two of them adventuring together in some remote place, far from the dull settlement streets. He had given her leave this morning to go and visit Holly, who had succumbed to the wasting sickness and now had not long to live. The old woman refused to leave her lonely hut and join Jenna, who had been taken into Medwin's household. Cara knew that Hanni walked up to see her each day, bringing food and fuel for the fire. Cara also visited often to listen to her foster-mother's rambling memories which grew more real to Holly as her body weakened. For her, the ravaged valley of the settlement was filled once again with the rustling forests of her childhood where she ran and laughed with her sisters.

Cara climbed the steep track up to the hut and opened the shabby door without knocking. Holly was propped up with a bolster on her high bed, wrapped in a faded blue blanket woven by Minna as a Karnavale gift the previous spring. The bed was pushed beside the single window which had been unshuttered, letting in the cool air and a glimpse of the distant mountain peaks, but the old woman's blue-veined eyelids were closed and she was sleeping, the fingers of one wrinkled hand tangled in her thin white hair. Cara drew up a stool and sat down by the bedside. The bare hut was as familiar to her as the palms of her hands, and because it reminded her of being a small child, it made her feel secure and peaceful. She stared up at the patch of bright sky which she could see through the window, and pondered again the odd conversation between herself and Anno that morning. They had arrived at the Lesson Hall together and were unlacing their boots in the lobby when he asked her if she still thought of leaving the valley.

She stared at him in surprise. 'You told me not to speak of it openly.'

'Do not waste time misunderstanding me, Cara. You may speak of it to me—fortunately it was I who found you when you were foolish enough to run away. The aldermen would not look kindly on your disobedience.' Anno spoke hastily and kept glancing towards the door as if he feared they would be interrupted. Cara was puzzled. She had not seen him in such a mood before, furtive and almost nervous.

She shrugged. 'Yes, I still think of it, but not of the desert any longer, now that I have been there and found what I was looking for.' She followed Anno as he strode into the inner room and stood beside him hesitantly. He produced a manuscript from his pocket and inspected it at arm's length.

Then he looked at her again. 'What would you do if the end of the settlement came and there was no longer any Assembly or any rules to restrain you?'

Cara frowned. 'If I could do whatever I pleased . . . I think I would go over the mountains, but I don't know if I could leave my sister behind, and I don't think she would want to leave the settlement.'

'You think your sister needs you?' Something in Anno's tone filled Cara with confusion. He was probing too deeply into her secret thoughts. She thought of her daydreams of the two of them journeying together and dug her nails hard into her palms, trying to keep her face expressionless. 'If she did not come, sir,' she said, 'I suppose I would have to go alone and that would be like going into exile, leaving all I had behind.'

Anno looked thoughtful. 'In my younger days I journeyed far on my own and it was more like freedom than anything I encountered before or since—but perhaps what you say is right, and humankind needs

65

the company of one another.' He paused and appeared to weigh his next words carefully. 'Perhaps it will not be long before we all leave, when nothing is left of the settlement except dust and chaos, but whether I would wish to go alone or not, I cannot say.' His eyes flickered over her and then turned back to his reading. She could leave at noon to visit Holly if she wished, he said and added, apparently as an after-thought, that she need not continue calling him 'sir'.

Remembering all this as she sat in Holly's hut, Cara still did not understand the purpose of Anno's questions, nor his strange manner. She did not really know herself whether she would have the courage to leave everything she had known as home, even if Minna came with her. Since her desert journey, her fierce longing for escape had lessened, and she no longer found herself falling into black moods or rages as often as before. Most of the time, she existed in a state of resigned melancholy and boredom, and she was content to remain that way for a while. It was less troublesome.

A moan came from the bed, and Cara rose to her feet and saw that old Holly was waking up.

Minna and Gethin were walking together in the fields further up the valley. They had arranged to meet there, near a roofless hut which Gethin was rebuilding for a young man who had acquired a wife and wanted to leave his overcrowded family home. Gethin had become a regular guest at Minna and Cara's hut ever since the night of Cara's disappearance. He usually visited Minna at noon-time, when his work brought him nearby, but she noticed that he would often walk right over from the other side of the settlement to see her then, which happened to be the time when Cara was sure to be away at Lesson Hall. Minna knew that he

66

thought himself in love with her—he had told her as much when they last met, three days before—and she was saddened because she had no stronger feelings for him than friendship and a touch of pity for his tortured emotions. Even so, she still enjoyed his company and his lively stories about settlement life, which made her realise how few people she knew and how little she saw from her hut in the secluded quarter of Eden.

They strolled arm-in-arm along a path of dried mud by a field budding with new bean vines, careful not to brush against the hairy, speckled leaves which could cause an angry red rash on the skin. Gethin was recounting the latest misadventure of his friend Ethan who lived with his beautiful, indiscreet wife Minella and five children in a grand two-storey hut. Minella had a weakness for other women's husbands and received many visitors while Ethan's skills as a surgeon kept him busy in households all over the settlement. Despite her weakness, Minella was very fond of Ethan; they seemed happy together, according to Gethin, although every now and then she would be caught out and Ethan would rage and storm for a while, spend the night at Gethin's hut and then return home in the morning after a good breakfast, his anger charmed away by sleep.

'It was little Alida who let out the secret this time,' Gethin began.

'Is she the youngest?' Minna interrupted, trying hard to recall the many different names and ages which Gethin assumed she knew.

'Yes, coming up to her sixth summer, and as bright as a sunbeam. Ethan is eating at table, telling Minella a stomach-turning tale about an old man's leg he had to take off at the knee, when little Alida sits up and says, "I saw a man with one leg today!" Minella's face goes

67

red, and Ethan says, "What's this?" and Alida chatters on about the kind man who came that morning and showed her his wooden peg leg and how he could take it off. He gave her a piece of cheese for being a good girl while he went upstairs to see her mother. Ethan pushes back his stool, picks up his dish of stew and throws it into the fireplace, and then marches out of the hut without another word,' Gethin could hardly contain his laughter and carried on with a sidelong glance at Minna, 'He told me last night, "You're a lucky man with no wife or family to burden you." I told him it wasn't for want of trying and he said, "You need a good quiet girl—you can marry my Alida when she's old enough!"'

'I am sure you would be very happy,' Minna answered politely, secretly hoping that he was not about to repeat the protestations and entreaties of their previous meeting, when he had all but asked her to come and live with him. Although she had tried hard not to sound unkind, she could not help revealing her own lack of interest in the offer.

'I suppose you feel no differently today from last time?' he asked rather sadly. Minna shook her head quickly.

Gethin sighed. 'I know you said you liked my friendship, but are you going to live with your sister for ever? I can build a fine hut for us, out here if you like, or down in the settlement close to all my companions. Cara could even come and live with us as well!'

When he said that, Minna knew he was making a final, valiant effort to win her and gave him a small smile before replying quietly, 'I am truly grateful for your kindness and respect your offer, but I cannot accept it. If you do love me as you say, then please take the friendship I offer you—it's the most I can give for

68

the moment.' Before he could answer, she continued, wanting to explain the reason for their meeting before he turned it into a quarrel, 'I've brought a gift I made for you, to thank you for your help when Cara disappeared. Here, take it.'

She unwrapped the bundle she had been carrying under one arm and handed him a light summer shirt, woven in brown and blue stripes. He held it up with a smile, although his eyes showed clearly that her second refusal of him was a crushing disappointment.

Minna could hardly bear to see his crestfallen face. Trying hard to swallow her guilt and pity, she touched his shoulder. 'Thank you for the walk this noon-time, and the stories, but I must hurry home now. If you are not busy tomorrow just before nightfall, you are welcome to come and celebrate the Karnavale with us. We are going to join the family of our foster-brother, Medwin, and I know they will be pleased to meet you.'

Gethin hesitated, unsure what to reply, but he saw how well the shirt fitted and how carefully she had woven it. He felt he could not appear ungrateful after her generosity, so he agreed to come along. They said goodbye and he watched her walk away, light brown hair glowing in the spring light, until she dwindled to a dark green speck in the distance. Pulling on his old work smock again, he trudged back to the half-ruin he had to finish roofing by the beginning of the scorching summer season, when outdoor labour was limited to dawn and dusk because of the heat. Retrieving his tool sack from its hiding-place in the tumbledown chimney, he set to work shoring up the crumbling walls, leaving gaps for the roof supports. These were to be fine, seasoned timbers, stolen and hoarded by the hut's new owner for his first home.

Gethin was proud of his skills and took great care

over the work, only jumping down from the wall when all the light had vanished over the horizon and the valley was deep in shadow. When he was hitching up his tool sack and setting off down the path, he remembered that the Karnavale began that night. He would be safer picking his own way across the fields and entering the settlement close by the Assembly Hall, rather than following the path Minna had taken, leading straight back to the main streets; it would be foolish to walk past the dark corners and blind alleys of Alden after nightfall.

He tramped through a plantation of juss bushes, the fleshy desert plant which some settlers had started growing as a crop. Gethin had heard that some households had begun to boil the swollen purple roots to make a tasteless hot mush. A network of winding tracks took him to the outskirts of the settlement, and he decided to take a short-cut along a narrow lane which would bring him close to the safety of his hut. Hurrying along, he turned a corner and walked straight into a huddle of ragged urchins. In the instant before they turned on him, he guessed they had gathered to plan a raid on a neighbouring household. He knew he was an easier target, and before he could even think of running, he was knocked to the ground and pinned down by his arms and legs. His attackers shrieked with delight, tearing at his clothes, pulling off his boots and emptying his sack to see what valuables he might be carrying. They tormented him with kicks and punches, spitting on his face and tugging his hair. There were perhaps fifteen of them, and although small and underfed, they were reckless and inflamed after drinking many jugs of tappa. Fortunately for Gethin, the contents of his tool sack distracted them from doing him serious harm. The grip on his limbs loosened, and with a sudden twist, he was able to struggle free. He ran off barefoot and half-naked, bruised and weeping with rage as their mocking laughter echoed after him. Not only had he lost his priceless tools but, no less precious to him, the shirt which Minna had woven was also gone.

Chapter Eight

Gethin's bruised face did not pass unnoticed at the Karnavale celebration, and he was obliged to tell his story to the assembled company as they stood warming themselves at a specially lit bonfire in the middle of Medwin's courtyard. Minna and Hanni were shocked and sympathetic and Cara was angry. Medwin, a broad-shouldered, hasty-tempered man, limped up and down the courtyard shouting curses on all wicked urchins. He ground his teeth and said he would go in person to the Assembly and demand an end to the lawlessness once and for all. Gethin was clearly embarrassed at the upset his news had caused and withdrew into a corner, where little Feya, her older brother Hal and plump, toddling Sanni, just three winters old, solemnly gathered round to inspect his wounds. Hanni tried to soothe the troubled mood of the gathering by announcing that supper was laid ready in the hut.

Hal helped his father to heap up the bonfire and then they all went indoors where the scrubbed table stood laden with festive delicacies. The Karnavale was the one night of the year when everybody had more than enough to eat, even in the poorest households. Hanni had prepared large meat pies, bean patties flavoured with thumon leaves, boiled cabbage with juss root and had toasted one of the hard brown cheeses until it was soft. She also set out a tiny dish of wheat soaked in eggs and milk. Everybody received a slice from a large wheaten loaf which Lina, Medwin's eldest daughter, had stolen from the house of one of the aldermen where she worked looking after a noisy pair of baby girls. Leathery potatoes, the last of the winter store, were roasting in the hearth. Cara and Minna had brought along a small, succulent pig's head which took pride of place in the centre of the table. Hanni wedged its grinning mouth open with a rag, and Sanni ran screaming into a corner when he saw it.

Everyone heaped a plate with food and ate until content. When the table was bare and the remains cleared away, Medwin scratched a rough circle on the floor. His was one of the last households where family and guests would stand in a circle and join hands to sing a Karnavale song whose ancient words and melody were said to have come on the first ship long ago. Minna stood with Hanni on one side and Gethin on the other, clasping her hand tightly, and she wondered whether this was what others meant by happiness—to be surrounded by friends, bound together by a time-honoured ritual. They sang the last verse twice, as was the custom.

> 'Fear no more the heat of sun,
> Nor the winter's angry rages,
> When all your worldly work is done,
> Home you're gone and took your wages.
> One day you and I must go,
> Like all good people, into dust.'

As Minna sang, she thought of the storm and the red dust sweeping down on Cara in the desert, and shuddered.

Soon it was time for the celebrations to end with much kissing and embracing. Feya threw her short arms round Gethin's knees and would not let go until Hanni laughingly pulled her away. The last Minna saw of the family was a crowd of cheerful figures standing round the smoking remains of the bonfire, as she looked back over her shoulder before turning out of the courtyard.

Gethin had begged permission to stay with the sisters that night, rather than walk home across the settlement. As they made their way back to the hut, they could hear drunken laughter and shouts floating up on the wind from the dwellings at the bottom of the hill. They did not stop to gaze at the milky trail of stars in the blue-black sky but hurried home and bolted the door.

Later that night, Minna lay curled in a nest of blankets on her hard corner bed, deep in dreams. She saw the bleak hills of her story and dreamed that she was running hard along the path to the top of the valley, the door of the hut hanging open behind her and the wind ruffling the thin grasses. She knew that a great danger was coming and that she must warn the prince so that he was not caught by it. She had to go and find him out in the wide world, but the harder she ran, the further the crest of the hills receded. Her laboured breathing burned her lungs. With a great effort, dragging herself on hands and knees, she reached the top and saw, too late, that beyond was nothing but darkness. Before she could stop herself, she was tumbling over the brink, cold earth crumbling beneath her palms. Then she was falling faster and faster into the abyss while all the time someone was calling her name.

She opened her eyes and saw night, tinged with a flickering red glow. Someone was leaning over her, shaking her hard and saying her name. It was Cara, and she noticed that her sister's hands were trembling and her eyes wide with fear. She was about to ask what was wrong, and then she heard the tumult outside and realised what the strange glow was—a fire, and the acrid smell of smoke was filling the hut.

'Get dressed, fast as you can,' Cara said in a frantic whisper. 'We might still be able to slip away before they turn to our hut.'

'Who? What's happening?' Minna asked nervously.

'Hush! Speak softly. There's a mob outside. I think there's a riot.' Cara pulled back the blankets and Minna stumbled out of bed and began pulling on her clothes. Gethin crouched by the door, lacing his boots and squinting through a crack to see what was happening outside.

He turned back to say to Cara, 'There's a huge crowd at the door of a tumbledown little hut, and they've all got torches. I think, yes, they've broken down the door and some of them have gone inside. Someone's screaming. And, oh, they're firing the roof, and it's blazing up like a torch!'

Minna rushed to look and was filled with horror when she saw the reddened sky and the swaying throng blocking the path leading to the main street. 'Cara, it's the hut of that old woman, Tilda. We must do something!'

Cara took no notice. She was struggling with the shutters which had been wedged shut as tightly as possible on the morning before the Karnavale. 'Come and help, will you?' she snapped, and then cursed as she cut her hand on a jagged splinter.

Gethin jumped to his feet and ran to assist but Minna stayed by the door, trying to see what was going on amid the swirling smoke and darkness and the

75

wavering flame-tinged shadows. Never before had a mob ventured to come so openly to rob and riot in Eden, and the numbers seemed to be increasing every moment—half-grown boys, women in tattered gowns, thick-set older men, all with drunken voices and distorted faces. Unsteady figures surged in and out of Tilda's hut, some carrying untidy bundles and others waving jugs and bowls in triumph. The old woman was nowhere to be seen. Minna noticed one or two rioters who appeared more purposeful than the rest. One ragged man was standing on the fringes of the crowd, shouting hoarsely and trying to gather the people's attention. Minna shook her head in disbelief. The Karnavale celebration had reached its wildest extreme, with the anger and hunger in people's hearts let loose so that they forgot themselves and wandered the streets maiming and tearing like maddened beasts.

'Come on!' Cara's frantic voice broke into Minna's thoughts, and she turned to see a black square of night framed by the open shutters and Gethin disappearing over the sill. Minna rushed to the window, but as she was climbing out, she thought of the treasured pictures she had forgotten in the confusion.

'I will follow after!' she shouted as Cara grabbed her arm in a fury of impatience, and jumped back into the room before her sister could stop her. But it was too late—they lost their slim chance of escape. There were shouts of 'Get him!' outside and heavy blows on the door.

Cara turned to the window only to see an agile man balancing on the sill, a curved knife in his hand. She seized a heavy stool and threw it at him as hard as she could, but he caught it in mid-air and tossed it over his shoulder to the baying crowd outside. Then he clambered into the room, followed by a horde of

76

whooping boys who started tearing down the hangings from the walls. The door was forced open and the hut filled with flaring torches and crazed voices. Somebody pinned Cara's arms in a harsh grip, and she was struck hard on the back of the head so that she collapsed in a rag-doll heap on the floor. Minna's scream was the last thing she heard before she drowned in a hot sea of pain.

When Cara woke, painfully, she found herself tightly bound back to back with her sister, lying on the grimy floor of the Lesson Hall. It was still dark, and in the distance she could hear the crackle of fire and the occasional crash of a falling roof. Unable to sit up, she twisted her head round to see if they were being guarded. To her relief, the room was empty. Perhaps they had been abandoned. Minna groaned and started struggling weakly.

'Lie still,' Cara muttered, her throat dry and raw. 'I don't think we're being watched, but we must be sure.' Both girls lay quiet, straining until their ears rang to hear approaching footsteps or voices. Nothing broke the silence. Cara tried to wriggle free of the ropes that bound them, but they were securely tied, and she only succeeded in rubbing the skin off her wrists. Although she felt sick and giddy, fury was slowly building up inside her at the way they had been treated.

Halting her efforts, she gasped to Minna, 'Where is Gethin? Surely it was not he who betrayed the secret of our cloth?'

'Don't be a fool, Cara.' Minna's voice was ragged with suppressed tears.

'Why doesn't—' Cara redoubled her attempts to loosen the ropes, 'somebody . . . come . . . and . . . rescue us?' Minna did not reply, and Cara grew too angry to speak further, writhing on the hard floor until she was exhausted. A grey dawn light began to glimmer through the shutters.

Then she lifted her head. She thought she could hear a faint scratching at the door. The noise came again, and the door creaked and slowly swung open, letting in the early morning and a solitary figure who hurried across to where the sisters lay. It was Gethin, carrying an extinguished torch in one hand and a knife in the other. One side of his face was swollen with bruises, and he was limping. He knelt beside them without a word and started cutting through the ropes, with some difficulty because the knife was blunt. Aching in every joint and suddenly shuddering with cold, Cara and Minna climbed to their feet. Laying a warning finger on his lips, Gethin beckoned them to follow. They hurried after him through the littered streets, not knowing where they were heading, catching glimpses of blackened ruins on either side and, once or twice, a body huddled shapelessly in the gutter. The air was heavy with smoke and other choking fumes. Nobody else was about, but Gethin still looked all round before leaving the shelter of an alley or crossing a street. At last he halted, and Cara saw that they had taken a roundabout route to the settlement wall. Glancing over his shoulder again, Gethin helped them down onto the rocky ground beyond. He did not allow them to stop until they had run across two fields and reached the first of the foothills.

Cara and Minna sat side by side, shivering, while he told them how he had escaped from the mob in the night and made his way to Anno's house, after he had seen them being dragged to the Lesson Hall.

'Why did you not go to Medwin?' asked Cara.

'Because the way to Medwin's house was—was blocked.' Gethin hesitated, then went on hurriedly,

'The streets were full of rioters, and almost every other hut in Eden was burning. Anno was still safe, though he was startled when I began hammering on the door. He said something about this being the end we'd all been waiting for and that I had to get you out of the settlement as soon as I could and bring you up here.'

Cara looked bewildered. 'And what did he do?'

'He said he had urgent business to attend to.'

'More urgent than rescuing us from that—that evil mob?'

'So he said. He gave me a key for the Hall and sent me off to rescue you. And now I'm to sneak back to the settlement and find food and warm clothing for you.'

Cara thought of arguing, but she felt too weak and ill. She slumped against a boulder and laid her head on her folded arms. Gethin rose to go, glancing at Minna, who was staring back at the shattered huts, sunk deep in unhappiness. He gave her arm a consoling squeeze. 'Don't be too anxious—you'll be safe now.'

She looked up quickly, clutching his wrist. She had been telling herself that she would never see her precious pictures again—but perhaps she could trust Gethin with the task of seeking and rescuing them. 'Will—will you do one thing for me?' she stammered, and when he nodded, she leaned forward and whispered, 'If you go back to our hut and—oh, this is a secret, Gethin, tell nobody, but there is a loose brick over the fireplace and in the gap behind is a wooden box. Please, please see if it is still there and bring it to me and please—do not look in the box.' His face showed his surprise, but he nodded and touched her cheek in farewell. Then, taking a firm grip on his knife, he set off for the settlement, while behind the dense grey clouds that shrouded the sky Sol climbed over the rim of the mountains. A chill wind was blowing.

Chapter Nine

The morning passed slowly as Cara and Minna huddled among the rocks, watching spirals of smoke from the settlement rise and twist in the wind. Ragged flocks of gryfons swooped and circled over the distant rooftops. Sometimes they thought they saw stealthy movements among the swaying grasses lower down the valley, and once Cara scrambled to her feet and threw a stone at an over-inquisitive chargul which had ventured too close. It bolted, squealing and snapping its yellow teeth. The scavenging creatures were abroad, scenting blood and chaos.

The settlement lay quiet under its pall of ash, and the outlying parts were silent and lifeless, save for the insistent bleat of a goat, desperate for milking time. As noon-time drew near, Cara wanted to go back to see what had become of Gethin.

In a rare burst of anger, Minna told her to stay where she was. 'You only think of your own impatience!' she said fiercely. 'For all we know, Gethin may be risking his life to help us, and you want to run off on your own when he promised he would return.'

'But I want to find out what has become of Medwin and Hanni and Holly! Perhaps they need our help.'

'Maybe we can best help by gathering our own strength and wits first,' retorted Minna. 'Do you think that I haven't been sitting here worrying about what they might have suffered?'

Cara did not reply, staring gloomily across at the high, dripping cliffs which reared up beyond the hills where the mountains began.

They did not notice Gethin and Anno approaching until they were almost upon them. The sisters scrambled to their feet and scanned the weary faces of the younger and the older man to see what news they brought. Gethin threw down a large bundle and unpacked a crumbling loaf of bread and two strips of smoked pork. These he handed to the girls, and while they satisfied their tearing hunger, he told them what he had seen in the settlement.

He had found his own hut still standing but deserted, he said, with no trace of his companions, so he left with as much food and clothing as he could carry. The streets were empty, with every door which had not been broken down firmly bolted.

'The mobs stripped everything from your hut,' he said bleakly. 'All they left were a few bits of cloth and the broken pieces of Minna's loom. But the first person I saw was your neighbour, Marris. He—they had killed him. He was crumpled in a heap, and his dead hands were still clutching the smashed remains of his clock.'

Cara and Minna stared at him speechlessly.

'The Assembly Hall was burned to the ground,' he went on after a heavy pause, 'but the only person I could find to tell me what had happened was one of those old fellows who used to sit outside. I found him poking about among the ruins and he said a mob had come looking for hoards and went mad with rage when the stewards held the doors against them, so they set the whole place ablaze.'

'Looking for hoards?' Minna caught her breath.

'The old man said—' Gethin hesitated. 'He said "Some of the rioters shouted about a mighty fine hoard of cloth in a hut in Eden and told the rest there were bound to be stores of wood or food in the hall because it was all the aldermen's doing".' He looked anxiously at Minna. 'Maybe they found other hoards besides yours.'

Cara interrupted, 'And what of our kin? Medwin and Hanni and old Holly? Are they safe?'

Gethin looked away, twisting the edge of his cloak in his hands. 'Holly died in her sleep last night. It was Hanni who told me. She almost walked past me in the street this morning, but I called to her. Her eyes were all red with crying and she was dressed for a journey.'

'A journey!' Cara gasped.

Anno straightened up from leaning against a boulder and spoke for the first time. 'It seems that since the end of last summer Medwin had been planning an escape for himself and his family. He dared not tell even you, his foster-sisters, or so his wife informed Gethin.'

'She would not say much more,' added Gethin miserably. 'Not even where they were going, although I don't know how a band of eleven could get away without being seen. They were even taking the goat with them.'

Cara smiled faintly. 'They would never leave her behind. But was there no message for us? Would they have left without a word?'

'Hanni said to tell you both that she still cared for you,' Gethin replied. 'I don't think she wanted to leave. She was glad to hear you were safe.'

In the ensuing silence, Minna tried and failed to imagine never again seeing Hanni or her children, or old Holly, and pictured Medwin's bright, warm hut standing empty and dark through the coming summers and winters.

Gethin was undoing the rest of his bundle, and she longed for a chance to ask him in secret whether he had found her box. He handed her a thick black tunic, folded neatly. It was heavier than she expected, and she almost dropped it. She looked up at him, and he gave an almost imperceptible nod. So he had found the box safe in its hiding place; it must have escaped the eyes of the mob, even though every wall-hanging had been torn down.

'I didn't open it,' he whispered, 'but will you tell me what it holds?'

She shook her head reluctantly. 'I cannot, not yet. Maybe—maybe I will one day. But Gethin—thank you.'

Cara had stood up and was pacing back and forth, rubbing her hands together to keep warm. 'What do we do now?' she asked Anno. 'Will there be more rioting? Can we go back to our ransacked home?'

'I think that there will be more rioting,' he answered sombrely. 'Do you not see that this is the end which I once said we were waiting for? Those who did not lose their huts or their lives are barricading their doors against all comers or taking the chance of leaving, although I do not think many will go far—perhaps they will flee to one of the narrower valleys close by the settlement, no more than three or four days' journey away. Few will venture the mountains.'

'But what about the Assembly? Surely the aldermen were not all burned along with their hall?'

'They have gone into hiding, as terrified as little children. When Gethin came to me last night, I was about to go in search of them, in the useless hope that they might try to rouse the better-hearted of our people to halt the destruction. But even those who listened to me refused to act, crying that the settlement was finished and that we would all be murdered in our beds by the morning. And as I ran from the last hut, where nobody had answered my knocking, I saw the flames leap into the sky as the Assembly Hall was fired, and I heard the screams of the stewards who died at their posts while the cowardly leaders trembled behind bolted doors.'

'But now, sir,' broke in Gethin, glancing up at the sunless sky, 'where can these two girls sleep tonight? Should we go back and protect the Lesson Hall?'

Anno shook his head. 'I think there will be no more Lesson Hall. Our settlement is crumbling.' He gazed up at towards the hills, his chin set resolutely. 'I have decided to leave, to journey over the mountains as I did many times before any of you were birthed. I once travelled for ten days and nights before hunger and thirst defeated me, and I turned back. This time I shall go on until the mountains come to an end and I find a better land beyond, or I die in the attempt.' Cara stared at him open-mouthed, and he turned to her. 'Remember I told you that my years of adventuring were over? Last night I knew that I would rather lie broken at the foot of a cliff in the wilderness, seeking the better land, than be killed in a musty hut by a drunken fool.'

Cara nodded in eager agreement.

Anno went on rapidly, almost angrily. 'I shall leave at nightfall, and if any of you wishes to accompany me, you may follow.'

Cara glanced back towards the settlement and then up at the mountains, avoiding Minna's imploring gaze.

She drew a deep breath. 'I will go with you, Anno.' It was the first time she had addressed him by name, and she flushed as she did so.

'Cara!' The cry burst out of Minna, and Gethin took a step forward.

'Well?' Anno looked at the three of them—Cara nervously defiant, Minna anguished and Gethin bewildered by the turn of events.

'I will go,' Cara declared in a low, determined voice. 'I cannot live in the settlement any longer. Minna must come too if she wants to stay with me.' Minna's eyes filled with tears, and her mouth trembled.

'Then—then I must go as well,' she said faintly.

Anno's face was expressionless, and Cara was torn between guilt and gladness, when Gethin spoke up. 'I shall come too. If Minna leaves the settlement, there is little else to keep me there.'

Anno unexpectedly flung back his head and laughed. 'So I shall be leading a walking-party instead of venturing alone on a dangerous journey. The way will not be easy, but you are all young and strong. And you are willing to leave home and go out into the wilderness with grim Anno, the Lesson Hall instructor?' He surveyed the three of them, and this time there was warmth in his face instead of the old mask of indifference and reserve.

And so it was that Cara was able to set out on the journey that she had longed for, and Minna and Gethin reluctantly chose to follow—Minna because Cara was all the family she had left, and Gethin because he would not leave Minna.

Gethin and Anno went back to the settlement one last time and returned with as much food as they could cram into a couple of sacks. When nightfall started creeping down the valley, the four gathered their bundles, laced their boots tightly and set off along a narrow track which wound up among the hills, getting steeper as the mountains drew near. They spent that night huddled in blankets in a draughty cave formed by a long-ago rockfall. The silence thundered in Cara's ears, and she could not sleep, so she took her blanket and sat looking over the valley where she had spent all her life. Where the settlement lay she could see only blackness, not even a glimmer of firelight.

Rising before daybreak, they started up towards the mountain pass which Anno had found years before. Here there were harsh black rocks underfoot, and as the travellers mounted higher, the air grew thin and searingly cold. They had left behind all paths and had to pick their way as best they could, sometimes venturing cautiously along the edge of a giddy cliff overhanging the valley far below, sometimes groping for whatever handholds they could find to haul themselves up a smooth rock-face. No vegetation clung to those dark slopes, but the travellers found swift icy streams where they could fill their water bottles. At night they slept the dead sleep of exhaustion, their hands torn and bruised and their limbs aching. Every hour they climbed, they glimpsed more of the desert which stretched red and hostile beyond the settlement, farther than the eye could reach, and caught sight of new peaks jaggedly rising ahead to bar their way.

Anno always strode forward on muscles of iron, and sometimes even Cara would halt and beg him to let them rest for a while. Gethin walked steadily, frowning with determination, and he made sure that Minna never fell too far behind. She sometimes cried because her legs were hurting so badly, and then Gethin, cursing Anno and Cara under his breath, would hold out his hand and pull Minna along behind him until she collapsed on her knees, unable to take another step without some rest. As the days passed, however, even she grew accustomed to the arduous climbing and the lack of food and water. Gradually the four inched their way up the vast shoulders of the mountains, and as they went, they heard always the moan of the wind among the crags.

On the fourth night after leaving the valley, they slept in the shelter of a jutting scar just below the pass. Cara woke shuddering with cold in the twilight before sunrise and crawled out from their hiding place to warm herself. She felt strong and rested, and decided to try and reach the top before the others rose. As she toiled up the steep slope, she grew hotter until she tingled down to her fingertips. When she neared the summit, she looked back towards the desert which was shrouded in an early morning haze, and then turned and hastened up the final ascent. She came to the pass as the first red-gold rays of Sol shot over the horizon.

She saw a fantastical landscape of tumbling, twisted snow-peaked mountains, glittering against the remote blue sky which trembled with light. The lower crags and cliffs were plunged in violet shadow and far, far below she glimpsed a streak of silver—a waterfall rushing through a distant gorge. She clung to the rock, dizzy with the unimaginable height and the dry, brilliant air, gazing and gazing at the vastness of the new world which had always lain about her, although she had never seen it in all the years of trudging the dirty settlement streets.

Chapter Ten

In the following days the four travellers made their slow and painful way through the wilderness that Cara had seen from the pass. They took the route which, as far as he could recall, Anno had travelled on his last and longest journey, although it was often hard to trace—blocked by falls of shattered boulders or split by deep chasms opened by a later upheaval of the mountains, which seemed to stir with life like uneasily sleeping giants. They took three days to toil round the outskirts of one high, broken-topped peak, and at times they heard groans and rumbles echoing from deep within its craggy sides. At night the summit cast an eerie red glow into the sky, and the ground would be shaken by faint tremors and the travellers woken by the tumble and thud of rocks falling in remote gullies.

They managed to cover a fair distance each day, their muscles hardening with exercise and their packs growing lighter as the food supplies dwindled. They rose before dawn to break their fast with a mouthful of stale bread and a few sips of water. At noon they would rest beneath a stony outcrop or stretch out their legs on a sun-warmed ledge and feast on slivers of cured meat and hard knobs of cheese, and when nightfall came,

Sol soon dipping behind the crimson-flushed snowy peaks, they ate some more bread and munched a handful of cold boiled beans to stave off hunger pangs while they slept. Gethin constantly watched over Minna to make sure she got enough rest and did not go too hungry. She spoke seldom, her thin face burned ruddy by the sun and wind, her hands scarred with climbing. Waking in the middle of one frosty night, he noticed that she was shivering and spread his own blanket over her. Her surprise at his faithful concern and care for her gradually turned to unquestioning acceptance and, day by day, she found their companionship deepening.

Sometimes, during their noon-time rest or when they had made camp at the end of the day, she would withdraw to one side and take out her pictures. Her old dreams of the girl in the little hut and the sheltered valley had become dim and insubstantial among the mountains, just as her settlement life was fading into half-forgotten memories. She pondered for several days, sunk deep in thought as she toiled after the others, wondering how she could keep the story alive. In the dreary days of weaving in the hut it had given her mind something to brood on, and now as she stumbled up a twisting ravine, every sinew of her body crying out for rest, she still wanted the story to be real to keep her thoughts from dwelling on the death which they all knew could end their journeying at any time.

One night, as she lay gazing up at the familiar patterns of the stars, she realised that she could pretend she was out in the wide world of her tale, and knew how she could fill the last two pictures—as yet an incomplete scene of the hut and hills and an unstitched piece of cloth which she had joined to the strip just before the Karnavale. She sat up and looked at the sleeping mounds of her companions. All was quiet, and

89

there was enough starlight for her sharp eyes to work by. She unwrapped the little wooden box, managed to thread a needle and, as much by touch as by sight, began stitching a jagged, mountainous outline on the final cloth. As she sewed, she whispered the beginning of a new story to herself.

When the lonely girl reached the top of the hills ringing her valley, she looked back for the last time at the hut which had kept her safe for as long as she could remember. She had left the door on the latch, open to any stranger who might need shelter. The girl was off to the wide world, following the path which had brought the prince to her so often. She had grown wise and strong in the long days since their last meeting and now his call had come for her to leave her home and journey to be with him.

Beyond the hills, a barren plain led up to the mountains where she would have to struggle to find the way to the prince's kingdom. She walked over bare, cracked soil, the sun scorching her back, and wondered how long it would be before she saw the green meadows and swift rivers of the prince's bright land where the silver roof of the great hall glinted and the people sang as they worked in the fields. She was not afraid of what might befall her on the journey because she trusted that he would come to her, wherever she was, if she needed his help. In her hand was a stout staff, and she carried a sack of provisions for the hard days ahead.

Minna laid aside the picture, too tired to continue. Lying down, she drew her tattered blanket over her head and imagined that she was the lonely girl going to sleep peacefully in a high and lonely place, secure in the knowledge that the prince was waiting for her and watching for her coming. The last thing she saw before her eyes closed were the blazing stars scattered across the night sky, and for an instant it seemed as if they started to swirl and circle one another in a stately dance.

Cara felt the hard outdoor life honing and strengthening her body, even though her lungs often burned and her heart pounded with the effort of climbing. Although she knew that their journey was perhaps no more than a hopeless gamble against huge odds, she felt her spirits slowly uncurling in their new-found freedom. She had felt reborn when she first set eyes on the great wilderness, and told Anno as much while they strode across a wind-swept plateau one crisp, cold forenoon. She could easily keep pace with him now, leaving Gethin and Minna behind, and as they walked, they talked together of Anno's past travels and the sort of future they could hope for if ever they came to the better land that he believed lay somewhere ahead. They never mentioned the settlement or the Lesson Hall—the masks of the stern instructor and his discontented pupil were forgotten. Cara listened eagerly as Anno pointed out a shining pinnacle of quartz, which he had named the Long Light on one of his earlier journeys, or found a cave where he had once slept.

Together they pondered names for the small brown lizards who clung to the rocks on six-clawed feet, and the spindly, dappled creatures, resembling the settlement goats save for the single twisting horns springing from their foreheads, who watched the travellers from a cautious distance. Anno would sometimes turn to look at Cara, remarking half under his breath that he had never found nor hoped for true companionship on his first journeys, and her gladness at his words kindled an answering glow in his face.

When she told him about the feeling of new birth on their escape from the settlement valley, he smiled. 'I remember how I was moved when I first looked out from that path. I was not much older than you are now, and I could not conceive how anyone would choose to stay in a miserable hut on the edge of the desert once they had heard about the splendours lying so close at hand. After the days I spent wandering in these mountains, anything else was no more than a half-life.'

'And now we are wandering here too, and you believe there is a better land somewhere.'

'I think you believe that too, Cara.' He gestured towards the peaks looming ahead. 'One day we might struggle up a ridge and see below us a green country where clear streams flow and the groves of trees are thick with fruit. Then we would travel onwards freely, finding new valleys and giving names to the hills and taming the strange creatures we found there. We would never be rooted and restrained in one place but wander on and on, moving slowly over the face of Osiris, our new home-world.'

Cara added in a dreamy voice, 'We will be a free people, living and journeying together through choice, not through custom, and our children will never be trapped by a roof over their heads and a door to shut out the light.'

'Think on that, then, and do not be discouraged if the path is a difficult one.' Anno stopped and pointed back to Gethin and Minna who had halted some distance back, resting against a boulder. He frowned, but all he said was, 'Do not lose your sister in your eagerness.' Cara felt guilty and resolved to share her bread ration with Minna that evening.

As the day drew to a close and the declining sun shone blood-red on the peaks, Anno gave a shout and beckoned the others over to a smooth grey rock set upright on a heap of smaller stones. Peering closely at it, Cara could just read the scratched message 'HERE ANNO TURNED BACK', and felt a faint thrill of fear. The others crowded round, fingering the inscription. Anno watched them impassively.

Turning to him, Cara asked half-accusingly, 'How do we know which way to take now? Do we still dare to go forward where you turned back?' Anno was gazing round as if to recall the moment years before when he abandoned his exploring and returned to the settlement.

'I had not realised how far I came on my last journey,' he said at last. His face was lined and tired. 'We must try to travel faster. We have taken nearly twice as long as the ten days I journeyed to get here.'

Gethin moved defensively towards Minna. 'But we've punished ourselves to get as far as this place. We don't know how long our food will last—tell us now if it's madness to go on. We could still return to the settlement.'

Cara stirred impatiently and Anno frowned, saying, 'You knew before you set out with me, Gethin, that this might prove a hopeless journey. Of course you may leave if you wish, but you might find that your homecoming was worse than the death you fear as you wander in the mountains.'

Minna ventured to speak. 'You would tell us, sir, if you thought there was no hope left?' Her eyes were dark with apprehension.

'From here onwards we have only our wits and good fortune to guide us,' Anno answered sombrely. 'But we can hope as long as we choose—it is better so. Perhaps we are close to the very edge of the mountains. Perhaps there is no end to them. I, for one, choose to hope and continue the journey as long as I can.' He touched the engraved stone lightly in farewell and then set off again on the steep course which they had been taking along the lip of a gorge. Cara hurried after him. Exchanging weary glances, Gethin and Minna picked up their bundles and followed.

Somehow from then on the journey began to go wrong. Anno sank into a dark, irritable mood and replied curtly when anybody spoke to him. Even Cara felt rebuffed. Their way became even rougher than before, as the mountains drew closer together, so that they had no choice but to start climbing higher to find a clear passage. The wilderness through which they had travelled earlier had been bleak, but at least clumps of mossy plants beside the streams and occasional smudges of red and orange lichens had brightened the monotonous blacks and greys of boulder and stone. What the travellers saw now was a blighted landscape—tortuous wastes of volcanic debris, gullies and ravines blocked by drifts of thick grey ash, a long hillside of splintered, knife-sharp rocks which would take them a whole day to cross and would shred the soles of their boots.

One strange happening broke the tedium of those days for Minna. Pausing for breath half-way through a grinding ascent, she wiped the sweat from her face and gazed at the hostile landscape on either side. Dry crags and ridges thrust against each other, screes spilled down precipitous slopes, and the crunch of boot on stone as the others climbed on ahead echoed into nothingness. She looked up at the pale Osirian sky where Sol seemed to hang motionless at the midpoint of the morning. Suddenly the light dimmed as if a veil had passed over, although Minna could see no trace of cloud. Then high, very high above, she thought she saw something. It was like a living creature, one with a long, thin body which appeared to be floating on the air. She rubbed her eyes and stared again. The creature was hovering above the travellers and even though it was still almost out of sight, she thought it had begun to glide downwards.

But as Minna drew breath to call the others, the creature checked its flight and to soar away so fast that in the next instant it had disappeared. As it fled, it must have uttered some cry because a high, remote wailing floated down to where Minna stood. Clearly none of the other three had heard anything—they tramped on without a backward glance. Minna hesitated, wondering if she should tell them, but then Cara turned and caught sight of her.

'Why have you halted again?' she called crossly. 'Can you not walk a little further?' Minna bit her lip, shamed. Perhaps she had imagined it all. She resolved not to speak of it.

Soon the weather grew colder as they left the more sheltered lower slopes and had to journey all day with an icy wind numbing their faces. At the same time their strength drained steadily away as the food grew less and the mountains still gave no sign of ending. Minna kept her own private reckoning on how many days they had travelled, and it was on the twenty-fourth day, eight days after they passed Anno's rock, that the storm struck.

They had spent a whole morning trudging drearily over a lava-waste under a heavy white sky when the first snowflakes began to fall. Cara, Minna and Gethin were at first excited. Snowfalls had been rare at the settlement, and the burning-cold touch of the flakes made them laugh and shout like children. Anno strode on unsmiling. Before long the floating white specks had turned to a dizzy whirl of powdered ice, growing thicker by the moment as the wind rose, driving snow into the eyes, mouth and hair and reducing garments to sodden rags. Minna stopped when she could no longer see the bowed figure of Gethin ahead.

'Wait!' she cried, her voice thin and uncertain against the deepening note of the storm. Uncertainly, she took another step forward, her arms held out in front of her. A dark shape came towards her out of the whiteness and grabbed her hand.

'Over here!' Gethin shouted, pulling her to the left and straight up the broken mountain slope which was fast disappearing under a snowy blanket. She staggered after him, falling over hidden rocks and getting thoroughly bruised and soaked, until he ducked and crawled into a cave that yawned unexpectedly at their feet. Minna followed and, blinking in the darkness, she found Cara and Anno already hunched together in the cramped space. The roof was barely high enough for Anno to sit upright, and they could only stretch out their legs if they braced themselves against the opposite wall. The ground underfoot was uneven and rough with broken stone. It was very cold.

They crouched in the cave while the blizzard roared round the mountain, more terrifying than the dust storm which struck Cara in the desert because of its bitter, chilling breath which felt as if it were slowly sucking the life out of them. The sun and sky were completely hidden, and only a forlorn grey light filtered through from time to time. Cara dozed, woke with a start and dozed again, and all the while the wind lashed the mountainside and the hoarse breathing of her companions filled the cave. Gethin sat bolt upright nearest the cave entrance and every now and then leaned over to kick away the snow which was threatening to build up and block the way out. Whenever his head started to nod, he would shake himself awake and start rubbing his face and hands to try and keep warm.

There came a time when Cara opened her eyes and saw Anno bowed forward, his head in his hands. The storm raged past the cave and gusts of wind blew eddies of snow inside. She sighed and Anno glanced up at her. Although she could not see the expression on his face clearly, she heard the edge of despair in his voice as he spoke.

'Perhaps this is the end we have been hoping against,' he said.

Cara felt as if she were drunk with fatigue, yet she struggled to reply. 'We . . . we will carry on . . . when the . . . storm is . . . over.'

'Cara, maybe the storm will still be blowing when our bodies are stiff and frozen—and even if it does end, I no longer know which way to go.'

'But—' Cara tried to think clearly. 'But we are going to the better land. You said so,' she finished stupidly.

'Maybe, Cara, maybe there is no better land,' said Anno very quietly. 'We only hope, we do not know, and our hopes may be groundless.' Then silence fell again and Cara drowsed, listening to the wind howling.

Later Gethin abandoned his unblocking of the cave mouth and a drift of snow soon filled the entrance, deadening the sound of the storm and even keeping out some of the cold. The night passed and almost all the next day, while the blizzard sang on with wild, fierce voices which crept into the dreams of the travellers so that sometimes Cara woke to hear one of her companions stirring and moaning, fearful in their sleep.

In Minna's dream, she was part of her story, wandering lost and frozen in the snow, clinging to a rock swept bare by the wind while the storm tried to pull her hands free and hurl her over a cliff. She was blind, choking, crying for help, knowing all the time that she was completely alone and far from any shelter. In her last desperation she called to the prince and tried to struggle forwards, but her legs would not move. She stumbled, fell, and lay helpless as the snow began to cover her.

Suddenly the storm was gone. She was lying on sun-warmed grass which was strewn with tiny flowers. Footsteps approached and she raised her head, and saw the prince standing beside her. He was clad in a sky-blue tunic and the light was so bright that she could not see his face.

'Did you doubt that I would come?' he said and bent down, lifting her to her feet. They were standing on the mountain slope by the cave, but the land was living and green and she heard the laughter of children floating up from the ravine far below.

'Come with me,' said the prince, and hand in hand they walked up the shining mountain. Ahead she could see a deep cleft in the rocks, splitting the peak in two, and there the prince pointed.

'Take that way,' he said, and kissed her forehead before releasing her hand and swiftly walking up to the pass. She was about to follow when she remembered that she had left her bundle behind. As she turned to go back for it, all the light drained out of the world and she stared down into a black void.

Minna woke with a start. She was hunched inside her blanket and achingly stiff all over. At first she did not know where she was, and then she saw the cave and the sleeping forms of Cara, Anno and Gethin. Then she noticed the silence. A sliver of palest blue was visible

through the half-blocked mouth of the cave. The
storm had blown itself out. She was ravenously hungry,
yet bursting with a curious fiery energy, still wrapped
in the mystery of her dream. Longing to stretch her
cramped limbs, she sat up cautiously and crawled past
Gethin, through a soft mound of snowdrift and out of
the cave. She was momentarily dazzled by the brilliant
sunlight on the smooth white wastes which spread out
as far as she could see. The snow came up to her knees
and she floundered round until she found a way of
stamping it down hard to make a path in front of her.

She wanted to climb higher, filled with a strange
desire to see if there really was a cleft in the peak as
there had been in her dream. The mountain-top was
hidden by a bulging spur and the going was slow, but
she was carried along by a feverish lightheartedness.
She had gone quite a distance when she heard sleepy,
anxious voices behind her and then a shout from Cara.

'Minna, what are you doing?'

She could now see that there was indeed a cleft in the
peak and she waved her arms, calling excitedly 'This
way!'.

'Don't worry, I'll get her.' Gethin was coming after
her, struggling up the path she had made.

Minna called back once more that they should follow
her and then pressed on, pulling off her wrap in the
heat of her exertions and carelessly letting it fall.

'Little fool—what are you doing? There might be a
snow-slide!' Anno's shout rang out behind her and
Minna gasped, trying not to laugh at the strangeness of
what was happening. She was close to the cleft now and
was almost running, punching a way through the snow
which flew up and melted on her flushed cheeks and
burning hands. As she reached the top, she was
suddenly afraid that she would see nothing but

another long range of mountains and she dropped to her hands and knees, muttering 'please' over and over again. She heard Gethin's laboured breathing as he toiled after her. Forcing herself to stand, she crept up to the cleft and looked through. Her cry brought Gethin running and when he saw what lay beyond, he yelled for the others to come, wild with excitement.

In the slanting yellow light of the setting sun they saw that they had come to the end of the mountains. The rocky slopes fell away, melting into gentler hills which bordered a green rolling landscape. On the very edge of sight, half-hidden by the haze of distance, was a vast stretch of shimmering water. A soft wind blew on their faces, bringing the scent of moist earth and warm grass, the last breath of a peaceful early summer's day.

Chapter Eleven

They did not start the journey down at once, but slept one more night in the little cave which had saved their lives in the storm. Rising at first light, they ate their last crusts of bread and set off, tightening belts round hollow stomachs. Minna said nothing about her dream because she never spoke of the prince or any other part of her story, and Cara was unusually talkative. As they climbed, she addressed the world at large, marvelling that Anno had been right all along about a better land and enthusing about what they might find there. She only fell silent when they began the treacherous descent of the cliff beyond the pass. The green country was still sleeping under the early morning mists, but the four travellers were too busy watching their next step to pause and admire the sight. They had to pick a way from ledge to ledge like wild goats, and often stones came loose beneath their boots and plummeted into empty space. At one point they thought they were stranded on the crumbling edge of a cliff until Anno managed to jump across to a narrow shelf and, clinging like a fly to the sheer rock, worked his way along to the safety of a broader ledge. It was a long time before Minna could pluck up enough courage to follow.

At last they found themselves among the foothills and felt earth instead of stone beneath their feet. The air was warm and the sun rode high in the gentle sky. The great lake glittered invitingly amid the grassy lowlands and the travellers only halted to stuff cloaks and jackets into their almost empty bundles before striding onwards. Presently they were walking through thick, short grasses, flourishing in more shades of green than they could have imagined possible. Anno looked about in growing astonishment. 'It is here as it used to be on the other side of the mountains,' he said at last. 'See!' He pointed a little way ahead to where many star-shaped flowers bloomed yellow and white among the grasses. 'The sida flowers, Cara, that used to cover the valley in summer when I was young.' Further on, Minna saw a nadel tree, thick with narrow, shiny leaves and growing no taller than her waist. Cara found a patch of what Anno said were roh bushes. The firm red berries were hidden beneath the clumps of heart-shaped foliage and brittle stems. Little flying creatures began to rise up from the ground and drone round their heads and Gethin caught one as it settled on his bare arm. Its glistening black back had a large blue spot in the middle and from tip to tail it was about as long as his thumb. He tried to touch one of the groping feelers which sprouted from its head but it buzzed fiercely and flew off, leaving him with a swollen red lump on his hand.

When they judged it to be about noon, they stopped at the foot of a rounded hillock for a rest and a few mouthfuls of the beans—the only food they had left. After he had eaten, Anno announced that he would sleep for a while and rolled his bundle under his head for a pillow. Gethin followed suit and Cara lay on her front, lazily surveying the sun-baked grasses. Nobody noticed when, after a moment, Minna rose quietly and wandered off. Cara plucked a few grasses and tried nibbling the juicy ends, but they burned her mouth and she spat them out, coughing. The air was very still in the midday heat except for the droning of the black insects and the quiet breathing of the two sleepers. From where Cara lay, she could see the ground dropping steadily down towards the lowlands and the lake which looked even larger now—a swathe of silver surrounded by dense patches of dark green. The heat haze made everything quiver, but as Cara twisted a bracelet of grasses for her wrist, she thought how the air was not as scorching as it was on the other side of the mountains.

When she looked up again, she saw a small animal perched on the ground in front of her, peering at her with tiny black eyes. Its body was covered in fine grey fur and it held its delicate forepaws against its chest. It was very like the hairless boras of the desert, and quite as bold. She stared at it and it gazed fearlessly back at her, making an enquiring chattering noise in its throat. Hardly daring to move, she extended a hand towards it and, dropping on all fours, it scurried closer to inspect her, sniffing at her boots and scrabbling at her leggings, bewildered by the coarse cloth which would not give way to its paws. When she tried to pick it up, it darted back out of her reach, scolding her in a shrill voice, and then with a whisk of its tail it vanished as suddenly as it had appeared. When she looked closely at the ground where it had stood, she found that it was honeycombed with burrows, each one cunningly concealed beneath a fringe of grasses and leading into a dark tunnel. Putting her ear to one hole, she thought she could hear a chorus of chirruping voices deep inside.

Meanwhile Minna was wandering farther and farther away, her feet leading her down from the moorlands to where the grasses grew longer, filling the air with a pungent fragrance as her feet crushed them. The mountain streams became languid ripples meandering through an undergrowth of bronze-stemmed reeds. Minna was sunk in a dream daze which deepened. How had the prince stepped into her dreams and foretold what she would find? She stood quite still beside one of the placid streams, listening to the ripple of water over stone and torn between fear and a wild hope that her tale might touch in some way on a greater, hidden world. A world which lay round her like the wilderness round the settlement valley, but which she had never perceived before. She realised that she was breathing hard and soaked in sweat.

'What does it mean?' she murmured out loud, her words falling like pebbles into the pool of still air, but she did not want to wait for an answer, not yet. She fought back both hope and fear and resolved to walk a short way farther before going back to the others. The grasslands lay so calm in the noon sun that she almost ceased to worry about hidden dangers, although up in the mountains she had constantly been afraid. Unfastening the neck of her tunic, she let the cooling breeze blow on her skin and wondered about bathing in one of the streams. She noticed something bright tangled in the thick branches of one of the trees, not far from where she was walking, and wondered idly what it was. Coming closer, she saw that it was neither an animal nor an exotic kind of flower, but something so wholly unexpected that she could not at first think what it was called.

Then she remembered how when she was very small, Holly had taken her to the edge of the desert to watch a crowd of youngsters flying bright scraps of cloth, stretched over thin struts and held on the end of a long piece of twine. Holly had told her that the boys and girls were playing with kites and that she had had one of her very own when she was little. The glowing object that Minna carefully disentangled from the tree looked like a kite, but far bigger and more beautiful than any of the clumsy settlement toys. It was almost as tall as she was, made from a sort of supple hide stretched to transparency and painted with swirls of bright red and gold. The light shone through the patterns, casting odd shadows on the ground. At the top of the kite were two golden eyes which seemed to be watching her, and at the other end was a tail of soft red plumes, far longer and finer than the feathers in Hanni's battered heirloom headress, brought from Earth on the first ship.

Minna stared at the kite, her thoughts spinning, wandering how it got there and who it was that could have made it. The craftsmanship surpassed anything she had ever seen in the settlement, and in a strange way it disturbed her, more than the thought that perhaps other settlement people had found their way over the mountains as well, losing a kite on their journey. Her heart began thumping in her chest and abruptly she turned and began to run back, clutching the kite in both hands, terror snapping at her heels.

As she hastened up the slope to where she had left her companions, she ran into Gethin, whose worried expression changed to astonishment when he saw the kite. Seizing his arm, she ignored his questions and dragged him back to where Anno and Cara stood arguing.

'I'm not my sister's keeper,' Cara was saying. 'If she is foolish enough to wander off in unknown country—' Suddenly she too caught sight of Minna and the kite, and her mouth fell open in wonder. She and Anno examined the find closely while Minna told her story.

'I, for one, do not understand it at all,' said Anno when she had finished. 'If anyone else had been journeying from the settlement, we would at least have noticed their trail—but I have never seen work like this among our people.'

'And look!' Cara held up a slender cord fastened to the centre of the kite. 'It must have broken free while someone was flying it.'

'And who was flying it?' asked Gethin, glancing over his shoulder at the empty hills.

Nobody replied. Eventually Anno spoke, almost to himself. "We may find stranger things in this new world than anything dreamed by humankind.'

A heated debate about the direction of their journey followed, ending with the decision to continue their downward course, heading for the lake as the clearest visible landmark and keeping a close watch for further signs of other travellers. Their path took them into the rich lower grasslands where Minna had found the kite, which they had left up on the hill-top. They walked among the clumps of nadel trees and sometimes saw one or two of Cara's small furry animals darting in and out of the shade beneath the branches. They had left the hills far behind, and Sol was sinking at their backs, elongating their shadows and outlining in black every blade and stem, when Cara found the huts.

She was walking ahead, a few paces in front of Anno, and rounded a grove of taller, broad-leaved trees which rose higher than her head. Huddled in a circle against the sheltering trunks, she saw five or six huts— but as she was poised to dart back into hiding, she noticed first that they were obviously abandoned, with broken roofs and crumbling walls, and then that they

106

were no larger than what would have passed for children's playhouses back in the settlement. Hearing the others approach, she motioned them to be quiet with a frantic wave of her hand. In a breathless whisper she told them what she had seen, and slowly the four travellers crept up to take a closer look. The thought uppermost in all their hearts was that here was final proof that they were not the first from the settlement to find the new country, and the disappointment was sharp. Cautiously, they came into the middle of the little circle of dwellings.

Minna gave a cry and pointed. Above each threshold was painted two bright gold eyes, just like the eyes on the kite. The bewilderment of the four grew as they peered inside the huts which were roofed with neatly cut turves and walled with interwoven branches. The inner walls were smooth with plastered mud and where they were not crumbling and fire-blackened, they were covered with frescoes as finely painted as the patterned kite. It took a moment for the companions to realise that the pictures showed the country through which they had been travelling but, inexplicably, seen from above. Ranged mountain peaks, an expanse of sapphire blue for the lake and many clusters of round, grass-roofed huts scattered across a vast swathe of greens and browns. And on the curve of the wall next to the empty doorway, there was an immense painting of a rearing winged creature—two stumpy legs, a long sinuous neck, two flaring wings covered with vivid red plumes, drawn with such precision that each tendril was clear. A pair of golden eyes on the huge head were turned to watch the onlookers.

Minna stood in front of the painting and her heart beat so fast that she felt sick with fear. Cara was telling Anno that outside were neglected patches of what

107

looked like a food crop, and ripe, dusky blue fruit growing on tangled bushes, but for Minna the words floated emptily in the close air of the hut. She stared at a dark stain on the floor, then bent to look at it more closely. It was dried blood.

'I think,' she said aloud in an unsteady voice, 'that something very evil has happened here.' She lifted her eyes and saw Gethin standing in the doorway, his face pale with shock despite his wind-browned skin.

'There—there is something you must see,' he stammered and beckoned them out of the hut, over to the far side of the circle and behind a half-ruined wall. Nothing in his manner quite prepared them for what they found there. A heap of broken bodies, dead perhaps only a few days. Small, delicate bodies with skins the colour of tarnished silver and slender, pointed faces framed by long blue-black hair. An arm, no larger than that of a six-year-old child, lay outflung on the trampled ground and on the exposed palm of the hand was tattoed a staring golden eye. Every body was bruised, torn and bloodied—whatever they were, the small beings had died struggling against a brutal enemy. Some of the bodies were pathetically smaller than the rest. The four humans stood looking at the dead creatures who had without doubt belonged to the little settlement, who had lived and borne offspring, flown kites and adorned their dwellings with mysterious paintings.

'In all the Earth years, nobody ever knew, but all humankind wondered whether they were alone among the stars and planets,' said Anno in a half-whisper. Minna found that she had bitten her lip so hard that it was bleeding.

'Surely,' Cara's voice broke the silence sharply, 'these

108

creatures were just strange off-shoots from some who came on the first ship.'

Anno shook his head. 'I have neither seen nor heard nor dreamed of anything like these. And—' he bent down and plucked a feathery grass, drawing it meditatively through his fingers, 'why should there not be other beings on a planet as vast as this?' Minna knelt and gently touched one of the smallest bodies. The slanting eyes of the tiny, perfectly formed head were open, staring rigidly at death.

'Maybe we should bury them,' she said. Then she saw that none of the others were listening. They were gazing up into the sky as if they had just heard something. She looked up as well and the sound came again, drawing nearer, a long-drawn-out wordless keening in the calm evening air. She knew it immediately as the mysterious cry she had heard in the mountains, but before she could speak, a firm grip dragged her roughly to her feet, and Anno was thrusting her after the others into the most secure of the nearby huts. As Minna lay on the earth floor, trodden hard by the feet of the small people, she saw through the gaping doorway a great winged creature, plummeting out of the gilded sky, out of all the legends and myths she had ever heard, the exact image of the one painted in rearing glory on the hut wall. The milk-white skin of its body shone against the glowing feathers on its outstretched wings as it hovered low over the circle of huts and the heaped bodies. Its golden eyes flashed in the yellow sunset light and from its open mouth came a lamenting cry, unlike any human voice, an unwavering note of mourning for the dead. Minna sensed that it held such a depth of sorrow that it almost broke her heart. Once, twice, three times, the creature circled the clearing, and all the while the keening never ceased. Then suddenly it beat its huge wings so that a wind rushed in the tree-tops and rose up and away, departing as swiftly as it had come.

Chapter Twelve

When the beating of the great wings faded, it was very quiet. Anno was the first to rise to his feet, rubbing his face wearily.

'It sounded like a lamentation, as if it were calling to the dead.' He spoke in the dry, precise tones of the Lesson Hall instructor and went over to scrutinise the wall-paintings again, pausing longest in front of the picture of the flying creature. The sun had gone behind the mountains and the clearing where the huts stood was shadowed and cold. Cara stayed by the door-way, staring blindly into the gathering dusk, and Gethin slumped at her feet. Only Minna stirred, remembering what she had seen and heard in the mountains. In a small voice she told of the brief episode.

'I think it was the same kind of creature as we saw now,' she ended. 'When I saw it before, I did not know what it was because it was flying so high, and the cry was faint.' The shadows were thickening and she could only see the others as silhouettes against the last of the light.

'I think,' said Anno, 'that we should start travelling by night, at least until we reach the lake. Come, we still

111

have time to gather some of the food crops Cara found outside. Our provisions are almost gone and I, for one, cannot live on air.' They did as he ordered, Gethin moving like a sleep-walker, and picked as much of the firm blue fruit as they could carry, while Cara unearthed misshapen creamy-white tubers from one of the overgrown patches of tilled earth. By the time they had finished, night had fallen. Although they were all tired after the day's journeying, nobody wanted to stay in that haunted little settlement and Anno urged them to walk on as far as they could.

'Anno,' said Cara breathlessly as she hurried to keep in step with him, 'were you not afraid of that—that creature, whatever it was?'

'Afraid? Not afraid, I think, but awed. Yet perhaps I am afraid, afraid for the wretched people we left behind us, stumbling about in a world that would drive them mad with terror if they knew half of it.'

'But for us—what will happen to us?'

'I do not know. Maybe we will die honourably defending the rest of those small people from their enemy. Maybe we will be mistaken for the enemy and killed. Maybe . . . '

'Maybe what?'

'Maybe we will see greater wonders than these if we do not give in to our fear, Cara.' Anno fell silent and they trudged on through the darkness until dawn was glimmering in the sky and they came to a sheltering copse of trees where they could sleep. Cara woke in the late afternoon and lay under the spreading branches, gazing at the play of the light on the rustling blue-green leaves. She ran a hand over the slender grey trunk beside her. For an instant the sun grew dim, as if a cloud had passed over, although the sky was clear. Then, faint and far off, she heard what was barely

112

more than an echo of the death-song, as if the winged creature were flying high over the plains, still mourning. She shivered and crouched lower in the tall grasses, fearing that it might see her and come swooping down again.

At sunset Anno roused the others, and they decided to risk tasting some of the food gathered from the ruined huts. The fruit was juicy and sweet beneath its hard blue rind and Gethin, too hungry to care about poison, crammed his mouth with it when the others were not looking. Even after the dirt had been washed from the tubers, they proved tough and tasteless when eaten raw, but Anno would not allow the lighting of a fire to try roasting them. Cara flexed her skinny arms and secretly wondered if they would starve to death or whether they could fight off the end by nibbling grass like goats. In that night's journey they drew steadily nearer the lake, passing the broken remains of more of the little people's settlements in the darkness.

'This country must have been overrun by them once,' Gethin muttered to Minna. 'All I hope is that whatever did away with them doesn't find us.'

At daybreak they finally arrived at the lake. On the left side, the shoreline ran on fairly straight, but on the right it curved away into the distance. Mist hung thick over the surface of the water and in the wan half-light they saw a huge tangled mat of dark green creeping plants stretching over the ground on all sides. The plants bore heavy purple blooms which filled the damp air with a syrupy scent. Minna plucked one, but it began to wither and lose its fragrance almost as soon as she broke the stem. As they walked along the shore, they came to what could only be another settlement, although nothing was left of it except a few fragments of wall and, in the middle of the circle of dwellings, a larger roofless hut which might once have had some special purpose. The desolation seemed complete, but as Gethin fought his way through the thickets back to the shore, he gave a yell of surprise and began tearing at the creepers. As the others ran up to help, he was uncovering a long flat structure made from short bundles of twigs bound tightly together, the cracks stuffed with the tough black moss which grew on the edge of the shore.

Anno stared hard at it and then turned to gaze at the water. Minna had taken off her boots and was paddling her sore feet in the warm shallows. Even though she had seen many awesome sights in their days of travelling, she still marvelled at so much clean water, though it was peculiarly salty to taste. In her heart she was walking in her own tale, telling her adventures to the prince.

'I believe,' said Anno slowly, 'that this may be meant to float upon the water. In some of the old Earth books, they spoke about—' He frowned, trying to remember. 'A—a raft,' he continued, searching for the right word. 'A means of crossing the lake, but where to, I wonder?' The daylight was growing stronger by the moment and the mist was thinning and blowing away in tatters in the steady breeze. The companions lifted the raft together and launched it into the shallows where it rested lightly on the surface, buoyant with air. Anno stood unsteadily at one end and propelled it along by pushing off the bottom with the long pole which he found lying close by. Cara and Minna watched his efforts, standing up to their knees in water, and laughed as he dropped the pole and reached out frantically to catch it as he drifted slowly away from the shore. They disturbed a shoal of incandescent water-creatures whose sinuous bodies snaked away into deeper water like shining green streamers. Cara shaded her eyes and peered across the wide expanse of the lake to see if the other side was visible. Her heart skipped a beat and she rubbed her eyes and peered again, trying to glimpse the far-off shape which had briefly loomed through the mist. Then she heard Minna gasp and knew that she could see it too.

'What is it?'

'I don't know—wait! No, the mist has blown across again. There!' Cara pointed and this time Anno looked up from the raft and they heard him catch his breath. Further away than they could have imagined, seeming to float between lake and morning sky, a tall white column rose and, as the air cleared, they could just see other vague shapes clustered round it, as remote and shifting as a desert mirage. The thought occured to both Cara and Minna that perhaps the little people's enemies had come from across the lake, and they exchanged fearful glances. Gethin came up behind them, returning from wandering among the ruined huts, and they pointed out what they had seen. His wide eyes showed that he too was afraid.

He ran up to Anno as the older man waded from the raft. 'What is it, sir? What should we do?'

Anno's frown showed that he was troubled, yet he spoke calmly. 'This is indeed a curious country. We thought all the while in the settlement that we were the only living beings on Osiris, did we not?'

Cara burst out, 'But what shall we do now?'

'I think that perhaps we should find somewhere to sleep and wait until nightfall.' He paused. 'What would you say then to crossing the lake by raft to observe without being seen ourselves? Perhaps it is only a grove of unnaturally tall rua trees or some strange Osirian plant which we have not encountered yet.' Tentatively, the other three agreed. None of them, not even Cara, felt able to form a better plan.

With Anno's help, they secured the raft at the lakeside and found a place where the ground-creepers formed a comfortable, springy bed so that they could rest unseen while the sun was in the sky.

When the welcome cover of darkness spread over the land, they returned to the shore. Stars filled every quarter of the sky and from time to time one would flame across the black expanse in a shower of meteoric sparks. As the water lapped at the pebbles, each ripple was outlined in pale fire and, looking more closely, Minna saw that hordes of almost invisible creatures were swimming about in the shallows, each one bathed in phosphorescence. She waded out with the others to launch the raft and then pulled herself up onto the knobbly twigs, soaked to the waist. The raft sat very low in the water when the four of them were on board, with the wavelets almost breaking over the top. First Anno and then Gethin stood upright at the stern, plying the pole with growing confidence, and they moved slowly away from the shore, making almost no sound at all. The water did not become too deep for the pole to touch the bottom, as Anno had feared.

At first they could see nothing on the far shore, but suddenly Anno gave an exclamation and pointed. Lights had appeared where the white column stood— three beacon-bright lights shining one above the other, and surrounding them were other, dimmer beams. Each of the four travellers was silent, seeing again after countless days in the wilderness what could only be the glow of fires and lamps burning. Cara crawled to Anno's side.

'What are they?' she whispered, overwhelmed for the first time by a longing for the confined, explicable streets of the old settlement.

116

'I do not know.' For a moment his hand rested gently on her hair. She shivered in the night wind, and he drew a fold of his cloak round her. They sat together, as the raft drifted on.

Minna sat alone, her bundle between her knees with the precious box of pictures inside. She had never finished stitching the mountain scene, too caught up in the rush of new happenings. Her dream in the blizzard had frightened her, too, giving unexpected life and independence to her own private creation. In her inmost heart, though, she was still the girl journeying to the prince's kingdom and she had shaped in her mind's eye the image of a sunlit courtyard with cool green ferns, white stones and a welling spring in the middle. There she would sit with the prince when at last she arrived, telling him the tale of her adventures, watching his bright eyes and feeling her hands clasped in his. Even as she crossed the lake, she was sitting in the courtyard with him and describing the stars, the glowing water-creatures and the beckoning lights.

Throughout the night the raft moved over the calm lake which mirrored in its depths the radiant stars above, while on the far shore the lights burned steadily. From time to time one of the others would take a turn at wielding the pole, but none of them proved quite so skilful as Gethin, who took to rafting as if he had done it since childhood.

After what felt like an eternity of darkness, the sky began to pale, and at the same time the mist rose again so that before the day was light enough to reveal what lay on the shore ahead, the raft was enveloped by thick fog, shut in on all sides by blank white walls.

Presently Gethin, who was poling again, sank down on his haunches and shook his head. 'It's no use going forward. We're travelling blind and we don't know what dangers there might be.'

Anno sat up and told him not to be a fool, and to try and head for the left shore. 'We will beach in secret if we can. Surely you knew we did not intend to paddle up meekly and tell the keepers of the lights that we were sorry but we had lost our way?' he added impatiently.

Gethin glowered and said nothing. He positioned the pole carefully and shoved so that the raft began to move to the left, although it was hard to tell whether or not they were simply going round in circles. He pushed on for as long as he could, trying to keep his bearings even though the rising sun could not penetrate the heavy air. Without realising it, they had been travelling close to the shore all night; sooner than they expected, they heard the soft hiss of surf sucking over pebbles, and suddenly the raft crunched aground.

The travellers tumbled off, staggering on cramped limbs, and dragged their craft higher up the narrow beach to where a steep bank rose, overhung with the same dark green creepers which they had seen before. They were able to conceal most of the raft under the curve of the bank and by the time they finished their labour, the fog had thinned considerably.

They saw walls, first, rising sheer above the veiled surface of the lake, gleaming faint yellow in the watery sunlight. Above the walls were many tall white columns with dark gaps in the stonework like watchful eyes, and standing among the columns were other buildings, compared to which the settlement Assembly Hall was no more than a clumsy shed. Ornamented roofs glittered, and carved rock sparkled against the pale sky. A warm wind began to blow, driving back the fog, and the travellers saw, farther off, a wide fertile country with dark woodlands and a line of hills beyond.

Then, closer at hand, there was movement. Through a clump of trees came a muffled figure, driving what looked to Cara's dazed eyes like a simple flock of goats. Their thin bleats broke the stillness and the figure threw back the hood covering its head. It was a man, and as his astonished eyes took in the bedraggled group standing on the shore, his ruddy face filled with pure terror. Abandoning the goats, he took to his heels and ran.

Cara heard a thud behind her and turned to see Minna lying in a crumpled heap on the pebbles. Gethin knelt beside her. Anno remained standing straight, staring at what lay before him, but his eyes brimmed with tears.

'Orion, the second ship,' he said, and the tears began to trickle down his hollow cheeks.

PART II

The Citadel

Chapter One

Before the four travellers could gather their wits and decide what to do, they heard shouts and footsteps coming through the grove. The goatherd reappeared with three other men, all dressed in loose brown tunics and work-stained breeches. They moved cautiously towards the strangers, regarding them with mingled fear and hostility. When Anno stepped forward, holding out his hands in friendship, they shrank back.

'We greet you!' he said, speaking slowly and clearly. 'We have journeyed far and need rest and refreshment.' None of the men replied, but they began to edge closer again, as if afraid that the four might try to dodge past and escape. Cara stood at Anno's side, marvelling at them: the men were taller and stronger than any of the settlement people, and dressed in finely woven garments, although the colours were dark and dull. They seemed to be waiting for something and kept glancing back over their shoulders and muttering inaudibly to one another. Minna had woken from her faint and was sitting up, supported by Gethin. She stared at the great buildings, at the walls rising above the lakeshore and at the threatening group of men.

Then they heard a trampling sound among the

trees, and out from under the branches came another man, even taller than the others, and leading a creature so magnificent that the travellers gazed with open mouths. Only Anno and Cara guessed that it must be a horse from certain passages in the old Lesson Hall manuscripts—but like Minna and Gethin they marvelled at its beauty and grace. Four slender, tapering silver-grey legs, a long neck, flowing tail, bright eyes and a soft, rounded muzzle. It stepped proudly down towards the shore, following its master who strode unhesitatingly through the others until he stood in front of Anno.

'Name and sector?' he snapped. The travellers stared at him, dumbfounded. His language was the same as theirs, although he spoke the words with a strange, thick accent.

Anno was the first to recover and bowed his head in greeting. 'My name is Anno, this is Cara, this her sister Minna and her friend Gethin.'

'I said name and sector only, not the family history.' The man's eyes were small and unfriendly, and he was dressed in a tight suit of scarlet and grey, all in one piece from neck to ankle. In the middle of his chest a shiny badge of office proclaimed him Captain of the Watch for the South-west Sector.

Cara dared to speak. 'We do not know what a sector is. We have just come from over the water.' Anno frowned at her to say no more, but the captain's face flushed with an ugly mixture of alarm and triumph. He stepped closer, away from the waiting labourers, and lowered his voice so that only the four strangers could hear.

'Rebels returning?' he sneered. 'Ran away and didn't like it out in the wild so you've come crawling back? The field men here don't like your faces, and I think they are right to be suspicious. We shall see what the Circle will say to you.' At that moment nine more men, all clad in the same scarlet and grey uniform, came hurrying through the trees. With a nod the captain dismissed the labourers. 'No alarm. These are strays from the North-east sector. Return to your work.' When they had gone, he turned to his patrol. 'Take them prisoner, and don't be too gentle.'

Cara's feet were kicked from under her and she fell so that all the breath was knocked out of her body. Struggling for air, she saw out of the corner of one eye that Anno was being overpowered by four stalwarts scarcely older than Gethin, who wrestled with him until he submitted to lying still. She heard a clink of metal and one of the men dragged her to her knees and chained her hands securely behind her back. The captain mounted his horse and watched while the prisoners' fetters were bound together to form a long line. Then he tugged the end and jerked them forward one step.

'You men!' he shouted. 'March ahead and clear the way so that nobody sees this little band. Send messages to the other companies and order a colony inspection. We'll enter the Citadel by the barracks gate.'

Three sentries remained to guard the prisoners and they waited in the silent grove, the sun beating down on their heads, until a breathless young Watch woman arrived with the news that the way was made ready. The captain urged his horse to a trot and the cavalcade set off, the prisoners forced to break into a stumbling run to keep up.

In spite of her bruises and fear, Cara could not help noticing the countryside through which they passed on their way to the Citadel. After the trees, they came to a shallow river flowing swiftly into the lake and they splashed through a ford, trying to keep a foothold on the slippery rocks. Shivering and dripping, they crossed a broad road, paved with carefully fitted slabs of black stone and lined on either side by the same graceful trees which they had seen by the lake. Among the pale leaves darted small creatures with big-eyed baby faces, framed by a cloud of white fur, and long clutching fingers and toes. From time to time the animals called to one another with shrill, plaintive cries. The Citadel walls loomed before the prisoners, pierced by great bronze and steel gates which were flanked by a guard of three stern Watch officers.

As they came down on the other side of the road, the captain suddenly hissed an order, and the prisoners were pushed to the ground. Cara glanced back and saw a company of children emerging from the gates, walking two by two and dressed alike in pale blue suits, fashioned in the same style as the Watch uniforms. A young man in a long orange robe accompanied them, and she heard him order them to step out for the pasture lands.

When the children had gone, the Watch men dragged the prisoners to their feet again. Cara saw that beyond them lay fields, green with budding crops and larger and better tilled than any she had seen before. Here and there lay scattered groups of huts, all built on the same regular lines—black stone walls, sloping turf roofs, the doorways opening onto a central enclosure. She could just see the inhabitants of one group marshalled together in their enclosure, gathered by a couple of Watch men for a cursory inspection. Nobody noticed the line of prisoners being led along the curve of the walls.

The captain seemed to grow nervous and barked at them to move faster, giving the chain such a tug that they almost fell over. After they had gone a little further, they came to a steep flight of steps and he dismounted and led them up to another gateway, small and insignificant this time, and guarded by one very young girl who stared wide-eyed at the prisoners as they stumbled past. They had a brief, confused impression of a large, unadorned stone building and a courtyard thronged with curious Watch sentries, and then they were hurried through a maze of winding streets. Whenever they crossed a wider thoroughfare, their guards clustered round to hide them from passers-by. Minna lifted her eyes and saw the gracious houses, the lofty white towers and the shaded gardens where fountains danced in the morning light, and wondered in her half-starved daze if she were not walking in the world of her story, the poor girl come to the prince's kingdom at last. Bewildered and feeling the chains galling her wrists, she began to cry.

The others dragged themselves along behind and before her, craning their necks for glimpses of the ornamented halls and homes, some still only half-built and others embellished with carvings of grotesque faces or moulded plasterwork. The main streets were thronged with people dressed far more richly than the fieldmen, draped in sumptuous layers of soft, flowing cloth in a rainbow of glowing colours. The prisoners saw bright faces, straight limbs, vigorous young bodies and also many children, for the most part walking in disciplined ranks. Then they were passing through back streets again, flanked on either side by featureless walls—here there were no paving-stones and the dust rose round them in grey clouds. They emerged from an alleyway and were jerked to a halt as the captain dismounted from his horse again. They were at the entrance of the tallest of the white towers, perhaps the same tower whose beacon lights had guided them over the lake. The captain spoke briefly to one of the Watch men standing to attention at the door and then removed the prisoners' chains.

'Don't think of trying to escape,' he said grimly. 'The Watch would have you before you took three steps down the street.' He saluted the tower and rode away towards the main gate, after delivering his captives into the hands of three silent women who emerged from the doorway, resplendent in their Watch uniforms and towering even above Anno.

Clearly, word of their arrival had preceded them because their escorts immediately led them up a flight of stone stairs which spiralled round inside the tower. The climb was a long one, past many narrow landings, and twice Minna's guard had to clutch her to stop her from falling. Eventually they halted before an immense nail-studded door. Anno's guard knocked twice, and the door was opened from within. The guards pushed the prisoners over the threshold and into a circular chamber, filled with light from the unshuttered window looking out over the shining waters of the lake.

'Captive rebels, brought here according to the Circle's orders. Caught by the shore, trying to waylay a field man,' announced Anno's guard, closing her mouth with a snap at the end of the sentence.

A large round table filled the middle of the room, and twenty young men and women with sharp, intelligent faces surveyed the dishevelled four ranged before them. One of the men rose to his feet, running one hand through his curly yellow hair. He yawned widely before he spoke. 'Address me as Chief Citizen Tav. What are your names and sectors?'

'We know nothing about sectors,' Anno replied,

shaping the words with difficulty because of his bruised mouth. 'We will answer no questions until you explain why we have been treated so harshly.'

Chief Citizen Tav looked surprised. He surveyed each of the prisoners in turn. Cara dropped her eyes as his curious gaze passed over her.

His manner became a little more patient. 'Even if you wish to stop resisting us and come back, you must be disciplined. Our people can only be safeguarded if we punish disobedience. If you tell us truthfully what you have done, the Circle may be merciful.'

He sat down with a sigh, and the prisoners exchanged glances. Cara looked pleadingly at Anno. If these arrogant people were indeed from the second ship, he could perhaps shock them with part, at least, of the truth. He held her gaze and then gave a tiny nod. Drawing a deep breath, he began recounting the tale of their journeying, being as vague as possible about the location and strength of the settlement and declaring their simple intention of exploring. He did not mention the flying creature nor the massacred heaps of little people which they had discovered.

The Circle members looked sceptically at one another when he had finished, evidently unsure whether to excuse him as a madman or dismiss him as a wicked, lying rebel.

'Tell us,' said a strapping carrot-haired young man, 'where did you say your settlement came from?'

At least they story had aroused their interest. Anno told in his best Lesson Hall manner the brief history of the settlement and the legend of the lost second ship. When he had finished, the twenty young men and women sat in shocked silence. Cara wondered if their people, like the settlement, told stories about another spaceship, and whether they ever credited the stories

129

with some truths. Perhaps they were reared in the belief that they alone guarded the future of human-kind because there was in all likelihood nobody else left—and maybe they sensed their authority shaken.

When Tav stood up again, however, his smile was disarmingly welcoming. 'You must forgive us!' he cried warmly. 'We treat you like lawbreakers and then discover that you are our brothers and sisters. The whole Citadel must hear of this finding!' He approached Anno and took hold of his arm, smiling into the cold grey eyes. 'We say we are descendents of the Orion, from the name of our ship. We always spoke of the people from Sirius as the lost ones. And now you are found! So what are your people like? How big is your settlement? Why did they make you travel so far and so hard?'

Anno drew back from the young man's firm grasp. 'We have no reason to trust you yet. You have told us little and treated us, as you say, like lawbreakers.'

'Give them something to eat,' shouted one of the other young men, amid general laughter. Obviously some of the Circle members were not yet inclined to believe Anno's story. Tav joined in the laughter and ordered one of the guards to bring refreshments and a bench for the guests.

'What can we tell you?' he mused, resuming his seat and smiling at them all. 'This is the Citadel, where the descendents of the starship Orion and the first col-onists live together happily and peacefully. We are the Circle, and we govern the people with the help of the Watch who are sometimes, we confess, more efficient than tender-hearted—but we are not used to stran-gers! Cassie,' he turned to a strikingly beautiful girl sit-ting near him, 'tell a little of the history of our people.'

Cassie looked over the heads of the four tattered

travellers. Her voice was languid and surprisingly deep.

'Orion and Sirius were coming from Earth. Orion was the bigger ship, but they were both intended to land near the site of the existing human colony on Osiris. They mistimed their approach and were caught in a freak storm. Sirius was swept away and only Orion arrived safely and united with the survivors of the old colony.'

'And so,' continued Tav eagerly, 'we have been living and working here, the last remnant. We have built a Citadel which is almost as great and strong as the cities we left behind on Earth. We wake each morning full of purpose,' he rose from his seat again and paced up and down, gesturing excitedly. 'We have the whole of this huge planet for humankind's new life, and now that we have discovered the lost Sirius, we can make Osiris as great a world as Earth ever was.'

The door opened slowly, and the food was brought in. The four travellers stared, not at the soft wheaten loaves, the cured meats and the bunches of shiny yellow fruit, but at the bearer—a short, dark, silvery skinned creature exactly like those they had last seen lying dead by a ruined hut. He moved quickly and nervously, setting the dishes on a small table and hurrying out again without raising his slanting eyes to the people in the crowded room.

Before Tav could invite them to sit and eat, Anno burst out angrily, 'What have you to do with the little people? We passed through a land filled with their broken huts and dead bodies. Was that your Citadel's doing?'

'So you came that way,' said Tav slowly. 'You saw but you did not understand.'

'Somebody had done the killing, brutal killing! We

131

understood that!'

'But you knew nothing of those creatures—the Scurriers, we call them.' Tav said the name with a sneer. 'Let me tell you that you were in great danger as you journeyed through that land. The first colonists were almost wiped out by the ceaseless, vicious attacks of those little people on their crops and homes. We subdued many of them after bitter fighting, but those of us whom they captured died cruelly. You were fortunate to come through unharmed!'

'Yet you keep them as servants?' retorted Anno sarcastically.

'Some did not want to fight us, so their own kind rejected them. They are not human, and we cannot reason with them, but they are content to serve and are very skilful with their fingers. We taught them to stitch clothes and build furniture for our homes.' Tav's smile faded and he raised his voice in annoyance at Anno's disbelieving expression. 'Out in the wilds they have these monstrous flying beasts like the dragons of the old world. They would tear you to pieces if they saw you.'

Cara and Minna glanced at one another, uncertain what to believe and almost too tired to care. They were desperately hungry, and Tav urged them to eat, explaining, as if to small children, what each food was. Anno looked as if he would have liked to refuse, but soon he too was tearing mouthfuls of bread and grasping the soft gelu fruit so greedily that the golden juice spilled out over his fingers. As they ate, the Circle members put their heads together across the table and debated in low voices.

At one point Cassie called out to Anno. 'You say you came across the bay?'

'Across the lake,' he answered shortly.

132

'Lake!' she stared at him. 'That's the sea, coming into a bay. Did you not know?' He stared back, uncomprehending. 'A tide sucks the bay dry every few days, sweeping all the water back into the ocean. If you had crossed tomorrow night, you would have been dragged away by the currents and drowned.' She turned back to her companions and the four travellers, their appetites satisfied for the moment, waited in a wretched silence, instinctively huddling together on their bench. Cara gazed at the floor, brooding on the chance which had brought them to the bay on a safe night and then allowed them to be taken captive.

At length Tav stood up and called for their attention. 'First, do you have any more questions?'

'The rebels,' said Anno quickly. 'Who are they and where do they hide?'

Tav dismissed the rebels with a wave of his hand. 'I regret that we cannot speak openly of that now. Perhaps some other time.' His manner became curt and businesslike. 'We have decided that you can join our people as full citizens, providing you prove to be sound in body and mind. Each of you will be examined and educated and allotted a suitable place, and then we will set about finding your settlement again.'

Cara's heart stood still and she felt as if the floor were falling away beneath her feet. She was dimly aware of Anno shouting something and Tav shouting louder that they should be grateful for the privilege which the Circle was extending to them. She felt nothing except fear of the unknown world of the Citadel. Too much had been new in one short day. Then, without warning, Anno and Gethin were gone, hustled down the stairs by a crowd of guards. Minna sat on the bench with tears rolling down her face, and Cara found that she was trembling from head to foot and struggling to cry out from a voiceless throat. There was a hand on her shoulder, and Tav was standing in front of her, genuinely puzzled at their distress.

'Listen,' he was saying, 'I shall take you and your sister to the infirmary myself. Nothing harmful will happen to you! Would you rather starve in the wilds or be eaten by a dragon? Come with me.' He took her hand as if she were a child and, too weak to resist, she allowed him to lead her away. Behind her, she heard Minna sobbing.

Chapter Two

Tav and Izak, one of his closest Circle companions, were out riding on the High Road which led from the Citadel gates to the hill country where they could be sure of good hunting among the dense woods, the scattered copses and coverts. As senior members of the Circle they had the pick of the Citadel horses—Tav rode a sure-footed grey mare and Izak a restless piebald stallion. Sol was climbing towards the top of the pale blue sky and the two young men were hoping to skewer at least one wild hoch with their long steel-tipped hunting spears. The hoch could move surprisingly fast on its short legs, despite its bulk and the weight of its shaggy grey coat. Hunting parties had to beware the creature's long tusk, which could gore a careless rider. Groups of field men and women saluted the Circle men as they passed, and they acknowledged each greeting with a courteous nod.

Tav was telling his friend about the state of the four strangers who had now spent twelve days in the Citadel infirmary. 'The physicians tell me they are growing stronger with rest and good food, but their spirits are low. The older man sulks alone in his cell, and the other shows little interest in anything beyond the next meal.'

'What about the two sisters?' asked Izak with a grin.

'Better-looking, even in infirmary gowns, now that they are clean. The smaller one cries often, but they say her older sister is quick to reply to any remark or question and is curious about our life here.'

'Are we going to pay them a visit?'

'Perhaps I'll call and offer the pleasures of a guided tour to make our guests feel welcome.'

Izak burst out laughing. 'You go and act the dutiful Chief Citizen, but you must arrange an introduction for me, if you think I would, let us say, enjoy their company.' Tav snorted and dug his heels into the mare's side so that she broke into a gallop, her metalled hooves striking sparks from the black paving stones, and Izak followed behind.

Meanwhile Cara was slowly wandering round a shaded courtyard formed by three blank stone walls and a low building with six windows. She and her companions lived on a separate corridor, isolated from the rest of the infirmary which stood near the main gate, with arched windows overlooking the fields and the curve of the bay. They each had a narrow white cell with a single window opening on to the courtyard, a firm couch for a bed and a three-legged stool. At one end of the row of cells was a larger room where they ate and at the other end was the chamber where their warden slept—an unsmiling woman with iron-grey hair who spent her day observing them in silence. The food, although abundant, was plain by Citadel standards, but no settlement table had ever been graced by such a wealth of fruits or such soft, light bread. The wardens had taken away and burned the ragged remains of the travellers' clothes when they arrived, and they were all dressed in the shapeless linen infirmary gowns.

Cara paced the courtyard, staring down at her bare feet on the dusty ground and thinking about what had happened in the past days. As Tav promised, no harm had come to them. Anno found the chance to impress on them not to mention the settlement wasting sickness, thinking it wisest not to admit anything which would further weaken their already precarious position. The physicians questioned them closely about the health of their people and found them to be in good health, if weak and underfed after their arduous journeying. A stern Watch officer came to instruct them in some of the laws of the Citadel: all citizens had to live within the encircling walls, while the field people dwelt in their own cabins, built together in strictly defined groups, or colonies, with no more than twenty colonies in each sector; the word of the Circle was inviolate at all times; the first duty of citizens and field people alike was to do their allotted work with diligence and energy. Most importantly, there were no rebels—the words were a figure of speech used only by the Circle and the Watch, and although the arrival of the four strangers provoked confusion, everybody knew that all rebellious elements had long since disappeared.

Three tutors came from the Academy where the children were educated, and spent a day testing their knowledge and skills. Cara effortlessly completed the calculations set for her and wrote an account of their travels in her clear sloping handwriting, as well as a few snatches of settlement history. While she worked, she heard Anno's angry voice coming from his cell as he argued with the earnest young man allocated to him. Over their meal that evening, Minna remarked that she had been told her weaving work was of no consequence in the Citadel because such tasks belonged to those who lacked her reasoning powers.

'They said I have a well-schooled mind which only needs a few months of discipline to flourish,' she added, darting a shy glance at Anno, whose sour face showed that he was in a fierce temper. He looked up as she spoke and then thumped his fist so hard on the table that the stew slopped from their bowls.

'You are playing into their hands, you foolish girl!' he shouted. 'Have you thought about what will happen to us when these games are finished?' Then the warden marched in to quell the uproar.

Cara sighed as she thought of Anno's refusal to co-operate with any of the Citadel people. Moving out of the shade into the hot sun, she crouched down to pick up a handful of the grey dust underfoot and let it trickle warmly through her fingers. The courtyard backed onto the Citadel wall on one side, and although she could not see over the top, she knew from what the warden had told them that on the other side was a Watch patrol to make sure none of them tried to escape. Above the roofs of the other infirmary buildings rose the white towers and majestic halls of the rest of the Citadel. Cara had begun to long to see more of it.

Later that day, as the sky began to fade into nightfall and a single star appeared above the hills, Tav came to the infirmary. He was pleasantly tired after the hunting expedition and had left Izak planning a hoch roast out on the vast expanse of shoals which would be exposed at low tide in the bay during the next few days. The Chief Physician, a stooping middle-aged man, welcomed him into his cluttered study-cell where he showed him the reports prepared on the four strangers. Gethin was judged suitable for some sort of labourer's work, Cara and Minna were both considered possible Citadel members, perhaps working in the Academy.

The Chief Physician tutted in exasperation as he produced the findings on Anno. 'They say he is abusive and withdrawn by turns. He says he wants nothing to do with the Citadel and tries to turn the other three against us.'

'Indeed?' yawned Tav, uninterested in Anno. 'But the sisters, Cara and Minna, would be willing to join our people?'

'Assuredly, once they are removed from the hostile older man. The dark-haired girl, Cara, asks many questions about the Citadel and shows much interest in all that takes place here.'

'I wondered,' said Tav in his easy Circle manner, 'whether I might beg a small favour of you.' Even the Chief Physician would not presume to deny the wishes of a senior Circle member and accordingly, the warden later brought a message to Cara saying that Chief Citizen Tav would call early the following morning to show her something of the Citadel.

'Please understand that this is a very great honour,' snapped the warden, staring hard at Cara who was lying indolently on the couch in her cell.

'Will I have to walk through the streets dressed in this?' Cara, with a wry smile, indicated the linen gown which enveloped her like a collapsed tent.

The warden did not smile back. 'Clothing will be brought to you in good time.' And she strode out of the cell, taking the tallow lamp with her so that Cara was left in star-lit dimness.

Shortly after sunrise, Cara was waiting for Tav in the Chief Physician's study-cell. The shapeless gown had been replaced by a crimson shift which fell to her knees, belted round the waist with three plaited thongs

139

of white leather, but she chose to go barefoot rather than wear what to her eyes looked like a pair of oddly-made strappings for a broken ankle. Tav's knock sounded at the gate and she was preparing to leave when the warden came hurrying up, the strappings in her hand.

'Do they wander barefoot like Scurriers where you come from, mountain girl?' she asked indignantly, and made Cara stay while she fastened the sandals. Tav smiled when he saw her, frowning as she tried to walk with the stiff leather constraining her feet.

'It's a pleasure to see you looking so well,' he said politely, offering her his hand. She was clearly unused to such ceremony and had not learned respect for her superiors, because she answered shortly that she had been perfectly well until these ridiculous—what were they?—sandals were forced on her.

Tav laughed. 'You can take them off when we are out of sight of the infirmary. The Citadel has much to show you and we will be walking a long way, so you may go barefoot if you please. Besides, it is always better to start the day in a good temper.' He kept his word and once they were round a corner, he knelt down in the middle of the busy street, disregarding the curious stares of passers-by, and showed Cara how to unfasten the lacing.

Cara grew accustomed to the stares during that day as Tav led her round almost every corner of the Citadel. Citizens continually pointed her out to each other as one of the four strangers who had arrived so suddenly, reputedly come from beyond the bay and even from the lost ship Sirius, although few believed that story. People also stopped to exclaim at the sight of a senior Circle member personally escorting one of the strangers, and many assumed that Cara must be a leader of her own people to merit such treatment. Men, women and children bowed as Tav passed and then stopped to whisper behind their hands about the pretty face of the dark-haired girl and the honour being paid to her. It was a bright, warm day and the clean walkways and the elegant buildings gleamed in the clear light.

Tav first took Cara up the twisting street from the infirmary to the Quadrangle, the unfinished square at the heart of the Citadel. It was bounded on one side by the Academy, which faced a half-built meeting hall across the broad expanse of black flagstones. He led her into the wide corridors of the Academy where the children, uniformly clad in pale blue, learned their lessons in pleasantly cool chambers, sitting on long benches drawn up to polished wooden tables. The orange-robed tutors read in calm, unhurried voices from carefully bound books of notes. When Cara exclaimed over the abundant wood, Tav told her that the Citadel had always taken care to preserve their trees, planting saplings of the grey-trunked kaim and the pale-leaved tabun wherever they were cut down, to ensure that the people's needs would always be supplied.

They went out again into the hot sunshine and he showed her the labourers at work on the new meeting hall, assisted by half a dozen nervous Scurriers who dodged out of sight whenever they could and never made a sound. Tav pointed out the firm stone foundations and ordered the foreman to bring the plans so that Cara could see how the hall would serve as a gathering-place for all the citizens, for pleasure as well as serious public debate.

'The Citadel players can perform some of the entertainments written by our scholars, and also the ancient

141

comedies and tragedies brought from Earth and preserved in the Bibliotheca—the hall of books,' Tav said, smiling at Cara's eagerness.

She had forgotten her awkwardness, and she pulled at his purple tunic sleeve. 'Take me to see the book hall, Chief Citizen Tav!"

He laughed. 'No need to call me Chief Citizen, now that we are better acquainted. My name is simply Tav.'

They crossed the Quadrangle again, dodging the horseback riders and the handcarts loaded with produce from the fields, the vigilant Watch patrols ordering the traffic and the crowds of brightly clothed citizens going about their business. Tav said that a great market was held in the Quadrangle once every seven days, when the field workers and their overseers came in to barter goods and livestock. 'The noise is deafening, and the little field children who are too young to attend the Academy run about screaming at everything they see!'

'I would like to be there,' said Cara hopefully. She felt as if she were walking in a dream or in one of the Earth tales which she had read in the draughty settlement Lesson Hall, which now seemed a distant age ago. They came to the sand-coloured walls of the Bibliotheca, standing next to the Academy and ornamented with grotesque stone heads along the parapet. They reminded Cara of the head of the flying creature which Tav had called a dragon. Through the heavy steel doors, taken from the body of the spaceship Orion, were whispering corridors filled with shadowy figures flitting in and out of doorways and up and down the winding staircases. Tav took Cara down to the underground storerooms where locked cases held the most ancient Earth books, the pages crumbling a little at the edges. Cara cradled one in her hands, inscribed with the date 2029 on the first page, and felt as if it would turn to dust at a breath.

'Who reads these?' she whispered.

'The tutors come here to prepare their lessons and the scholars work here all the time, preparing new books and studying the old texts.' Back near the entrance hall he showed her brighter rooms full of newly written volumes. Some were on parchment leaves, others on fine vellum scrolls, but most were inscribed on thin pieces of a rustling yellow material which Cara had never seen before. She turned a page carelessly and the corner tore in her hand.

'Take care!' Tav warned with a smile. 'The scholars are jealous keepers of their books. This is paper, frailer than parchment but quicker to prepare. It comes from wortweed which grows in the bay. It is gathered at low tide, beaten to a pulp and then dried in the sun in sheets.'

Climbing the staircase, they came to the sunlit rooms where the scholars worked in plain grey gowns pulled over their Citadel finery. The silence was unbroken except for the turning of a page, the scratching of pen nibs and the echo of footsteps along the corridors. The lofty glazed windows were embellished with coloured patterns which threw gold, green and scarlet shadows onto the ranged desks, and through the windows Cara saw the chiselled stone of sand-coloured turrets against the flawless sky. They went up a final flight of stairs to the topmost level, a bare, dingy place where the Circle records were kept, dating back to the time of the starship landing. Dominating the room, though, was what Cara thought at first was a perfect statue of one of the wilderness dragons, rising on outstretched wings with its gilded eyes turned to gaze at the onlooker, just like the wall-paintings in the ruined Scurrier huts.

143

Cara's mouth was dry and her voice shook slightly. 'What is that?'

'A fine trophy.' Tav went up to it and stroked the long red pinions, and she realised that it was not a statue but the preserved body of one of the flying creatures, every plume intact. Tav continued, 'It has stood here for years as a reminder of the bitter battles fought by the first settlers. When I was a child, I would sometimes escape from the Academy and come up here and look at it.' He paused, thinking, perhaps, of quiet afternoons when the small boy had sat there alone, marvelling at the strange beast. 'Come, we must go now.' He took her hand and hurried her through the corridors and back into the Quadrangle. Blinking in the light, they made their way across to the broad avenue where the Citadel nurseries lay. In a garden full of squirming babies and bright-eyed toddlers playing round a fountain, Cara was soon distracted from the thought of the great creature locked up in the gloom of the Bibliotheca.

In the hottest part of the day they rested and ate a meal with one of the most important Citadel households: the family of Cassie, the beautiful Circle girl who was one of Tav's oldest friends. Cara was awed by the large house with its pillared central courtyard and many rooms with patterned rugs spread on every floor. An unobtrusive Scurrier servant served their meal in the courtyard, and their hosts ate with them—Cassie's silver-haired father, Julan, and Tasha, her elegantly groomed mother. Cara blushed and dropped her food whenever they spoke to her, so they tactfully adressed their conversation to Tav, dealing for the most part with Citadel matters of which Cara knew nothing. She ate in silence, relishing the cold spiced meat coated in a sweet, sticky paste, and the oily cakes which dissolved

144

in the mouth. One of the blue-spotted insects which the travellers had first seen on the moorlands droned peacefully round the shaded room. Tav told Cara that the scholars had named them smalt flies.

Later he took her to see the workshops where the Scurriers toiled with quick, slender fingers, spinning and weaving and stitching garments, building graceful tables and couches, curing animal hides and mending children's broken playthings. Cara looked on in fascination, forgetting for a moment the slaughter she had seen in the wilderness. They went to the cluster of white towers where the administration of the Citadel was conducted in hushed, shuttered study chambers, and then down to where the Watch were quartered in their swept and polished barracks, next to the stables housing the Citadel horses. Cara put out her hand and timidly stroked the smooth neck of Tav's mare and felt the soft lips and warm breath on her palm.

When at last it was time for her to return to the infirmary, she felt worn out with exertion and by all that she had seen. She halted at the top of the infirmary street to retie the hated sandals on her feet and then took Tav's proferred arm. Before they knocked at the gate, she thanked him gravely for the day's entertainment.

He bowed. 'It was pleasure for me as well. Will you care to come out again some time?' She nodded eagerly and then scowled as one of the wardens hurried out to meet them. Seeing the expression on her face, he laughed. 'You will not be staying there for many more days, I think.' Then he bowed courteously in farewell and passed into the infirmary ahead of her to speak briefly with the Chief Physician.

Full of high spirits, Cara did not even grudge exchanging her shift for the unbecoming infirmary

gown, and the warden's dour face did not suppress
her. She almost skipped along the corridors back to her
cell and was quite unprepared for the storm awaiting
her. Ignoring Minna's tear-stained face and Gethin's
anxious frown, she rushed to find Anno, eager to tell
him what had happened that day. He was waiting for
her on the couch in the dining chamber. She stopped
short when she saw his face, which was pale with anger.
Closing the door, she stood with her back to it, looking
at him.

'Why did you not tell me where you were going
today?' he said at last, his voice tight with suppressed
rage.

Even though his mood frightened her, Cara felt her
hold on her own temper begin to weaken. 'Surely the
warden told you where I was?' she snapped.

'The warden, yes,' Anno replied through clenched
teeth. 'She told me with a mocking smile that one of my
women had more sense than I did, and had taken some
Chief Citizen's offer of a tour round the Citadel. "You
can't keep them to your way of thinking," she said, and
laughed at me.'

'And so? I cannot help what the warden may say.
Anno, I learned many useful things today. The
Citadel—'

'Cara,' Anno cut in icily, 'you went without consult-
ing me, or even your sister or Gethin. How can we
safeguard ourselves if we do not act together?'

'I went because Tav asked me. I am old enough to
know my own mind. Why should it concern you? You
were not asked to come.' Cara knew she was shouting
but did not try to control herself. She was furious.

'*Tav* now, is it? So you are on intimate terms with the
Circle already? You are no wiser than your sister.
You're both going along with their games, won over by

146

a smile and a clever word or two.'

For a moment Cara hated him. 'I see,' she spat out. 'You're angry because I'm not obedient enough. More than that—you're jealous. Jealous because I dared to spend a day with somebody young and pleasant, not bitter and distrustful like yourself. I—'

He was across the room in a couple of strides, his hand raised, and before she could dodge away, he struck her hard across the face. Gasping with pain, she wrenched at the door and was out in the corridor before he could strike again. The warden was hurrying towards her, evidently summoned by Minna, who hovered anxiously behind.

'In there,' Cara panted. 'I—I think he's gone mad. He hit me.'

Chapter Three

The warden made a stony-faced report to the Chief
Physician later that evening, when Anno had been
locked in his cell and Cara was nursing her hurt over a
late supper of bread, curd cheese and boiled nappes,
the swollen white tubers which the travellers had first
found by the Scurrier huts. When the Chief Physician
heard that Anno was becoming violent and disorderly,
he made a note in the margin of his bulky yellow-paged
book which contained all the records of the infirmary
inmates. Then he told the warden to keep Anno locked
in his cell, isolated from the others even at meal times,
and to let him out into the courtyard for exercise only
at noon when nobody else was about. The warden carried out the order with relish—she did not like Anno—
and if she sometimes forgot to bring him his food or
remove a brimming slop-pail, nobody heard his complaints. She preferred serving the other three strangers who at least treated her with some degree of
deference and who were clearly impressed by what
they had heard of the Citadel.

Cara told Minna and Gethin about what she had
seen during her day with Tav, but while they wanted to
hear about the Citadel, they were still more concerned

with what might happen to them when their time at the infirmary was over. Cara realised with annoyance that the two of them had been spending their time talking over Anno's dark warnings and sharing their fears. Accordingly, when Tav sent a message asking if Minna wanted to accompany them to the weekly Quadrangle market, Cara shrugged impatiently and said that her sister preferred to spend the day brooding in her cell and did not like being disturbed.

Tav came to take her to the market a few days later. It was as entertaining as he promised, and together they wandered past gaudy stalls, pens of bleating goats and squealing crowds of children who were bartering bruised apples for sticky slabs of honey cake. Tav told Cara about the Citadel's great beehives which were tended out near the bean fields, remarking that he would take her there soon. She saw plump chickens offered for sale by stout matrons in dark brown smocks, a bird tucked securely under each arm, and laughed at the sturdy little sheep with blotched fleeces of creamy white, deep brown and grey and their neatly curving horns, and marvelled again and again at the bounty of the Citadel, created with the wealth of long-ago Orion, the last and biggest ship to leave Earth.

Instead of bartering for goods, Circle members bought them using earthenware discs stamped with their badge of three clustered stars. Tav gave Cara a handful, telling her to find something for herself and also a gift for her sister. Eventually she found a leather belt studded with squares of polished metal for herself, and for Minna a delicately woven triangle of sheep's wool which, the stall woman said, should be worn as a scarf wrapped round the head when the weather turned cold. Cara fingered the bronze and white stripes and thanked the woman for her advice with a

149

newly learned courtesy that almost matched Tav's. When she came back to the infirmary that evening, after dining with Tav in the Circle refectory, she gave Minna the scarf and a colourful description of the goings-on at the market. Minna had passed a dreary day sitting alone in the courtyard—Anno was locked away and Gethin was unexpectedly tired and spent hours resting on his couch—so when Cara mentioned that Tav requested Minna's company for a visit to the countryside beyond the Citadel walls, she surprised both Cara and herself by accepting.

They went two days later, the morning after the Circle hoch-roast. Although Tav was heavy-eyed and weary, he was so charming to Minna that before long she forgot to be shy and began talking almost as freely as Cara. The hills were hazy with summer heat by the time they walked out of the gates, the Watch guards saluting Tav as he went past. They saw the fields of root crops and wheat, the bean fields which were kept by the Citadel only for animal fodder, the beehives where three labourers were trying to catch a swarm, the pasture lands near the sea-cliffs where the sheep and goats grazed, hogs rooted and flocks of chickens darted about, scratching up the soft turf. Dotted everywhere in colonies of six or seven were the snug cabins of the field people and the larger dwellings of the overseers, each with a tidy garden patch beside the open door. Brown babies played in dusty patches of sunlight while their mothers baked bread for the mid-day meal and roasted cunies, the little furry creatures which Cara had found on the moorlands. Tave told the sisters that the hills beyond the Citadel were riddled with warrens.

He took them down a long path winding through groves of kaim trees to the fields of cotton and flax grown to make the fine Citadel cloth, and then led them to one of the many deep clear pools which stored water for the drier seasons. It stood in a plantation of orange and lemon trees, next to a flourishing gelu vineyard. As a Circle member, Tav could pick the crops as he pleased and he gave the sisters some of the juicy, sharp-sweet oranges and told them about the intricate process of turning the shiny gelu fruit into the sweet yellow wine drunk only in the highest Citadel households.

To her disappointment, Minna was not asked out again for a few days, while Cara went back with Tav to the Bibliotheca and the Circle tower and explored the Citadel further. She stayed at the infirmary while Gethin slept or rested on his stool in a sunny corner of the courtyard. Even though she had managed to keep her pictures hidden from the warden, they now lay untouched while she lounged on her couch, chin cupped in her hands, staring through the window at the buildings rising beyond the infirmary. When the call came for her to join Cara, Tav and his friend Izak on a visit to the hills, she was delighted and could hardly contain her excitement.

They set off early in the morning, taking only two horses since neither of the sisters could ride, although, as Tav remarked, it would not take long to teach them. Izak was a lively companion and his witty stories kept Minna laughing as she sat behind him. By noon they had left the fields behind and were among the hills where they halted to eat cold chicken and honey cake by a clump of thorny gerst bushes. The four lounged in the warm grass and looked back at the towers of the Citadel standing proudly against the bay. Presently Izak announced that he wanted to ride further up and called Minna to go with him. She scrambled onto the

151

horse's back and they rode off together. Cara watched until they were out of sight and Tav lay beside her, seemingly daydreaming with eyes closed and hands behind his head.

He said without opening his eyes, 'My companion is as pleased by your sister as I told him he would be. He noticed her pretty face that first time we saw you.'

Cara could not contain her curiosity. 'Why have you been so kind to us? And how long must we stay in the infirmary? What will happen to us afterwards?'

'You ask too many questions. This is not a session of the Circle.'

Cara shifted restlessly. 'We have been given no answers at all. Sometimes I fear that we will be thrown out into the wilderness again to starve to death when the Citadel has finished with us.'

Tav opened one eye. 'So you would rather belong to our people? That is good. The time in the infirmary will be over sooner than you think, and then you will hear where you will go next.' He rolled over and peered up at her. 'That older fellow with you—why is he always so angry?'

'Anno?' Cara hesitated, reluctant to sound disloyal to Anno, yet eager to dissociate herself from his hostility to the Citadel. 'He hates being held in the infirmary against his will, and maybe he does not want to belong to another people. I—I do not really understand why he is so,' she finished awkwardly and winced at her own untruth.

'No matter,' Tav sighed and jumped to his feet. 'Come, let's go after Izak and your sister. I want to show you the plains.' They rode on for some way through the dense undergrowth that covered the higher hills and came at last to the highest which rose flat-topped above all the rest. Beyond they saw a wide grassy plateau stretching off to the horizon.

Tav pointed straight ahead. 'That is where Orion landed, out in the middle of the plain. Some say you can still see a hollow in the ground. Below us, at the foot of these hills, is where the colony was when the ship came, sheltering from the attacks of the Scurriers and the dragons.'

Cara looked at the swaying grasslands. 'It is beautiful. More beautiful than the desert by our settlement.'

'Tell me about it,' said Tav quickly, twisting round in the saddle to catch her expression. Cara bit her lip, remembering Anno's warning about speaking too freely too soon. Then they both heard a shout from down below and saw Izak urging his horse up the slopes from the plain, Minna clinging on behind. Tav seemed to forget his question and welcomed his friend's suggestion of races down on the flat.

Much later when they were on their way back to the Citadel, travelling at the pace of the tired horses, he turned to whisper to Cara, 'You will have plenty of time to tell me about your people and where they live.' He smiled. 'I want you to show me your city as I have shown you mine.'

Back at the infirmary, Cara and Minna were seized by the warden who gave them freshly laundered gowns and told them to hurry to the dining chamber. When they entered, they were surprised to see Anno seated at one end of the table, looking pale and grim, with Gethin placed opposite him. The warden made the sisters sit together at the other end and then ordered them to rise for the Chief Physician. He entered carrying his record book and nodded at them to resume their seats.

Opening the heavy volume, he ran his finger down a column of names and began reading aloud. 'The

153

infirmary inmates known as Anno, Gethin, Cara and Minna, the last two being sisters, have been resident for twenty-one days and are found to be in good health by the physicians. After examination by the Academy tutors and observation by their warden, their futures are settled. Gethin will join the quarry labourers in the North-east Sector and learn to work stone and live with the people there. The sisters will join the ranks of citizens and study in the Academy for a term, after which time their places will be reviewed. Anno—' the Chief Physician paused. 'Anno will remain in the infirmary for further guidance until he is fit to join the Citadel, when he also will work in the Academy.' He closed the book carefully, bowed his head and left.

Cara looked round cautiously at the others. Her expression was a careful blank but inside she was exulting that she and Minna were judged equals of the Citadel people with their priceless books and great buildings. Minna was twisting her hands in her lap, gazing at Gethin, whose face was filled with helpless indignation. Anno sat quite still and stared straight ahead, his eyes cold and forbidding. Then the warden entered with dishes of food for the evening meal and the four had to turn their attention to eating under her watchful eye. Anno was allowed to remain in the room with them and the warden ordered them to say their farewells that evening because they would be leaving at daybreak the next morning. Minna and Gethin both wept as they embraced, and Cara also hugged him, a little awkwardly, but when they turned to Anno, they found he had already gone to his cell and the closed door did not open to their knocking.

Cara fell asleep almost immediately when she retired later on, worn out by fresh air and exercise. In the middle of the night she dreamed she was back in the settlement hut, surrounded by the terrible Karnavale mob, and someone was tapping persistently on the window shutter, demanding to be let in. She woke with a bound and saw that it was still dark. Lying rigid on her couch, she listened for the tapping which had come into the dream. The night was silent. Then she heard it again—a swift knocking on the shutters just above her head and the faintest whisper of her name. Clenching her teeth to stop them from chattering with fear, she steeled herself to sit up and open the shutters a crack. Outside, a tall figure loomed against the black sky and a hand groped through the crack and touched her fingers. It was Anno.

'Will you let me in for a moment?' He spoke so softly that she had to strain to catch his words. Clambering over the sill, he stood shivering beside the couch, dressed in what looked like the uniform of a Watch sentry.

'What are you doing?' Cara asked, horrified.

'Not so loud! Listen and decide quickly. I have planned an escape. I am going to climb the wall, after the patrol has passed by, and run to the hills. If you wish to come, you must help me rouse the others, and we will try to leave together. I know Minna will not go unless she follows you, and Gethin would never leave her behind.'

'But why are you running away? The Watch will hunt you down, and we are at least safe here from the dragons and the little people.'

'So you believe what you have been told? I thought you saw more clearly than that, Cara. Something within me does not trust these people. Their Citadel is too ordered, and may be a crueller trap for us than our old settlement.'

'But what will you do?'

'Discover more about this country. Observe it in hid-

155

ing—and perhaps my suspicions are empty and I will return and pledge allegiance to the Circle. If not, we can return to the wandering we abandoned so soon, across the plains or over the ocean or wherever we wish to go. Come with me.'

Cara clenched her fists. She had forgotten their quarrel and was torn between the remembered freedom of their journeying and the thought of Tav's pleasant smile as he led her through the bright Citadel streets.

Anno grasped her arm. 'What will you do? I must leave now, but I want you with me. It was good when we travelled together.'

Feeling tears stinging her eyes, Cara blinked hard to keep them back. She knew suddenly that she could not bear the thought of Anno going away without her, yet the Citadel had captivated her. She did not want to become a wanderer again, not yet.

'Will you not stay just a while longer?' she pleaded, impulsively taking hold of his hand. 'I think they are good people here, but they have found you hard to understand. Stay a little longer, and we can work in the Academy togther. Later, perhaps, it will be right for us all to leave. Do not go so soon.'

'Cara, I have decided. You cannot change my mind. For the last time, will you or will you not come too?'

Shaking her head, she said in a cracked whisper, 'No, I cannot. You will have to go without me this time. But tell me before you journey right away and perhaps—perhaps I shall go with you then.' She heard him sigh, and could not stop the tears spilling down. A sudden thought struck her and, detaining Anno again, she reached beneath her couch to where she had concealed the green stone clasp that she had found in the desert. When their old clothes were taken away, she had remembered to unpin it and hide it in her hand—her one remaining link with her former life.

She thrust it at Anno. 'Take this. I found it when I went looking—for Sirius in the desert.'

He took it from her gently. 'But you will not come with me?'

'I—not yet, I cannot say.' She touched the Watch badge of office on his chest, trying to delay the last farewell. 'How did you get this?'

'Cara, I must go.' He embraced her quickly, kissing her on both cheeks. Then he was over the sill and out into the courtyard, and as Cara watched, he clambered up onto the wall, balancing on the top for an instant and then disappearing onto the other side. She closed the shutters as quietly as she could and then huddled under her coverlet, unable to sleep until the darkness began turning to pearly grey.

She told nobody about her midnight meeting and watched the confusion when Anno's absence was discovered in the morning. The Chief Physician questioned them all closely and then ordered them to prepare for departing the infirmary. Minna cried again when she saw Gethin dressed in the drab olive green of the quarry workers while she and Cara were splendidly arrayed in Citadel colours—Cara in the crimson shift she had worn when she first accompanied Tav, and Minna in a trailing emerald gown. The warden permitted herself a rusty smile as she led them through the quiet corridors to the gate where the escorts were waiting to take them to their new homes. They could see the wide street outside, already filling with people busily going about their duties, but in the distance Cara heard the tramp of booted feet and knew that the Watch patrols were abroad, and that they would not rest in their searching until they had found the missing Anno.

Chapter Four

It was high summer. The Citadel lazed in the sticky heat, and a crowd of country women came to the Quadrangle at daybreak each morning to sell freshly-picked kaim leaf fans. Out in the pasture lands, sheep huddled wherever they found shade and goats sprawled groaning on the dry turf. The waters of the bay stretched blue and inviting round the Citadel but only Circle members could bathe whenever they pleased. The field people had to wait for the sunset evenings, and then the city walls echoed with their splashes and shouts until long after nightfall. Tav and Izak liked to bathe as soon as they finished their day's work, when Sol still blazed high in the bleached sky.

On one hot afternoon they were floating on their backs near the shoals where they had been diving down to chase the scuttling orange sea-spiders hiding among the roots of the wortweeds. Tav was telling Izak how the sisters Cara and Minna were faring at the Academy.

'I have seen little of them since our ride to the hills,' he added, 'but I hear the tutors are delighted with their progress even though their minds have been unskilfully trained. They remember all that they're taught and are quick to join in the discourses with other pupils.'

'Indeed?' Izak blew a waterspout into the air.

'They say Cara has the makings of a fine scholar and her sister could one day serve as tutor for the youngest children.' Tav glanced impatiently at his friend who was not paying much attention, and then began swimming with slow strokes to where a ridge of the shoals broke the placid water. He hauled himself up onto a rock and lay down to bask in the sun. A moment later Izak crawled up beside him.

'Have there been any sightings of the older man, the one who ran away?' he panted.

'The Watch followed his trail to the hills but the ground was hard, and he left few traces. It is a pity that we did not get him teaching the Watch some of his wilderness skills. He might even have made a good captain.'

'Why not First Captain? He looked fierce enough to keep all the rest of them in order,' said Izak lazily.

'More than that,' said Tav shortly. 'He was the one who could have told us how to find this settlement that they mention so seldom. The sisters must know something, but I think he was the leader and they and their other companion simply followed after him.'

Izak scratched his head. 'Surely they would soon remember the way if the Watch marched them to the mountains?'

'Maybe. But first we must try persuading them to tell us freely. I think Cara, for one, is easily flattered. I think she would listen to my persuasion.' Tav winked at his friend. 'Do you want to hear the whole of my plan for the stranger girls?'

Izak settled his back comfortably against the curve of the sun-warmed rock. 'Speak on!'

159

'You and I have to set about finding partners soon. As good Circle members we can take whom we please, I propose you and I take the mountain girls as our partners. Wait!' he continued, as Izak sat up in surprise. 'The Academy is grooming them into respectable citizens, and they are already amusing companions and pleasing enough to look at. If we joined with them, the citizens would see it as a sign of the future joining of the two starships, when this settlement, whatever it might be, will be brought to swell our numbers. What do you say?'

Izak thought for a moment and then shrugged. 'Certainly I hadn't seriously considered any other Citadel girls, but I thought you were pledged to Cassie.'

Tav grinned. 'Cassie and I are old friends, and we need not put aside our friendship simply because I partner somebody else. It would be diverting to join with those sisters—they come from outside the Citadel. We have not known them all our lives or watched them grow up alongside us. And it will give us a chance of learning the truth about their settlement. What do you say to taking the younger girl while I have Cara?'

Izak burst out laughing. 'You mean I'll be satisfied with pretty looks and you want the one with sharp wits. I'll consider this diverting idea of yours. Perhaps Cassie will chase after the other fellow who came with them.'

'I think not.' Tav joined in his laughter. 'Some poor country girl is getting him, and I hear that the sisters are using their Citadel privileges and going out to watch the ceremony.'

A few days later, on a patch of beaten earth between the cabins of the quarry labourers, a crowd gathered to watch the joining of their kinswoman Ria with Gethin, whom they called the stranger. Black-haired Ria wore an unbecoming scowl on her round face, and the blue gown which her mother had made for her own joining ceremony years before. Ria and her five younger sisters had formed a low opinion of Gethin in the time he had lodged in their father's household, slowly learning the skills of quarrying. He spoke seldom and never smiled, and Ria protested hotly when she heard that he had been chosen for her. Her complaints that he was too young and too dull were swept aside because at twenty-five years she was already old for partnering and her father wanted to be rid of her.

The brief ceremony was conducted by the Watch captain for the North-east Sector who rode away as soon as it was over, leaving the crowd to gobble down the prepared banquet and exclaim over the guests of honour, the two mountain girls who had been allowed to join the people of the Citadel. Cara and Minna stood apart in their gaudy clothes, receiving the good wishes of a long line of country people. Minna's face was blotched with tears, although she tried to hide her feelings for the sake of Gethin, who looked as unhappy as his new partner. The couple were soon hustled away to their own cabin by Ria's sisters who pushed them inside and shut the door with a great deal of giggling. There seemed no reason to stay longer and, declining further offers of food and drink, Cara and Minna set off back to the Citadel in silence.

Once Minna said in a voice which was almost a sob, 'Do you think that is what Gethin hoped for when he left his home to come with us?'

'And what would you have instead? Death by hunger and thirst on a mountainside?' Cara snapped back.

Minna did not speak again.

They made their way though the busy Citadel streets to a lane running along the back of the Academy where they lodged in a hostel for young women. Their chambers were two flights up the broad staircase and three landings below the flat roof that provided a retreat in the cool of the day for drinking iced cordials and watching the setting sun gild the waters of the bay. As the sisters stepped into the dark entranceway, the doorkeeper bustled up to them.

'From the Circle,' she said importantly, handing Cara an ornamented parchment bearing the Circle seal of the three clustered stars. The words 'To the sisters Cara and Minna' appeared at the top in flowing script and line after line of closely written text followed, ending with the scrawled signatures of Tav and Izak.

'What is it?' Cara asked.

The doorkeeper smirked. 'Read it. A great honour for this hostel.'

Minna peered over Cara's shoulder, skimming the words, and then cried in amazement, 'They want to partner us!'

'You have one month to walk out together before the joining day,' said the doorkeeper smugly. 'You will have to entertain each another and hold public assemblies, maybe a roof-top gathering here with the families of high standing. A great honour for us all!'

Later that evening the two sisters sat together in Minna's chamber, still turning over the Circle proposal. Even though the shutters were wide open, no breeze entered to chase away the heat and stuffiness. The letter lay in Cara's lap, the inks smudged from the touch of damp fingers.

'And what if Anno returns? He would not journey far without you, would he?' Minna said suddenly.

Cara stood up and went to the window which overlooked the sand-coloured turrets of the Bibliotheca. They had talked for hours and all the while she had been secretly turning over thoughts of what it would be like to live in the Citadel as Tav's partner. She thoughtfully ran her fingers over her face, wondering how it was that she had captivated someone so fine-looking, so well-mannered and powerful as he.

In a rush of pride she turned back to Minna. 'I shall accept,' she said impulsively. 'Why should I wait for Anno to come back? I still do not want to leave the Citadel. And perhaps, when Anno does return, Tav can persuade him to stay.' She sighed as she saw Minna's puzzled, doubting expression. 'Would you rather sit by yourself in your chamber and cry? For what? Struggling through deserts and up mountains till you lie down and die of weariness? Weaving in a tumbledown hut with a mob outside waiting to tear you to pieces? Listen,' she gripped Minna's hand tightly. 'In the next hour I shall go to the Circle tower to declare my acceptance. You can come with me to say what you have decided.' And she rose and left the chamber for her own room.

Left alone at last, Minna knelt before her linen chest, opened it and drew out the battered wooden box, spreading out the shabby strip of pictures and looking once again at the old make-believe. She had not thought of her stories since the first days at the infirmary and now she had begun to feel ashamed of them. She thought of Izak's cheerful grin and the day when they had raced on horseback over the grassy plain. He had kissed her as they hid from the others in a hollow of the hills. Her needle-worked pictures looked clumsy and childish against the delicate stitching on her cotton gown, and she blushed as she imagined what her Academy tutors would say if they heard about the foolish tales she had spun and treasured. Cara's footsteps sounded in the corridor and she thrust the box and its contents under the couch.

'So are you coming with me to the Circle?' Cara called through the closed door.

'Give me just a while longer,' Minna called back, and waited until she heard Cara's door close again before retrieving the pictures. She took the worn cloth strip in both hands. Slowly and deliberately she tore it to pieces which she gathered up and threw, one by one, out of the window. The fragments were caught by a sudden gust of wind from the bay and carried off over the rooftops and towers. When they were all gone, she closed the shutters. Then, with heart beating fast, she went in search of Cara to say that she too would accept the offer.

In the following days, the sisters and their future partners were excused their usual duties so that they could carry out the many observances of walking out. They attended sessions of the Circle, festivals of verse and song performed by the Citadel players, and public gatherings in the Academy halls when tutors and scholars conducted complicated debates which always ended with a speech extolling the glories of the descendants of Orion and the shining future awaiting them. The Circle members had seats of honour on the dais, where they sat and yawned behind their hands and whispered private jokes to one another. The sisters learned to ride, and Izak took Minna hunting with a group of his companions. A magnificent feast took place on the shoals three days later, with enough roasted hoch to feed the whole Citadel. New, exquisitely fashioned garments arrived at the hostel every day so that the two girls would always appear in suitable grandeur. Cara received the gift of a rare scrap of looking-glass, and she dressed up in an embroidered turquoise gown and smiled at her reflection over her shoulder.

She learned to converse lightheartedly and make impudent remarks in the presence of older, forbiddingly haughty citizens whose very age made them slightly ridiculous in the eyes of the Circle. All the members made her feel welcome among them, save for Cassie who, with her languid voice and beautiful, ironic mouth was only coldly polite, avoiding conversation with Cara whenever she could. Plans were drawn up to hold the joining ceremony in the new meeting hall which was almost completed, and everybody was promised two days' holiday, even the labourers in the remotest field colonies, who cheered when a Watch officer rode up to read the news from a scrap of twice-used vellum. The doorkeeper at the sisters' hostel got her heart's desire when they held a lavish roof-top assembly there with coloured lanterns, trays of gilded sweetmeats and cups of spiced yellow wine.

The month of walking out passed swiftly. Cara woke very early one morning and lay in the half-light, weighing up the knowledge that on the next day she and Minna would be escorted through streets lined with onlookers to the Quadrangle where the meeting hall stood filled with noise and colour in honour of two mountain girls who had strayed to the Citadel by accident. An unexpected feeling of panic rose inside her at the thought of all those faces turned towards them and the relentless scrutiny of hundreds of pairs of eyes. She rolled off the couch and went to the window to pull back the shutters. The sun had only just risen in the white dawn sky and few people were stirring. She would use her new privileges and ride out to the hills before the day began, to spend a last few hours alone.

Dressed in her riding tunic and breeches and defiantly barefoot, she hurried down to the stables, leaving a message for the hostel doorkeeper on the way. A lively chestnut filly was reserved for her by right, as Tav's future partner, and as she trotted through the gateway, the Watch saluting as she passed, she remembered the morning when she first entered the Citadel, a prisoner on foot and in chains. The fields were already busy with men and women bent over the rows of plants which they cherished so carefully, but Cara did not spare them a second look. Urging her horse to a gallop down the High Road, she stared straight ahead to where the blue hills rose in gentle curves.

When she reached the winding paths that led up the slopes, she aimed for the flat-topped summit where she had stood with Tav and seen the plains for the first time. When she reached it, she dismounted and turned the horse loose to graze, and then sat down with her back to the Citadel, gazing at the undulating leagues of yellow and green. A breath of hot wind stirred her hair and the rustling of the grasses reached her ears like a long sigh. She hugged her knees with her folded arms and closed her eyes.

'Cara.' The whisper was as faint as the wind in the grasses. 'Cara.' Something touched her foot, jerking her awake from her daydream. Anno was crouched before her just below the summit of the hill. She opened her mouth to cry out and he dragged her down beside him, his hand firmly over her lips.

'If you value my life at all, do not make a sound,' he murmured. 'Come lower, where nobody can see us.' Unable to escape his grip, she crawled down the slope beside him, noticing with a pang of guilt how thin and ragged he was, with a half-healed scar on one cheek.

She stopped. 'Anno, who's there to see us out here?'

He glanced at her, a twisted smile on his face. 'Surely

you know you were followed? Look!' He made her inch back up the hill until she could peer over the top, and pointed to a distant bushy hillock. In the clear morning light, she saw a hunched figure sitting there.

'Probably a field man stopped for a rest,' she said disbelievingly, scrambling down again. 'But where have you been, Anno, and why have you come back now?'

Anno ignored her questions. 'Do you think they would dare let so valuable a prize as you slip away? They need you to find the way to the settlement so that they can deal with our people as they dealt with the Scurriers in the wilderness.' He grabbed her shoulders, angered by her doubting face. 'I have learned much through wandering on the margins of the Citadel, much that you have not seen even though you live there.'

'I do not understand,' Cara said bleakly. 'Are you not glad to see me again?'

Anno relaxed his hold and made her sit beside him. Taking both her hands in his, he carried on rapidly, 'Cara, there are rebels out on the plains, far beyond any Watch patrols. They are the ones who escaped with nothing but their lives from your Citadel, and few remember them, even among their own kin. But I have been with them and learned their ways of survival— which overseer turns a blind eye to some missing roots or a half-emptied sack of meal, where news can be gleaned, where the patrols pass. I know what is happening to you and your sister tomorrow, and had you not walked into my hands just now, I would have risked my life and come to you one more time to give you warning. Besides, I was going to return as you asked, before I journeyed far away.'

'I still do not understand,' she said fearfully.

'Cara, a great evil feeds the very heart, the very roots

of the Citadel. It does not spring from the Circle, yet those young rulers shape the laws which keep the evil alive. Do you not see, Cara, that for the Citadel, each person is worthless or even dangerous unless he fits the pattern? Gethin becomes a quarry labourer, you will be a scholar—not because you wish it, but because that is what will benefit the Citadel. Our settlement was lawless—here there is nothing but law. The people are watched night and day, and those who dare to be disobedient are punished. They disappear, and nobody speaks of them any longer. And where are the old and the crippled and the weak? Have you wondered, Cara, why you have not encountered any old women here like your foster-mother Holly? Nobody with any wasting diseases or imperfect minds or bodies?'

'I have seen nothing which others have not explained to me,' replied Cara weakly, beginning to hate his fierce gaze.

'What I see is that you have forgotten that you always have a right to ask questions. I met a wretched man out on the plains who told me how he ran away after his partner was delivered of their first child. When the birthing-time was over, he returned to his hut to see her and found a Watch officer riding away with a tiny bundle under one arm. He had to fight his way in to see the woman who was screaming that they had killed her daughter before her very eyes because she had been born with a crooked back. They came to take her to the infirmary, saying she was maddened by pain and would not recover. He never saw her again.' Anno rose to his feet and glared down at her. 'And why is there no public place where the dead are buried?'

Cara writhed under his interrogation. 'Perhaps—perhaps the Circle would say it's better to take care of the living instead of commemorating the dead.'

'I think you know that would be a lie, Cara. You would not be told that all the dead—young and old, broken and whole—are burned down into fine ash, deep within the infirmary walls so that nobody ever finds out how many die before their time.'

She refused to look him in the face and frowned angrily at the ground, trying to shut out what he was saying and at the same time match it with Tav's smile and the riotous, good-natured Circle members who could turn so easily to their task of governing the people with due seriousness and authority.

'Cara.' He was pleading with her. 'Come with me— you still have time to bring Minna and even Gethin. Arrange for the three of you to meet in secret out on these hills, and even though you will be followed, you may still have a chance of escape. Osiris is a huge world, Cara, and I have heard talk of other lands across the ocean and beyond the plains. A handful of us will journey together and be a free people. And Cara, I would have you with me.'

For a moment Cara was almost swayed. His hands clasped hers tightly, and she saw with a shock that his eyes were full of pain. She had a brief vision of herself galloping away on her horse, leaving behind the ordeal of the joining ceremony and the vague, unacknow-ledged fears about what her future life might hold. She saw herself with Anno, walking at the head of a great gathering of people, and her heart wavered. Then far away she heard the Academy bell ring, and remem-bered that Tav was calling for her at mid-morning to go riding along the shore.

Suddenly she felt that Anno was using dark words to frighten her into doing what he desired, and she grew indignant because he was trying to snatch her from the place where she was admired and entertained as a person of distinction, and turn her back into a dirty, tattered wanderer who lurked in the undergrowth like an outlaw.

'No,' she said abruptly, standing up and backing away from him. 'Go if you wish, but I will not come with you. You have been lying to me, and I will not listen any longer.'

He tried to seize hold of her, but she fled back to the top of the hill, calling to the horse who was grazing peacefully. Grabbing the reins, she mounted and then turned to see if Anno had followed, hoping to give him a final stinging retort. Behind her was nothing except the wind-blown plains stretching to the horizon. Facing the Citadel once more, she looked nervously for the waiting figure on the hillock, but he too had vanished. Her limbs trembling, she urged the horse downhill as fast as she could. She was almost back at the High Road when she realised that she was crying, and furiously rubbed the tears from her cheeks.

Chapter Five

In the country where the Citadel stood, summer heat changed gradually to a winter of clouded skies, mild winds and endlessly drizzling rain. The High Road grew slippery with mud which was carried into the Citadel on cart wheels and horses' hooves, to splatter carven doorposts, stain handsome garments and leave gritty traces on the wooden floors of the Academy. Out in the fields, the labourers' cabins filled with the smell of damp woollen garments drying over fires built from wood that sizzled with moisture and burned with more smoke than heat.

It was the day of the Quadrangle market, and a cart from the quarriers' colony was clattering down the road to the Citadel, laden with men and women who were gossiping and laughing at the tops of their voices despite the rain falling steadily from the leaden sky. Wedged between their knees were bags of coloured stones which they gathered from the quarries, polished and cut into pleasing shapes, and then exchanged at the market for food and cloth at rates controlled by the Watch. Both men and women bought the gems to wear as glittering rings and necklets.

At the back of the noisy cart sat Gethin and his

partner. He too clutched a bag of stones but did not join in the chatter, watching instead the glistening paving slabs stretching away behind them. From time to time he glanced at Ria, whose face was twisted with pain. Whenever the cart jolted, she winced and tried to settle herself more comfortably on the hard seat. The cart trundled through the Citadel gates and then took the left turn leading to the infirmary. When they reached the cluster of rainwashed stone buildings, the carter reined in the horse and halted long enough for Gethin to climb down and carry Ria to the entrance. A poker-faced warden answered his knock and listened to his brief explanation, before disappearing inside. Returning almost immediately, she took Ria from him without another word, hurrying her off down the shadowy passage. Gethin hesitated on the threshold until the heavy gate was shut in his face, but his partner did not look back. The cart had not waited for him, so he slung the heavy sack over his shoulder and set off for the Quadrangle.

He was seldom allowed to make the trip to the Citadel, and whenever he did come, he cherished a secret hope that he might see Minna again, although he had not set eyes on her since the day of his joining. He heard all about the joining of the two sisters with the Circle men at summer's end and spent many days sunk to such a depth of unhappiness that he thought he would never recover. But at last the monotony of his hours in the quarry and the evenings of bickering with Ria wore down even his despair into resigned misery, lightened from time to time by visits to the Citadel or, as now, by the absence of his partner. He felt a sudden pang of guilt as he remembered her sickness and then stubbornly shut out all thought of her, determined to enjoy his solitude.

The Quadrangle was thronged with citizens and country people even though the drizzle had turned to a drenching downpour. Gethin shouldered his way through the crowds and found himself at one end of a crammed row of stalls opposite the Academy. The bell was ringing loudly for the noon-time break, and a handful of pupils and tutors were pulling up their hoods and hurrying out into the storm. He paused to rest his bag on the ground, straightening his aching back. When he looked up again, he saw Minna.

She stood on the threshold of the Academy, dressed in an orange tutor's gown beneath a bright yellow wrap which she was fastening at the neck. Their eyes met and in the instant before she recognised him, he saw the misery in her gaze. Then it had gone and she was running towards him, forgetting all the Citadel rules of conduct. Heads turned as she caught hold of his arm, checking herself before she embraced him in public. Conscious of the disapproving stares of nearby citizens, she drew back and greeted him with a formal salute. Gethin bowed awkwardly in reply and bent to pick up his sack.

'Wait!' Minna touched his arm as the inquisitive onlookers turned away. 'We can spend a little time together. Walk behind me as I go back to my chambers. They cannot begrudge me a few words with an old friend,' she added under her breath.

Anxious lest anyone should notice what he was doing, Gethin followed Minna through the crowds which thinned as they reached the side-streets near the tower where she lodged with Izak and other Circle members. It stood in the choicest quarter of the Citadel, next to the outer walls and not far from the spacious home of Cassie's family. Nobody else was about as they entered the building and climbed the staircase leading to the top of the tower which narrowed until it was no more than one room wide. Minna unlocked the door of the topmost chamber and bolted it securely when both she and Gethin were inside. He could see a panorama of rooftops through the unshuttered window and by the door a ladder led up to a trapdoor in the ceiling. Minna followed his gaze.

'They say this is the best chamber in the whole tower. I was given it because of my important partner,' she said bleakly. 'The doorkeeeper told me how Izak likes to sleep under the stars when the nights are warmer, and next summer I can join him.' Her face crumpled and she slumped down on a stool, crying terribly. Gethin knelt beside her, his arms round her shoulders, wondering what he could say to comfort her. His heart was still full of the sisters' betrayal in joining with the Circle men.

Eventually she grew calmer and leaned against him, wiping her eyes on her sleeve until she was able to speak. 'We are safe here for a while. My partner has been away for two days and will not return for another three. He has gone with a party of Circle members and Watch officers to survey the land we travelled through, as far as the mountains. This is my private chamber and nobody except—except my partner can come against my wishes.' She sat up and faced Gethin. 'Tell me how it has been with you. So much time has passed since we last spoke together.'

He sighed and told her about the hard, never-ending labour in the quarries, splitting and shaping harsh black stone and working the crumbling sand-coloured rocks. He described his hateful life with Ria and how she had come to the infirmary after losing the third child she had conceived since their joining.

'And you?' he finished. 'You don't like the partner

you chose?' He ground out the last word savagely.

'It—it is not quite as you think,' Minna faltered. 'I was chosen by him, and although his flattery swayed me for a while, in the end I joined with him because I was afraid to refuse, not because I—I cared for him. Now I teach in the Academy, and I have to hide what I feel because otherwise he and his friends laugh at me for being foolish and dull. What they care about is increasing the power and wealth of the Citadel, and the rest of their lives is just idle play. I thought Izak cared for me, but before long he grew tired of me because I was not high-spirited or amusing enough and did not like to hunt as much as he did. Cara has become one of them, but I belong nowhere.' Her voice sank to a whisper. 'For a while I wanted to die because my days were so black and empty.'

'And now?'

She hesitated. 'I have—something. I shall tell you about it, but—' she hesitated again. 'It is started years ago, back in the settlement. Do you remember the box you rescued from my hut after the Karnavale riot? The story concerns what I kept hidden in that box.' And huddled on a stool at the top of a Citadel tower, she told the whole tale of her prince, even describing the dream she had in the mountains and the hour when she finally tore the old pictures in pieces.

'You must understand,' she said, looking pleadingly at Gethin, 'that for a time I thought Izak could be the story made real, even though he cared a good deal more for himself than he did for me. I thought I could exchange a worn-out daydream for a living person. I was mistaken.' Gethin said nothing. 'And now,' she went on, 'I will show you what I have made.' She knelt in front of the heavy wooden chest that was pushed against the window. Drawing aside her wrap, she

175

produced a small key from the belt at her waist, unlocked the chest and took out a roll of cloth. She shook it undone and laid it on the floor in front of Gethin. It was a stack of embroidered pictures, worked on what looked like linen coverlets.

Aware of Minna watching him nervously, Gethin began to inspect one after another. He saw mountains, seas, clouds drifting in a pale sky, winding rivers—and the awesome flying creatures and strange little people of the wilderness. In the middle of the biggest picture was a vast, impossibly peaked mountain rising sheer out of a forest. At the summit stood a man with golden eyes holding out his arms in welcome, or perhaps invocation. Crudely stylised beams of light streamed from his face to the plains below. Gethin shook his head, trying to understand, searching for some clue as to what the scenes showed.

'Who is that?' he asked eventually, pointing to the man on the mountain-top.

Minna drew a deep breath. 'I will tell you.' She started speaking softly, almost chanting the words as if she had recited them many times before.

The chronicler sits in her tower and gathers the lost tales, remembering the past days when the Master of Osiris had not been forgotten, when he dwelt openly on the highest mountain and filled the whole land with his light.

In the first days, he kindled a fire which burned for many lifetimes until it dwindled to a great heap of ash. The Master blew on the ash and there beneath it lay the little people, shaped in the heat of the burning. He called them and they awoke, but when they saw the brightness of his eyes, they were terrified and ran from him until they were scattered over the face of the world, dumb, ignorant and nameless.

Then the Master was grieved and knew he must make mes-

176

sengers to go between him and the little people, to give them instruction and guide them in the right ways. So he kindled fire once again, on the topmost pinnacle of the mountain, and gazed into the flames to see what sort of beings he should create. And he saw, and he took the everlasting snows of the mountain-tops for whiteness of skin, the soft light of sunset for plumes of deepest red, yellow drops of wild honey for sweetness of voice, and last of all he took the very heart of the fire for golden eyes to mirror the radiance of his own gaze. Then he spoke a word and there were hosts of winged creatures who flew at his summons, eager to do his bidding. They gathered round him, hovering about the mountain, and the beating of their red wings tossed the branches of the mighty forest trees like a storm.

The Master sent the creatures out to find the little people and they flew over the wide expanse of the world, seeking the hiding-places. They found the little people in the cool of the day and won their hearts with their beauty and the sweetness of their voices. The little people learned to love the flying creatures who taught them to speak and build dwellings and till the ground for food. And with their new speech, the little people named themselves the Children of Aesha, because they had been drawn from the ashes of the Master's fire, and they named the winged creatures the naigas, meaning the Wise Ones. The naigas also taught them to sing songs and tell tales and shape likenesses of the living world on the walls of their dwellings, and sometimes the Children would fly on the backs of the naigas until they came in sight of the greatest of all mountains, where the radiance of the Master shone clear.

But the light was veiled when the Earth ships came, because the Master knew the hearts of humankind and that their coming would begin the breaking of all things. He hid his face and made Sol to ride in the sky instead, to show his Children that he would not forget them, and the greatest of all mountains was cloaked in mists and darkness and is now lost. And only frag-

ments of the tales of the first days remain, like dead leaves whirled downstream.

Minna fell silent, staring blindly at the heap of tapestries, and then suddenly buried her face in her hands. 'Now you will mock me.' Her voice was muffled.

'Mock you? Why should I?' Gethin stared at her, puzzled.

She looked up again, speaking with unexpected vehemence. 'Tell nobody about it! Promise me!'

'Of course I promise. But Minna, why have you made all this?'

She avoided his gaze, blushing hotly as she replied, 'On one of my blackest days I went to the Bibliotheca, to a part forbidden to everyone except the highest scholars. On that day I was past caring about what might happen to me, so I climbed the stairs and entered the room. It was empty but one of the locked cases had been left unfastened. I dared to open it and found a few Earth volumes among the shelves of Osirian writings. The bindings were cracked and the pages torn and much of the writing was in strange lettering or languages I could not read, but I found one book which I could understand. The covers held nothing but a few loose sheets of print, and it began in the middle of a sentence. It said . . . ' Minna screwed up her eyes to remember and her words came haltingly, ' . . . "this barren universe where once the gods walked in the black inter-stellar spaces and wore the constellations like a coronet." I read those words over and over again. They—they moved me—it was like the day in the settlement when I first thought of the prince. The idea came to me that here was something for me to do—I could make stories, make "gods", beings higher and wiser than any human princes, for Osiris, the

178

empty world. Maybe in some way the stories would fill the blankness inside me. You could call it a game, but maybe even the power-seeking of the Circle is no more than a game. I wonder sometimes,' her voice slowed dreamily, 'whether I could almost make it true by believing it. My own true world, more real than the rain and the grey sky and the dreary Academy corridors.'

Her reverie was abruptly broken by the high, insistent ringing of a bell, signalling the end of the citizens' noon rest.

'We must go.' Gethin found his tongue again. 'My people will be looking for me. Come, Minna, you have to return to the Academy. I hope it is not too many months before we meet again.' He rose hastily, straightening his cloak and gathering up the bag of stones. Minna followed slowly after him, smiling secretly to herself, absorbed in the remote land of her tales. She unbolted the door and let Gethin out with a farewell embrace. He raced down the steep stairs, consumed with worry in case anyone should catch him as he left the tower, but as he hurried back to the Quadrangle, his heart was filled with one single thought—that Minna was losing her reason, and unless she escaped from the Citadel, she would either die or descend the tortured path of madness.

Chapter Six

The angry voices snapped back and forth, one harsher and deeper than the other. Even though the people gathered in the room below could not catch the words exchanged, they could still follow the quarrel quite easily. Dayva, the newest Circle member, was hosting a gathering in her chamber, and her cheeks were flushing hot with shame. She was afraid to remark on the noisy behaviour going on above in case she gave offence by speaking rudely about senior Circle members. Suddenly footsteps rushed across the ceiling, followed by a muffled crash.

Dayva started as someone behind her guffawed with laughter.

'Fight back, Tav!' he shouted. 'Don't let your woman get the better of you!'

His companion, a sallow-cheeked girl who hung on his arm and giggled incessantly, dug him in the ribs and told him to leave his friend's private affairs alone.

'Dayva,' she added, speaking a little too loudly, 'Izak here is much impressed by the food and drink you have provided. Tell us how you found such excellent wine at this season.'

In the room above, Cara stood sullenly by the

window while her partner gathered up the pieces of the enamelled clay dish which had smashed against the wall as she threw it at him. A clear blue spring sky was emerging from behind a pall of cloud and the light made the wet streets sparkle. She was thinking that it was almost exactly two years to the day since she left the settlement, and when summer's end came again, two years would have passed since her joining day. She heard the door open and looked round. Tav was standing on the threshold, wrapped in his cloak.

'I shall be busy with my own affairs for the next few days,' he said coldly.

Cara ignored him and he left, closing the door behind him with more force than was necessary. She was still seething with fury after their quarrel and began drumming her fingers on the windowsill, reviewing all that they had said. She had been demanding, yet again, to join the expedition to the settlement which Tav was preparing for the first month of summer. He told her, as he had done many times, that she had already played her part by telling him as much as she could remember about the journey. The Circle had decided that she should devote her time to her work as a newly elected scholar, helping to compile the record of the Citadel's years.

'You take your duties too lightly,' Tav had said. 'You have not yet begun to prepare your discourse for the Fifty Year Feast. You should be concerned with that, not with conjuring excuses to go riding in the wilderness.'

She was incensed and said that if he reminded her of her duties again, she would stand up at the Feast with nothing to say and shame him publicly, on the day when the founding of the Citadel would be commemorated with greater festivities than ever before. It was then that he came towards her as if he were going to strike her, and she threw the dish at him with more anger than accuracy.

Recalling this, she mouthed some of his words contemptuously. 'We in the Circle must exercise our privileges wisely . . . our duties must override all else . . . your behaviour has disappointed us . . . and at least your sister is bearing us a child!'

Minna's pale, closed face came to mind. The sisters met seldom, and when they did see one another, Minna was more silent than she had ever been in the settlement days. According to Academy reports, she made a worthy tutor at first, but her pupils had begun complaining that her lessons were dreary. Eventually she was excused most of her work and now spent the day confined in her room, her body growing sickly and tired as the birthing-time drew near.

The large window of Cara's chamber overlooked the Academy, and the bell for the end of the noon-time break was ringing. Cara knew she should return to her desk in the Bibliotheca where she had left her papers in an untidy heap, but she still felt fiercely defiant. She scowled out of the window at the smug Academy walls and decided to show her contempt for Citadel rules by going back to work without her scholar's gown.

When she arrived at the steel entranceway of the Bibliotheca, the doorkeeper bowed his head respectfully and reminded her that she had forgotten her gown. He was a revered citizen, with a stern hook-nosed face and streaks of silver in his black hair, and Cara quaked inwardly as she walked by, feigning deafness. She heard his voice behind her as she hurried down the corridor, avoiding the astonished eyes of the other scholars who were all obediently wearing the unadorned grey robe which draped them from chin to ground. She began to feel proud of her daring as she climbed the staircase to the study rooms, and by the time she reached her desk she found it hard to smother her laughter at the prim, shocked faces glancing up from their work as she strode past in garish purple tunic and turquoise leggings.

Sitting down heavily on her backless stool, she scowled at the stacks of dusty books and tattered sheaves of wortweed paper. She was supposed to be summarising the works of the Citadel's earliest bard who flourished in the first years after the coming of Orion. He was the grandfather of the Chief Physician and so merited a whole passage of the Citadel history to himself. Cara hated his overwrought rhapsodies on the wonder and form of humankind's new world but she had been ordered to read them all and compose a discourse on his life and work for the Fifty Year Feast. As she fingered the crumbling volumes, her defiance surged up again, and she picked up her best reed pen, dipped it in the thick red ink and wrote ENOUGH in large, angry letters on a fresh sheet of paper. She stared at it and added the word ESCAPE underneath. Then she screwed up the paper and threw it hard into a corner, before dutifully drawing up her stool and opening one of the books.

Since the secret winter meeting of Gethin and Minna in the chamber at the top of the tower, more than a year had passed. It was now common knowledge among Circle members that a rift had opened between Tav and Izak over the partnering with the mountain girls, and that Izak continued to lodge with Minna only to preserve the Circle's honour in the eyes of the citizens. Cara had begun avoiding her sister because she was ashamed of her timid nature, which put her at odds with the high-spirited, quick-witted Circle

183

members. Vague rumours had also spread about the younger mountain girl spending her time doing clumsy stitchery, foolish pictures such as a child might make, knowing no better way of passing time.

For a while Cara enjoyed a place in the very midst of the Circle, happy to serve her time as a novice among the scholars during the day and ride out hunting with Tav and his companions in the warm summer twilights or join the riotous winter evenings of wine and debate in the Circle refectory. But as the first year of their partnering drew to a close, she found that Tav began to spare less time for her. He had become more and more concerned with plans for an expedition to find the Sirius settlement—and to Cara's surprise and anger, she was not asked to take any active part in it. Sometimes, in the first bewildered days when she realised that he was drawing away from her, she wondered if he had started to pay less attention to her as soon as he had gleaned every last detail she could recall about the settlement. She also realised with great disappointment that she was never going to be made a Circle member herself, but would remain at the Bibliotheca until she conceived a child, and even then she would have to return to her studies afterwards unless the Circle decided that she would be better employed elsewhere.

The rules and meticulously observed customs of the Citadel started to try her short supply of patience, especially the decree that she have an escort whenever she went out into the countryside. When she tried leaving alone and secretly at unexpected times of day, she found that a watch was kept on her from a distance, just as Anno had pointed out when they met in the hills before her joining. One day she rode to the man set to guard her as she wandered on the plains, and ordered

184

him to leave. He looked past her with a bored, bland face as if he had not heard, and she was filled with such rage that she lashed out with her whip, leaving a swollen red weal on his cheek, before galloping back to the Citadel in a storm of tears. That night Tav lectured her for hours on her disgraceful conduct, and she retorted by refusing to accompany him to the meeting hall for the Night of Welcome in honour of three new Circle members. When he accused her of trying to prevent herself from conceiving a child, they quarrelled so bitterly that they did not speak to each other for three days.

On the morning after Cara had walked defiantly ungowned past the doorkeeper, she received a summons to the Chief Scholar's study-cell which opened off a dark landing in the heart of the Bibliotheca. When she was admitted to the small room, lit only by a single window high in one corner as if the Chief Scholar were afraid of light, she was surprised to see the Chief Physician and the First Captain of the Watch, as well as Cassie, Tav's most constant companion from the Circle. They stared at her without a smile or word of greeting, and something like fear began to tug at her as she took her seat before them.

The Chief Scholar spoke first. Although she was not many years older than Cara, she had taken the post early as the most brilliant pupil to have ever graduated from the Academy. Her expression was severe and her cheeks colourless from long days spent shut away with her beloved books.

'We know how you pride yourself on speaking your mind, Cara, so we will not waste words with you. When you first came here, we gave you the honour of becoming a citizen, and you repaid us by working diligently and even rising to the rank of scholar. All the Citadel spoke well of you. You promised to abide by our rules, and we treated you with due respect. We do not understand why you are now behaving so strangely. I will not speak for the moment of your childish action yesterday over the matter of the gown.' She turned to the First Captain. 'Give us your report.'

He cleared his throat. 'On several occasions in recent days this citizen has rebuffed my officers, refusing to heed their lawful requests. She has been caught on market days giving her Circle tokens to field people or even Scurriers and urging them to buy for themselves, although they protested against her actions. She was also found trying to barter one of her own garments in Citadel colours for a dish of honey cakes offered by a woman labourer, when she knows that such exchanges are forbidden.'

The Chief Scholar spread her hands. 'Do not be tempted to smile, Cara. It seems to us that you are trying to work mischief in the orderly lives of our people, on some whim of your own. I shall speak plainly—no citizen breaks the law and remains unpunished, not even the partner of a senior Circle member. You know as well as we do that the First Captain speaks of no more than the latest in a series of petty defiances.'

Cara darted a look at Cassie and saw that her expression was grim. The Chief Scholar continued, 'We summoned you here to give you a warning. You have no privilege or protection if you are willfully disobedient, and it would be well if you accepted your good fortune in being Tav's partner. Devote yourself to supporting him in his burdensome duties and carrying out your own tasks as a scholar so that he is not ashamed of having chosen an outsider for his joining when many others might have been better suited.' She paused eloquently and the faintest shadow of a sneer appeared at the corner of Cassie's mouth.

'And—and if I do not heed the warning?' Cara dared to ask.

The Chief Scholar indicated the Chief Physician standing beside her. 'You would return to the infirmary. We would be charitable and tell ourselves that your mind is diseased. You would be observed and perhaps given some cure—but the wardens would not be as patient as the first time. If you still refused to mend your ways, we would no longer be charitable, and your life would become, we might say, unpleasant.'

There was an ominous pause. Then Cassie leaned towards Cara and said calmly. 'But we are reasonable people, just as I am sure you are reasonable. I think you find it hard to understand our ways, coming as you do from the mountains. You are excused from your duties for seven days to examine your conduct and see how much better it would be if you worked with us, not against us.'

'You may leave now,' said the Chief Scholar pleasantly. 'Do you have any request or final word to say to us?'

Cara found that she had to force her lips to move. 'I would ask that no watch is set on me when I go out from the Citadel, and I promise,' her voice rose as she saw the doubt on the others' faces, 'I promise that I will not try to run away.'

'That would be wise,' replied Cassie serenely. 'The Watch are sometimes impatient with straying citizens. We shall take you at your word and grant your request. Let us hope that you prove trustworthy.' And at a nod from the Chief Scholar, Cara was allowed to go.

She fought back tears of panic as she descended the staircase, and when she reached the corridor below and heard footsteps approaching, she darted into a tiny ante-room where broken stools and a few unused gowns were stored. Even after the footsteps had faded into echoes, Cara stayed huddled in the gloom, pressed against the cold stone wall, fighting the dread which had taken hold of her, reminding her of all Anno's dark warnings about the Citadel which she had once treated so scornfully. At the same time, beating inside her head was the knowledge that he had offered her escape from the Citadel and she had rejected him. Now he had been gone almost two years, and probably lay dead somewhere in the wilderness. She would never find him again.

Chapter Seven

Cara spent the first three days following her summons to the Chief Scholar biting her nails and wringing her hands in a corner of her chamber. Tav passed in and out, but they had exchanged no words since their quarrel, although he must have known about the reprimand she had received. One small fact gave her some consolation. The Fifty Year Feast would take place on the fifth of her free days, and because she had been excused her duties, she would no longer have to prepare a discourse and might even be excused attending altogether.

On the evening of the third day she grew quite exhausted with weighing up and fighting her fears, and decided that she must put Anno's words to the test. Surely she would find some proof of them, no matter how frail, if she went out among the field people and watched and examined everything done and said. She had questioned Tav once about what happened to the dead and why there were none among the Citadel people who were aged or sickly—to no avail.

He had stared straight back at her and said, 'We are healthy stock but not as long-lived as we should wish. As for the dead, the infirmary takes charge of the bodies to spare the families further pain. Was it not the same in your settlement?' She could get nothing further from him and at that time had made herself believe that he told her the whole truth of it. Now she was foundering in a sea of uncertainty, growing more and more determined to test everything before venturing to believe it.

Very early one morning, while it was still dark, she muffled herself in a hooded cloak and slipped noiselessly through the streets, pressing herself against walls and hiding in shadowy doorways as she made her way towards the Watch barracks where the postern gate was concealed in the wall, the only exit from the Citadel other than the main gateway which stayed locked until dawn broke over the hills. She approached the gate cautiously, edging round a corner until it was clear that nobody was about apart from the young guard who looked half-asleep, leaning against her lance. Cara decided to gamble on not being recognised. She stepped out confidently and was upon the dazed girl before she had time to salute, although she managed to struggle to attention and ask for a gate pass.

Cara waved what appeared to be a Circle badge, saying, 'Private business of some urgency, Watch, so let me through and I will not report you for falling asleep on duty!' The girl hastily unbolted the gate and watched Cara hurry down the steps into the dimness. Scratching her head, she wondered why she had not recognised the Circle member's voice, but then perhaps she was one of the newcomers. Dayva, was it?—The guard could not remember the name—but, whoever she was, she had saved her from a whipping by promising not to report her. She shivered in the chilly breeze and tried to rub the drowsiness out of her eyes.

Meanwhile Cara had turned off the High Road onto one of the well-trodden paths between the fields, leading to a scattering of overseers' farmsteads and labourers' cabins.

Sol had risen behind a mass of thick cloud which had gradually filled the sky as she walked along. The dampness in the air turned to a fine mist of rain, and dense white fog shrouded the hills. She neared a cluster of cabins which rose by the edge of the bean fields, far enough from the High Road to be hidden from the curious eyes of passing Citadel folk. Smoke rose from the neat chimney-pipes; and she smelled baking bread, a sudden, sharp reminder of old Holly and the long-ago settlement mornings. A woman appeared, emptying dirty water from a cooking pot onto a garden patch, and before Cara could dodge behind the nearest cabin, she was observed.

She politely wished the woman a good morning, hoping secretly that if she could not watch unseen, then at least she could talk without being immediately known as a stray from the Citadel, dressed as she was in her oldest, most faded garments and her face shielded by a hood.

'I have walked far this morning and would welcome some refreshment,' she said. The women came closer, peering at her suspiciously.

'Which sector are you from?' she asked, and then Cara saw to her dismay that she recognised her. The woman stepped back, dropping the cooking pot in confusion and saluting with fluttering hands. 'Forgive me for not knowing you, Citizen Cara! An honour for us, and on such a morning too! Please, come with me and we will give you the best of what we have.' She scurried back to her cabin, beckoning Cara to follow and calling her family to rise and make ready, for the partner of

Chief Citizen Tav had come to visit them.

Cara was glad enough for the warm bread and cup of broth thrust into her hands, and the comforting blaze of the fire which was heaped higher and higher until she had to protest that she would be roasted. She soon wearied of the attentions of her hosts, who hovered round, agreeing with every remark she made and begging her to tell them about the wonderful life she led in the Citadel. Besides the woman, who said her name was Linnie, there was her partner, a grizzled, heavy-limbed man called Colem, their three daughters and five sons. The older children had partners of their own and lived in the surrounding cabins, each with a brood of young ones who clustered round the doorway to stare at the guest until Linnie proudly brought them in for Cara to hear their names and receive their greetings. Clearly the whole family would wait for her to leave before resuming their everyday tasks, and they would only say how grateful they were to the Circle and how much they respected those fortunate enough to be citizens.

On an impulse Cara turned to Colem, asking, 'Are the people out here ever afraid of the Watch?'

He looked at her blankly, unable to answer, and Linnie broke in with a quick, nervous smile, 'Nobody has reason to be afraid, Citizen Cara. We work hard and carry out our duties, as even the Circle have to do.' Sighing inwardly, Cara knew that she would not learn anything of importance from the family, so she thanked them for their kindness and took her leave. Linnie came after her, anxiously smoothing her patched gown.

'You will say that we are good people, won't you?' she begged, putting out a hand as if to hold Cara back. 'Colem is a worthy man, but he is not quick with words

192

like the people of the Citadel. We wish you well.' Cara reassured her as best she could and walked slowly back towards the High Road, shaking her head over the family's behaviour.

The fields were already busy with labourers, but few glanced up as she passed. In the drizzle and dull light they were no more than shapeless bundles of cloth lumbering through the sticky mud or bending anxiously over a row of frail seedlings. When she was out of sight of Linnie's colony, Cara took a turning at random which led off to the left, away from the Citadel. She would continue her search for the rest of her seven free days if necessary. She would prove to herself whether or not there was any evidence for Anno's doom-laden pronouncements, which were beginning to beat on inside her head night and day.

As the hours passed and the light began fading to pallid dusk, Cara started to lose hope of making any fresh discoveries that day. She had criss-crossed the muddy paths and tracks among the fields, wandering from colony to colony, trying in vain to engage the people in conversation. At almost every cabin she approached, someone recognised her as belonging to the Citadel or even identified her as Tav's partner. At another time, she might have been flattered that so many knew her face and had been present at her joining, but she began to curse inwardly each time a cautious welcome turned to fawning and gratitude for her kind visit. She had not realised how closely the various clans of the labourers and overseers were linked, nor how suspicious they were of strangers. At the few, remoter colonies where they did not recognise her, the women refused to reply to her questions until she gave a name and sector, and even then they mistrusted her, turning aside together to discuss her unfamiliar face

193

and doubting her words. Some wanted her to describe her own colony, her partner and even their lineages, until she was forced to abandon her attempts at conversation and move elsewhere.

Cara did not notice how quickly night was coming down until she halted to ask for directions back to the High Road and found that scarcely anyone else was about. The field people trooped home when it grew too dark for work, to wring the moisture out of their garments and fill their empty stomachs with hot, savoury stews and heavy cakes of fried dough. Cara was still out in the far reaches of the North-west Sector, among the hummocks and slopes at the foot of the hills, and after nearly two years in the Citadel, she knew that the main gateway closed at nightfall and the postern rarely opened to someone knocking from the outside. If she was locked out for the night, she ran the danger of being caught by the Watch and publicly disgraced—or worse still, taken to the infirmary and imprisoned as a mad troublemaker as the Chief Scholar had warned.

Then for the first time in many weeks she thought of Gethin, and realised, with a spark of hope, that it was not far to the North-east Sector where his colony lay. He could give her shelter for the night and would not betray her to a Watch patrol; he might even offer her some help in her search. Straining to see through the deepening gloom, she began stumbling along the path which led, as far as she could tell, towards the quarries. Her footsteps were very loud in the still night air, and from time to time she paused, convinced that she heard a following tread behind. As she neared the High Road, she stopped again, listening intently for sounds of other wayfarers. She was about to walk on when she sensed a faint stirring of the air, a breath of

194

wind that brought with it an echo of movement. Then she heard faint and far off, but approaching swiftly, the tramp of many feet. Only a Watch patrol would be on the move at that hour and Cara had no wish to meet one. She crossed the road quickly and went on in the direction of Gethin's colony.

Before long, however, she realised that the patrol were rapidly drawing closer and were in fact following the path she had taken. She broke into a run, trying to move as quietly as possible, and came in sight of the huddled group of cabins just as she felt too tired to go any further. None of the dwellings showed any light or sign of life and she got no answer when she knocked at the low doors. She was about to peer between the window shutters to see if there was indeed anyone within, when she heard stealthy voices on the path. Noiselessly, the Watch had surrounded the colony, and Cara barely had time to slip behind the cabin and disappear in the thickets covering the earth mounds thrown up by the quarrying work. Just as she settled herself in her hiding-place, she heard metal gauntlets thudding on wooden doors and the pitiless voice of the captain giving orders. Torches flared blindingly and Cara saw the people being dragged out and lined up in the muddy enclosure which lay in the middle of the circle of dwellings. The captain did not stop shouting, but Cara found it hard to catch the words. Hardly daring to breathe, she crawled closer again and saw him striding up and down in front of the quaking labourers.

'Tell me what you know,' he snarled, 'and it will be better for you. Keep up this stubborn silence and your colony will be dealt with more harshly than you can imagine.'

One of the women dared to reply. 'We cannot tell you what we don't know,' she quavered. 'We never took much account of the stranger. I tended his partner till she died, and she talked of him as a grim man who always kept to himself. He neglected her unkindly. He would not tell us about any plot he might hatch.' The Captain turned on her.

'And what else do you know, Zeah?' he demanded, spitting out the words venemously. 'What about the two from the Citadel, his former companions? How often have they come here and plotted with you?' Zeah burst into tears, as one of the Watch sentries ran up to the captain and saluted.

'We have found no trace of anything amiss here, Captain,' he reported.

The captain gestured him away impatiently and turned back to the waiting people. His tone grew softer, yet somehow more menacing. 'I may be willing to believe that you knew nothing of Gethin's deeds—though I find it strange that you did not pry into his affairs with your usual curiosity—but I'll offer you a final chance of telling me what I believe you're concealing. When did you last see him? Did he ever reveal his plan to any of you? And surely there is one of you who can confess to being part of his conspiracy?'

'Please,' said a man with a slow, bewildered voice, 'we don't even know what he's done yet.'

The captain laughed unpleasantly. 'Some of us, Dorby, need to hear things many times before we understand, don't we? Your companion Gethin has only made a spectacle of himself and tried to carry off one of the women he first came with, the timid one. He accosted her in her own chamber at noon today and said he'd come to take her away with him. Fortunately for her, Chief Citizen Izak happened to come in, and the besotted quarry labourer has been packed off to the infirmary, clearly quite deranged. I doubt if you

196

will see him again.'

Cara sank down in the bushes, unable to believe what she had heard. The voices in the enclosure continued and she realised that one of the other women was speaking, pleading with the captain, sobbing that they had never known that Gethin was so wicked, exclaiming that they were fortunate to be rid of him, that they had never trusted him. She fell to the ground, clutching at the captain's boots, wailing that the good name of their colony was ruined and their children shamed.

'Get up, Brenna,' said the captain irritably. 'We will accept your pleas and believe that the treacherous stranger did not draw you into his schemes—but be warned!' he glared round at the silent people. 'The Circle may be prepared to hold the colony blameless in this matter, but you will all be watched closely in the coming days. We hope for your sake that you are all as faithful as you declare. Return to your beds and think hard on what has happened.' The people began shuffling back into the cabins, their heads bowed. The captain called to the woman named Zeah and took her on one side. The little he said to her made her stifle a cry and look wildly over to where the patrol were waiting, ready to march off. This time someone else stood with them.

In the light of the torches, Cara glimpsed a wrinkled, elderly face and a frail body supported between the shoulders of two strong Watch men—one of the oldest women she had seen in the Citadel lands. She was crying out for her daughter in a piping, fretful voice, and her guards were telling her to hush and behave herself. Zeah ran up and kissed her on both cheeks, clinging to her until the captain pulled her away. All the other quarry families had disappeared indoors, and as the patrol departed, Zeah stood alone on the edge of the enclosure.

The hollow where Cara had hidden was empty, and she was following behind the Watch company as closely as she dared, although their trampling boots hid any noise she made. The old woman was being marched almost off her feet, still managing to keep up a mumbled stream of questions and complaints which her two guards ignored. Cara trailed behind in the hope that they were returning to the Citadel, so that she could slip through the postern with them and find out what had happened to Minna and Gethin.

It was getting close to midnight, and the old woman turned to complaining about the cold. As she paused for breath, one of her guards remarked jovially that she would be warm enough where she was going. She seemed as witless as a small child and told the men again and again that all she wanted was a seat by a fire and a crust of bread to chew. Then her whines turned to tears, and she cried to go back to her daughter, and the captain turned round furiously and ordered his men keep her quiet. From the sounds that followed, Cara guessed the old woman was being gagged.

At last the Citadel walls loomed in front and Cara readied herself to try and dart through the postern behind the patrol—she doubted she would escape unnoticed, but she felt too weak and wretched to care. Her fears proved groundless, because as the cavalcade in front started up the steps, the old woman suddenly began struggling so violently that her guards lost their grip, and she tumbled back onto the rocky ground below. In the ensuing confusion, Cara managed to squeeze past the bewildered gate sentry, muttering something about bringing reinforcements. Glancing back, she saw that the old woman had been overpowered by four large men who pinned her down to stop her from kicking while she was chained.

As Cara fled homewards through the dark streets, something nagged at the back of her mind, some vague, troubling idea that she could not consciously grasp. In the alarm of hearing about Gethin's disastrous actions, she had forgotten her original reason for going out into the fields. A turning brought her onto the shadowed expanse of the Quadrangle, and there came like a thunderclap the realisation of what she had just witnessed. Anno's hints and warnings flooded back, and she saw again the old woman—the oldest woman she had yet encountered in the Citadel lands—and her weeping daughter, the harsh grip of the Watch sentries on their frail captive, the insistence on silence as they neared the postern.

Anno had spoken of all-consuming fires deep within the infirmary, of bodies burned to ash, of a deformed child murdered in the hour of its birth, of rebels who uncovered hidden, evil things and were driven by their knowledge to run away and wander on the plains. Had Cara not told herself that she would look for proof, no matter how small, and had she not found it? Surely the Watch had no honourable reason for hauling an elderly, harmless field woman from her cabin under the cover of night and taking her in secret to an unknown resting-place.

And yet—and yet Cara hardly dared believe it. Was the word of Anno, whom Tav called an embittered outlaw, more trustworthy than the reassurances of the Circle? Her thoughts raged and battled with one another, her body shook and she felt sick, even as her legs carried her on towards the safety of her chamber. If Anno had spoken truly, though, then her own chamber was no retreat but a steel-jawed trap, baited with poisonous lies. Again, as the tumult grew inside her, she thought of Gethin and perceived the horrible danger he was in—and with a rush of foresight she pictured the Circle expedition setting off over the mountains, seeking the old settlement. If the heart of the Citadel was indeed black and wicked, she had been deceived by that wickedness into betraying her own people, and her faulty recollections of her journey would be twisted into instruments of destruction and enslavement for even more defenceless creatures.

She came to her tower, slipped through the unbolted door, and began climbing the stairs. A slow tide of grief and weariness seemed to flow round her, engulfing body and mind and dulling even her fevered imaginings. It was too much—she could not grasp the enormity of it. She had to sleep before she even set about discovering what had become of Gethin. Reeling with exhaustion, she opened the door of her chamber. Inside was light, not the darkness she expected, and in the light she saw Tav sitting by a reading lamp, a book in his hand. His tired face relaxed as he saw her on the threshold.

'I will not ask where you have been,' he said gently. 'I must try to be patient with you, Cara. Come, wash the mud from your face and hands, and then we shall sleep. I have been waiting for you to return.'

Chapter Eight

It was in the days after Gethin first visited her chamber in secret that Minna fell to a new depth of unhappiness. Izak came to her at an unexpected hour, flushed with too much wine, and caught her sitting on the floor with the pictures laid out round her. When she refused to explain them, a quarrel erupted. Izak grabbed a handful of the tapestries, tearing them in pieces and thrusting the scraps into the fire. He bore the largest one off in triumph to laugh over with some of his Circle companions. After that, Minna's life became infinitely more wretched for a while. She salvaged as much of her work as she could and set about patching and mending, but she could not close her ears to the stream of tiresome jokes with which Izak and his friends goaded her for a few weeks. She took to sitting for hours at a time on her couch, wondering if her hold on life was weakening at last, as the outside world grew remote and insubstantial, like the colourless spring mists blowing in tatters past the window.

One afternoon, when the mists had rolled back to reveal a serene blue sky holding the first promise of approaching summer heat, Minna fled from her Academy class, weeping shamefully because of the crude jests of her young pupils. They had heard rumours of her pictures and seized the chance of ridiculing a tutor whom they despised for her dwindling authority. In desperation, she ran back to her tower, bursting into her chamber where she could hide from curious stares and mocking laughter. Crouched on the floor, clutching one of the ragged cloth pictures, was a female Scurrier, horrorstruck at her sudden entry. The wooden chest which held the pictures had been dragged into the middle of the room and stood wide open, the lock broken.

Speechless, Minna gazed at the creature. Blue-black hair fell to her shoulders and in the shaded chamber her skin gleamed a faint silver. It was the closest Minna had come to one of the Scurriers since the day in the wilderness when she saw the pile of slaughtered bodies. Like Cara, she had been told many times that the Scurriers were dangerous, half-tamed beasts who could only be trained to understand enough simple orders for serving in the larger Citadel households or labouring at wood-shaping, stitching and smithying in the workshops. She had almost forgotten that the Children of Aesha in her tales had living counterparts.

The creature remained frozen while her slanting eyes flitted over Minna's face. Then she did something which astonished her even more. Reverently laying aside the picture, she prostrated herself, the palms of the hands upwards as if presenting to Minna the marks of the two golden eyes she bore.

Minna forgot that she would not understand ordinary speech. 'Please—please get up,' she said, her words tumbling over each other in her anxiety. 'Please go—you should not be here. They are only foolish stories. Please do not look at the pictures.'

The creature lifted her head and her strange eyes

searched Minna's face again. Her lips moved, and Minna took a step backwards, suddenly afraid that she might utter some hideous noise or even spring at her like a wild animal.

'Ah-ron.' The creature rose to her feet and placed one hand on her forehead. 'Ah-ron.'

'Arron, yes, I understand.' Minna almost laughed with relief. The creature was only saying her name. She pointed to herself. 'Minna. I am Minna. Go now, Arron, or—or you will be caught and punished.'

'We know of you. We wait for your coming a long time.' The Scurrier's voice was high-pitched and slightly hoarse. Although she used the words clumsily, she spoke in recognisable human speech. 'You come to us tonight. I come and lead you. Wait and watch for me.'

Minna gasped, unable to believe what she heard. 'But you can speak!' she said stupidly. 'I—I thought—'

The Scurrier bowed. 'It is a . . . hidden thing. We watch and learn from men. Only you know.' Minna shook her head, wondering wildly if she had slipped into a waking dream. Seeing her bewilderment, Arron stepped forward and touched her hand with delicate, dry fingers. 'We wait for you tonight. Watch for my coming. My words are . . . are true.'

'Come where? Why tonight?' Minna's questions remained unanswered. Footsteps sounded on the stairs, and immediately Arron was gone through the open window. Minna ran to the sill but she saw no sign of the Scurrier until she looked upwards. A small figure was swiftly climbing the sheer wall, clinging to invisible crevices in the stone. The towers crowded close together in that quarter of the Citadel, and she saw Arron poised to jump from one roof parapet to the next. Then the wall was empty and the creature was gone.

The remaining daylight hours passed very slowly. Minna went over every gesture and word of the extraordinary encounter, trying in vain to understand. Even though she was apprehensive at the thought of walking off into the night with such a companion, she shivered with excitement—yet she did not know whether she would have the courage to accept the summons when the Scurrier returned. She was also in a fever of anxiety lest Izak decide to call and find her gone, but he sent a message at dusk to say that he was leaving on a hunting trip and would not return until the following evening. When the last traces of daylight faded from the sky, Minna decided she would be brave and left the shutters unfastened. She had not waited long before she saw a furtive movement in the twilight and Arron sprang onto the floor, panting from the climb.

She was barefoot and naked apart from a strip of coarse cloth wound round her thin body. As she waited silently for Minna to prepare herself, she lifted a hand and pointed to the wooden chest, and Minna knew she was expected to bring her tapestries to wherever she was going. Summoning all her courage, she drew a shawl round her shoulders, bundled the pictures under one arm and turned to Arron, who was beckoning her down the stairs. Thankful that she was not expected to scale the rooftops, Minna followed the fleeting figure.

She kept a careful watch for other passers-by, but Arron was leading her by alleys and back streets so distant from the main Citadel thoroughfares that they were rarely used even in daytime. Clouds hid the stars and muffled the buildings in darkness. As they hurried along, Minna caught sight of the shadowy outlines of the Academy and the Bibliotheca rising high above the other parapets and towers. The streets round the Circle tower were still busy, and here Arron vanished ahead of Minna after pointing out the direction she must take. They met again under the arch of a bridge which spanned the gap between two immense halls where lamplight gleamed through the windows and the cheerful voices of households at table floated out into the lane. The final stretch of their journey led them to the edge of the Scurriers' quarter, diligently patrolled by the Watch at all hours of day and night. Minna hung back in dismay when they rounded a corner and saw the knot of uniformed men loitering ahead.

Arron pulled at the hem of her shawl, pointing to the ground. She looked and saw that her guide was climbing down into a black hole which opened at their feet where before had been solid stone pavement. There was no time to lose—Minna could see that the Watch was about to turn and begin walking back towards them—so she despairingly threw herself down and thrust one leg into the opening. To her surprise, her foot found the rung of a ladder and a small hand tugged her ankle, warning her to hurry. Someone was balancing beside her, and as she climbed lower, she heard a faint chink and the trapdoor closed, blotting out the square of night sky. Now the darkness pressed against her eyes like thick felt and when Minna reached the bottom of the ladder, she groped forward with her hands spread out uncertainly. A slender grasp encircled her wrist.

'Come with us,' said Arron's voice. A tiny light was kindled by the Scurrier who had closed the trapdoor and Minna saw that they were in a tunnel. The walls were slick with moisture and the roof rapidly dropped so low that she had to stoop to pass underneath. Illuminated by the sickly glow of the torch, they passed along tunnel after tunnel, always sloping down-hill and sometimes only high enough to let Minna through on her hands and knees. They took a sharp turn to the right and then two left turns and suddenly came to a dead end where another ladder stood. Minna climbed after the others, her bones aching with weari-ness. Before she could see where she had come to, she felt many hands reaching down to help her up and heard the murmur of alien voices, speaking what could only be their own whispering, hissing tongue.

She was standing in the lamp-lit room of a roughly built shack, crowded with more Scurriers that she had ever seen gathered together before. As she rose to her feet, every voice hushed, every head bowed and a forest of golden eyes stared back at her from upraised palms. She realised that they were showing her the same homage as Arron had paid, but in that crowded space they had no room to kneel. Then the crowd parted like a sea and Arron was pulling her by the hand towards a heap of rags at the far end of the room.

'Sit!' she urged, patting the makeshift chair proudly and Minna warily settled herself down, noticing that the rags gave off a sharp, animal smell as they were dis-turbed. When she was still, Arron stood beside her and began to speak, first in human words and then in the Scurriers' own language.

'We are glad for your coming, Talemaker. We hear of you through men's talk, and I go to find if the talk is true. I see your . . . your pictures. You show them to us now and make tales in the true way.' Every creature in the room was perfectly still.

Minna shook her head. 'I don't understand what you are saying. I—I made the pictures and the tales for myself, because I was lonely. I am no—no Talemaker.'

206

Arron broke in quickly, stretching out a skinny hand, 'Wait and watch. I tell you all things, and you remember as I speak. Talemaker's heart sleeps till we wake it.' Wonderingly, Minna shifted herself into a more comfortable position and listened as Arron began.

'Know,' said the hoarse little voice, 'that in the first days, before men's coming, we live here in all the land. We and the winged ones, the . . . ' she groped for a word, 'the See-ers. They keep our tales and our . . . our past. In the first days we ride together and they make . . . make dreams for us. They tell us how they dream of a day when the Brightness comes and we see all things and know all things. At men's coming, there is smoke and flames, and we say it is the Brightness at last. The See-ers look and say men are . . . are wise. We come with gifts, but men do not know us. They take our people and put them in . . . in cages. They want our secrets but we are silent and the words and tales are hidden safe. We fight for our people and the best of our See-ers is taken. Men make him like stone and lock him in the great hall. We see him there now.

'Then more men come in smoke and flames. The most wise of the See-ers speaks to us and says this is the . . . the Dimness, when men rule us. But one comes, one day, from among men—the Talemaker. Talemaker gives us new, true names and makes wiser, better tales than even in the first days, and Talemaker comes to lead us out from men and bring us to the Brightness at last. We wait and watch long days for you and now you come.'

When Arron fell silent, Minna looked round and saw that every eye was fixed on her, and in every eye was a flicker of hope. Although she felt she must be losing the last traces of her reason, she knew she could not destroy their forlorn dreams, remembering only too clearly her own sense of desolation as she sat, a virtual prisoner, in her tower chamber. It was mad, it was beyond madness, that she should allow the little people to honour her, mistaking her for some mythic hero of their own, yet she had used them for her own consolation in her tales, and it would be a cruel betrayal to dismiss their stories as worthless. They felt they had some special claim on her and maybe, maybe she could accept it.

The words that had brought her out of her black despair came back to her, and she said, half to herself, 'A barren universe, where once the gods walked . . . ' Then she laughed out loud. If they wanted tales, she would give them tales. It would be better than the life of walled-in silences which had kept her shut away for so long. Arron had turned to her enquiringly.

'Very well, I am Talemaker,' she said and the host of alien faces were instantly radiant. 'Listen to my story.' She drew out the bundle of pictures from beneath her shawl. Arron spoke to the crowd, and there was a ripple of movement as the Scurriers seated themselves on the hard floor, waiting for her to begin. The night breeze shook the flames of the guttering lamps and shadows danced on the dusty walls while Minna told the tale of the Master and the shaping of Osiris.

In the months since that first visit, Minna returned as often as they summoned her. Although she knew that she could not give them any real hope of escape from their slavery, she played the part they had thrust upon her, spinning tale after tale about the Children of Aesha and the lost world of the first days. Humankind had seized the little people, branded them with a mocking name and hunted their See-ers as monsters, creatures straying from old nightmares. The little people had waited for the Talemaker to come and give them new names, and as they heard Minna's first tale unfold, they had cried out in wonder. They were reborn as the Children of Aesha, just as Talemaker declared, and the See-ers were indeed the Wise Ones, the naigas.

Sometimes the dark alien faces filled Minna with an unexpected rush of fear as she surveyed them ranged before her, waiting expectantly for her to begin. She was half tempted to believe the Circle warnings about the little people—that they were irrational creatures who, if given their freedom, would strike to kill and maim humankind without mercy. At other times, she would gaze at them and see how small and defenceless they were, like human children, and then she would imagine herself as a liberating warrior, a great leader, and would shape bizarre plots and schemes, even though she knew they were all in vain.

Sometimes she told them about the settlement, the journey, her sister and Anno, and about Gethin, but if she dwelt on such matters, a discontented murmuring would break out among the crowded rows and Arron would pull at Minna's sleeve, whispering, 'Talemaker, Talemaker, do not speak too much of men. The Children do not want to hear of them and their ways.'

As time passed, however, the Children's trust in her deepened, and they would sometimes acknowledge her concern with her own kind, bringing her news through Arron of happenings in the Citadel—news of the planned expedition to the settlement, of the preparations for the Fifty Year Feast, of Cara's reprimand from the Chief Scholar. Minna was astonished at how much they knew and observed, although she seldom learned anything that touched her closely.

Her life became strangely fragmented as the months went by. She still worked in the Academy, struggling in the face of her pupils' scorn and disrespect, and at the same time she was growing in stature as Talemaker, the Children of Aesha's longed-for one. And again she was simply Minna, sustainer and centre of all Gethin's love and faithfulness and desire.

After he first came to her chamber, they saw one another again and again. Sometimes they met at noon in the tower, but sometimes they clasped hands out in the distant fields of the North East sector, when Minna managed to escape her duties for a while. She had valued his friendship in the settlement, depended on his watchful care as they journeyed in the mountains, and now she gave herself to him completely, yielding at last to his unreserved love. One summer evening, they met briefly by the shore and pledged themselves to one another for all time.

'You are my true partner. Nobody else matters,' she said in a rush of joy, tracing the line of his lips with one finger as he smiled.

At the end of that summer, Gethin was removed from quarrying work because his strength flagged so quickly. Instead, he became a carter, conveying goods to and from his sector and the Quadrangle market. He and Minna were able to meet more frequently, and before long Minna realised she was carrying a child, and that the child could only be Gethin's.

For her, their secret joy together was like a dream, moments of intense happiness quite separate from the real world where Izak neglected her and the Academy tutors laughed at her shyness. She and Gethin never spoke of the other parts of their lives, although she had once or twice attempted a faltering explanation of her times as Talemaker for the Children of Aesha. But

210

Gethin had stared at her so strangely and told her not to mind such things in such an anxious voice, that she did not try again.

She had not known, she never could have guessed, what he had been scheming ever since their first reunion.

Gethin burst into her chamber without warning. Before Minna could speak, he was spilling out his plans, his arms round her in a tight embrace. 'Come with me now. See, I have a disguise for you. Come with me and hide in my cart and we'll drive to the hills and then escape into the wilderness.' He did not wait for her to finish explaining that Izak was about to arrive. 'See, Minna, we can escape together, as we hoped. You and me and the child, free in the wide world. No more worry about talemaking or blackness or the old days.'

She had barely absorbed what he was saying when the chamber door opened and Izak entered. Minna screamed a warning, but Izak moved fast, knocking Gethin to the floor and roaring for the Watch to come. Minna sank onto the couch, weeping and wringing her hands, begging Izak to let Gethin go free. 'It is a mistake, a misunderstanding. Please, please don't harm him.'

Izak ignored her, and a Watch patrol was already pounding up the stairs when Gethin managed to gasp, 'She knows nothing of this. I am to blame. Don't punish her.' Four strong guards appeared in the doorway and proceeded to bind and gag the prisoner before dragging him to the covered infirmary cart which stood waiting at the foot of the tower.

Izak stood over Minna while she tried to calm herself. At length he said heavily, 'Whether I believe the quarryman or not, I can't say. Perhaps you are, as he

211

claims, blameless.' He stared at her. 'We have not been happy together, you and I. I came today with a plan for you to move to chambers in the Academy. We can tell the Circle that it's because you're pining for your tutor work and you would rather lodge alone for a time. If you go quietly, I'll believe that there has been no scandal between you and that fellow.'

Minna could not speak, but shrugged. She did not care what happened to her now.

'You consent, then?' Izak went on. 'I shall attend to the arrangements—but first I shall see that the infirmary knows how to deal with their new, foolish inmate.' He left the chamber abruptly, without a backward glance.

Minna wept quietly for Gethin. She felt completely helpless, afraid of what he might suffer and afraid of revealing too much concern for him lest the full truth of their clandestine meetings was uncovered. When her tears ceased at last, she sat deep in thought. Suddenly she saw what she could do. Perhaps the Children of Aesha could help her. Many of them were employed as servers in the infirmary, and they could watch over Gethin for her. Maybe she could even help him in some way through them. The thought was a tiny flicker of comfort. She rose, bolted the door and hung a length of white cloth over the window sill, like a linen shift put out to dry in the sunlight. It was a sign to certain watchers that her chamber was safe, and not long after, there was a scrabbling by the shutters and Arron's small figure slipped into the room, her pointed face alight with greeting.

'Welcome, Arron,' said Minna gently, and Arron held out her hands in reply, palms upward to show the staring golden eyes tattooed there. 'They have taken my Gethin, my true partner, to the infirmary because he

212

did a foolish thing.' Minna spoke slowly and sadly, watching to see that Arron understood. 'I must know what they are doing to him. Can you and the Children help me?'

Arron nodded. 'We watch him for you, Talemaker. You come to us tonight? As before?'

'I think—yes, I will,' Minna answered slowly. 'I have a new tale for you to hear.' The Scurrier placed her narrow hands together in farewell, before turning and slipping through the open window as silently as she had come. Once she was alone again, Minna tugged out her wooden linen chest from its hiding-place under the couch. Drawing out and laying aside a pile of blankets, she unearthed a thick winter cloak fastened in a tight bundle. As she unfastened it, her remaining hoard of pictures tumbled from the folds. Her fingers smoothed the fine stitches of the topmost tapestry which showed a darkening sky over jagged mountains. The tiny bodies of the Children of Aesha could just be seen clinging between the wings of the naigas who outflamed the setting sun as they flew. Minna rested on her heels and gazed at the picture for a long time, her eyes half-closed.

Before she went to the Children that evening, Izak returned. The pictures were safely stowed away long before he came, and when he entered the room, she was lying on the couch, hands clasped round her child-swollen body. He announced that he had decided she was ignorant of Gethin's plans for escape. She said nothing.

'I hope you have recovered from your fright,' he mumbled after a pause, shifting from foot to foot. 'I have arranged for you to move to the Academy to-morrow afternoon, before the feast. It will be better that way.' He waited, but she made no reply. Sighing impatiently, he marched out again, but not before she heard him mutter a curse on Tav for ever persuading him to join with such an empty-headed girl.

Chapter Nine

The day of the Fifty Year Feast dawned fresh and
clear, pink and gold clouds drifting over the hills as the
sun rose and made every glazed window in the Citadel
flash like lightning. All normal work was suspended by
special order of the Circle so that everyone could prepare for the evening of celebration. Out in the fields
the labourers and overseers organised their own feasts
on battered wooden tables arranged in rows between
the huts. Grubby children squealed and stole scraps of
roasted cuny, while the women hurried in and out with
steaming, newly-baked loaves wrapped in leaves to
protect them from the dirt. In the quarriers' colony,
the people averted their eyes from Gethin's empty hut
and Zeah sobbed as she raked warm embers over the
nappes roasting in the hearth, mourning her lost
mother whose old hands had always tended the fire so
lovingly.

Up in the Citadel the citizens were woken by the tolling of the great brass bell which hung at the top of the
Circle tower, sounded only for festivals and holidays.
Wreaths of fragment blooms festooned the pillars of
the meeting hall which was filled with long trestle tables
spread with embroidered cloths, worked by a dozen

specially chosen patterners who had spent many days stitching away in a small white chamber, high in one of the towers. Breathless master cooks thronged every kitchen, placing the final twist of painted dough on the lid of a gargantuan pie, throwing another cupful of wine into a seething, murky broth or sprinkling spiced salt over a roasting haunch of meat. Each hoped to win the honour of being chosen as the creator of the best dish. In every household, men and women laid out their freshest, most colourful garments and smoothed the red sashes warn by all the citizens on feast days in accordance with a Circle decree.

At the top of another tower, Minna and Cara were having a stilted, formal conversation, the first time they had spoken at length for months. They sat on Minna's couch, neither looking the other in the eye, while Minna described what had happened to Gethin.

'Is all well with you?' said Cara with an effort.

Minna shrugged slightly. 'You know that I move to new lodgings in the Academy this afternoon?'

'So I have heard. Do you know what will happen to your child?'

'No. Perhaps it will be reared in the nurseries. Perhaps I will take care of it. They have not told me.'

They were silent for an awkward moment, and then Cara ventured, 'Have you—have you any fresh news of Gethin?'

Minna turned and looked her full in the face. 'You know as well as I do that the Chief Physician will say nothing about any of the infirmary inmates.'

Cara rose to leave. 'I must start preparing for the feast.' Minna only nodded in reply. She never considered even hinting to her sister about her encounters with the Scurriers, and while Cara's mind was wearily circling her fears about the true nature of the Citadel,

216

she had grown too far from her sister to think of sharing them with her.

When she returned to her own chamber, Tav was already there, painstakingly sleeking back his curly hair with oil. She was as shaken by his unexpected kindness the night before as she had been by his earlier indifference. Now he made her sit on a stool so that he could coil and braid her thick brown hair high on her head.

'Who taught you to do this?' she asked, leaning back against his knees as he worked.

He hesitated before replying smoothly, 'I had a younger sister. Her hair was as dark as yours, but it hung below her waist. She loved me to dress it for her.'

'You did not tell me you had a younger sister,' said Cara, puzzled.

'I had no reason to speak of her before. She drowned out on the shoals a few days after she reached her fifteenth year.' His quiet voice soothed her, and as his hands smoothed the glossy braids of hair, the disturbing events of the previous day grew more and more remote. The last traces of her panic fade as he talked on about the splendour of the feast day, held every spring to celebrate the establishing of the Citadel. He told her about the ceaseless contests in his Academy class when he was only a child, to see who would be elected for training as future Circle members and how proud he had been when his name was read out at the feast in the year he was chosen.

He talked about the hard years when the winters froze and the summers burned and everyone went short of food except the Circle children who ate their meat and bread at a separate table, forbidden to pass scraps to their hungry friends. His voice ran on, remembering the bounty years when the Citadel folk joined the labourers out in the fields, toiling from sunrise to sundown in order to harvest the mounds of fruit and grain and roots, when all the ewes bore twin lambs and the pasturelands were loud with the bleats of baby goats, when every household drank gelu wine and spread their bread with dripping honeycomb.

As he spoke, the fifty long years of Citadel life stretched before Cara's eyes. She saw a small, trusting Tav growing older as his people grew in strength, moving from brute survival to dreams of rebuilding the glories of Earth, lost in the final years of chaos and tumult on the old world. Suddenly seizing his hand, she kissed it, marvelling at his steadiness and determination, and full of gratitude once again that he had chosen her as his partner out of all the Citadel women. Tav saw that her troubled look had gone and became the brisk Circle member again, telling her that he had to return to the Circle tower to complete some final preparations for the evening, and that she must rest a while before bathing and dressing in her festal garments.

His parting remark was over his shoulder as he left the room. 'There'll be dancing on the shoals for the Circle and their companions when the feast is over. I don't want it said that my partner does not know how to enjoy herself—I want to see you celebrating till dawn!'

When Sol had set over the bay, painting a dazzling path of light from the Citadel walls to the horizon, the Circle bell sounded its deep, rich note again, and the streets filled with hordes of peacock-bright citizens making their way to the Quadrangle for the start of the festivities. Only the infirmary gates remained closed, after reluctantly opening to let out the Chief Physician, robed in sapphire and scarlet, and a handful of senior wardens in demure ivory gowns.

When Cara arrived at the Quadrangle in the procession from the Circle tower, she was amazed the orderliness of the huge crowd, waiting in disciplined ranks and respectfully saluting the Circle members and their families who, for that one night, were allowed to share the exalted status of their offspring and eat at the high table on the dais. It was the task of Dayva, as the newest Circle member, to call the people to attention, and her hand shook as she raised it for silence.

'Children of Orion!' Her voice was thin with fright. 'Children of Orion, we have gathered to remember the founding of our Citadel fifty years ago this day. The hall is ready for us to celebrate with banqueting and song, and hear the tale of our unfolding greatness. Will you celebrate with good cheer?'

The answer came roaring back from hundreds of throats. 'We will celebrate!'

'Then let us begin!' Dayva squeaked and almost forgot to take her place on Tav's arm at the head of the procession to lead the citizens into the hall.

The Circle had planned the Fifty Year Feast to honour the power and splendour of the descendants of Orion, and the evening was rich in music and pageantry as well as food and drink. A chorus from the Citadel players kept the feasters entertained with a series of scenes from the past fifty years and songs newly written for that night, besides long-preserved verses and melodies from Earth. Cara laughed at a witty dialogue between the characters of a credulous young pupil and Merrow, founder of the Academy. She remembered briefly the tawdry Karnavale and felt, not for the first time, deeply ashamed of her own people. The lavishness of the banquet, however, was a ready distraction from serious thought—the tables were groaning with

219

provender, and bearers went back and forth replenishing the dishes and platters.

The master cooks had prepared whole roasted hogs stuffed with roasted chickens which were stuffed in turn with eggs, long skewers of smoked meat coated with herbs and dipped in lemon juice and honey, mutton pies with tiny flocks of pastry sheep grazing on the crust, concoctions of pickled sea-spiders and soft mounds of stewed potato, heaped pyramids of gelu fruit and apples, and stacked sweetmeats oozing syrup and shaped like towers, bells, horses, and thunderclouds. Spiced wine filled every cup and left stains on many fine garments.

When nothing was left except crumbled pie-crusts and sucked bones, the bearers cleared the tables and brought out more flasks of wine and small dishes of oranges dipped in a sugar-glaze. The citizens loosened their sashes and prepared to listen to the succession of speeches and commendations which they always had to endure at the end of a feast. Firstly the winning master cook was announced and applauded for his creation of minced cuny livers in a wheat and honey sauce, baked in a pasty shaped like one of the little burrowing creatures perched on its hind legs. Then the hall hushed as the Chief Scholar rose to read out the names of the twenty children selected for Circle training. None of them was aged more than seven years, and they looked even younger as they walked between the cheering tables to the dais where they received their Circle badges and a summons to the tower at noon on the following day.

Other awards were made—for good citizenship, noted scholarship, the most skilful tutor—and Cara's attention wandered. She glanced at Minna, a few seats down the table on her left, and wondered what

220

thoughts were passing behind her dreamy expression. Watching the people sitting below her, she became absorbed in the sight of a plump, balding man who was trying hard to stifle an enormous yawn. Then a familiar voice summoned her attention. Tav was on his feet, his clear tones ringing to the very back of the hall. He was telling the people about the expedition to find the Sirius settlement which would depart on the first day of summer.

'We shall journey to seek out our lost brothers and sisters and bring them back to be united with us, and after fifty years of separation, Sirius and Orion will be together again.' He gestured towards Minna. 'A first child of that future union will soon be birthed and as it grows, it will be a sign of the greater beauty and strength of our united peoples. Little did we know,' his eyes flitted to Cara as he continued, 'that when four strangers stumbled into our midst, it would herald a new dawn for us. They found us by chance, but that chance will lead to greater good than any of us can yet imagine.' He sat down as the people cheered and hammered on the tables.

Cara stared down at the crumbs on the table as she fought against an unaccountable picture appearing in her mind's eye: a picture of the dead lying in heaps in the reddened settlement streets, faces which she had known from Lesson Hall twisted in agony, babies crying beside the broken bodies of their mothers, chained lines of prisoners marshalling under the crack of a whip. The unreasoning fear was like a bitter taste on her tongue, and she gulped a mouthful of wine from her brimming cup, trying to steady her fingers. The Chief Scholar was speaking again, giving the climactic Fifty Year speech about the past achievements and coming ambitions of the citizens. Cara had not been listening but her ear caught words and phrases which made her realise that significant matters were being weighed.

'What has made us a great people,' the Chief Scholar pronounced, her white neck stark against the glaring orange and lemon yellow of her gown, 'is that though we are a free people we choose to sacrifice our own freedom for the good of all. We work hard and give ourselves to our allotted tasks so that the Citadel will thrive and be a home for our chidren and our children's children. We give greater comfort and privilege to those who earn it with their greater labour and duties, and we are satisfied with what we receive for ourselves, for that is how we preserve peace and keep faction at bay. We enjoy our pleasures the more because we live for our labour, and through the wisdom of the Circle none is left without work and none is overburdened. Let us drink to our fifty years of greatness and to the fifty thousand years to come when the Citadel's light will burn brighter and brighter until the whole planet of Osiris is radiant with the glory of what humankind has done.'

She sat down as the hall roared its approval and downed cupful after cupful of wine. The end of her speech signified the ending of the feast, and those seated at the high table were pushing back the benches and beginning to file out of the hall. Cara saw that Izak had to nudge Minna to bring her to her feet. They came out into the Quadrangle under a glittering, starry sky—a jostling, laughing crowd heading for the shoals which had been left bare and dry by the receeding tide. In the sudden darkness after the glare of torchlight in the hall, Cara could not see Tav. But she felt she must talk to him, to pour out her fears about the Citadel and her nightmare vision of the settlement expedition, and

222

hear his reassurances that she had misunderstood, that all was well.

She hurried through the crowd as it spilled out of the main gates, past the grinning Watch officers, and on to the path leading to the river and then to the shore, but she could not find her partner. The crowd began to run, splashing across the ford and racing to see who would be first to reach the shoal ridge where the vats of wine were heating and the bonfire throwing showers of sparks into the air. Ahead, they could already hear the musicians tuning their fiddles, blowing their flutes and playing quick bursts of the dancing tunes.

Cara soon arrived at the ridge, but she could still see no sign of Tav. Faces glowed red in the leaping flames and the darkness closed in behind them. There were screams and yelps of merriment as more and more people arrived, and once or twice Cara thought she heard Izak's loud laughter. She loitered disconsolately near a knot of girls she did not recognise. Their voices were hushed and they were evidently enjoying a piece of gossip.

'You're wrong even to speak about a Circle member in that way,' said one.

'But it's true!' insisted the girl next to her, who seemed to be the source of the story.

'But we should look to the Circle as a pattern of good citizenship and loyalty,' objected the first girl.

'So we have always been told,' said the second. 'And when I hear that in fact they have worse faults than the rest of us, I do not believe it at first, especially when the story concerns Tav—but it's different when I see proof of it with my own eyes.'

Cara froze and, trying to move nearer without being observed, she listened as hard as she could.

The second girl dropped her voice to a whisper. 'He and Cassie were always friends, and we all wondered when he joined with the mountain girl, but he only did that for the sake of the Citadel. I saw Cassie and him together. They are lovers. Even when she is joined, they will still meet together.'

Another girl interrupted, her voice deeper than the rest. 'If it were not for the scandal of it, I believe he would take any girl in the Citadel who pleased him. Of course Izak is far worse—but I hear he may be ordered to change his ways soon.'

'I pity Tav's partner,' added the second speaker. 'The mountain girl, Cara. She knows nothing of the affair and must think he chose her for love, when he only took her for the good of the people and to find more about this Sirius settlement. But hush! Nobody else must know of this!'

The voices buzzed softer, and Cara backed away, blind and sick with disbelief. She could not bear the thought that anybody could flatter and deceive her so effortlessly—if what she had overheard was true.

Despite her determination to trust her partner, however, the whispered rumours tormented her. She was afraid that nobody would dare invent so monstrous a story without some basis of fact, and she could not fight the growing suspicion that she had in some way been betrayed. All round her the crowd was taking partners for the dancing, but she angrily brushed aside the hands that came clutching for hers. Savage, horrifying ideas crowded her heart—she wanted to walk far out beyond the shoals until she came to the sea, and lay her face in the water and die. She wanted to kill Tav and Cassie. She wanted to set the Circle tower on fire. The music soared up and down, singing of brittle, heartless pleasures while the dancers bounded back and forth.

The air was heavy with the smell of woodsmoke and spilt wine and sweat.

Then through the music came shouts, harsh, urgent shouts and the sound of galloping hoofs on the pebbles. The dancers halted, panting, and the instruments squawked and fell silent. Torches flared in the breeze and Cara saw the grim faces of a Watch patrol bearing down on the revellers. Their leader was calling for Tav, for Izak, for the Circle. Tav stepped calmly into the firelight. Cara could not see if Cassie was with him.

'Why have you disturbed our celebration?' he demanded.

'Lights, lights on the hills!' The Watch captain was short of breath after the ride across the shore and his voice quivered with emotion—whether anger or fear, Cara could not tell.

'What lights?' Tav spoke courteously but a little impatiently, perhaps suspecting the patrol of indulging themselves with festal wine while on duty.

The captain cried out, 'There are beacons. The field people have fired warning beacons on the hill-tops. The Watch must be gathered. An army, a great army of people is out on the plains. They crept up stealthily and made camp, and at every corner they have set guards, men and women with unsheathed blades in their hands.

PART III

The Awakening

Chapter One

After a night of confusion and troubled rumours, the people of the Citadel woke to a morning of fear. The news brought by the Watch patrol was whispered in every quarter, from the pillared courtyards of the wealthiest households to the infirmary cell where Gethin lay imprisoned, his body showing all too clearly the first signs of the terrible wasting disease which he had unknowingly carried from the settlement in his blood. People said that a great host of strangers were gathered on the plains, intending to besiege the Citadel, and that a Watch captain and a handful of field people were already taken hostage. Nobody knew where the host came from, although many believed that the two mountain girls had been in league with spies from their own settlement, and some even whispered secretly of rebels.

The Circle had been in emergency session ever since the first warnings came in the middle of the night, and at daybreak they were debating whether to keep a close watch on Cara or whether to lock her up on a charge of conspiring with the host of strangers on the plain. The matter was far from settled when two grim-faced Watch sentries entered, escorting a ragged man who smiled insolently at the crowded chamber.

'What is this man doing here? Where has he come from?' Tav was on his feet with a bound, shouting at the guards.

One of them saluted, muttering sullenly, 'By your leave, Chief Citizen, he bears a message from the captain of the rebel army. He demanded that we bring him to the Circle.' Tav took a step closer to the man, who stared back at him coolly.

'Your name is Tharm, is it not?' he said. 'No doubt you can tell us much about rebels.'

The man nodded and gave a careless salute. 'It must be a full five years since you ordered my execution, Tav, but power has not worn you out. You look as youthful as ever. My untimely escape did not spoil your ascendancy, and I can see you have been busy turning the Citadel into a fine place, a very fine place indeed!' His mocking tone made Tav flush red and grit his teeth.

'Deliver the message from your captain,' he said in disgust.

Tharm inclined his head stiffly and produced a grubby scrap of vellum from the folds of his threadbare tunic. Seizing it, Tav read aloud the few words scrawled inside: 'The Free People offer their greetings to the Citadel. We intend no harm and bring no warfare with us. We ask to meet with the Circle and the citizens in the Quadrangle before dusk today. I, Anno, sign this for the Free People.'

Everything was still for a moment and the grey morning light showed up the red-rimmed eyes and anxious faces of the Circle members. Tav threw the message onto the table and stood staring down at it, his fists clenched by his sides.

'Tell Anno,' he said with as much scorn as he could

muster, "that he and some of his followers may come to such an assembly, but they must leave their weapons at the gates and lay not a finger on any person either within or without the Citadel walls.' Tharm cast a cynical glance over them all and then, with a brief bow, left. A smell of woodsmoke and unwashed clothing hung in the air behind him.

Secluded in their tower overlooking the placid bay, the Circle had not seen the spreading panic in the streets as the citizens abandoned their regular duties and ran hither and thither, seeking out friends and relations to gossip over the alarming news about the host. Tharm was seen going to the Circle tower and returning later on, despite his guards' attempts to keep him hidden. Many citizens recognised the rebel, including his own sister who collapsed in a faint when she caught sight of him. Some of the scholars and many of the Academy tutors kept to their usual tasks but undercurrents of fear and excitement were everywhere, and an infectious sense of chaos made the blood tingle and the heart beat faster.

In the middle of it all, Cara slipped out through the gates, muffled in a dun-coloured cloak that made her look like a young field woman. She had heard nothing of the message to the Circle and was consumed with curiosity about the identity of the strangers. Refusing to admit her secret hopes even to herself, and temporarily laying aside her fears about Tav's faithfulness, she hurried through the crowds of labourers and squealing children on the High Road. Every now and then a Watch patrol marched by, brushing all other people aside. Cara knew that the hardest part of her journey would be crossing the line of guards posted on the hills, and when she had passed the flax and cotton fields, she took a seldom-used path which skirted the quarriers' colony and lost itself in the thickets where the uplands began. Moving cautiously through the undergrowth, she worked a zig-zag path up the slopes. Fortunately for her, the Watch had little woodcraft and she could easily spot the straggling line of sentries as they crouched uncomfortably among the thorny branches and leathery leaves of the gerst bushes. Once she had passed them, she breathed more easily but quickened her pace because there was less cover higher up, forcing her to dart from copse to copse.

When she had at last put the first range of hills between herself and the Watch, she paused for a rest, rubbing her tired legs. A final punishing climb would bring her to a high place where she hoped she could look down at the stranger host without being seen. She pulled her hood lower to hide her face and was about to go on, when she heard the faintest cracking of a twig behind her. Before she could turn round, a large hand was clamped firmly over her mouth and something cold and sharp was pressing against her throat.

'Don't move or make a sound,' said a fierce whisper, 'and no harm will come to you.' She was pushed forward three paces and then gripped even more tightly. 'Who are you?' Cara suddenly felt that the voice was somehow familiar.

'Only a poor field woman from the North-east Sector,' she gasped.

'And what do you want, poor field woman?'

'To—to see the stranger host that everyone is speaking of, and discover where it comes from.'

'And how do I know you are not a spy from the Citadel?' The man's hold was loosening on her arms.

'You have my word.' As she spoke, Cara remembered why the voice was familiar and forgetting the knife and the warnings, she spun round, pushing the hood back so that he would recognise her. It was Medwin, her foster-brother, whom she had last seen on the eve of the Karnavale. He knew her immediately, his face a picture of astonishment before he seized her in a hug so powerful that she could hardly breathe.

When they drew apart, he began to lead her along a twisting trail over and round the hills, towards the rebel camp. She marvelled at how quickly and quietly he moved, despite his lame leg. As they went, she heard that what she had secretly wondered was true—the host was led by Anno who had collected together not only the stray Citadel outcasts, but the scattered remnants of the settlement who had listened to his words and decided to follow him.

'But when did he return to the settlement? What has been happening there?' Question after question burst from Cara, and Medwin shook his head, smiling.

'It's a long story, and Hanni will tell it better than I. Yes, she has come with me, and—and most of the children.' He fell silent as they came to the crest of a ridge and Cara saw the broad plains stretching away before them. Almost immediately below was a large circle of tents, coarse brown and grey cloth stretched over poles and secured with rope. Thin columns of smoke rose unwavering into the pale sky, and the new sun rimmed every blade of grass with its own shadow. As they approached, a man seemed to rise straight out of the ground at their feet, an unsheathed knife in his hand. When he saw Medwin, he relaxed his guard although he gave Cara a suspicious glance.

'I vouch for her,' said Medwin with a nod in her direction. 'I'm taking her to Anno.'

'No! Not Anno! I don't want to see him. Not yet.' Both men started at Cara's vehemence. She pushed a lock of hair out of her eyes, trying to steady herself

233

before she spoke again. 'Take me to Hanni first. I want to hear all your stories and—and I do not wish to see Anno yet.'

Medwin shrugged. 'Very well, but he'll think it strange if he hears of your coming in secret.'

'Then say nothing of my coming, please.'

Medwin and the guard looked doubtfully at one another and then Medwin jerked his thumb in the direction of one of the tents. 'Come and talk to Hanni then.'

The dwellings were crowded together and Cara hid her face in her hood as they passed each canopied entrance, even when she thought she heard a voice she knew from the settlement or glimpsed a half-remembered face. She had no desire to come upon Anno unexpectedly after their last bitter parting—she had told herself too often that, were he still alive, he would hate her because she had deserted him, choosing the Citadel instead of their dream of the Free People. The grass was already beaten down into a maze of tracks between the tents, and here and there goats grazed, tethered two or three to a pole. She followed Medwin as he ducked under the fringed awning of his home, and found herself in a dark, stuffy enclosure filled with blankets and sleeping children. Hanni had her back to them, coaxing a fire into life, and when she turned round, Cara saw that her face had grown thinner and her golden hair was cut short—but once the shock of recognition was over, her smile was as warm as ever, and she made Cara sit on a pile of sacking beside the fire while she made a stew of smoked hoch meat and a bulbous pink root which Cara had never seen before.

Cara guessed that Anno would have told of the journey from the settlement to the Citadel, so she spoke

234

about what had passed since then, painting a black picture of the lives she and Minna and Gethin had been tricked into accepting. Hanni's face grew puzzled and then grave as she listened.

'Anno said you chose freely to stay there,' she said, when Cara finished.

Cara bit her lip. 'So it may have seemed to him, but we were deceived by cunning people. We—we did not choose freely, and now Gethin is a prisoner and Minna is very unhappy.' But she knew as she spoke that she knew nothing of what Minna might really be feeling.

Medwin said slowly, 'So you wish to leave and join with us?'

'I cannot say until I have heard your tale and know what you will do now,' Cara replied.

Hanni scolded Medwin for asking such a foolish question. She was busy rousing the children from their beds, and soon there was a row of six tousled, sleepy heads by the fire. Cara recognised Jenna, who smiled at her shyly, and Feya and Sanni, but Medwin's three eldest children were missing and she could see no sign of the baby Hanni had been carrying when Cara saw her last.

'Lina and her brother would not come with us,' Hanni said sadly, 'and Hal fell from a rock and was killed in the summer after you left. The baby lived four hours.' She turned her face away and ladled the hot stew into an assortment of dishes. The youngest children ate straight out of the pot. Even though Cara was hungry, she had to force herself to swallow the bland slop and tried not to think of the tables crammed with seasoned delicacies at the Fifty Year Feast. Nobody spoke until every trace of the stew had vanished, and then Hanni put down her dish with a sigh.

'Now for our tale,' she said. Cara pretended not to

235

notice Sanni who had found her half-finished portion and was busy licking the bowl clean.

'We did not journey far when we left the settlement after the Karnavale,' Hanni began. 'Medwin knew of a hidden valley not more than two days' walk away where we would be safe. We found a few juss bushes which we could dry for fuel and a bit of stony ground for crops, but it was no kinder a place to live than the settlement. The wind still blew and the sun burned us in the summer. Sometimes one or two of us would venture back to the old place to see what had happened. Many of the better people had disappeared, and many of those who stayed were in a pitiful way, with scarcely any food or shelter and stealing and fighting like animals. Without Anno the Lesson Hall closed, and the Assembly was gone too. We had a hard summer and a grim winter. When spring came, nobody celebrated the Karnavale. Then one evening, just before nightfall, Anno came back.'

'He found his way to our hut and knocked on the door for a bit of food,' Medwin added. 'We thought you and he were long dead, but what he told us was even stranger news than his return.'

'We didn't believe him at first,' said Hanni. 'We thought he had lost you all and gone mad, wandering alone in the wilderness, but then he said he'd brought with him twenty-five men and women who were sheltering in a cave higher up the valley. They'd come with him from this Citadel. People from Orion! We couldn't believe it until they came to the hut and greeted us like lost kin. Anno said they'd found a new route over plains and rivers so they didn't have to cross the mountains, and that they'd come to gather everyone who would leave the settlement to travel away to the better land he had found and the great Citadel. You should

236

have seen him, Cara, searching the tumbledown market for people to join him and standing in the ruins of the Assembly Hall, talking about the grass stretching as far as you could see, and all the trees and the warm light. The wiser ones listened and came, but too many refused, saying they wanted to die in their own beds.

'We believed what he told and came with him, and in the end he led away the host you see here. Although,' Hanni paused, struck by a sudden thought, 'he never made us take him as leader. It seemed right that he should be the one we followed. He never lied to us—he said the way would be hard and it was. We've been footsore and hungry and we've left graves along the way. We lost some of the young and strong, as well as the oldest and weakest. He told us, too, that we'd see greater marvels than anything we could dream of, and we've seen lands which were nothing but bare orange rock from one horizon to the other. He led us by ways where we saw boiling water rising straight out of the ground and where waterfalls poured over jagged cliffs, making a huge lake and a foaming river, and we saw meadows full of blue flowers and crooked mountains where the rocks were speckled with coloured stones.

'We found living creatures which were good to eat and, Cara, they had no names till we made them! Creatures like the paith with its long, coiling body and many tiny legs, and the lumbering urso who cried like a baby as it died. We gathered roots and fruit tasting finer than anything we harvested at the settlement, but we turned aside to come near the Citadel in this emptier land, and now we're only waiting to see who will join us before we go back and continue our journeying.'

'And what does Anno promise you?' asked Cara.

'He says we are a free people and that if we want, we can journey on and on, finding new lands, perhaps even crossing the ocean one day. He says this world is greater than we know, and it lies empty, waiting for us to walk in it.'

'Did he not tell you about the little people?'

'He spoke of them,' said Medwin, 'but we've travelled in lands where no people have ever been, large or small.'

'And now, Cara,' Hanni took her hand, 'will you bring your sister and Gethin to join us? If you hurry, you can eat with us here at nightfall. I long to see Minna again.'

Cara shook her head. 'We cannot come so easily. I shall return to the Citadel and tell Minna your tales, and perhaps we shall be able to leave when Anno calls for people to join him.' Her voice was confident, but she was inwardly perturbed. Surely Anno's people knew how strong the rule of the Citadel was? But she had not time for further talk. Sol was high in the sky now and she knew she must return before her absence was noticed.

Medwin rose to accompany her back over the hills and Hanni gave her a final hug of farewell, begging her to make haste and join them as soon as she could. The last Cara saw of her were her thin arms reaching out to her smallest son who lay curled up in the warm ashes, dreaming in a happy daze of stew.

Chapter Two

Later that day Cara and Minna stood together on the edge of the teeming crowd that filled the Quadrangle. Word had gone round quickly that the leaders of the host were coming to a gathering of the Circle and the citizens, and the Watch was hard pressed to keep out the hordes of field people who lingered at the gates and milled about on the High Road, stirred to a tumult by the rumours and whispered tales concerning the great army encamped on the plains. As the hour of the gathering drew near, Watch patrols began forcing a clear way down the High Road on horseback, beating away the over-curious with angry shouts and blows. The sky was hidden behind mist which turned blood-red as the invisible sun sank to the horizon.

The crowd in the Quadrangle shuffled and murmured, stamping booted feet and rubbing hands as the air grew colder. Cara was shivering in spite of the woollen cape which fell below her knees, but Minna stood straight and unflagging, even though she felt within her body that her birthing-time was almost upon her. Cara had found her lying dreamily in her lonely Academy chamber and had told in headlong, reckless fashion of her meeting with Medwin and Hanni and

239

the tale of the Free People's wanderings, as well as her deepening suspicions about Tav and Cassie. Minna took a long time to reply, staring down at a crack in the floorboards and running a finger round a neatly patched hole in her coverlet.

At last she said quietly, 'I have often longed to see Medwin and Hanni again, and I knew that Anno would return one day.'

'How could you know?' Cara broke in impatiently.

'Because he cared too much for you to leave you behind and never come back,' replied Minna simply.

Cara stared at her sister and then abruptly looked away, biting her lip and frowning. When she spoke again, her voice barely trembled. 'I will return just before dusk so that we can go together to the gathering, if you wish.'

As they waited on the black flagstones of the Quadrangle, Minna was pitying her sister who had forsaken one ideal for another which proved hollow. Cara abandoned her home and her people to follow Anno with his talk of wandering through the new world. She forsook him for the glorious Citadel and one of the strong young men who governed it. Now she was no longer sure of Tav and, worst of all, she was confronted by Anno again, triumphantly leading a host of free people, just as he and Cara had once dreamed.

'And I,' thought Minna, 'have no hopes, nothing except a clutch of my own tales—but at least they cannot cheat me.'

Suddenly shouts rang out in the distance. Heads turned, and an excited whispering ran from one end of the crowd to the other. The leaders of the host had arrived. Craning to see past the Watch men standing in front of them, the sisters glimpsed seven, eight, nine figures stepping up onto the platform which had been hastily built that afternoon to receive them. The coloured garments of the Circle members flamed gold, silver, emerald, sapphire and vermillion in the fading light. They could see Tav stepping forward to greet the newcomers. At a word of command, the sentries standing at each corner of the platform lit their torches and in the sudden glow, the faces of the nine strangers were clearly visible. Many in the crowd caught their breath as they recognised not only the lean figure of Tharm, but also others who had not set foot in the Citadel since their unexplained disappearance many years before.

Cara searched for Anno among them, and at first she feared that he was not there—that he had been taken captive as soon as he set foot through the gates. Then she caught sight of him standing to one side, taller and more hollow-cheeked than she remembered and wrapped in a dirty brown cloak, fastened at the shoulder with the green and silver clasp she had given him on the night of his escape from the infirmary, almost two years ago. Was he wearing it as a sign of reconciliation? She could not guess and hardly dared hope, yet as his gaze ranged over the upturned faces in front of the platform, she told herself he was searching for her. She huddled deeper into her cape, hoping he would not notice her as she gazed at him, yet unable to stop herself from tracing every feature of his face again and again.

Tav was speaking, welcoming the rebels in formal terms, expressing astonishment at seeing again those thought lost, passing smoothly over the question of the field people who had been taken captive, hinting at the Citadel's curiosity regarding the origins of the host, inviting Anno to explain their coming and calm the anxieties of the citizens.

A breathless hush fell as Anno moved to the centre of the platform, lifting his right arm in a gesture indicating that all were included in his words. His voice rang out clearly and the silence of the listening crowd grew more profound as he spoke.

'We are the Free People, drawn from the remnants of Sirius who lived in a settlement beyond the mountains, and from the outcasts of this Citadel who have been in hiding out on the plains for many lonely years. We have become one people and come now not to offer violence to the Citadel but to secure certain terms. Those of your labourers whom we hold hostage will be freed when the terms are met. They are that—'

'Your messenger did not say you wished to discuss any terms,' interrupted Tav.

'They are that we be granted leave to barter for provisions for our journeying,' Anno went on, as if he had not heard Tav, 'and leave to depart for anybody who wishes to come with us, from Citadel or field.'

'And who,' Tav retorted with withering scorn, 'would wish to accompany such as you? The citizens want to know who you are and what you are doing on our plains, not listen to your foolish demands.' Then, to his amazement, came cries from the crowd of 'Silence!' and 'Let the rebel speak!' Tav's face turned scarlet with anger. Never before had the authority of the Circle been challenged so openly and so humiliatingly.

Anno turned his back on the Circle to gaze out at the crowd and said gravely, 'We, the Free People, have no homes except the tents we make with our own hands and no meat except our scanty flocks of goats who can only snatch grazing as we travel. We harvest the wild roots and fruits growing far beyond any tilled fields and drink nothing finer than soured milk and spring

242

water. But if you join us, you will have no duties and no call to submission except to one another. The way will often be hard, but we will see a greater world than you could ever build here by your own strength. It will not be a gentle life, but it will be an unfettered one. Any man, woman or child can join us, the noblest scholar or the humblest of the little people that you call the Scurriers.'

The buzz of troubled voices in the crowd swelled to an uproar as Anno finished, and even the Circle members on the platform were painfully agitated. Obedient to Tav's shouted command, the Watch threw down their torches, plunging the Quadrangle into shadow. Above the disorder, his cry could barely be heard: 'The gathering is at an end. Return to your chambers at once.' Cara and Minna were caught up in a jostling, pushing crowd, stumbling in the blackness and strung to a pitch of nervous excitement after the threat and challenge of Anno's words. Cara soon lost sight of her sister and after a moment's hesitation, she began pushing and fighting her way back towards the platform. When she got there, it was empty except for a Watch officer who seized her roughly, not knowing her face in the dark.

'Did—did the Circle get away safely?' she panted, not daring to ask about Anno.

'They did,' said the man gruffly, 'and you should be returning to your chamber.'

'But—' Cara could not contain her anxiety. 'But the stranger leaders, are they still free?'

The man stared at her. 'Of course, until they commit a punishable deed. Do you think the Citadel takes innocent people captive?' Then he gave Cara's arm a shake and told her to make haste and leave the Quadrangle as she had been ordered. She pulled free and hurried away down a short-cut of alleys to her tower, picturing the nine men and women striding back unhindered to their camp on the star-lit plains, and Anno one of those nine strangers, sharing with them the dreams he had first shaped with her in the mountains. Then she stopped short in the middle of the street as another picture formed in her mind. She saw herself marching towards the host encampment at the head of a joyful army of liberated citizens and labourers, and meeting Anno surrounded by freed people who had escaped through her efforts, leaving behind a bereft and broken Citadel. She would not return to him in shameful secrecy, begging to be accepted, but in triumph, proving by her actions that she was truly deserving of the trust he had once placed in her.

Gradually the Citadel grew calm again, and soon everything was quiet except for the occasional footfall of a Watch sentry pacing to and fro on ceaseless patrol. Night thickened as the lights shining from chamber windows were extinguished, but out on the hills the beacons flared, driving back the dancing shadows, and the Citadel sentinels heaped the fires with dead wood, always glancing over their shoulders for fear of a rebel knife in the back. High in the Circle tower, behind the heavy nail-studded door, the lamps were still lit and twenty young men and women ran fingers through tangled hair as they wearily turned the same questions over and over. Most of them were afraid—afraid for their own safety as they never imagined they could be, afraid that the strong walls of the Citadel were not invulnerable, afraid of the ragged, mysterious barbarians who had come within their gates.

'This talk of free people,' said Cassie, 'hides their true motive. These rebels want to overthrow the

Citadel and rule it for themselves. They want to take what we have built and use it for their own purposes.'
A murmur of assent greeted her words.

Tav irritably slammed his palm down on the polished wooden table. 'And can't we devise a plan between us to defeat this absurd threat?' Nobody spoke. 'Perhaps,' he continued, 'I can shape a plan.' Nineteen pairs of eyes turned to him at once. 'I know it is against the Circle code for one person to lead, but in a matter as complex as what I will propose, we could have only one mind at the centre of the web.'

'Speak on,' said Izak sullenly. 'None of the rest of us is any use.'

'First, we humour the madman Anno with his futile chatter of terms. We allow the strangers to barter for food, while making sure the rates are fixed as high as possible, but on no account must any one of our people, whether from Citadel or fields, be allowed to join the host. We will give the hill-top sentinels the powers of life and death over any caught trying to flee. To the rebel host, we announce a day of festival and games to celebrate the coming of summer, and we announce that all who wish to leave may do so on that day. We will make a show of the Citadel's power and splendour so that our citizens can see how broken and wretched these so-called free people are.

'The Watch will have been mustered and when the celebrations are over, we will order the rebels to exile themselves from the Citadel lands forever. I believe that they will be foolhardy and choose to resist instead, and then the Watch can take its lances and slay every single law breaker. At the same time, the company will march to the encampment to make an end of those left behind.'

Nineteen faces were turned to his, marked by varying expressions of horror, incredulity and delight at the boldness of the plan.

'Must we shed so much blood?' asked Izak suddenly.

Tav frowned angrily. 'What do you propose instead? Letting the rebels go with as much of our food and as many of our people as they wish? Do you think they would go quietly into the wilderness? Would they not rather return, take us unawares and destroy us?'

Izak shrugged. 'Is there no easier, less costly way? Why make war when we have no pressing need to do so?'

Tav stared hard at him. 'I think you should be silent, Izak,' he said at last. 'Your words make us doubt the depth of your loyalty to the Citadel.'

Izak did not reply, and slowly the debate resumed and continued along a tortuous course until the coldest, darkest hour of the night—when the Circle voted to follow Tav's plan and chose him to lead them in carrying it out.

Chapter Three

At the end of a windowless corridor on the third level of the Academy, a worn staircase spiralled upwards into shadows. Very few passed that way and disturbed the dust on the elaborately whorled balustrade, and some of the pupils terrified one another with tales of cold hands clutching at the ankles of anyone rash enough to climb the stairs, sending them plunging to their death. All that a venturer would have found, however, was a low-ceilinged passageway at the top, closed by a blank stone wall at each end and with half a dozen doors opening off either side. Footsteps echoed hollowly on the creaking boards, and the breath of the venturer might stir some of the grimy nets of cobwebs floating overhead, work of the offspring of the stow-away spiders carried from their own planet by the last spaceship. Some of the doors would open to reveal nothing more alarming than empty, mouldering closets, but others would remain obstinately closed, and then the venturer would take fright at a faint movement or scuffle in one of the locked chambers and run off, noisily clattering down the staircase until it sounded as if a whole pack of nightmare beasts were chasing behind.

Minna lodged in one of those isolated rooms, just wide enough to hold her couch, a stool and the screened alcove where she hung her clothes. A tiny window in the sloping roof opened reluctantly to let in a breath of air, and an unexpectedly luxuriant woollen rug covered the floor, woven in blue and amber spirals. She chose the remote passageway herself, rather against the wishes of the Chief Scholar who knew that a woman as close to her birthing-time as Minna should not stay in so inaccessible a chamber. But there were in fact few other places where Minna could go, because the rapidly growing numbers of the Citadel people filled every tower and hall; scarcely any room remained within the walls for new building work.

So in the end Minna had her way. She installed her belongings in her new home on the afternoon of the Fifty Year Feast and had passed only one night there before the meeting in the Quadrangle. During the next three days she wandered through the streets, watching the passers-by and listening to the muttered gossip of the loiterers who had appeared at every corner. When she grew tired, she would return to her chamber and rest there, pondering the strange events since the feast day and waiting for the soft tap of Arron on the window, come to take her to another assembly of the Children of Aesha.

The whole Citadel seethed with excitement, as restless as a hive of bees on a thundery summer's day. Minna overheard two women's conspiratorial conversation as they rested on the sunny steps of the meeting hall after a morning of scrubbing pots in the Circle refectory, unaware that she was leaning in the shade of the cool stone entranceway.

'It makes me tremble just to think of that stranger host out on the plains,' said one.

248

'I knew you were afraid, just as I am!' replied her friend, busily peeling a flaum, one of the dusty blue fruits which Minna had first seen among the ruined Scurrier huts beyond the lake.

'Nonsense, Lisha. I am excited, not afraid!'

'Hush!' said Lisha who was now tearing the flaum into dripping segments. 'I have heard that the host are no more than a dirty band of thieves.'

'But there are rebels among them—Lisha, there really are rebels. That Tharm, now. His sister told everybody that he'd been killed by a dragon, but all the time he was living out on the plains. Did you not hear the tales about rebels when you were a girl?'

'Tales, yes. Stories to frighten us into working hard at the Academy and growing up into good citizens. Perhaps the Sirius settlement does exist, but the people might well be no better than Scurriers, not a powerful fighting force. You saw how the mountain girls were when they came.' And Lisha filled her mouth with flaum so that purple juice spurted from between her lips and dribbled down her chin.

'But the man who spoke to the crowd, the man called Anno—you could see from his face that he was a good man, not a vagabond.' The woman dropped her voice so that Minna could hardly hear. 'If I were younger, Lisha, I would dare to think about going to join them. I've heard that some have vanished even from the Citadel. They crept over the hills and went to hide in the camp.'

Lisha choked on her fruit. 'Melina! You should not say such things, not even to me. Those barbarians probably slit the throats of any who get there, after tearing the clothes off their backs first.'

'And why do you believe that? Who has been feeding you with rumours?' The two women began squabbling,

249

and Minna edged away before they noticed her.

The evenings were lengthening as spring turned to summer, and people began to congregate in the Quadrangle at sunset when the day's work was over, as had always been the custom. Crowds of children shrieked and tumbled and chased one another, while their fathers and mothers strolled round arm-in-arm or met with their companions for a sip from a communal flask of wine, a rare indulgence for the lower ranks of citizens. But after the gathering with the leaders of the Free People, the light-hearted mood of those Quadrangle evenings changed. The first stirrings of summer heat brought a feverish restlessness, not the old holidaying mood. Minna strayed into the Quadrangle at dusk one day and was drawn to the fringes of a group clustered round one man who was talking in a rapid, urgent voice.

'Listen to me!' he kept saying. 'I have seen them. They laugh, they have no fear, their faces shine. They all belong to one another. Nobody rules their hours with decrees or tells them where to live. Listen to me! Who will go with me to join them?' Everyone round him said 'Hush!' and glanced about uneasily. When the upright figure of a Watch officer appeared on the edge of the Quadrangle, the group instantly melted away into the twilight, leaving Minna standing alone.

In the black night hours, she was Talemaker for the little people. With the weight of the child in her body, she found it hard to climb the ladders leading in and out of the secret tunnels, and she often felt faint in the crowded shack where the Children of Aesha spread their palms before her, waiting for her to speak and transport them from their world of slavery and hopelessness to the enchanted realm that she shaped for them. A world where the naigas soared and sang and the Children grew so mighty that they banished humankind from their lands, so their children and their children's children could live fearless and free under the open sky. But when she told them of the coming of the stranger host and the turmoil in the Citadel, their faces remained expressionless, row upon row of slanting eyes glinting in the light of the single smoking lamp which stood on the floor next to her.

Puzzled, she turned to Arron who waited, as always, at her right hand. 'Are the Children not concerned even with these events?'

Arron touched Minna's knee with a twig-like finger. 'Know that the Children do not care for men's troubles. Men never bring good, only harm. Only you, Talemaker, concern us.'

Minna said desperately, 'But there are other good people besides me. Anno, who leads the host, is a good man. He said the Children should be allowed to walk free and join with them. He could help you better than I could. I can only make tales.'

Others besides Arron now understood some, at least, of Minna's words, and a tremor ran through the packed ranks before Arron could finish translating. From corner to corner a hiss of concern spread and broken phrases were muttered. Some of the little people began shuffling forward, pressing closer to Minna, reaching out to touch her as if to reassure themselves that she was real. The whispering voices grew louder, and it seemed to her that the stifling air of the room began to throb. She gasped and put her hands to her head, shutting her eyes as the narrow alien faces crowded nearer. Dimly, she heard Arron scolding in shrill tones and gradually, the press of bodies about her receeded. After a moment she lifted her head and saw that they were settling back on the

251

floor. There was a light pressure on her shoulder.

'The Children are afraid, Talemaker,' said Arron. 'You must be the one who saves us.' Minna could only shake her head speechlessly. 'We know,' Arron went on, 'that you are the one to lead us out, one day. Then we go to our lost homes and bury the dead, and the naigas come and we fly together to a new home and always you lead us. You make the tales and Talemaker cannot lie. We know you are true. We watch and wait and listen to the tales until the time is ready. Men cannot save us, only Talemaker.'

Their trust in her had become absolute. Minna stared at the upturned faces and a sea of golden eyes stared back as each creature raised its palms in homage. She was beginning to fear them, not least because of their trust in her and because of the role they had thrust upon her—yet they loved her because for them, she was the saviour. She drew a deep breath and told herself that somehow she would help them. Not simply with tales, but in some way that would provide the key to their liberation, and maybe Anno could be part of that key. Suddenly she was so overwhelmed by fatigue that the room swayed about her.

Arron's breath was on her cheek. 'You wish to go back now, Talemaker?'

Minna nodded wearily, struggling to her feet and drawing her shawl round her shoulders. As she followed her guide to the tunnel entrance, the crowds melted away to let her through, but before the trapdoor closed over her head, she heard the whistling murmur of their speech start up again and felt certain they were discussing her.

She woke early on the next morning and lay in a pleasant half-dream until the Academy bell rang for the first meal of the day, eaten by tutors and pupils together in the refectory before classes began. She rose, pulled on a loose-fitting gown and knotted her hair at the back of her neck before carefully making her way down the staircase, through the corridors and down further steps to the sun-lit room which was already filling with chattering children and heavy-eyed tutors. Minna took a hunk from a freshly baked loaf and a handful of gelu fruit from the serving table and went to sit in her customary place, a stool by one of the open windows. Breaking off a small piece of the warm brown bread, she looked out at the Quadrangle basking in the yellow morning light. The towers of the Citadel thrust up arrogantly into the sky which had been swept clean of its dawn veil of mist.

Suddenly the babble of voices all about her was hushed. Minna glanced up and saw that one of the Citadel Watch captains had entered with the Chief Scholar who had lifted her hand for silence. When the chamber was still, she turned to the captain and nodded at him to begin.

With an elaborate flourish, he produced a leaf of vellum from the folds of his uniform. He was a very young, pompous captain, and his new badge of office winked on his chest. He read slowly and carefully, giving due emphasis to each word. 'The Circle gives this decree to the citizens, the descendants of Orion. That ten days from this reading, there shall be Games held to celebrate the strength, beauty and power of our people. That the Games shall take place on the sands of the great bay when the tide is at the lowest ebb. That the leaders and people of the stranger host encamped on the plains shall be welcomed to these Games and see the greatness of the Citadel. That a banquet will be held at noon on the day of the Games, and that every citizen shall be there, excepting only those at their birthing-time. That those chosen to take part in the Games shall do their utmost, so that the glory of the Citadel is increased. That those of our people who wish to leave and join the host may do so when the Games are over. This the Circle decrees, and it shall be done!'

Chapter Four

The activity unleashed to ready the Citadel for the Games dwarfed even the preparations for the Fifty Year Feast. Regiments of patterners set to work stitching flags and banners and cutting lengths of multi-coloured ribbon for knotting into victory sashes. A group from the Circle scoured every household and every field colony to find the swiftest, the strongest and the most agile descendants of Orion, and whole Academy classes were drilled for hours with newly-composed songs and ancient Earth dances. The master cook who had won honour at the feast was set to create a monstrous cake as the centrepiece of the noon banquet, and at every turn, the Watch was there, reminding citizen and labourer alike that they were striving together to increase the glory of their people.

Yet for all the bustle and excitement, Minna sensed a troubling undercurrent, different from the intrigue stirred up by the first news of the stranger host. She began to feel that new rumours were abroad in the streets and byways unlike anything she had heard in the Citadel before. As she went about, she caught snatches of conversation echoing down a hall corridor, muted phrases exchanged by women waiting at the infirmary gate, stifled remarks passed between buyer and seller on a market-day stall. One day the Academy doorkeeper sat by her in the refectory for the morning meal and began whispering a long story about corruption in the Circle.

'Who told you these things?' asked Minna cautiously.

'She would not say her name, but she said she spoke the truth. She said the Circle abuses its privileges,' the doorkeeper said, after a careful look round to see that nobody else was listening.

'So what are the members doing wrong?'

'They are always drinking too much wine. They reserve the best vintage for themselves and then drink it like water. And they are unfaithful to their—their partners.' The doorkeeper bit her lip and blushed, suddenly remembering who Minna's partner was. 'Of course,' she added hastily, 'it's all wicked lies. I said to the woman who told me that I would report her to the Watch, but she ran away before I saw her face. She spoke to me at twilight in a corridor of the Bibliotheca.' And the doorkeeper rumbled an excuse and hurried away, leaving Minna to finish her meal alone.

On a black midnight, four days after the announcement of the Games, Minna was jerked from sleep by a tortured, gurgling noise which sounded as if it came from right below her open window. As she listened, it rose to a wordless moaning and became an animal cry, rising higher and higher before ebbing away into broken silence. She shuddered, her body drenched in the cold sweat of fear, and waited for the cry to come again. She heard nothing. After an agonising moment of indecision, she plucked up enough courage to creep out of bed and down the staircase to the lower passageway where a window opened onto the Quadrangle. Easing back the shutters, she looked out on a sky blazing with so many stars that she could clearly see the man tumbled in a heap outside the Academy, groaning and tearing at his hair. After her first shock, she recognised him as a respected older citizen who spent his days compounding remedies in the infirmary. He was on his knees, beating his head on the flagstones so that blood poured from his forehead.

Minna was filled with horrified pity. Evidently the man had lost his reason, and she could do nothing to help him—every street in the Citadel was paced by the Watch at night, and even now they would be marshalling a patrol to deal with the disturbance.

'Cleanse the Circle!'

Minna started, leaning further out of the window. It was the crazed man who had shouted, and now he flung his arms about wildly. 'Share the privileges! There is enough for everyone! Call the Circle to account!'

Already Minna could see the Watch approaching from the other side of the Quadrangle.

'Cleanse the Circle! Let the people be free!' The man turned as the six patrol men drew in and surrounded him. He began screaming, a steady unbearable shriek which was cut off abruptly as rough hands snatched at him. Other shutters started to creak open, but when the onlookers saw that the commotion was over, they slammed them shut again, vexed at having their rest disturbed. Minna remained by the window long after the Quadrangle had been restored to its earlier emptiness and peace. She was sickened by what she had seen—the ravings of the tormented man and the brutal efficiency of the Watch—but beneath that, she was shaken by the thought that someone, or some group, was daring to spread doubts about the Circle's honour, and she could not shake off the suspicion that Cara was involved in it, whatever it was. Sighing, she closed the shutters and dragged herself back to bed, resolving to seek out her sister and discover whether she had been reckless enough to get caught up in such a dark conspiracy.

It was Cara who sought her out, however, as the following day was fading into dusk. She came hesitantly up the staircase and knocked softly at Minna's door. Minna was resting on her couch and putting a few stitches into the little white smock she was making for her child. When Cara entered, she immediately sat up and put her work aside at the sight of her expression. Cara's eyes were bleared and heavy-lidded in her white face, and tight lines had appeared round her mouth.

Closing the door securely, she said in a strained voice, 'Can anyone hear us up here?'

'No, if we speak softly. What brings you out at this hour, Cara?'

Cara rubbed her face, visibly close to complete exhaustion. 'I do not know where to begin . . . I am so tired. Minna, there have been—there have been rumours, new rumours in the Citadel in the past few days. Have you heard them?'

Minna drew a sharp breath. 'I have heard them. Oh Cara, how have you become concerned with such an affair?'

Cara closed her eyes and spoke slowly, almost as if she were in a trance, as if she had recited the same words many times before. 'The Citadel and the Circle are based on corruption, built on profound evil. Anno warned me before he went away, and I refused to listen. I discovered, too late, that he had told me the truth.'

'Evil? What kind of evil?' Minna was bewildered. The fate of the Children of Aesha showed that the Citadel could be harsh, and she had found herself that the Circle were sometimes cruelly indifferent to one person's hopes and wishes, but Cara seemed to be speaking of deeper matters.

'Have you never questioned where the old, the crippled, the sickly people are?' Cara's voice grew more passionate. 'They are taken to the infirmary in secret and their bodies destroyed. The Citadel has no place for imperfection. Only the healthy and strong are allowed to survive—and any who persistently fight the laws that govern our lives vanish without trace. The lucky ones escape to become the rebels out on the plains.'

'Stop!' Minna could not grasp what Cara was saying. 'What proof do you have?'

'I saw an old woman dragged from her home to the infirmary. She had lived too long and grown too feeble and lost her right to life. It was then that I chose to believe what Anno told me, and he told me what the rebels had told him. And now I have learned more from others. Much of it is scarcely more than rumour, unanswered questions, unexplained happenings, but put together in the light of understanding, it is proof enough.'

Minna stared speechlessly at the tiny smock in her lap. She was afraid of what Cara would say next.

'Minna, you must listen to me. I have good reason not to trust the Circle, and I believe they will harm Anno's people if they can. They would never let anyone walk away freely from the Citadel. I—I have resolved to stage an uprising. It will break out at the Games and create enough confusion to allow as many as possible to flee to the encampment.' Cara leaned closer to Minna, breathing quickly. 'I decided to risk everything and see if I could find other citizens to assist me. I have collected a handful but I do not know how trustworthy they are. Some I won over with bribes. Minna, I need you to help me too.'

Minna forced her words from a dry throat. 'How could I help you with my birthing-time so near?'

'I can confide in you to ease my own heart and ask your advice. The others look to me for guidance, and I do not always know what to say.'

'Who are these people?'

'One was passed over when the Circle was chosen and has nursed his bitterness ever since. Others are restless, bored citizens who welcome intrigue and excitement, no matter what the risk. But Minna, you can surely play some part. If you are in the infirmary with your child, you can be the centre of the plot to liberate the people held there, people like Gethin.'

At the mention of Gethin's name, Minna hung her head, filled with guilt. She was the cause of his downfall and had been unable to help him since, knowing only that he was held in a secure infirmary cell. Seeing Cara's desperate gaze upon her, she marvelled that her sister should feel so much need of her. At last she nodded reluctantly. 'I will help you, Cara, although I have none of your strength and courage.'

Cara's eyes shone, and some of the lines of tension round her mouth were smoothed away. 'We are meeting together just before the Games, when I will explain our final plans. We are spreading rumours to sow doubt and distrust so that when the uprising begins the citizens will not be taken completely by surprise, and some will be ready to flee with us. Oh Minna, my heart is lighter already!'

She stayed a while longer, turning the talk to other matters—Minna's child, the Games, gossip about the scholastic feuds in the Bibliotheca—as if she had forgotten her own belief that the world of the Citadel concealed an underlying horror. Although Minna answered lightly, she was inwardly turning over what Cara had revealed. Despite her sister's vehemence, she still could not fully believe what she had heard and resolved to question Arron closely. The Children knew of everything that took place within the city walls, and she was certain that they would never lie to her or invent tales to win her favour. Sadly, she admitted to herself that her trust in Cara's word was slight.

Not long after Cara had left, pledging to return soon, Arron's familiar tap came on the skylight. Minna's heart sank at the prospect of returning yet again to the packed, stuffy hut, but she smiled at Arron and allowed herself to be led away, even though the safe cloak of darkness had only just fallen over the streets. They took a different route from their usual way, to a tunnel entrance lying on the very outskirts of the quarter where the Children were housed, near the workshops where many of them slaved day after day fashioning delicate rings and necklets, spinning cloth, carving tracery to adorn a handsome chair. As Minna clambered into the shaft, she felt a surge of panic at entering the blind, constricted place once again. Clenching her teeth, she forced herself to follow Arron although her legs shook on the ladder and her stomach lurched with nausea.

She stumbled along the damp passage, straining to

keep her foothold in the uncertain torch light. Several times she had to rest and catch her breath while Arron and the nervous little tunnel-keeper hovered about her. But they came at last to the gathering-place, and Minna forced her tired body through the expectant crowd and sank onto the rag-heap set aside for her. The Children settled themselves on the floor and waited for her to start speaking. She felt blank inside, as if she had lost her store of tales and memories. Casting about for a beginning, she remembered Cara's tired voice describing her plot, and realised that perhaps she could share it with the crowd. As she dwelt on it, she saw with growing excitement that it could be the key for which she had been searching—the key to their freedom. At least it was something true, not merely a homespun legend.

'I have good news,' she began, while Arron busily took her place beside her and started translating into the Children's own sibilant tongue. 'You will know that the rulers of the Citadel are holding a festival of games and celebration five days from now. On that day, it may be that you will walk free from this place.' She hesitated, unsure how to explain Cara's plans. 'Some—some of the citizens are unhappy with their life here and want to leave. They will make an uprising at the Games, a—a disturbance so that whoever wishes it can join the stranger host. If the Children are ready, they too can seize that moment and flee. I know little more than this, but perhaps the time is drawing near when you will be liberated.' A murmur of anticipation ran through the crowd, and Arron turned to Minna in delight.

'We watch and wait, trusting you, our Talemaker!' she cried.

'But there is something more,' Minna said

nervously. 'Something I must know. I have heard—I have been told that the people of the Citadel do not allow the old or the sick, or any lawbreakers to live.' Arron made a soft noise in her throat as if to interrupt, but Minna was determined to finish. 'And I have heard that any rebels have to flee into exile on the plains to save themselves from imprisonment and worse.' She held out her hands to the crowded room. 'Do you know any of this?'

Every face was still, and they were all so quiet that she could hear the tiny sputtering of the tallow lamp. Then the whispering began and the troubled movement of slender hands, covering mouths and gesturing distractedly in the air.

'What are they saying?' Minna begged Arron. 'You must tell me what they are saying!'

Arron's brow was furrowed with anxiety. 'Why do you speak of such things? Why do you ask us? You know we do not watch men's work. They do not touch our world.'

'But I am not only Talemaker—I am concerned with my own kind. Please, Arron!' Distraught, Arron squeaked to herself in her own tongue and spoke sharply to the crowd who subsided into silence.

'Know,' she said to Minna, her voice thin with disapproval, 'that the Children of Aesha see everything passing in the Citadel. Some of us serve in the infirmary. Men hide nothing from us because they do not believe we truly see and understand.'

'What do you see?' Minna whispered.

'Death of many people,' said Arron with cold detachment. 'You ask us, Talemaker, and we must tell. From the streets and the fields come the feeble, the old men and women. They go to a chamber and drink from a cup. Their bodies grow stiff and cold.

263

Then we take them to the room of the great fire and they become smoke and soft, soft ashes, blowing out into the bay when the wind comes.'

'What if they do not want to drink?' Minna felt as if a band of steel was tightening round her head.

Arron's face was impassive. 'The physicians come and they drink, in the end. And the little children, the babies born crooked or weak, they go to the chamber and their bodies come out stiff and cold. I see it. It is always so.'

'But my true partner, Gethin, he is still living, locked up there?' Minna burst out hysterically.

'Sometimes they come out from the infirmary when they forget their rebel ways. They have new names. They go quietly and work far out in the fields till they die—only a short time. Many do not come out because they cannot change. They go to the little chamber and drink the cup. But your friend is safe, Talemaker. We watch him for you. Talemaker, are you sick?'

For Minna was doubled over, clasping her temples and engulfed in a stormy flood of tears. She tried to speak and choked on the words.

'Dead! They are dead, worthless!' she sobbed at last.

'He is not dead, Talemaker. Your friend lives.' Arron tried vainly to console her.

'Not Gethin. Oh, I did not believe her—but it is worse, far worse than I thought. It is all blackness, all evil.'

'Speak to us, Talemaker, tell us of the Master and the naigas. Make our hearts bright. Do not be troubled about men,' pleaded Arron but Minna was past understanding.

Shaking her head, rocking back and forth on her

264

stool, she wept inconsolably. 'It is too late. The tales are dead, they are all dead. It is finished. The blackness swallows it all. I can say no more.'

Chapter Five

She was staggering, falling, limping on again, feeling a warm trickle of blood down one leg from her torn knee. She still had to cross the Quadrangle before she came to the shelter of the Academy and above the blurring panic, she clung to the single hope that she would not be caught by a passing Watch patrol. Thick clouds had rolled in from the hills to shroud the sky and the night was impenetrable black. Here and there a shutter banged or a doorbolt was slammed home, but no one else was walking out. Minna was alone. The little people had watched in astonishment as she ran from them, without waiting for Arron to escort her. She could not have explained her extreme anguish to them even if she had entirely understood it herself—she was lost in a nightmare maelstrom, falling faster and faster into a pit of horror. Like the madman she had pitied the night before, she wanted to throw herself on the unyielding flagstones and scream. And after that she would die.

The darkness was kind to her, though, and she was able to pick her way unseen through the tangled alleys of the Children's quarter and across the Citadel. In a last, agonising effort, she ran across the

Quadrangle to the looming bulk of the Academy. Round a corner stood a small door which was left unbolted until midnight for any tutors returning late to their chambers after studying in the Bibliotheca. Pushing it open as quietly as she could and groping her way in the unlit passage, she found the main flight of stairs without rousing the doorkeeper. Along the corridors, up further staircases and finally clutching the worn balustrade of winding stairs, Minna came back safely to her chamber. She forced herself to close the door securely before collapsing onto the couch, unable to swallow the lump of grief rising in her throat. The muffled sound of her weeping crept out of the room and strayed into the lower passageways, but there was nobody to hear.

Eventually her crying ceased. She lay quite still, listening to the wind moaning through the hinge of the skylight. Looking up, she could see three clustered stars, brilliant in a gap between the clouds. She had deceived herself with her own tale. The stars blazed in an empty universe—they were not radiant crowns for some great being, but simply pinpricks of cold light. She began talking aloud to herself, and the sound gave her some slight comfort in the indifferent night.

'Worthless, empty tales,' she muttered. She thought of the Children and their narrow, silvery faces. Had she ever thought them beautiful? No, they were as pitiless as the humans they despise. 'I have no shield left,' she murmured. 'Nothing to shield me against the cruelty and the violence.'

She thought of Cara who planned to fight for freedom—but even in her uprising innocent people would suffer and die. But perhaps it was a privilege of the innocent to die and so escape from a cruel world while she lived to see her dreams mocked and shattered in pieces. Her tales were worthless, idle dreams; and beyond them, in the everyday world where the Citadel lay, was an empty universe. No gods, no lies, nothing but the unbearable knowledge that the old and the weak and the feeble would always be pushed aside. They would die in dust and ashes while the rest of humankind pressed forward with their so-called glorious deeds, leaving the slaughtered bodies in heaps behind them.

'And for me,' she said aloud, 'there is nothing . . . nothing. I cannot fight like Cara. I can do nothing except hide the true horror beneath a handful of day-dreams.'

Again she began to weep, and this time her tears were for Gethin, for old Holly, for the madman, for every child and every man and woman who had clutched the deadly cup of the infirmary chamber, choking on the sour dregs as their life drained out of them. Minna's torment grew until she felt crushed by the weight of it—yet her body was exhausted, and after a while her breathing became calmer and the tortured expression on her face faded. She slept.

As she slept, she dreamed: dreamed that she was lost among the wheeling patterns of stars that filled the night sky—but even as fear gripped her, she found that she was being carried along faster than sound or thought, on a path through vast spheres of fire, luminous clouds of gas, showers of flaming rocks. About her were the stately movements of whole galaxies, stars bursting into new life and withering away into solid blackness as if she were passing through time as well as space.

'Look back.' A voice spoke, and she knew there was someone beside her, although she could not see who.

Not daring to disobey, she glanced over her shoulder. Behind her stretched the unfathomable reaches of space, trails of light shimmering across the stillness of the original void.

'See Osiris,' the voice commanded, and Minna looked, and found she could see a large, pale globe, spinning on its axis round the white-heat of the star she knew as Sol.

Her own voice was tiny in the emptiness. 'They are lost, lost on that strange new world.'

'They have strayed far from their first home,' said the one beside her. 'Come.'

Then she was standing on a mountain ridge that towered above a huge, barren plain. The air was dry and sulphurous, and not a single green or living thing grew in all that wasteland. Overhead seethed a mass of storm-clouds, thunderous black and harsh yellow.

The voice spoke sorrowfully. 'See how Earth grieves. She has been left desolate.' And in the choking air Minna heard a ceaseless lamentation, sometimes as if many tongues were mourning together, sometimes a single wail, rising about her in a litany of grief and then dwindling into a remote thread of sound.

'There is much to weep for,' said the voice. 'The heart of humankind does not change. Come.'

She saw beneath her another plain, a great battlefield—many battlefields. Men's blood ran red on the trampled soil, wave upon wave of grim young faces pressing forward to be beaten down into trampled bodies. Mighty cities ringed the horizon, a thousand times stronger than the Citadel, but burning, crumbling, laid waste, each one rearing up and then falling on the ruins of its predecessor. The smoke of blazing forests hung about her in a reeking pall, and hooded carrion birds glided and circled through the murk, swooping down to fatten themselves on their prey. She saw numberless hosts marching out against one another, weighed down with deadly weapons. Then through the battlestorm three horses came galloping, galloping on the wind, one white, one fiery red and the third black, and their riders spurred them on with fierce cries. When the hosts saw them, they shouted, and the clash of their weapons was like the breaking of a storm. But behind the three came a moon-pale horse, and when the people saw its dark rider, they screamed and threw themselves down, hiding their faces.

In the middle of the confusion, Minna saw what looked like two stars rising above the scarred plain. Something within her made her cry out, and at her cry a sudden, absolute silence fell. A dying wind hissed over the bare rock at her feet, and she saw the two stars, one after the other, soar higher and higher into the twilight sky until they vanished.

'Orion and Sirius, the Hunter and the faithful Hound, last of the great ships to leave Earth, taking the remnant of humankind to a new home,' said the voice. 'They fled fear and death, but fear and death went with them.'

Then Minna was alone, wearily dragging herself along a dusty path that wound between harsh, stony hills, like the hills she gazed at in childhood when she sat safe on the threshold of Holly's hut, dreaming as the sun set over the desert. Her limbs were growing weaker, but she knew she must force herself to carry on until she reached the muffled figure striding far ahead of her on the same path. Even as she struggled to catch up, the weight of the child in her body pulled her back so that she sank down on the cold ground.

With a final flicker of strength, she willed the figure to wait, to turn and come to her, to save her from the wild white dogs who were gathering on the slopes above her, licking their jaws and slavering, watching for the moment when she stopped moving. Just as the world turned to night, she thought she felt strong arms about her, lifting her up.

She was in darkness; warm, gentle darkness so complete that she could not see her hand before her face. She did not know whether she was standing or lying down or simply floating, but her body was bathed in content. There was no fear in the darkness, no time passing. Gradually she began to sense a presence about her, the same presence she had encountered earlier. Yet now it was closer, surrounding and enfolding her, holding her secure. After a while—she did not know how long—the desire grew within her to know what this presence was.

'Who are you?' she whispered, and almost immediately the answer came, although whether a voice spoke aloud or whether the thought came into her own head, she could not tell.

'The one who has known you from the beginning.'

She lay drowsing in the stillness again, until another question formed itself. 'Where am I?'

The voice spoke tenderly. 'Safe in my keeping.'

'And you—where are you?'

'You will find me at the end of your seeking.'

The loving voice and soothing touch of the presence caressed Minna, but the darkness was starting to pale. Her body lost its weightlessness and her eyes screwed up tight against the light. Even as she knew she was waking, she fought to cling to the dream, but even as she fought, she opened her eyes and saw the bare chamber in the cheerless dawn. Her face was stiff with dried tears and the child within her stirred and thrashed its limbs until she clenched her fists and cried out for it to stop.

Chapter Six

The memory of the dream and the mysterious presence stayed with Minna in the following days. She remained secluded in her chamber, seeing no sign either of Cara or of Arron, and spending many hours withdrawn in thought. She still trembled when she remembered the grim truths she had learned about the Citadel, yet at the same time she felt, inexplicably, a wayward spark of hope. She did not know what it was she hoped for, nor how the hope had been kindled, but it warmed her heart a little as she lay wrapped in silence for hour after hour, gazing up at the square of pale blue sky framed by the window.

Cara, meanwhile, was feverishly busy, as she had been ever since her meeting with Minna. Outwardly, she was a model of diligence, arriving early at the Bibliotheca and working her allotted hours while many of the other scholars wandered from desk to desk chattering to one another, distracted by the news of the Games and the troubling rumours abroad in the Citadel. She saw nothing of Tav, who spent all his waking hours in session with the Circle and had taken to sleeping in his old chamber at the Circle tower. Cara was grateful to be left alone, consumed as she was with the shaping of her plot and terrified in case it was betrayed by a careless slip on her part or by her fellow conspirators.

Some of them met for a noon gathering, two days after Cara had brought Minna into the plot. They came one by one to a cramped chamber opening off an isolated staircase in the Bibliotheca, each giving a signal of two rapid and three slow knocks. The door was kept bolted, and they spoke in whispers, huddling together like excited children playing a secret game. Each brought along food and drink, and they spread cloaks on the floor, sharing out mutton, ripe cheese and handfuls of flaums, stifling their laughter and mouthing jests to one another across the room. Cara sat apart, slowly crumbling a hunk of dry bread between her fingers and surveying in turn the curious assortment of citizens she had found to help her—or would they prove a hindrance in the end? The question tormented her every night as she tossed restlessly on her couch.

Her gaze fell on Halin, a stooping, morose man who had spent many years toiling in the white towers where the administration of the Citadel was carried out, jealously nursing a grudge from his boyhood when he had been unjustly passed over in one of the first Circle selections. Beside him sat Jassa, a junior warden in the infirmary who had left her country family to become a citizen. She had hated the Chief Physician ever since he allowed her grandmother to die, decreeing that if the old woman was foolish enough to drink contaminated water, she had brought her sickness upon herself and, furthermore, his precious remedies were only for younger, stronger sufferers. It was Jassa who confirmed some of the tales Cara had heard about the secret happenings in the infirmary.

Hunched on the floor next to Jassa was Ginia, a

274

respected scholar who had been the first of Cara's fellow-conspirators and had helped to seek out the others. Cara had overheard the sly comments of other scholars about the stout red-haired woman who, they said, refused all offers of partnership and was allowed by the Circle to have her way because they valued her work so highly. It was also said that she had no close companions, only a sharp word for everybody. She spent her days in a shuttered room in the Bibliotheca, carelessly dressed in a stained gown and examining the native plants found in the neighbourhood of the Citadel.

On the morning after the meeting with Anno's people in the Quadrangle, Cara encountered Ginia in an empty corridor and, suddenly reckless, looked her straight in the eye and asked whether she thought the Circle should let people go freely to join the host.

Ginia had looked straight back at her, remarking in her blunt way, 'You consider yourself something of a rebel, perhaps, Cara? But I am not afraid to say that I think the present Circle is worthless and could make no right decision. Now I expect you will turn good citizen and report what I have said to the Watch, but they cannot touch me!' Cara warmed to her forthright manner and by the time twilight fell that day, Ginia had been taken into her confidence.

Lounging next to Ginia was Shen, fifteen years old and the youngest of the rebels. He was in his final, graduating year at the Academy and craved change, captivated by the idea of Anno's Free People and longing more than anything else to be able to ride under an open sky from dawn to dusk. Perched on his shoulder was one of the furry baby-faced creatures that lived among the trees lining the High Road. The Academy pupils called them simmies and were forever trying to

275

catch and tame them as pets. Shen had kept his simmie since the previous summer, giving it the name Tok. He stroked its silky white fur with one hand as he ate.

In a few minutes Cara called them to attention. They did not have long for their gathering and there were urgent matters to discuss. Two or three others besides Minna were absent, and Cara was secretly worried that interest in the plot might be flagging. She asked for word of how the rumours were being received in the Citadel.

Jassa shrugged. 'The people talk all day long of the host and the Games.'

'But are they being stirred up? Do they question the wisdom of the Circle? Do they talk of the need for justice?' asked Cara urgently.

Halin shrugged. 'The third tower of administration is rapidly filling with intrigue and dispute. Some are starting to look sharply at any Circle demand.'

'But this is good!' broke in Ginia eagerly. 'For too long the people have lived without questioning their blind trust in the Circle and in the whole government of the Citadel. It is very good! Take heart, Cara!'

'Has mention of the uprising been made to anyone else? Have you found others who might prove trustworthy?' Cara demanded.

'I have mentioned it further in the infirmary,' said Jassa. 'I think I know of ears that will turn to me.' The others agreed that their veiled hints were often favourably received.

'And now,' Cara went on, 'I have important news for you all.' She looked round at the circle of expectant faces. 'Early this morning, Owin set out for the host encampment with a message warning them of our plans.' Every eye was round with astonishment. Owin was the newest member of the conspiracy, a highly regarded young Watch officer.

'Why Owin?' Shen felt vaguely snubbed at not being chosen himself.

'Because he has the woodcraft to dodge the guards on the hill-tops,' Cara answered shortly. 'He has taken a day's leave to visit his family colony in the fields, but instead he will make his way to Anno and tell him that some citizens will fight for him and that he must be ready for the shout of uprising at the Games.'

'Why does he not speak more clearly to the host leaders?' asked Halin.

'Because we may have to change the detail of our plot and we could not give our allies a message which might prove false when the day comes.' Cara did not add that she was still reluctant to reveal herself to Anno, afraid that he would despise her schemes and have nothing to do with her. The gathering broke up shortly afterwards when an impatient hand tried the door of the chamber. The conspirators slipped away, exchanging significant glances and winks, full of their own importance. Cara waited until the room was empty and checked that all traces of their meeting had been removed. She brushed some crumbs into a corner and scuffled the dust until the footprints were obscured. Pushing aside, for the moment, her fears about the soundness of her plans, she straightened her gown and set off back to her desk for the afternoon's work.

That same noontide, in a small colony amid the cotton fields of the North-west Sector, Watch officer and would-be rebel Owin was seated on a stool in his widowed mother's hut, watching her stirring a pot over the smoky fire, preparing some cuny broth for him. He had decided to call and see her on his way to the hills, giving himself time to gather enough courage for venturing among the stranger host. She came running to embrace him as he trudged up the path, exclaiming at how strong, how well, how noble he looked even though he was not wearing his Watch uniform. As the eldest of her six children and her only son, he was her favourite, not least because of the way he had excelled at the Academy and gained a posting in the Watch, bestowing on her a wellspring of happiness.

Stopping her work, she came to him, putting out a timid hand to stroke his hair. 'You are quiet, lad,' she said. 'Surely nothing is wrong?'

He shrugged away her caress. 'Nothing, nothing. We are being sent on more patrols than ever. I am tired.'

She smiled fondly at him. 'You're a good lad. I am proud of you. The Citadel needs all its brave men to defend us against the terrible savages on the plains. I've heard they snatch children off the field paths and carry them away to their camp and eat them.'

Owin's mouth went dry. 'But—but surely those are just gossiping tales?'

His mother shook her head knowingly. 'They are monsters, lawless barbarians, not true humankind. I've heard that when the mountain girls first came to the Citadel, they had to be chained and would only eat raw meat, tearing it up with their fingers and teeth.'

Owin knew this could not be true, but even so it stirred up a vague, unreasoning fear of Cara who, after all, had burst into the Citadel with her three companions from the unknowable outside. When he first heard of her bold plot, he decided he would be safer joining the rebels so that if the Citadel fell to them, he would at least save his own skin. Yet the more he thought about the host, the more anxious he became. He would have no defence against them, no respect

278

accorded to him because of his position and insignia. Then his mother thrust a brimming bowl of broth into his hands, and settled herself down to watch him eat.

An hour or so later, he was painfully inching his way through needle-sharp gerst bushes towards a hill summit which would give him a sheltered view of the encampment on the plains. A cold wind rustled in the undergrowth, hiding any noise he made, and he was able to reach the top of the slope quickly. He lay there panting, congratulating himself on his woodcraft and beginning to feel that perhaps he could face any number of stranger hosts. When he was rested, he cautiously raised his head so that he could peer over at the land spread out below. Instead, he looked straight into the wide eyes of a half-naked barbarian man.

Owin was on his feet with a bound, heedless of whether any Citadel guards were about. The barbarian was clutching an unsheathed knife and as Owin yelled in surprise, the man lunged at him with the jagged nails of one hand, as if he were trying to tear his face. Racing back down the slope, not daring to look behind him, Owin stumbled and rolled over in the lacerating bushes. He recovered his senses just before he crashed into the line of Citadel guards who were already hurrying about, trying to discover the cause of the disturbance. Crawling into the middle of a dense thicket, heedless of his torn garments and bleeding hands, he vomited.

When he had recovered, he huddled up in his battered jacket, shivering and vowing to have no more to do with Cara or the conspiracy. But he was afraid of what she would say when she heard that his mission had failed. She had promised him a handsome reward of three flasks of wine and a steel blade, and he felt he deserved some recompense for the dangers he had endured. Wiping his mouth on his sleeve, he decided that he would lie. He would tell Cara that Anno welcomed the message, and hope that she had expected nothing more. Then he would take his reward and leave the rebel band—not to betray them, of course, for that might lead to his connection being discovered, but simply to spare himself any further trials.

And Cara believed his falsehood, even though he told it badly, blushing and shuffling his feet. She hardly acknowledged his muttered reasons for leaving the conspiracy, and absently handed over the wine and the blade and saw him to the door of her chamber. Her mind was wholly preoccupied with resolving the final intricacies of the uprising, too absorbed now to care about the loss of one rebel.

On the night before the Games, the conspirators met for the last time, in Minna's chamber. Nine of them were present and most spoke of secret support from others who dared not take part in the actual plotting. Nobody jested now, and every face was grim. From time to time the darkness outside was broken by glittering bursts of coloured light and a series of thunderclaps while an unseen crowd whooped and shrieked approval. The Circle had organised a firecracker display in the Quadrangle to stir up the citizens in anticipation of the festival day to come, but none of the conspirators took any notice, even when a shower of green stars broke right over the roof of the Academy. They were listening to Cara describing what would happen on the morrow.

Her face was tense with anxiety as she spoke. 'The signal will be the handing of the victor's sash to the winner of the wrestling trials. Then we must cry together "Cleanse the Circle, share the privileges, let the people go free." You will be standing with some of those who have pledged support, and they must take up the cry.

Watch for the host. Those liberating the infirmary—make your way there as fast as you can. I will come with you. We must release as many prisoners as possible and, above all, our companion Gethin. Those of you attacking the Watch and the Circle—use violence only if you must, but make sure the people are free to follow the host. We must create as much confusion as we can.' She turned to Minna, who was curled up on a corner of the couch, cradling her tired body.

'Minna, I do not know what part you can play, but even if you are too weak to leave your couch, we will make sure you escape with us. Perhaps you will be able to come down to the shoals just before we strike and urge those around you to join with us.' Minna nodded, a tiny smile flickering at the corner of her mouth.

'And now I speak to all of us,' Cara looked in turn at each conspirator. 'We know that the uprising could fail. Some of us may not survive till nightfall tomorrow. If it looks to be failing, then flee with any who will go with you—but let us at least try to throw open the infirmary gates and cleanse that place before we leave the Citadel behind us.'

Later that night Minna lay awake remembering Cara's brave words and reassurances. Despite the absurd hope still flickering in her heart, she felt sure that many lives would be lost in the next few days, including her own. The thought of dying did not frighten her, but she grieved for her unborn child, so restless inside her. She was also waiting for the light tap which she knew would come on the window. Since she had fled weeping from the little people, she had not returned to their meeting place, but that morning she had sent a message summoning Arron for what would probably be her final dealing with the Children of Aesha.

At last the knock came and Arron's slender body slipped into the chamber. She approached the couch on trembling limbs, covering her face with her hands, afraid to look at Minna.

'Arron,' said Minna patiently. 'Arron, I am not angry with your people. Look at me.' Arron hesitantly withdrew her hands, but her eyes were still downcast.

'Look at me,' Minna repeated. 'All will be well. I am going to tell you how your people can walk free tomorrow.' Arron raised her head.

'Talemaker?' she said timidly.

'I am not angry, but my concerns must be with my own kind as well as you and your kin,' Minna said. 'Listen. My child is coming soon, maybe in the morning, and I cannot promise to lead you out myself—but I shall tell you how you will know the right time to leave. Your people must be gathered and ready then.' And she repeated to Arron as much of Cara's plot as she could recall. 'If I can, I will come to you again,' she ended.

Arron's slanting eyes shone. 'We watch and wait for you always, Talemaker. You never desert us.'

'But do not wait for me in the Citadel. Your people must walk free tomorrow,' urged Minna.

'We understand, Talemaker. You make us wise. We watch for you.' Arron held out her palms and the golden tattoos gleamed faintly. Minna beckoned her closer, reached out to hold the narrow hand and kissed her gently on the forehead. Then Arron was gone, nimbly clambering back through the skylight. They had both heard shuffling feet on the staircase and then a heavy knock on the door.

'Who is it?' Minna called.

'The infirmary. Unbolt your chamber.' Three unsmiling wardens entered, together with the

282

Academy doorkeeper.

Minna shrank back onto the couch. 'Why have you come?'

'Make haste and pack your belongings. You are to come to the infirmary tonight for the birthing of your child. You have kept yourself in secret up here for too long already.'

Chapter Seven

The sun had not yet risen on the morning of the
Games when the tolling of the brass festival bell roused
the Citadel people. In barely an hour the bell would
ring again, summoning them to assemble in the
Quadrangle and march out to the shoals, accompanied
by the music of drums and bass-flutes. Patrols of Watch
men were already marching up and down the field
paths, appointing overseers to take charge of groups of
twenty labourers, with orders to lead them to the bay as
soon as a horn blast gave the signal. Up in their meeting chamber, the twenty members of the Circle clasped
hands with one another, agreed on their plan of cam-
paign and boldly anticipating the complete victory that
they were going to win over the stranger host, defeat-
ing with the same stroke any rebel factions lurking
within the Citadel walls.

Cara had not slept at all, and when the bell rang, she
was sitting by her window, half-dressed and staring out
at the streets and rooftops which looked flat and drab,
drained of colour by the grey sky. Her spirits were low.
The tower doorkeeper had brought a message from
the infirmary with Cara's morning dish of bread and
cold nappes, saying that Minna had been taken into the

charge of the physicians and was even now beginning the weary struggle of birthing her child. In the dull morning light, Cara's schemes appeared hollow and worthless, and she was beginning to admit to herself that she was, in truth, very much afraid.

It was peaceful among the tents of the host encampment, in stark contrast to the bustle of the Citadel. A young girl in a tattered blue gown was milking a goat and singing softly to her baby daughter who lay beside her, snugly wrapped in a shawl. Anno sat in the entrance of Medwin's tent, talking earnestly to the men and women gathered round him. A pot of roasted beans, covertly harvested from the Citadel fodder fields, stood in the middle and the listeners took a handful from time to time, spitting the tough skins into the trampled grass.

'We must go in peace outwardly,' Anno was saying, 'but keep a grip on your blades and be ready to run if I give the order. We cannot trust the smooth words of the Circle.'

From a neighbouring tent emerged the dazed face of a young labourer who had escaped over the hills to join the encampment during the previous night. He gazed about in astonishment and growing wonder at the goats, the other shelters and the group sitting with Anno. They did not look like the savage barbarians described in the lurid tales of the field huts. A woman with yellow hair and a kind face came over and offered him a cup of fermented milk which he gulped down gratefully. She sat down beside him, told him her name was Hanni and began asking who he was and where he had come from.

'Do you know anything of two girls, Cara and Minna? They live in the Citadel,' she added, a wistful expression replacing her smile.

The labourer wiped the last drops of milk from his lips. 'The mountain girls? I have never seen them. They say one of them is mad.'

'No matter.' Hanni turned away, her eyes brimming with tears.

Out on the shoals work had been going on all night, levelling a smooth track of sand, marking out a course with rows of black stones, preparing the long line of trestles for the noon banquet. The Circle called for contests of running, leaping, throwing, wrestling and acrobatics, when the most agile and lithe among the citizens and field people would try to outdo one another in tumbling and somersaults. Already the first athletes were congregating in their own enclosure, limbering up and gradually shedding layers of garments as their bodies warmed and grew supple. Nearby, a band of musicians were turning their fiddles and breathing on their horns to take the chill off the ancient metal.

At last the festival bell rang for the second time, and the hordes began streaming out of the Citadel gates, the shuffle of their feet mingling with the marching rhythmn played by the musicians who strode alongside them. Towards the front of the procession was a company of giggling children dressed alike in green and yellow. They would entertain the people with their singing before the contests began. The air hummed with anticipation as companies of labourers and overseers joined the citizens, coarse sage green, russet brown and black clothes mingling with fine scarlet, emerald and sapphire. The country-dwellers would not sit down to the banquet with the people of the Citadel, but would have their own fare handed out in baskets by a small army of Scurriers.

In a bare cell at the end of an infirmary corridor, Minna was groaning in a daze of pain. The linen coverlet beneath her was crumpled and damp with sweat, and the warden tending her had unshuttered the window to let in some daylight and clean air. Minna opened her eyes to see a sliver of sunless sky and feel a faint breath of wind on her face. The warden wiped her forehead with a rag and then gave her a cup of water which had a gritty white powder stirred into it.

Easing herself down onto a stool, she regarded Minna with a practised eye, remarking, 'You need not worry about the child's safety, no matter how long the birthing takes. His father's from strong stock, and I've never known of a Circle child who was not born healthy!'

A thought rose to the surface of Minna's clouded mind and she spoke it without thinking. 'Gethin—my former companion—how does it go with him?'

'Gethin?' The warden sounded puzzled that she should ask. 'He is kept here still, but he is ailing. A lingering sickness in the blood, I think, and each day he grows weaker. The Chief Physician says it's a mercy he sired no children. We cannot have any blood taints among our people.'

Minna turned her face to the wall and did not reply.

On the curving sands of the bay, a fanfare of horns burst into the troubled air like hot explosions of colour and the noisy hordes of onlookers quietened. The Circle members were approaching along the broad shore path from the Citadel, crossing the tide-line of smooth pebbles and coming in solemn procession through the crowds. A line of benches awaited them beside the victors' dais in the centre of the oval track. Cara walked with the retinue of partners, friends and

287

favoured relatives who followed behind, acknowledging the salutes of the people on either side. The twenty Circle members were splendidly arrayed in shimmering rainbow colours and they held their heads proudly as they took their seats. They had planned the day as a celebration of their own greatness, and the knowledge shone in their eyes. There was no sign of the stranger host.

Tav rose and in a loud voice spoke greeting to the huge assembly. The proceedings would begin, he said, even though their guests had not the courtesy to arrive on time—but what more could be expected of barbarians? Uneasy laughter swept through the crowds. At a sign from Tav, the companies of Academy children were marched out by their tutors and ranged in a tidy crescent. Their young, breathless voices filled the air with a song about the ripening summer and the budding fruits of the new world. Then they joined hands in two circles, one inside the other, and started treading an old Earth dance. The woman seated on Cara's left remarked to her that simple people used to dance it long ago, believing it would bring a fine harvest. The children danced now to the plaintive melody of a single bass-flute and a drum-beat which they echoed with the thud of their feet on the sand.

Just as they were joining hands for the final round, a disturbance broke out at the back of the crowds, a confused murmuring and shuffling. People craned over the heads of those behind them to see what was happening. The Circle and their retinue exchanged rapid glances. Then, unexpectedly, a ragged cheer broke out among the spectators standing nearest the shore path. At the same time the disturbance grew until the cheering dissolved into angry shouts. As the dance tune faltered into silence, the crowds parted to let the stranger host through.

At their head walked Anno, as proud as any Circle man, with the rebel Tharm at his side. Cara's heart thudded painfully as she recognised many from the settlement with him—Hanni, carrying Sanni on her hip and clutching Jenna's hand, Medwin with his halting step, and even Amma, whom she had known long ago at Lesson Hall. With them were others she could not name but who were known to the citizens or field people. Many gasped in surprise at the sight of those who had fled to the host in the past few days and now dared to walk openly with them. Cara glanced over at Tav and saw him forcing a smile of welcome over his frown. Nervous Watch sentries shepherded the host into the area laid aside for them, adjoining the rest of the crowds but separated off by a hastily erected rope fence.

Tav's gaze was frosty above his false smile. 'We welcome you,' he said with faultless courtesy. 'I regret that you have come too late for the songs and dancing of the children of our Academy, but perhaps you are eager only for the contests themselves. Then let them begin!' The staring Academy children were hurried away by the tutors, and Izak took charge as Master of the Games, calling for the runners to make themselves ready and come to the track. Two dozen clean-limbed descendants of Orion stepped forward, twelve men and twelve women chosen from the fleetest of Citadel and country. Izak looked disdainfully towards the stranger rabble who seemed to be disputing as to who should go. At last they pushed forward five, among them Amma and a young man whom Cara was sure she knew from the settlement days. She cast about in her mind and at last recalled that he was a distant cousin of Gethin, and that his name was Randal.

Izak gave the call for the first race—the young women would run a single fast lap of the track. The crowds settled down comfortably on the sand, preparing to enjoy themselves and gossiping busily about every member of the host. Cara shifted her stool so that Anno could not see her, and watched Amma shyly take her place beside the other girls who all towered above her in their tight, short tunics. Cara found herself wishing furiously that the settlement girl might win. A horn blast signalled the start of the race and the four runners were off. Although Amma started well, her spindly legs were no match for her taller, better-fed rivals, and when they came round to the finish, she was trailing far behind. Even so, she was smiling as she passed the post and the crowds applauded her politely. The young men lined up immediately afterwards for the next race, but Cara watched Amma making her way back to the host enclosure and saw how they hugged and congratulated her, Anno with the rest. She suddenly felt a twinge of jealousy mingled with overwhelming loneliness and was tempted to run from her seat right then, forgetting the conspiracy, and defiantly reunite herself with her old friends in front of the whole Circle.

Her thoughts were interrupted by a surge of cheering. She turned to the track and saw to her amazement that the settlement boy, Randal, was neck and neck with a heavily built young citizen as they began the last stretch. The other two competitors laboured after them, their faces showing that they could hardly believe what they saw—the Citadel's honour threatened by one of the barbarians. Even some of the Circle retinue rose to their feet as the two runners neared the finish. Across the track, field men and scholars alike were cheering themselves hoarse. With a shock Cara realised that many were shouting for Randal, calling him simply 'the boy' because they did not know his name. In the last few yards, though, the Citadel runner managed to draw one pace ahead, and then the race was over. Randal had lost by a hand's breadth. He almost fell as he came to a halt, and Cara saw that his breath was coming in shuddering gasps. One of the other host runners helped him back to the enclosure, and as he passed by, the onlookers gazed at him wonderingly and whispered to one another behind their hands.

Under Izak's orders contest followed contest without a pause, and none of the other host athletes finished better than last—or once, second to last when a Citadel girl tripped and fell as she rounded the first bend in the track. The crowds were generous with their applause, however, and by the time of the last race, many were cheering the barbarians as loudly as their own side. A few half-hearted attempts were made to call Randal back, but he shook his head with a grin. Circle members presented sashes to the winners of each race as they stood high on the victory dais, glowing with arrogant health, the finest specimens of young humankind to be found on Osiris. When the calls came for the leaping and throwing contests, the stranger host could not always put forward a competitor, although two young men, newly escaped from the South-east Sector, put up a brave show in jumping the high rope and finally took third and fourth places out of the six contestants, to the delight of their former kin. Cara saw how Tav's face darkened whenever a shout of support went up for Anno's people. His aim of humiliating the host was not succeeding as easily as he had expected.

Back at the infirmary, muffled cries floated from behind a bolted door into the gloomy corridor. Inside, Minna was writhing and moaning, and the warden was sponging her face with an impatient hand.

She leaned over her, hissing in her ear, 'You're disgracing us, and yourself! There's no reason to scream. If you calm yourself, you'll feel nothing but a little discomfort. Hush now! Are you a country brat, to make such a fuss? A woman of the Citadel shouldn't behave so!'

As the pain ebbed away, Minna sank back onto the couch, trying not to sob with every breath she took and conscious above all of profound exhaustion, a dragging fatigue in every limb. Dazed by what she had endured in the past hours, her mind floated on a remote plane, detached from the cell, the infirmary, even the Citadel. She thought she was in the mountains again, journeying away from the settlement, gazing up at the steep slope that she had to climb, hoping Gethin would turn back and help her. Then her mind flickered, and she remembered a far-off winter morning when she was a very small child. She had woken long before daybreak, crying from a dream of tumbling helplessly over one of the high cliffs lining the settlement valley. Neither Cara nor Holly heard her crying, and she lay frightened and alone in the dark for many hours until the cocks began to crow.

She was brought back to the present as a shudder ran through her body. A fresh wave of pain was coming. She bit hard on her knuckles until she drew blood. In desperation her mind groped for some comfort, some consoling image or feeling. And then for the first time since her labour began, she remembered the presence—the warm, dark presence which had enfolded her at the end of her dream.

292

Without thinking, she called out to it silently, 'Help me! Help me, save me, now!' Then the black tide swallowed her and she drowned beneath the pounding waves.

At noon the contests halted and citizens, Circle members, field people and host began feasting together. Although the strangers sat at separate row of tables, they too received the rich Citadel fare by Tav's orders. Many of the citizens were too busy watching the barbarians eat to enjoy the banquet themselves, and to the disappointment of some, none of the outsiders called for their meat raw or thrust their faces into their dishes like hogs. From where she sat, Cara could see the eyes of the younger barbarians shining at the food offered to them, but they all behaved graciously, thanking the Scurrier servants, who were strangely agitated, dropping trays and colliding with one another. All round her, Cara heard curious voices discussing the guests.

'Not a healthy body between them . . . that poor young girl in filthy rags . . . they have at least some breeding . . . they should be rounded up and set to work with the Scurriers . . . look at that child, smacking its lips over a piece of pie . . . a shame there are no sashes for brave losers . . . '

Tav and Izak conferred together for most of the meal, leaving their food almost untouched, although Izak downed cup after cup of wine. At length Tav nodded to the First Captain of the Watch, and immediately the sentries started calling for silence up and down the tables and among the groups of field people.

When all was still, Tav cleared his throat. 'I hope the athletes have eaten lightly enough to continue their efforts when the banquet is over.' There was a polite ripple of amusement. 'The next contest is for the acrobats and tumblers who have leave to begin preparing themselves.'

Shortly afterwards, the revellers resumed their places round the track. A square of soft sand had been measured out in the centre, and seven acrobats stood there already, stretching limbs and flexing muscles. No contestant had yet come forward from the host, but then a cheer went up as Randal stripped off his outer tunic and hurried to join the others.

Each contestant had to perform a tumbling trick, and the rest had to match it before displaying their own skill. Any who failed to execute a trick was disqualified. After a few rounds of somersaults, forward and backward springs and cartwheels, only four contestants were left—two Citadel girls who made up for lesser strength with greater agility, a wiry young Watch officer, and Randal. One of the girls dropped out next after failing to land five backward somersaults in a straight line. Her companion injured her ankle in the following round and had to retire. Suddenly it was a straight fight between barbarian and citizen.

The spectators were frantic with excitement, dividing into factions and violently arguing the merits of the two contestants, while the young men rested briefly and drank some honey-water. Sol had emerged from behind the clouds, and the afternoon was growing hotter.

Randal flexed his back, bowed to his rival and jumped high in the air. He somersaulted forward twice before his feet hit the sand and then contrived to spring backwards and twist at the same time so that he landed facing the other way. Then, springing nimbly onto his hands and dangling his legs elegantly over his head, he ran two perfect circles in the sand. The

294

crowds cheered and yelled their approval. The Watch officer sighed and prepared to match the trick. Although he was stronger than Randal, his size had become a disadvantage, making him tire so that he was moving ponderously. He landed so heavily after the somersaults that the wind was knocked out of him, and as he threw himself into the spring, his hands seemed to miss the ground. All the onlookers were on their feet, unable to believe that the Citadel champion was beaten—but he lay in a groaning heap on the sand while Randal heartlessly spun round him in a string of victory rolls. The host athletes had forgotten their reserve and were cheering louder than their opponents.

Tav stood up to make an announcement, but the crowds went on clamouring until Izak ordered the musicians to sound the drums and horns as loudly as they could. Even then, the noise subsided only slowly and Tav was hard put to it to suppress his anger.

'I regret that the contest used more than its alloted span of the Games,' he said icily. 'We have no time to present the sash to the victor.' The people shouted with outrage at this, and order could not be restored until a Watch horn was sounded. Ignoring the interruption, Tav continued, 'The Circle decided at noon that the Games should finish sooner than was planned, so we will not hold a wrestling contest. Perhaps it will be fought on some other day. We thank our guests for coming to us.' He no longer bothered to conceal the contempt in his tone. 'Let the younger ones leave now, and if the host can restrain themselves, the Games will close with a word of commendation from a respected citizen.'

Cassie's father, Julan, took Tav's place and embarked on a rambling address while the companies of children marched away.

Numb with shock, Cara could only stare at her hands as they twisted in her lap. Her plans were foundering even before they were set in motion. She caught the anxious gazes of Halin and Ginia who had found places next to the Circle retinue. They were waiting for her to tell them what to do. She had to act before it was too late, before the moment was lost.

In the shadowy corners of the infirmary, small, darker shadows darted to and fro, congregating and dispersing on noiseless bare feet. Word had come to the Children of Aesha that Talemaker was suffering in the birthing of her child and they came to be near her, slipping in through hidden entrances known only to themselves. No sound came from the cell where Minna lay, and in the throbbing air every footfall was magnified. The wardens had unbarred many shutters to let a cooling draught into the stuffy passages, and the stiff hinges creaked faintly as a sea-breeze stirred them.

Then through the open windows floated unexpected sounds, brought from the shoals by the rising wind. Shouts—not the earlier shouts of admiration for a brave contestant, but shouts of fear and fury—and shrill screams, a swelling chorus of anger and confusion.

Cara's conspirators had struck, and the consequences far exceeded her fading hopes. The temper of the crowds had grown uncertain during the long day, and now it flamed into anarchy. Even the Watch was thrown into turmoil as order became disorder all about them. Tables were overturned, women and children trampled underfoot, weapons seized and passed from hand to hand. Nobody knew who was attacking whom and many were simply terrified and fought to escape, running back to the Citadel in fear for their lives. As Cara jumped up to give the rallying cry, she saw blank astonishment on the face of Anno and realised he knew nothing of her plans.

For an appalled moment she hesitated. Then battle frenzy overtook her. The other conspirators had done their work well, and on every side the chaos was mounting. She had no time for thought. Anno was fleeing with the rest of his people, fending off the blows and pinioning arms of the Watch sentries who were attempting to carry out the Circle's orders. Cara was still trying to see how many had managed to escape with him when Ginia pulled her over to the group making for the infirmary. The crisis had come, and it was too late to pull back. She put her head down and ran for the Citadel.

In the cell where Minna had laboured for so many hours, the Chief Physician and the warden were staring with distaste at the boy child who lay on the couch feebly moving his blood-stained limbs. Minna's eyes were closed in a drugged sleep—she did not know that the birthing was over. The Chief Physician and the warden exchanged glances.

'What's to be done?' murmured the warden.

The Chief Physician's mouth curled in disgust. 'A monstrous child. You ask me what should be done with a monstrous child?' He pointed at the baby's unnaturally swollen head, the misshapen body, the watery, sightless eyes. 'The girl must have some foul taint in her blood. Or worse, there was some trickery over the parenting. No Circle man could have fathered this child. Take it away before she wakes.'

The warden was used to obeying such orders. Picking up the baby at arm's length, she wrapped him in a strip of coarse black blanket, handling him none too

297

gently even though he was beginning to shudder with cold. As she opened the door of the cell, Minna's eyelids fluttered and she stirred, trying to sit up.

'The child—where is it? Is it safe?' she asked weakly.

But neither the warden nor the Chief Physician paid any attention because, as Minna spoke, they heard a tumult in the corridor—anxious voices and the approach of hurried feet. And echoing from a distance down the warren of passageways, came another, greater tumult. They heard a roar of voices and a storm of blows, hammering at the very gates of the infirmary.

Chapter Eight

As the warden and the Chief Physician stared at one another, a junior warden burst through the doorway, his eyes wide with alarm.

'There is madness—madness outside!' he cried. 'A mob with knives demanding entry. We cannot hold the gates against them much longer.'

Even as he spoke, wood splintered in the distance and the cries of the rebels turned to cheers. The Chief Physician clutched the younger man's shoulder with a trembling hand.

'Summon—summon the Watch,' he gasped. 'Tell them the barbarians are upon us.'

'Master,' said the junior warden desperately. 'it is not barbarians—at least, some barbarians, perhaps—but the mob is led by our own citizens!' Hurried footsteps sounded behind him in the corridor, and he was suddenly pushed aside by the stern woman who had once kept the four travellers in her charge. Panic distorted her normally impassive face, and her cheeks were smeared with blood.

The woman was hysterical, shouting incoherently and flailing her arms. Through the open doorway, the Chief Physician saw the flitting shadows of thronging

Scurriers, but now there seemed to be hundreds of them and their slanting eyes glowed at him in the half-light. He looked back at Minna, who was trying to pull herself into a sitting position, and an instinct told him that she and her sister could be at the root of the mob disturbance. Perhaps he could make use of her in some way to save himself.

Moving fast, he thrust the screaming woman out into the corridor so that she staggered into a cluster of Scurriers who were lingering just outside. As he pushed the other two after her, he ordered them to take the child and dispose of it, quickly. Before they could protest, he had slammed and bolted the door. Minna opened her mouth to cry out, but he crossed the room in a bound and struck her hard on the chin so that she fell back and lay motionless and silent, her hands limp on the tangled coverlet.

The Chief Physician leaned against the doorpost, trying to master his fear. In a few minutes he heard running feet in the corridor. They paused outside the cell and the latch was lifted gently. When the door did not open, the unseen person began to kick and wrestle with it, calling out for help. Soon others ran up and joined the struggle and the stout door yielded. Long cracks opened in the wood and the heavy bolts weakened. Then it gave way and a crowd of thirteen armed men and women, led by Cara, rushed through.

They stopped short when they saw who was inside. The Chief Physician was crouched in the corner, holding a knife to the throat of a fainting girl dressed only in a stained, soaking shift which was torn in several places. Cara had to look twice before she realised that the girl was Minna. The Chief Physician's shaking hands showed his terror but he clutched the knife tightly and Cara knew that he was also very dangerous, a snarling dog caught in a snare. She moved towards him slowly, handing her blade to Ginia who stood beside her.

'We will do you no harm as long as you do not resist us,' she said, trying to speak calmly.

The cornered man scowled. 'Why should I trust the word of a treacherous young girl? If you come any closer, you will see your sister die like a skewered hoch.' And he pressed the blade against Minna's skin until a thin ribbon of blood trickled down the greasy metal.

Cara swallowed hard. 'The Citadel is in chaos. If you leave peacefully now, you will still have safe passage. Soon it may be too dangerous to walk the streets.' The man stared at her blankly. 'We have come to release any held here against their will—above all, Gethin and my sister and her child.'

The Chief Physician staggered to his feet, leaving Minna slumped on the ground. 'Take her then,' he cried with a high, sobbing laugh. 'But Gethin—' his laugh changed to a scream, 'I signed the order for his execution this morning.' Cara's followers began to crowd closer.

'The child, Minna's baby, where is it?' asked Cara fiercely. The Chief Physician dropped his knife and cowered away from her. Saliva ran down his chin.

'Don't harm me!' he shrieked. 'I only obey orders. The child is dead by now. Don't touch me!' But they merely dragged him onto the couch and tied him up securely after removing the keys which hung at his waist. A tall young man, who had deserted the Watch for the rebels only an hour before, effortlessly swung Minna into his arms. Then the room was empty, leaving the Chief Physician babbling to himself and writhing to and fro until he fell from the couch onto the hard, cold floor.

When they were back in the corridor, Cara turned hopelessly to Jassa who had served in the infirmary for two years and knew every turn of the passageways. 'Should we bother searching further? You heard what the Chief Physician said.'

Jassa shook her head. 'He may have been lying. We must still search every cell, if only to free the other inmates. But your sister looks very weak. She should leave to join the host without delay. You must give us orders, Cara!'

Cara hardly dared glance at Minna who was lying barely conscious in the arms of the tall rebel. 'Go, take her and get out. Make your way to the host as we agreed and we will come when we can. Find some covering to keep her warm and tell her we are searching for her child. And hurry!' She did not watch him stride away but turned back to Jassa. 'Where would they take a newly-birthed child?'

Under Jassa's direction the crowd split into twos, each taking a different turning. They had very little time before their search would be interrupted. Cara followed Jassa down a maze of corridors, forcing open every door they found. Although many of the cells were empty, others held solitary inmates whose eyes almost started from their thin faces when they heard they were free to go. Every now and then a fleet-footed Scurrier twisted past, too swift to catch, although Cara tried to clutch at a fluttering tunic or a skinny shoulder. One or two of the stronger inmates joined them after their release and soon their search party numbered six—but still they found no trace of Gethin.

Eventually they came to a dingy, windowless passage, lit only by flickering lamps and leading straight ahead to a securely barred door. Jassa pointed to it.

'The furnace room,' she said briefly.

Cara caught hold of her companion's arm. 'So that is where they—'

'They dispose of the bodies.' Jassa's voice was stony. 'And along here are the cells where inmates awaiting disposal are held.'

'So Gethin—'

'He may be here. Maybe the child. Maybe we are too late.'

While the others set to work opening the cells, Jassa ran over to where the furnace door stood. She soon returned and drew Cara to one side. 'The door is cold, which means they have done no firing in the last few days. Perhaps they have begun stacking up fresh bodies in there, but—'

'But we have no use for dead bodies,' interrupted Cara. 'And we cannot break into the furnace room?'

'No. It would take a band of strong men with steel cudgels more time than we have now. Search for your friend in these cells. If he is not here, then we have come too late for him.'

As door after door swung open or fell shattered in pieces, Cara's hopes faded. They heard no answering shouts to their calls and knocks and each cell they entered was empty and undisturbed. At last just one door remained. They braced themselves against the unyielding wood and began to push, but the bolts proved stronger than before and they paused for breath, easing their strained muscles. Jassa idly flicked the latch. The door was unlocked. Hastily, Cara flung it open, and saw an empty cell. The couch was disarranged as if someone had slept there and a strip of torn cloth lay on the floor, but that was all. She saw Jassa watching her from the doorway while the others crowded behind.

'Cara,' Jassa said gently, 'we must leave this place.

303

The Watch will attack an any moment. At least we can save these people.' Bewildered and crushed with disappointment, Cara put down the strip of cloth. It seemed that Jassa was right. They had come too late to save both Gethin and Minna's child, and although she longed to know why the new-born baby had deserved death, she agreed to abandon the search. As they set off down the shadowy passageway, she looked back at the furnace door. A lonely resting-place for a settlement carpenter, perhaps side by side with a child just a few hours old. She grieved that Gethin had ever left his valley home to follow them on their journey. It had brought him only pain.

They hurried towards the infirmary entrance, joined as they went by other rebels in twos or threes who hurriedly told stories of what they had found—rooms full of discarded clothing, a whole family kept isolated in a single cell because of the unsightly skin disease on their arms and legs, an old woman who had been shut away without food or water for three days, awaiting her trip to the furnace room. They were almost at the main gate when Jassa pulled up short and ran to a small door which had so far escaped the rebels' attention. She searched the Chief Physician's bunch of keys and picked out a short grey one with two white spots painted on the shaft. Unlocking the cell after a brief struggle, she beckoned to Cara and the others and showed them the infirmary stores inside, crammed with phials of coloured liquid and jars filled to the brim with finely ground powders and smooth ointments.

'Here, take these.' Jassa rapidly seized several handfuls of preparations and handed them out. 'This is for fevers, this for bad stomachs, this numbs pain . . .' She passed Cara a little flask filled with an oily brown cordial. 'We call this a restorative. It revives people's energies for a time. Your sister will need it if she is to reach the host.'

She was still speaking when they heard renewed commotion outside. All the while the corridors had echoed with raised voices and confused movements, but now they could hear shouted orders and the disciplined tread of a Watch company approaching. Jassa grabbed as many phials as she could hold and set off at a run, leading the others to the hidden gate known only to the wardens and physicians. One by one they slipped through, just as the Watch were streaming in through the main entrance, lances at the ready. Cara barely had time to clutch Jassa's hand in farewell before they all scattered in different directions that would eventually lead them through the Citadel gates and over the hills to the host—if luck was with them.

A winding alley led down from the wardens' gate to an intricate criss-crossing of gloomy side streets, and Cara ran fast, hoping at every turn to see Minna and her rescuer. She had settled with him beforehand which paths he should take so that she could meet them when her business at the infirmary was done. The sky above her was darkening ominously, and a few fat drops of rain began to fall. As she went, she could hear angry cries in the distance, brought to her on the cold breeze which also carried the thickening smell of smoke. She wondered, with a throb of panic, whether her uprising was turning to open war. A few more turnings brought her close to the Quadrangle and she started to move more cautiously, dodging from doorway to doorway and pulling her hood well forward to cover her face. Then she saw where the smoke was coming from. The Bibliotheca was ablaze.

Sinking to the ground, Cara closed her eyes in disbelief. She had never intended matters to come to this pass. She was at the rear of the meeting hall and roused herself to peer round the corner into the Quadrangle, determined to see the worst. Flames were shooting out of the arched windows, and she could hear the roar of the fire even from where she crouched. Evidently the shelves of frail volumes had been tinder-dry and swift to kindle. A crowd was gathered in front of the burning building, passing futile buckets of water back and forth, the heat too intense for them to venture closer.

Suddenly something struck Cara a stinging blow on the cheek. She spun round. Behind her was a semicircle of young boys and as she stared at them, she realised that their hands were full of stones.

'Mountain girl!' shouted one. 'It's you who brings this trouble on us!' And he hurled a stone which caught her on the side of the face even as she flinched. As if that was a signal, they all began pelting her and calling at the tops of their voices for help. 'She's here! The traitor! Come and seize her!'

Before their cries could be answered, Cara had gone, but she could hear them running after her, still shouting. She crossed the street leading to the infirmary, glimpsing out of the corner of her eye a band of Watch men guarding the gates. Perhaps they too began chasing her—she dared not look back to see. Her only hope was that she could shake off the pursuit before she drew near the postern gate. Minna and her rescuer would be waiting for her just beyond the Citadel walls, and she was clinging to the hope that the Watch barracks would be almost deserted because of the uprising. At last footsteps no longer sounded behind her, and she slackened her pace.

Thunderclouds were rumbling and brewing in the blackening sky as she approached the barracks. Even though nobody seemed to be about, she knew she could not hope to find the postern completely unguarded. She tightened her grip on her knife and went on. It was almost eerily quiet as she passed by the stables, as if the blazing Bibliotheca had consumed the whole life of the Citadel in a single inferno. She came to the wall, turned left and saw the gate swinging open in the wind with no sentry beside it, but on the ground nearby were three bodies.

Cara reached them in a few swift strides. What had happened was only too clear—a young Watch sentry lay dead from a dozen deep wounds, next to Minna's rescuer, who had clearly been killed in the same struggle. Minna herself was propped against the rough stone of the wall, her eyes closed and her face a bloodless white—to all appearances, she was also dead.

Chapter Nine

As Cara stared in disbelief at her sister's body, the storm broke. The wind had risen to a furious gale and now the rain started lashing down in solid rods, turning the thickening pools of blood into foaming crimson lakes. A savage crack of lightning tore the sky in half. In the deafening thunder that followed, Minna stirred and moaned, slowly waking from the faint which had taken her as her rescuer was attacked by the Watch man.

Tears of relief filled Cara's eyes and trickled down her cheeks. She knelt at her sister's side, smoothing back her damp hair and trying to shield her from the rain with the rough blanket which was her only covering besides the soiled infirmary shift. Minna did not speak, clinging feebly to Cara's arm.

Trying to calm them both, Cara urged her to take a sip from Jassa's flask. Minna pulled a face when she first tasted the liquid, but it soon brought some colour to her cheeks and cleared away her drugged, dazed expression. Another mouthful, and she said she felt strong enough to stand. Cara helped her to her feet and the two of them were able to begin inching their way towards the gate. Long, painful minutes passed before they were safely through the archway and creeping down the steep steps beyond. They were already close to the tilled expanse of the South-east Sector where there were few hiding places, but Cara shut her mind to the chance of someone seeing them before they reached the comparative shelter of the field paths. In spite of the restorative, Minna still had to stop and rest every few yards. The rain had become a pounding deluge, and both girls were soon drenched.

When they reached the bottom of the steps, they took to the paths leading well away from the High Road, cowering behind the scrubby gerst bushes that bordered many of the fields. Cara took most of her sister's weight on her shoulders, muttering encouragement to her as they went. Peering ahead, she could see one or two colonies, but the muddy cabins looked dead and deserted. She guessed that the field people who had escaped the chaos had fled to their homes to shelter behind closed doors. Far off on their left, bordering the High Road, a lazy column of blue-black smoke rose from the smouldering ruins of a farmstead, the only visible sign that anything had ever happened to disturb the prosperous, well-tended countryside. From time to time Minna had to pause and take another sip from the flask, wiping the rainwater from her face and pulling the blanket closer round her shoulders. They had spoken only once or twice since leaving the Citadel, but Cara was dreading the moment when her sister asked about Gethin and the baby.

As they trudged on, the storm gradually dwindled to a steady downpour. They had covered perhaps one third of the distance between the Citadel and the hills, and Cara felt they could allow themselves a longer rest. Not far away stood a weather-beaten shack in the middle of a field of young flax. The door was ajar and inside Cara found it offered reasonable shelter from the rain, even though the roof leaked in places. It was probably used only as a harvest-time store. She carried Minna over the rough ground and settled her in the driest corner on a heap of straw.

As she struggled unsuccessfully to shut the rickety door, Minna spoke.

'So my baby, and Gethin—they have gone on ahead of us? You found them safe?'

Cara's mouth opened but no sound came out. She heard Minna draw a sharp breath.

'You did find them—they are safe, are they not?'

Cara stared at the ground, not daring to meet her sister's gaze as she slowly shook her head.

'Tell me, speak to me, Cara! Could you not find them? Did you find them dead? Tell me!' Minna seized her tunic and was almost shaking her.

Cara sighed heavily. 'We found nothing. We searched everywhere but we came too late to save them. The Watch were coming and we had to run to save ourselves.'

Minna made no immediate reply. Then she said slowly, 'So you left them behind in the Citadel?'

Cara's temper began to rise. 'I told you, we searched everywhere,' she answered, a little too loudly. 'We were forced to leave when the Watch came. We had to save the inmates we managed to free.'

It was as if Minna had not heard her. 'You left them behind. They are waiting for you to find them, but you left them behind.'

'Minna!' Cara's anger turned to anxiety. 'You are not yet in your right mind. Do not think about them. We did all we could to save them, and it was not enough. Rest now, and soon we will be with Anno and his people.' Even as she said this, she knew she secretly

310

doubted whether Minna would ever reach the hills.
Minna rose unsteadily to her feet, tugging the blanket
round her shivering body.

'I must go back now. They are waiting for me,' she
said rapidly. 'How could they be dead? They are waiting for me to come to them.'

'Stop!' Cara had to drag her back from the door by
force. Minna was fired with a feverish, unnatural
strength and Cara pinioned her against the far wall.
'Listen! Whatever plans you have, you cannot go wandering back to the Citadel tonight, weak as you are.'
She glanced out at the dull curtain of rain. The daylight was draining away under the dense clouds and
dusk was falling early. Minna tried weakly to wriggle
free, but Cara forced her to be still. 'We can rest here
until it is quite dark and then we can travel on
quickly, or—or decide what we should do. You cannot go back just now. And look, I have food and
drink with me. You must eat something before you
go.'

Beneath her cloak she had slung a small bag over
one shoulder, and she opened it and brought out
bread, cheese and a piece of cold mutton saved from
the noon feast. She had also brought a full bottle of
wine. At the sight of the food, Minna quietened and
slowly took her seat again on the pile of straw, meekly
eating whatever Cara gave her and making no further
attempt to leave the hut. The light was failing fast and
Cara guessed that they had perhaps a couple of hours
before it was completely dark. She made Minna lie
down, covered with her own cloak, while she sat bolt
upright beside her, determined to watch in case her sister tried to slip away again. They seemed safe for the
present, and as Cara watched the shadows thicken
imperceptibly, she allowed herself to hope that no

311

Citadel search parties would venture out as far as their hiding-place.

The rain became a light drizzle as Minna slept and Cara sat with her chin resting on her knees. Eventually the clouds broke up, leaving a clear night sky in which the first pinprick stars were emerging. Cara stretched her stiff joints and wondered whether she should rouse Minna to continue their journey. Then, in the quiet darkness, she heard a sound outside which froze her limbs. Hooves—maybe four or five horses approaching the hut at walking pace down the track leading from the main path.

Suddenly Cara felt utterly calm. Any movement she made would be heard, and she and Minna could not hide themselves in the bare little hut. Their running was over. She made herself sit motionless, waiting for the door to swing open. The hooves clattered to a halt, and the riders dismounted. Hushed voices exchanged a few inaudible words and someone pushed the door. It yielded on protesting hinges. Somebody was standing on the threshold, black against the brightening stars. Before anyone moved or spoke, Cara knew that beyond all hope it was Anno. He had come back for her.

He held out his arms and she was crushed against him. As his lips pressed against hers, she knew that their last, unhappy meeting on the hill-top was forgotten, and a great joy and relief filled her. Three other men crowded into the hut behind him, but their faces were unfamiliar, and Cara hardly looked at them. One of them went over to where Minna was sleeping and carried her out to the waiting horses.

'We have no time for lengthy explanations,' said Anno at last, releasing Cara from his grasp. 'Word came to the host that you were trying to reach us, and

312

we came as soon as we could. Fortunately we did not have to search long, but now we must make haste.'

'Are—are the host safe?'

'We suspected treachery at the Games, and most of us had already begun journeying away over the plains. We travel swiftly when we need, and I think the Citadel are more concerned with finding their own rebels than pursuing us. You and your sister are in grave danger.'

'Gethin is dead,' said Cara in a choked voice. 'And Minna's child too. She—' They were interrupted by the sounds of a struggle outside the hut. Minna had woken from her sleep and was trying to fight free of the three men.

Cara hurried to calm her. 'Minna, you are safe! These are Anno's men, come to take us to join the host.'

Minna drew herself up very straight. Even in the darkness, Cara could see the mixture of pity and impatience on her face. 'I cannot join the host, Cara. Not until I have gone back for Gethin and my child.'

Then Anno was beside her, and although he held her firmly, his voice was very gentle. 'What is this talk, Minna? We must all flee for our lives. You cannot save the dead, you can only grieve for them.'

Minna, who had always been so timid, stared back at Anno fearlessly. 'I need some clothing and some food. I am not mad, as Cara thinks. I simply know that I must go back for them. They are not dead. They are waiting for me. I have eaten, I have rested, I have recovered a little of my strength. I must return.'

Anno shook his head. 'Cara says that Gethin is dead. You cannot help him. You have lost your child, and the wound may never completely heal, but would you have gained much joy in a child forced on you by a Circle man? Minna, you will find others who will love you

313

truly and give you more children.'

'I would love my own child whoever fathered him,' Minna answered quickly. 'But Gethin himself gave me this child, and so he is doubly loved.' Cara stared at her in astonishment. 'You may say that I will die, that my strength will fail—but at least I will die obedient to what my own heart is telling me. The host cannot call itself a free people if it will not let one girl do what she knows is right.'

While Minna spoke, the other men were shifting from foot to foot, looking nervously about them. One of them touched Anno's arm. 'We cannot stay any longer. The Circle will soon be sending the Watch out here. The price on the heads of the mountain girls will be very high.'

Anno nodded and turned back to Minna. 'You are right when you call the host a free people—but those who care for you will be heartbroken if you do not return with us. Hanni speaks often of her longing to see you again. You will be comforted in your loss.'

'But I can still fill that loss. I do not believe that Cara has seen the dead bodies and I cannot rest until I have found Gethin and my child. Yes, you must go now. Go and tell Hanni that she will see me again one day. It may be hard for us to join the host, but we will follow after you, perhaps. You cannot keep me from what I know to be right!'

Then to Cara's astonishment, Anno bowed his head. 'If your mind is made up, I will not venture to change it. We will give you what food we can spare, and we will linger on our path as long as we can. You are too weak to walk far, so we will saddle one of the horses with soft cloths and see if you can bear to ride. And here, we brought garments for you and your sister. You cannot go far in those rags.'

314

Exchanging bewildered glances with his companions, one of the men unstrapped a pack and handed Minna a warm jacket, woollen leggings and a fringed shawl such as a field woman might wear round her head on a cold day—clean, home-spun clothing, stolen from a farmstead. As Minna went back inside the hut to change, Cara turned furiously on Anno. 'She is going to her death, and you know it!'

'Cara, your sister is right. We cannot claim to be the Free People and then force her to come with us against her will.'

'But she is out of her mind! She does not know what she is saying.'

'Was it not in the Citadel, Cara, that they branded people as mad and locked them up if they gainsaid a single word uttered by the Circle? And even if we force her to come with us, she might escape at the first opportunity. And who knows? She may return, against all odds, with the ones she is seeking.'

Minna stepped out of the shadows, looking like a slender young labourer in her new clothes. Her eyes were very bright in the starlight. She came to Cara and gave her both her hands.

'May you travel swiftly and safely,' she said, using the words of an old settlement farewell and added, 'I know I shall find them, but it may be some time before I see you again. You saved my life by rescuing me from the infirmary. Do not think me ungrateful for going back.'

Cara could not speak, and the two sisters embraced. Before she mounted the impatient horse, Minna clasped Anno's hand, and he touched her cheek lightly. Then he helped her ease herself onto the thickly padded saddle that had been prepared for her. Her face showed her unfaltering determination, even as she bit her lip with pain. Anno tied a small sack of

315

provisions beside her. Sitting as straight as she could, Minna nudged the horse with her heels and pulled its head round in the direction of the Citadel. The darkness soon swallowed her, but they heard the hooves trotting away into the distance for a while until the noise faded into the night.

The tears grew cold on Cara's cheeks for the second time that day. She felt herself being lifted onto a horse, seated behind Anno with her hands tucked into his belt. As they left the shack behind, he spoke briefly to his men, telling them they must ride without stopping to cross the hills before the line of Citadel guards was reinforced. They spurred the horses to a canter and Cara shivered in the rushing air.

She leaned closer to Anno, whispering so that the others would not hear. 'Do you forgive me for all I have done?'

'Cara, you too did what you thought was right. You are still young and have much to learn. Maybe your uprising has freed many people. Maybe it made the innocent suffer. Some might say you were brave to try and overturn such a proud, powerful city. Others might say you were foolish.'

'But you, did you think I was foolish?'

'I do not judge you. I am glad that now you choose to come with us. Many will grieve for Minna, and whether she was very brave or whether she was indeed driven mad by her loss, I cannot say.'

They were both silent then, thinking of Minna riding back to the dark Citadel, and Cara's tears fell again, mourning her sister as if she were already dead.

'The clasp with the green stones,' Cara said abruptly, when they had ridden some way farther. 'You wore it on your cloak when you came back to the Citadel. I—I wondered whether it was meant for a sign.'

Anno glanced back at her. 'A sign?'

'That you were not still angry with me for refusing to leave the Citadel and come with you.'

'I was not angry. I kept the clasp until I could return it to you. Take it.' He held out his hand and the star-light winked on the silver tracery and the green gems. 'It was your token, taken from the desert on your first journey. It is right that you should be its keeper again as you journey into the new world.'

Cara's fingers closed over it and she held it tightly as the riders travelled along seldom-trodden paths which grew steeper and stonier as they climbed the lowest slopes of the hills dividing the Citadel domains from the vast hinterland. They reached the last ridge at the coldest hour of the night. Cara turned in the saddle and saw the far-off bulk of the Citadel looming against the stars and the glimmering waters of the bay. A few tiny lights burned high up in some of the towers but the countryside round about was black and lifeless. Then the horses began the tortuous climb down to the empty plains, and the wind brought Cara the scent of warm earth and the wordless whispering of the grasses, and she did not look back again.

Chapter Ten

Minna's thoughts raced far ahead of the briskly trotting horse. Her body ached all over, and her hands felt oddly weak as they gripped the halter, yet every sense was heightened, and her mind flowed like quicksilver. She could hear distinctly the faint rustlings in the bushes as unseen night creatures passed furtively to and fro. The lights of the Citadel pierced the darkness like flaring beacons, and the cool air was crowded with the odours of damp soil, crushed leaves and the distant, brackish smell of the shore, laid bare by the outflowing tide.

As she rode, she tried without success to fathom why she felt so determined to go back. She could find no reason except the unassailable conviction which seized her as soon as she heard that Gethin and the child were not safe—the conviction that they were alive and awaiting her return. It was as if she herself had been reborn in the anguished struggle in the infirmary cell, entering a life purged of the old doubts and fears which formerly governed her actions. Now she was filled only with unshakeable certainty about the path she should take. With the realisation of this certainty came the memory of the little people, those the

Citadel dismissed as 'Scurriers'—the Children of Aesha. With an effort she recalled the last time she had spoken with Arron—scarcely more than a day ago and yet at the same time immeasurably remote. She could hear Arron's husky voice repeating that they would watch and wait for her, their Talemaker, to lead them to a new homeland. Even though Minna was beginning to weary of the whole Talemaker business, she could not rid herself of the thought that her own life and the fate of the little people were still bound together in some way.

On horseback, the return to the Citadel took less than half the time of the sisters' tortuous journey that afternoon. At the black hour before the first glow of sunrise, as Cara stood on the hills looking back at the towers for the last time, Minna came within a stone's throw of the walls and the lofty, barred gates. She knew that dressed as a labourer she could not ride a horse into the Citadel, yet if she left it tethered on a patch of grazing ground, someone would probably have led it away by the time she returned—if she returned. Eventually she decided to dismount and turn the horse loose. Since the gates would not open until dawn and she dared not venture the postern again, she found a cramped, uncomfortable hiding place among the thorny stems of a clump of gerst bushes. She had no clear plans except to get back into the Citadel somehow and trace the whereabouts of Gethin and the child, starting at the infirmary. Settling down to wait until first light, she rolled herself in her shawl and went to sleep.

She was awakened by the crash of metal on metal as the Citadel gates swung open. Sol was newly risen and every shadow stretched out long and wavering. Peering out from under the bushes, she saw to her surprise that already a crowd of people was emerging from the Citadel, shuffling forward in complete silence and urged on by countless Watch men and women carrying sputtering torches which burned with pallid flames in the morning light. The crowd was so large that it spilled off the High Road towards the field paths on either side, and Minna saw that she might be able to slip among the throng unseen. Moving with the utmost caution, she wound her dew-soaked shawl round her head and shoulders until her face was almost completely covered. She saw some other field people among the crowd, and guessed that they had taken shelter within the Citadel walls while the disorder was at its height.

More and more citizens and labourers were spilling through the gates, and finally Minna felt it was safe to emerge. Nobody noticed the crumpled figure mingling with the rest and slowly working her way nearer the gates. When she was close to the edge of the crowd, she stopped short as a shouted order was given and the Watch threw down their torches, extinguishing them. As the smoke rose, she saw that the crowd had become perfectly still and a line of guards had formed across the open gateway. Then she caught her breath as the line parted to let through a group of all too familiar figures.

First came Tav, a linen dressing tied round his head and one arm supported in a sling. His face was chalk-white and his mouth set in a grim line. Behind him walked Cassie, Dayva and a dozen other Circle members, many injured in some way and each one wearing an expression of mingled loathing and fear. Minna could not see Izak among them. They passed along the High Road as far as the first of the tabun trees which lined the way, and drew to one side to allow through those coming behind. When the crowd saw the second group, the silence became a deathly hush. Bloodied, chained hand and foot, shaking with terror, came ten men and women. As Minna recognised face after face, a surge of nausea rose in her throat. Ginia, her red hair matted with dust and her eyes almost swollen shut; Shen, limping heavily and trying to choke down his sobs; Halin, his pinched face blackened with bruises. Following them were others whose names she did not know. And at the end of the stumbling line, his head hanging down to hide his shame, was Izak, manacled so heavily that he could hardly walk. No movement, no sound came from the watching crowd. The Watch men accompanying the prisoners herded them forward until they halted in front of the Circle. From where she stood, Minna could see everything.

Tav had no need to lift his hand to gather the crowd's attention before he spoke. 'You are gathered to watch the execution of ten ringleaders. These people are among the chief of those who treacherously schemed for the downfall of our Citadel and the overthrow of what we laboured over many years to accomplish. Some, perhaps, had futile dreams of glory, joining themselves with the two traitors who were allowed the rank of citizenship. One—and I will not even speak his name—forgot himself and his position so far as to arrange for one of those same two traitors to move to the Academy where plots could be hatched in her chamber. He still refuses to confess his part in the uprising at the Games, although he surely knew what was going to happen.' The officer standing beside Izak jerked the prisoner's hair so that his face was lifted to meet his accuser's gaze.

Tav showed not a flicker of emotion. 'The plotting was deeper than any of us imagined, and we can only be rid of it by destroying it from the root. That is why we cannot pardon these offenders. They will be put to death in our sight and their families disgraced and sent to work in the fields with the humblest labourers, no matter how much they cry to the Circle for mercy. It will take many years to restore the Bibliotheca from its blackened foundations, and even when it stands again, the greatest treasures will still be lost. But we can begin to exact full retribution for that deed now, and for all the other wrongs committed.'

He paused, surveying the crowd. 'Do not think that these will be the only punishments. We will not rest until we have hunted out every last rebel. If any of you lays hands on either of those traitor girls who came from the mountains to sow discord and corruption among our people, bring them before me at once. Anyone found sheltering a traitor will be dealt with as harshly as the worst offender.'

As he finished speaking, the First Captain of the Watch ordered his men to drive the prisoners along the road. Only then did Minna see the rope nooses swinging gently from the branches of the trees. Ten nooses, five on each side of the High Road. She wanted to turn and run away, but it was too late. Although she averted her eyes from the actual executions, she could not stop her ears from the sounds of each death. A woman near her in the crowd fainted, but the people were so tightly packed that she remained wedged upright, her head flopping on one side, her mouth sagging open.

When the last victim hung limply in the air, bowing the branch beneath the weight, the First Captain saluted Tav, and he turned and led the Circle members back inside the Citadel. The crowd followed in a movement like a slow sigh, hundreds of feet dragging in unison. Minna walked with them, never turning her head in case she caught sight of one of the lifeless bodies. A numbing weakness had taken hold of her again, and she was afraid that she might collapse and be trampled by the crowd. Worse, someone might discover her true identity. Companies of Watch men and women patrolled alongside the people, shouting that everyone should return to his own home and remain there awaiting further instructions. Calls went out for all country-dwellers to leave the Citadel before noon, and Minna tried to keep in the very middle of the throng so that her costume was not noticed. Suddenly she realised that the turning to the infirmary was drawing near on her left. Frantically, she began pushing through the packed masses, suffering many kicks and curses as she did so. At last she had come close enough to break from the ranks and make for the side street. No guards stood nearby, and before she had time to be afraid at her own daring, she ran, clutching the shawl round her head as she went.

'Stop!' The shout echoed behind her, and she glanced back to see a burly Watch captain staring after her. 'You cannot pass that way!' She heard him rapidly giving orders, and then came the thunder of pursuit. There was a bend in the street ahead and as she rounded it, she came in sight of the infirmary gate, which had five sentries posted in front. Looking desperately for a way of escape, she saw only high, blank walls rising on either side. The sentries had seen her now and were brandishing their lances, warning her not to approach. Just before her pursuers appeared round the corner, she saw an opening on her right between two imposing halls, a narrow lane scarcely wide enough to enter. Gasping for breath, she dodged into it and took another and then another turn in the web of alleys beyond, still hearing the footsteps pounding after her. Panic filled her, crushing her previous assurance and purpose. She was blind, crazed, her feet leading her into a sprawling maze, and always she heard the pursuers coming, sometimes from in front, sometimes behind, never in sight but always within a few strides of overtaking her.

Suddenly her foot caught on a loosened paving slab and she crashed to the ground and lay there, winded and stunned. When she opened her eyes, she saw she was in what had once been a thoroughfare and was now a dead end. On three sides were featureless walls and she was sprawled in a shallow pool of rainwater. She had no recollection of the paths she had taken and did not know where she was. The ringing in her ears was too loud for her to hear if the Watch were close on her trail, and as she tried to rise, the walls began spinning round her, faster and faster, until she dropped back dizzily to the ground. The ringing became a deafening roar, and the broken slabs beneath her undulated like a sea-swell.

Minutes—or perhaps it was hours—later, a feather-soft touch on her forehead woke her. Her limbs were powerless and she barely had strength to raise her eyelids, past fear or caring who it was that had found her. Above her hovered the dusky faces and slanting eyes of two of the little people. When they saw she was awake, they quickly lifted their hands in homage. Clearly, they knew her as their Talemaker and although they could not speak except in their own hissing tongue, their gestures were eloquent enough. They wanted her to follow them—they pointed to a dark gap in the ground where one of the paving slabs had been pushed aside to reveal an entrance to their secret passageways. They looked back fearfully at the way she had come—perhaps the Watch were still following her. She could not stay there. She must trust them. Exhausted beyond belief, drained of emotion, Minna dragged herself to her feet and allowed them to lead her down a shaky rope ladder into the yawning hole. When they stood on the smooth tunnel floor, the Children's dry hands clutched hers, tugging her on until she was forced to break into a run, and all the while the rustle of their alien voices filled the air, urging her forward.

After a hurried, twisting journey, they emerged onto the littered floor of a ruinous shack. Minna had never entered one of the Children's dwellings which was not packed with the little people, and she gazed round curiously. A nest of torn blankets lay in one corner, and the floor was criss-crossed with the tracks of bare feet. One of her rescuers put his fingers to his lips and whistled four quick notes, giving some kind of signal.

The heap of blankets stirred and, to Minna's relief, Arron crawled out and greeted her gladly.

'Talemaker, we watch for you, and we know you come back to us. Our people wait outside the Citadel, and we must join them. The men come soon, angry, and burn down our dwellings.' Her black eyes surveyed Minna's drawn face. 'You come with us. They wait for you in a far place—the Children of Aesha, your Gethin and your little one. Everyone is safe.'

'How . . . when . . . ' Minna's mouth trembled and her gaze was suddenly hard to focus on the restless figure standing before her.

'No more time to speak,' whispered Arron, reaching out to stroke Minna's sleeve. 'You come with us.'

They took Minna to a corner of the shack where another hole opened in the floor, leading to a newly dug passageway more like a burrow than a tunnel. In places Minna had to crawl on her face to force a way through the clinging earth, fighting against thoughts of the moist walls collapsing and burying them. Before her last reserve of strength ran out, the way came to an abrupt end, dropping down several feet to meet a tunnel far larger than any she had yet seen, hewn from the very rock on which the Citadel was built. Minna tumbled out after Arron and found that the walls were almost high enough for her to stand upright. A sluggish stream flowed through it, running downhill into the distance where the tunnel dwindled to a round speck of light. The air was foul, and as Arron turned to urge her on, Minna realised they were in the great sewer which ran under the Citadel, carrying the people's waste down to the sea.

The Children's eyes gleamed in the darkness and they beckoned Minna to follow them towards the light. She splashed after them, wiping the filth from her face with the back of her hand. Once her legs gave way and she staggered against the slimy walls, but before she fell, Arron's arms were supporting her, waiting until she had recovered and could walk on. As she went, the speck of light gradually grew to a circle and soon after that she was close enough to hear the boom of surf against the rocks and feel fresher air on her face. Then she was standing on the lip of a wave-washed precipice, staring in astonishment at a glittering infinity of sea and sky. The Children were busy fastening a length of rope-ladder to an outcrop of shiny black stone and already the first of the three had disappeared over the edge, climbing down into apparent emptiness.

Arron was beside her again, telling her to set her foot on the topmost rung.

'But what if I fall? Where are you climbing to?' asked Minna anxiously. Even Arron's impassive face showed some concern.

'We must climb,' she chattered. 'There is a ledge below. The bay fills with the waters but the ledge is safe. Make haste!'

The ladder shook under Minna's weight, throwing her against the cliff so that her knuckles were bruised and torn. She closed her eyes against the plunging drop and her mind against the thought that if they did not fall to their deaths, they would be sucked away by the pounding of the waves. When her feet touched solid ground, her eyes opened. The sea crashed against the cliff just below the jutting ledge where she stood, sheltered from the Citadel walls by the overhang of the precipice, and before long she was drenched with spray. Crouching as close to the cliff face as she could, she watched while Arron climbed nimbly down and then knelt before her, looking up timidly into her eyes.

'Is it well with you, Talemaker?'

'What plans do you have for me now, Arron?' Minna asked wearily. 'Will we float away like sea-spiders or grow wings and fly?'

Arron's face was grave. 'We must set our sign on the rocks so that only the right eyes see. We are not safe yet, Talemaker.'

Wondering what she could mean, Minna watched as the little people set about burrowing beneath some loose stones not far from where she sat. Her wonder grew as she saw them unearth a round steel dish, such as was found only in the highest Citadel households. One of the Children stripped off his filthy, ragged loincloth and used it to polish the dish to a high sheen. Then Arron took it in both hands, lifting it to catch the hot rays of Sol as the star climbed towards noon. Again and again she tilted it so that long reflected rays of light shivered across the bay and at last Minna thought she

327

glimpsed an answering gleam. Arron noticed it at the same moment and dropped the dish with a squeal of joy.

'See, Talemaker!' she cried, almost dancing with excitement.

Minna saw a swift flash of crimson and gold, at first remote in the sky but speeding towards them as fast as an arrow. Milk-white skin and red plumes were a brilliant blur of colour and the beat of the outstretched wings stirred the waves to a fresh tumult. Golden eyes swept over her as the naiga, the winged Wise One, hovered above the waters. It extended one of its clawed legs and gripped the rock, furling its wings and inching its way onto the ledge where Minna and the three Children of Aesha waited.

'Come!' called Arron, tugging Minna towards the creature. The huge head turned on the sinuous neck to gaze at her as she was heaved onto a perch between the creature's wings. The others scrambled up behind and before her. Minna felt the warmth of the feathers on her cold hands and the surging power of the body beneath her as the wings spread again and the creature leapt out from the cliff. As it rose in flight, she heard shouts from the Citadel walls and saw a dozen Watch sentries running to stare at their escape. A lance sang through the air and landed harmlessly in the water beneath them. Already the shouts were growing faint as the naiga rose higher and higher, and when Minna looked back again, the lofty towers had dwindled to a pin-size cluster, dwarfed by the spreading plains on one side and the reaches of the open sea on the other.

Chapter Eleven

The naiga flew on, cutting a bright path between pale sky and white-capped waves. The mountains were a dark smudge on the horizon, and although Minna screwed up her eyes against the glare, trying to see something of the land she had once crossed, she could not make out the purple moorlands where the four travellers had rested and found the first traces of the little people. The keen air and the wonder of flying had renewed Minna's strength somewhat, and her heart grew lighter as they left the Citadel farther and farther behind. As the naiga flew, it lifted its beautiful, inhuman voice in a haunting cry. Minna remembered the lament she had heard sung by such a creature over the dead bodies of the Children. The song now sung was a fierce, wild, joyful one, stirring her heart and filling her with thoughts of desolate places and far journeys to unknown lands. The little people joined the cry with their own ecstatic pipings. And they flew on.

In the quivering heat of midday, they came in sight of a wide bay where blindingly white dunes spilled onto the shore, glittering with mica and tufted with coarse grasses. A dense haze shrouded the distant mountains and Minna could not even guess how far they had come. As they plummeted down to land, she realised that the shore was swarming with small figures, and as the naiga came to rest on the edge of the dunes, she saw that they had been brought to the gathering place of the liberated Children of Aesha. Here and there she glimpsed the glaring plumage of other naigas, wings furled, basking on the warm sand, and she was glad because the little people were reunited with their See-ers at last.

When the newcomers were sighted, the air filled at once with hundreds of jubilant voices, and teeming multitudes crowded round Minna and her companions as they climbed from their mount. As Minna looked about, she saw a primitive shelter nearby, roughly built with loose-woven grasses and bleached wood. She was gazing at it with faint curiosity, wondering if it was set there in her honour, when something moved inside, shaking the flimsy walls. A gaunt human figure appeared in the entrance, peering out to discover the cause of the disturbance, and Minna stared at it, puzzled. Then she realised that it was Gethin.

She walked slowly towards him as he pulled himself upright, twisting his wasted features into the ghost of a smile.

'Minna.' His weakness made it hard for him even to speak, and he often had to pause for breath. 'We've been . . . waiting for you, and you've . . . come.'

Minna tried to return his smile but her face was suddenly stiff and awkward, and she could hardly bring herself to look at him. Then she heard another, smaller sound coming from within the shelter—an almost inaudible cry which sent a bewildering jolt of power through her whole body. Gethin took her hand and drew her inside.

330

She saw her son lying in a hollow in the sand, wrapped only in the black infirmary blanket. The little people had washed him and his skin glowed translucent pink. Minna saw at a glance his misshapen head, the crooked back and withered limbs, his sightless eyes—yet she loved him. Hot tears spilled down her cheeks as she knelt and lifted the baby in her arms, rocking him to and fro until his plaintive cries ceased. She held him to her breast and he suckled, drawing what little nourishment her body could give him.

Gethin had his arms round her. 'The Scurriers saved him . . . as they saved me. I knew . . . my own death was coming . . . yesterday morning, and in the last hour . . . the door opened and they rescued me . . . When they carried me from my cell, I saw them . . . thrusting a warden's body into . . . the furnace room. They had taken the . . . child from her.'

Minna stroked the baby's head as she replied, 'Cara took me from the infirmary and we met with Anno out in the fields, but I had to come back. I knew you were both waiting for me.' And as they sat together, she told him of everything that had happened since the day when he was first imprisoned in the infirmary, and how the little people had served her by keeping watch over him in his cell. Then they were silent again, looking at one another.

'We have come far together since the day Cara brought you to our settlement hut,' said Minna eventually. 'You know that this is your child?'

Gethin gently grasped one of the baby's fists. 'I thought it . . . must be so. I've wept as you have . . . because he has to suffer from the . . . taints in our blood. The wasting disease has hold of me, Minna . . . I'm dying.' Minna took his hand and they rested in the quiet of the shelter, their baby in her arms.

After a while they heard a soft babble of voices outside, and Arron appeared in the entrance, extending her palms in greeting before she spoke. 'Talemaker, the Children of Aesha and the naigas await your coming. They want to hear the tale of our escape. Come now.' And she called in four more of the little people to help Gethin walk out. Minna followed, clutching the child to her closely and pitying Gethin's faltering steps.

When she saw the horde of little people on the shore and the naigas rising tall behind them, she was overcome and stopped short, wondering if she could disappear into the safety of the shelter again—but Arron was at her elbow, hurrying her to where a dozen tunics were spread out on the sand as a seat of honour. When Minna, Gethin and the child were in place, Arron turned to the assembled crowd, spreading her silvery arms in a gesture of welcome.

'See!' she said in human speech, 'our Talemaker, her true partner and her child!' And then she spoke in the Children's own tongue and every palm was raised in honour of Minna, while the naigas shook their fanned tailfeathers until clouds of sand sparkled in the air.

'And now,' announced Arron, turning to the three on the seat of honour, 'we will make a tale for you.' The crowd seated itself expectantly and Minna watched in amazement as one of the naigas moved ponderously on its short legs to take its place at Arron's side, towering over her even when settled. Then she remembered how Arron had told her on her very first visit to the Children of Aesha that the See-ers, the naigas, were the keepers of the little people's tales and the record of their past days, the ones who dreamed dreams and saw visions for them. As she recalled this, the naiga began to sing and now she could clearly hear the Children's hissing speech in its song, only in the mouth of the naiga the sounds took on a finely wrought shape and harmony. Arron spoke at the same time in human words, telling the tale of the leaving of the Children of Aesha.

'It is a good leaving we make. We wait long years for Talemaker, and she comes and shows us the right time for us to go. The Children dig in the earth and find the tunnel to the sea. We wait for Talemaker and take the true partner and the child with us. In the stamping and screaming of men on that day, the Children go their own way and leave the huts empty. The See-ers watch in the skies and see the smoke of the burning we make. We cannot leave the body of the best of our See-ers in the hands of men, so we light a fire in the hall of the books, and it burns well.' Minna and Gethin exchanged wide-eyed glances. 'The See-ers wonder at the burning, and we see the gold of their gaze as they fly above and they see the sign we make, shining light back with the white metal so that it flashes like their eyes. And in the dark of night, when the bay is dry, the Children take the true partner and the child and go through the tunnel and across the dry shoals. And because the See-ers wait for us, they too gather and their eyes see even in the darkness and they bear the Children up on their backs and fly to this place of rest. And so the leaving of the Children of Aesha and the joining with the naigas is made,' Arron ended, as the See-er's song finished. 'It is a good leaving, is it not, Talemaker?'

Minna bowed in answer and then bent over the baby so that her long hair fell like a curtain, shielding her face. She was achingly weary and longed only to lie down beside Gethin in the shelter, but Arron had not yet finished.

'You are with us now, Talemaker, and you must rest so that you are ready to go with us to find a new home, far from men. You sing with the naigas and weave tales round us till we are a mighty people and the Brightness comes quickly. You have your true partner and the child and you set aside the doings of men forever. We wait for you, Talemaker, and now you come and begin your true work and the Children of Aesha grow greater than the citadels of men.' Arron's tone was commanding, and Minna looked up in surprise. Rows of narrow faces gazed back at her unblinkingly. They all knew what she must do—for was she not Talemaker who had liberated them and had now a life of service to give?

Minna's tongue felt clumsy in her mouth as she groped for an answer. She felt that she had become a dried husk, emptied of all life and strength, all tales and dreams. The bitter night of suffering in the infirmary, and everything she had endured since, had only completed what had begun many days before, when she first realised that the Children of Aesha were concerned only with their own affairs and cared nothing for humankind. She had no more to give them.

With an effort she said, 'I think the time for Talemaker is passed. Believe that the Brightness will come, although I do not think it will be yet. Watch and wait for its dawning yourselves. I—I cannot come with you.' The rows of faces stared at her blankly. 'I think my place should be with my own people.' Before that moment she had not known what it was that she should do, but suddenly she knew that she wanted to see Hanni again, to take Gethin to Anno's host so that he could at least end his days peacefully among his own kind. 'I cannot be your Talemaker any longer. I served you by pointing the way to leaving the Citadel.' She hesitated, but not even Arron spoke. 'I would ask of you one thing. You brought me here where Gethin and the child waited in safety. Can you grant me one other gift? May the three of us mount on the back of a naiga and fly to the plains beyond the Citadel where the Free People are journeying? The naiga will return when we are done, but my true partner is too weak to journey so far, and I think my strength is gone.' Still there were only rows of expressionless faces. She said desperately, 'If it were not for the Free People, the Children of Aesha would not have been able to make their leaving.'

In the absolute hush that followed, Minna heard the whisper of the wavelets lapping the shoreline and the breeze rattling the dune grasses. Beside her, Gethin's breathing sounded harshly in his throat, and in her arms the baby made a convulsive movement. For what seemed like an age, every slanting eye was turned on her and then Arron, her face like carven stone, held out her palms in a gesture of dismissal and told them to return to the hut. Nobody came forward to escort Gethin, so he walked back leaning on Minna's arm. Behind them they heard a hissing confusion of speech break out, and Arron's shriek rising angrily above the rest.

Minna lay on the sandy floor of the shelter, cradling her child and staring up through the cracks in the roof of the shelter at the fathomless blue sky. Gethin had fallen into a deep sleep, sprawling next to her with his hollow cheek pillowed on a work-worn hand. Even though she knew that the little people were displeased with what she had told them, she was not afraid. Besides the gladness of finding Gethin and her son again, she felt only a great emptiness, and when she heard scuffling footsteps outside the shelter and knew that she had to go out and hear the fate decreed for her, the emptiness grew until she was lost in it altogether.

Arron was waiting for her with a crowd of others surrounding the hut and began speaking rapidly, keeping her gaze downcast. 'Some of the Children say you cannot be the true Talemaker. All say that if you are no longer Talemaker, the Children can have no dealing with you. The Children have no dealings with men. Even the See-ers fear death at the hands of men and will not pass over the Citadel again. The Children can do nothing more for you.'

'So you will leave without me?' Minna heard herself say.

Arron knotted her fingers together and the others moved closer, as if urging her to continue. 'The See-ers say it is time for us to be gone. They take us far away to a land where no men ever come. You have shelter here and there is no evil thing to hurt you.'

'We will die without food and water,' Minna's voice said dispassionately.

'Beyond the shore it is not an empty land.' Arron's impassive mask threatened to crack and one hand reached out as if to touch Minna—then it was hastily withdrawn and Arron spoke again, this time with brittle formality. 'We grieve that you refuse to be Talemaker. We go now.' And Minna watched as she and the other little people turned their backs on her and hurried away.

Sol had begun the journey down the sky towards the mountains, and the shadows were lengthening when Minna stood outside the shelter, hugging her son and watching as rank after rank of naigas rose up, filling the bay with the beating of their wings, a mass of little people clinging perilously on each back. There had been more of the great creatures among the dunes than she had known, and she marvelled how room was found for every one of the Children so that they could

336

all depart at once. Gazing towards the open sea, she saw lines of red wings soaring away into the distance, and then they were gone, leaving a single plume floating in the foamy shallows.

As Minna stared after the departing naigas, she felt no bitterness in her heart at the betrayal, nothing except the peaceful emptiness. The rays of Sol broadened and deepened in hue until the bay was molten gold. Gethin stirred within the shelter and called her name.

Getting no answer, he dragged himself out and surveyed the deserted shore in disbelief. 'Where have they gone?'

'They have gone far away,' Minna answered, still staring out towards the open sea. 'They said they would have nothing more to do with men.'

'But . . . you were Talemaker!'

'No longer, and now I am nothing to them,' Minna replied. Gethin was silent, trying to understand the turn of events. He shook his head.

'Are you . . . not afraid of dying here?' he asked. Minna seated herself beside him as he lay down with a sigh. Soon he would be unable even to prop himself upright without help. She began to comb his matted hair with her fingers.

'We may be able to find food and water beyond the dunes,' she said quietly. 'But no, Gethin, I am not afraid. Perhaps death is not so terrible. I have to face it now as well as you and maybe we can be brave together.'

'I . . . was never truly brave.'

'Oh no, Gethin. Without your bravery Cara and I might have died at the hands of the settlement mob. But forget the old days. It is all past—the settlement, the Citadel, the Free People, and we are left here on

337

the edge of the world. We have been written out of every other tale, and it will not be long before ours comes to an end.'

With a sigh, Gethin closed his eyes as Minna stroked his forehead. She saw that he was beginning to burn with a fever which she knew would consume him to the last breath.

She carried on in a soft voice, 'I said to the little people that the tales were finished, but I have saved one for you, Gethin, one to tell you at the end. Listen now to my story.'

Chapter Twelve

There was once a girl who lived alone in a hut hidden in a deep valley between the mountains. She had dwelt there as long as she could remember, and every evening the light died behind the cliffs in glory and fire and splendour, and every morning a new light rose up beyond the end of the world. Every morning, when the light touched the pillow where she laid her head, she left her bed to milk her goat, feed her hens and tend her garden patch. She drew water from a stream running among the rocks of the valley and wove her garments on a loom strung with goathair, trimming them with brown and white feathers.

She had always been content with her lot, but one morning she woke early, while it was still dark, and looked out on a grey world where shadow and substance were one and the same. She saw the embers of light beginning to glow beyond the end of the world and as she watched, the light grew until at last it filled the whole valley with its radiance. And something stirred in her heart so that she cried out for the wonder of it, and she was filled with desire to see the far place where the light was kindled. That same morning, she shut up the hut, turned her animals loose, made a bundle of what she might need for the journey and set off into exile.

She wandered for days on hard mountain paths and over

the empty plains which lay on the other side, and when very many days had passed, she had come close to the end of the world. Then she entered a strange land where bottomless ravines opened at her feet, and the ground shook and hot ash fell like rain. The air swirled with mist and yellow smoke, and the girl soon lost her way. At last she was too tired to walk any more and huddled among the rocks, hiding her face from death.

Then a young man came to the girl, clad in garments rich enough for a prince, yet stained and threadbare with travel. His face was kind and he comforted her, giving her meat and drink and binding her sore feet.

'Where are you going?' he asked her.

'Beyond the end of the world,' she said.

'What are you seeking?' he asked her.

'The place where the light is kindled,' she said and blushed, for she felt it was a foolish answer to make. The young man smiled.

'I live there,' he said, 'and I have been waiting for you to come. Although I must go on ahead of you, you will see me again if you follow the path I take. The way may be hard but you are strong to have come so far on your own.' When he had finished speaking, he was gone, and where he had passed, the mists thinned and she could see clearly enough to follow him.

As she went, she came to a smooth meadow of the finest grass. The light was very strong now and the colours of the grass and the meadow flowers were almost more than she could bear. The young man's path was marked here and there with a freshly dug strip of turf, and the way soothed her feet after the days of journeying in stony places.

Then the meadow became a grassy slope, and at the bottom of the slope she saw what looked like a mighty hall. Although the path did not lead to that place, she turned aside and drew closer, and saw that it was indeed a hall and the doors were shut. She knocked and the sound echoed inside. The doors

340

opened and she saw a crowd of men and women in splendid garments standing on the threshold, their beautiful, noble faces surveying her curiously.

'Where are you going?' asked one of the men.

'Beyond the end of the world,' the girl said.

'And what might you be seeking?' asked one of the women.

'The place where the light is kindled each morning,' the girl replied.

The people laughed at her. 'You are too young and pretty to chase after such idle dreams,' said one of the men.

'Come and stay with us a while, and perhaps you will reconsider your plans,' said one of the women.

'They took her and dressed her in clothes as fine as theirs, and set before her an elegant meal. When she had eaten and rested, the people showed her how they spent their days, sheltering in the hall from the light outside. They were busy ornamenting their home with many clever pictures and carvings, and spent much time spinning tales. They also took it in turns to work on the flat roof of the hall where they were building a soaring tower to fill with their writings. Neither hall nor tower had any windows, and the doors were always kept shut.

When the daylight was gone from the world, they unrolled mats on the floor and prepared themselves for sleep, the girl with them. But at the black midnight hour, she was woken by terrible dreams, and when she opened her eyes, she saw something more terrible still. The people had risen from their mats and were standing in a circle. And as the girl watched, each man and woman lifted up their hands and began tearing at their faces. The noble features peeled off like masks and underneath there were the heads of hideous beasts, horned and savage. As the beast heads slowly turned towards her, the girl cried for help in hopeless fear.

As her cry echoed in the rafters, a wondrous thing happened. A great light began to burn in the middle of the hall, blazing with white heat and driving the shadows and

341

monstrous creatures into the farthermost corners. The girl thought she saw a face in the light, a face like that of the young man, but older—yet at the same time ageless; wiser—yet also as innocent as a tiny child; awesome—yet still infinitely tender. Then she felt herself seized by a violent wind, and she knew nothing until her eyes opened again. She was lying in the warm sunshine, not far from where a heap of stones marked the path. When she looked back, she saw the meadow and the green slope, but the hall had disappeared.

The path led her to where the land rose up again in an immense cliff and on to the very foot of the precipice where the way disappeared into a narrow cave. She crawled inside and saw that the cave became a tunnel, leading farther and farther into the darkness of the earth, and yet even here there was some light, although she could not see its source.

Before she ventured further, she knew she must rest, so she rolled up her bundle beneath her head and went to sleep. And as she slept, she dreamed that someone came to her and spoke tender words to her. Although the face was hidden, the voice was like, and also unlike, the voice of the young man. She awoke, and even though she could not remember the words she had heard, the presence still lingered round her like a shield, and she knew that she could never be very afraid again.

Then she picked up her bundle and set off through the tunnel. The air blew fresh and cool on her face, and she had hardly wearied of walking when she saw the end ahead. The light grew stronger and stronger, and at last she stepped out of the tunnel on to the shore of a boundless sea. The light filled the sky and shone all round her, but she knew that she had not yet come to the place beyond the end of the world, where the young man dwelt. Then the path came to an end at the water and she saw that she could never cross that endless sea alone. She felt that the light swallowed up everything, even the lingering presence, leaving nothing but herself, a single speck on the rocky shoals at the very edge of the world.

342

And perhaps her seeking will go on for ever. She waits still on the shore where the light never fades, night or day, watching the waves lapping the pebbles until they have washed away everything inside her except the knowledge of herself and the waiting.

Minna stopped speaking, the story complete. Night had fallen and as she glanced down at Gethin, she saw that he was fast asleep, one skinny arm flung out protectively towards their slumbering baby son. Noiselessly, she crawled out of the shelter and crouched at the water's edge. In the waves floated swarms of the glowing sea creatures she had first seen on the night when the four travellers crossed the bay to the Citadel. She trailed her hand in the shallows, and the threads of light slipped through her fingers. Looking up, she saw how much brighter and closer the stars were, now that she was far from the lamps of the Citadel. The glittering constellations of the Tower and the Sickle seemed to swing just over her head. Minna's gaze wandered over the whole expanse of the sky, and she began talking softly to herself. 'How far we came! And perhaps they are waiting for us on Earth, waiting for us to come back, wondering what new world we found . . .'

Her voice trailed away into silence, and suddenly she cowered on the sand, terrified at the enormous empty spaces above her head, where once the gods walked before men and women laid the old memories aside. Then as the moment passed, it was as if a breathless hush blanketed the world so that even the slow waves, breaking at her feet, were quietened. Everything was sleeping except for her, alone in the star-lit dark.

Then the emptiness was gone. Suddenly the night had become more than blackness and wheeling stars.

343

Above her, beside her, hemming her in on all sides, she felt again the presence which had come at the end of her dream in the lonely Academy chamber, a vast and yet intimate presence. Now it was brooding over the whole world, filling the sky and also penetrating the core of her being. A breath of warm wind ruffled the placid waters, and then all was still again. Without knowing why, she rose to her feet.

Over the far horizon, where the sky met the sea, light began to grow. It was neither yellow like the beams of Sol nor remote like starlight, but a pure, incandescent blaze which grew and strengthened until every grain of sand on the shore was outlined in fierce shadow. Even as the radiance increased, Minna found that she was still able to stare straight into it, and though her heart beat fast, it was not with fear but with a strange excitement.

The light formed a shining path over the sea, and as she watched, Minna saw what looked like the giant figure of a man gradually detach itself from the heart of the brightness. He was walking towards her down the shining path, and as he came closer, he was no longer a giant but simply a tall man, every limb ablaze and his eyes like golden fire. He drew nearer and still she stood unmoving, and she knew his face, although at each step it changed. At first it was the face of her prince in the long-ago settlement days. Then it was as glorious as the Master she had shaped for the little people, and then it even bore a fleeting resemblance to one of the naigas. And by the time his foot touched the shore, his face was both unknown and also one she somehow recalled from her earliest dreams.

The golden eyes caught and held her gaze and she dared to speak, her voice thin and piping in the silence that lay on the world.

344

'Is this death or madness? Will I wake from it?'

The man answered her and his voice was filled with the sonorities of a thousand oceans, the surging power of flood and tide.

'You sought me, and now you see me plainly.'

'Who are you?'

'The first and last word in every tale. I am the Prince and the Master, and also the Brightness, yet I have had and will have many other names in other times and other worlds.' He held out a shining hand and drew her towards him.

'Minna.' As he said her name, she knew that it was he who had been at the end of her years of tales and seeking. His golden eyes read her thoughts as if she had spoken them aloud, for he said, 'You have spent your days making stories for yourself and for many others. You have been Talemaker. I want you now to be my Truth-bearer.'

'I do not understand.' Minna felt that she was being consumed in his gaze.

'The people are lost in the dark. All are blind, but some have been seeking light. Not only are they themselves lost, but they have lost their greatest treasure. They left it behind on Earth and carried with them only withered memories of it, locked away in books which no one ever read.'

'I do not know any truth to tell.'

He laid his fingers on her lips, silencing her, and the touch burned like fire. 'My words are in your mouth and you must speak them, write them down. Tell the people they have strayed far, but not too far to return, although the journey will be a long one. Tell them they must remember old, forgotten ways, search their hearts, forget their pride and call on me, and then the broken places will be made whole and the lost found.'

'On whom should I tell them to call?' Minna faltered.

'Tell them that I am the Brightness.' Then Minna despaired because she thought he was telling her that the little people's stories had been right and that she would be bound to them for the rest of her days, when all she wanted was to be with her own kind.

Again she was answered before she had spoken aloud, and she felt the burning touch on her head, telling her not to be downcast.

'Your place is not with the little people, but with the host who are even now grieving for you, thinking you dead. Among them there are others who have sought me as as you have, and those you must seek out and tell first.'

A last doubt shook Minna. 'How will I know that this is true and no dream?'

'I will set a sign in the sky for you, a light in the dark as radiant as the Earth moon which the people still mourn in the blackness of the Osirian night. See!' He pointed into the void, and as Minna watched, one star began increasing in size, shining stronger than all the rest until it was bright enough to cast her shadow at her feet. 'Far out on the plains and even in the Citadel, they will see that star, and you will bring them its meaning. Come.'

He walked towards the shelter, his feet leaving firm prints in the sand and the radiance dimming a little. In the gloom beneath the roof of the shelter, Minna could just see the bodies of the two sleepers.

'Gethin has loved you and served you, but he is worn out in body and mind so that no sleep in this world can heal him. He will walk now with me, and you must go on without him.'

Minna felt as if part of her body was being torn away, but she could not weep yet. Dumbly, she stared at her

346

child, and the love ached inside her.

'Your son has no name.'

She shook her head, unable to speak.

'Let him be called Joram. He is the fruit and memory of his father's faithfulness, and he too will be a sign.' Strong, loving hands reached into the shelter and picked up the sleeping baby who stirred without waking.

'Joram,' said the voice commandingly, 'be whole!' And Minna was holding her son in her arms, and saw in wonder and amazement that the crooked body was straight, the withered little limbs plump, the swollen head neatly rounded and the sightless eyes open and staring intently at the tall man.

'It is time for you to depart this place. Look, not all the naigas turned away from you.' Minna glanced up as he pointed and there, circling above them, was one of the flying creatures, humbled now and come obedient to its true master's bidding. Even so, it did not appear to see the shining one standing on the shore, for it landed not far from the shelter and gazed only at Minna.

'It will carry you to where the host is encamped. Your sister has lingered as long as she dared in the wild hope that you would return. Go to her and be patient if she is slow to believe what you have to tell her. She loves you more than she knows.'

Then, with a last glance at Gethin, Minna climbed up on the naiga's back, holding Joram tightly.

'Do not forget what I have told you.' The voice rang in her ears, but when she looked back, the radiant figure was gone and in that instant the world stirred and began to wake. Even the new star was paling as the first streaks of dawn appeared in the sky. Joram wriggled in his mother's arms and his wide blue eyes scanned her face gravely. The naiga turned its gaze on her as well, listening for her instruction.

'Wait,' she stammered, unsure whether it knew human speech. She slid off its back and ran to the shelter. It was empty. There was the hollow where Gethin had slept, but his body was gone. Slowly she retraced her steps and climbed again onto the warm perch between the fire-bright wings.

'Go now,' she said and the naiga spread its wings and sprang into the air, swiftly climbing higher and higher so that soon the shelter was no more than a speck on a thin white crescent of shore. Although tears for the passing of Gethin were running down Minna's cheeks, at the same time she looked down at Joram and laughed out loud for the joy of what had happened that night. Sol was climbing over the jagged summits of the mountains and she saw the new world, the world of Osiris, spread out beneath her, more beautiful than any picture that human hands could weave.

'It has begun,' she said.

The Gates Of Zion

by Bodie Thoene

A monumental story in the tradition of Leon Uris' *Exodus*.
PALESTINE, 1947.

When young American jounalist Ellie Warne photographs the Dead Sea Scrolls—without realising their significance—she is caught up in battles between Jewish underground agencies, Arab Terrorists, and the British occupying forces. Should she trust Moshe, the quiet Hebrew scholar, or David, her lifelong sweetheart? As she tries to make sense of her friends' talk of the God of Israel, and as escaped Nazis hunt her down, her path is crossed and recrossed by:

• YACOV, streetwise orphan, whose only friends are his grandfather the Rabbi, and his dog, Shaul.
• RACHEL, embittered survivor of the death camps, hungry for food and tenderness.
• IBRAHIM EL HASSAN, the terrorist who will stop at nothing to take revenge on Rachel.
• EHUD, intrepid fisherman whose cargo boat brings in not sardines but survivors of Auschwitz.

BODIE THOENE (pronounced TANEY) interviewed many Jewish families before beginning this the first of five Zion Chronicles. She has worked as a writer/researcher for John Wayne's Batjac Productions and ABC Circle Films. Married with four children, she now lives in California.

Minstrel
Monarch Publications

The Hawk And The Dove

by Penelope Wilcock

'Lifts and transports us into another world...I was hungry to read more.'

JANE GRAYSHON

THE HAWK. An aristocrat of the thirteenth century and a renegrade from his own passions, Peregrine entered monastic life still fierce and proud. When thugs from his past beat and crippled him, they left him helpless as a child. Bereft of his independence, he could finally teach true strength to his brothers.

THE DOVE. Melissa is a modern teenager, direct descendent of the hawkish abbot, who encounters the same struggles he did. As she listens to her mother's stories of her distant ancestor, Mellissa discovers that times do not change: that people, pride, resentment and love stay much the same, and that it is the grace of God on the inside that changes things.

'I enjoyed reading this book and saw once again more of Jesus - for me always the final test of a good book.'

ROGER FORSTER

'Not only a joy to read, but also the kind of experience from which you come away feeling cleansed, whole and determined to live life more generously.'

JOYCE HUGGETT

Minstrel
Monarch Publications

Monarch Publications

Monarch Publications was founded to produce books from a Christian perspective which challenge the way people think and feel. Our books are intended to appeal to a very wide constituency, in order to encourage Christian values which currently seem to be in decline.

Monarch Publications has three imprints:

<u>Monarch</u> is concerned with issues, to develop the mind.

<u>MARC</u> is a skills-based list, concentrating on leadership and mission.

<u>Minstrel</u> concentrates on creative writing, to stimulate the imagination.

Monarch Publications is owned by The Servant Trust, a Christian charity run by representatives of the evangelical church in Britain, committed to serve God in publishing and music..

For further information on the Trust, including details of how you may be able to support its work, please write to:

> The Secretary
> The Servant Trust
> 1 St Anne's Road
> Eastbourne
> East Sussex BN21 3UN
> England